Prologue

Love and Grief

Prologue

Newport Beach, California
May 26, 1969

It was one of those days—a picture-postcard, wish-you-were-here kind of moment that couldn't have been better. Beaches along the southern California coast were packed with Memorial Day crowds, the air heavy and rich with the smell of sea-water and coconut oil, as slippery bodies up and down the sand turned to toast. Around the patch of ground that eight-year-old Mallory and her family had staked out, "Hey Jude" blared from a dozen transistor radios. Sun-drunk, half the beach was chanting by the time the song reached its hypnotic, monosyllabic final refrain. Sea gulls dived and squealed in protest at the invasion of their territory, but their complaints were lost in the din of music and voices and crashing surf.

Mallory watched as her older sister, Diana, placed shells along the ramparts of the sand castle they'd made. It had two towers, crenellated walls and a moat filled with water. Their father had helped them build it, but had then stretched out for a snooze on the beach chair next to their mother's. She sat drowsily turning the pages of a magazine.

Mallory slithered a twig around the moat toward her sister's side of the castle. "Better watch out, or my alligator will get your guys!"

"No way. My guys are princesses, and they're in the tower, and alligators can't climb walls."

"This alligator can."

"Can *not*. Don't you dare! Mom, tell Mallory not to let her alligator eat my princesses!"

Their mother looked up briefly from her magazine. "Mallory, keep your alligator on your side of the castle." With her soft English accent, it came out "cah-stle."

Mallory pulled a face. Her father opened one eye and shot her a grin. Her grimace vanished and she dropped the twig-alligator into the moat, stood and headed for the water's edge, toes squishing in the wet sand as her eyes scanned the ground for a good piece of driftwood.

What this game really needed was a nice, big, fire-breathing dragon.

A mile or so inland, as the crow flies, a man in a stolen southern California Edison truck drove the Esmerelda Canyon Road, following its twists and turns until he reached the unpaved driveway of a new home, the yard still littered with builders' clutter. Turning the truck into the gravel driveway, he gunned it up an incline and pulled to a halt behind a boat and trailer, then climbed out and surveyed his surroundings.

The sprawling, stepped house had been sited well back on the cliff, overlooking the canyon and the blue Pacific Ocean, twinkling beyond. The bogus electrician noted that most builders, thinking themselves somehow immune to the law of gravity, would not have been able to resist the temptation to perch the house on the very edge of the precipice, which was why a couple of them seemed to collapse like Tinkertoys every time the ground shook. In this case, since the architect had designed the house for himself and his family, he must have decided to sacrifice a few feet of scenery in favor of security. Maybe architects should always be forced to live in the places they design so they wouldn't do such goddam stupid things as put them hanging off cliffs smack in the middle of earthquake country.

The man glanced around, watching for nosy neighbors, but the nearest house was a half mile down the road and well out of sight. Satisfying himself that the area was free of hikers and horseback riders—it was too hot for shit like that, he thought, wiping the sweat from his face with his sleeve—he turned back to the stolen truck. He withdrew a fifty-foot roll of rubber hose, then walked across the lawn. The new sod felt springy under his feet. Rounding the house, he came upon the swimming pool, set into one side of the lot. There was construction rubble on the deck, but the pool looked dry and ready for filling. About forty feet long and half as wide, it was the kind of pool you could take maybe six strokes in before you had to turn around, but it had a small diving board and a slide for kids. This place was the ultimate symbol of California success, he thought—the big fancy house, the pool, the view.

Rolling up his sleeves, he dropped the rubber hose next to the pool heater and went to work. He pulled a wrench from his pocket and loosened the pipe connecting the heater to its propane fuel tank. Esmerelda Canyon was too sparsely populated for California Gas to have gotten around to running in a line yet. Pocketing a coupling joint, he slipped one end of the rubber hose onto the fuel line, just below the supply valve, and secured it with duct tape. Then, working backward, he unrolled the hose, running it around the edge of the pool and across the patio. Using a glass cutter, he made a circular hole in the pane of a French door and fed the hose through, snaking it across the Mexican tile floor of the kitchen until the hose was fully extended. Satisfied that the line was kink-free from fuel tank to house, he ripped off a little more duct tape to secure the hose in the door and seal the opening around it. He glanced at his watch and smiled. Walking back to the fuel tank, he gave the valve a twist and listened for the soft hiss that indicated the propane was flowing.

Before leaving, the man made a call on his two-way radio, and by three thirty-four, the California Edison truck was long gone from Esmerelda Canyon and approaching the on-ramp of the San Diego Freeway.

Back at the house, the heavy propane gas streamed through the open fuel-tank valve, along the hose and into the kitchen, pouring out over the floor—invisible and deadly. Heavier than air, it seeped through the house, room by room, clinging to tiles and deep carpets. It spread from the kitchen to the family room, covering packing boxes and unhung paintings propped against walls. It drifted into the dining room and living room,

wrapping around furniture legs, insinuating itself over door-
jambs, then into the main-floor powder room and the den, with
its twin drafting tables, balsa-wood models and rolled-up
blueprints.

When the gas had filled every crack and crevice at floor level,
it began to rise, flowing up freshly painted walls and around
vases of celebratory new-home flowers, swirling around the
brass-and-teak chandelier in the dining room, wafting to the arc
of the living room's cathedral ceiling. Then the deadly cloud
paused; all the windows in the house were closed tight against
the midday heat.

A staircase provided a new avenue of advance. The poison-
ous vapor threaded its way up, step by step, spreading out when
it reached the top landing. Invisible tendrils extended into the
master bedroom and its still-disorganized dressing area and
bath. Into the guest room, used now as a catchall for clutter
from the move. Into the main bath, where pink bubble bath
and a family of yellow rubber duckies stood in a line along the
tub.

Last of all, the gas crept into the one room of the house that
was as settled as it was ever going to be—unpacked but messy,
with books, paper, crayons and an Etch-A-Sketch on the floor,
and mismatched socks already hiding under twin canopy beds
that were covered with identical white eyelet spreads. On the
floor between the beds, a small, gray-and-white Persian kitten
was sleeping in a soft, padded basket. The kitten's still-blue eyes
never opened when the gas washed over her, but she began to
convulse. Her little body shuddered for a minute or two, then
the spasms stopped abruptly and she was still.

The lethal vapor filled every corner of the room, rising to the
ceiling. Finally, its advance halted, it hovered. Waiting.

"Mallory, why did you do that?" Their mother stood between the girls, one hand shading her eyes as she looked down
at them, her pretty face etched with a frown.

Mallory stared at her brown toes, tracing a line in the sand.
"It was an accident."

"It was not!" Diana protested. "You broke my tower on
purpose!"

"It was *your* fault, because you pulled your guy away at the last minute, and the dragon fell on the tower."

"Mallory, apologize, please."

"Sor-ry," Mallory grumbled. Diana made an equally grudging reply.

"That's my lovelies." Their mother's face softened and she gave each forehead a kiss. "Sisters shouldn't fight. Sisters are best friends. You have to take care of each other."

Their father put his arms around their shoulders. "Come on, beach bunnies. It's time to go home."

Mallory jammed her feet into her plastic flip-flops, their center straps gritty between her toes. Diana was watching, she noticed, and she didn't look so mad anymore. Mallory wasn't, either. The castle game was getting kind of boring, anyway. Maybe they'd play Barbies when they got home. If they did, Mallory decided, she was going to let Diana use Malibu Barbie *and* Skipper, just to show she really hadn't meant to break her tower. She gave her sister a poke in the side, then screeched with glee as Diana chased her up the beach.

When they finally stopped to catch their breath, Mallory glanced back at her parents, who were gathering up the beach chairs, blanket and picnic hamper. Behind them, at the water's edge, a wave crashed over the sand castle, washing it away.

The car pulled into the driveway of their house, and the girls' father climbed out and opened the trunk. "Rinse off the sand toys before you put them away, please," he said.

Mallory and Diana made the usual complaints, but lifted out the pails and shovels while he gathered the beach chairs, blanket and picnic hamper. After they had spread the toys on the driveway, Diana looked up. "You unwind the hose and I'll go get the kitten. She must be lonely. We'll let her play on the grass while we do this."

Mallory nodded and walked over to the tap at the side of the house, turned it on and dragged the hose back to the toys at the bottom of the driveway. Then, seeing her parents going arm in arm up the front steps, Diana right behind them, she was seized with devilish inspiration. She lifted the hose nozzle and aimed it at her sister, waiting to squeeze the trigger until her parents had just stepped inside the house. Diana's hand was already on the handle of the big oak front door, but when the water hit her back, she let out a shriek and spun around.

Suddenly, there was a flash, and Diana was being hurled through the air. The front door was flying, too, Diana's hand still holding the handle. The last thing Mallory remembered, before everything went black, was hearing a thunderous boom.

When she opened her eyes, Mallory sensed that she was on her back, and that her skin had been scraped raw. Her legs, her arms, her face, even her bare belly with its bikini tan were stinging something awful, and her ears rang from the thunderbolt that had knocked her down. She blinked at the clear blue sky, then rolled over onto her stomach and lifted her head to see that she was lying at the bottom of the driveway. It was a good thing the construction trucks weren't around today, she thought, or she could have been run over. She pulled herself up on her elbows and peered toward the house, but it wasn't where it was supposed to be. She must have gotten turned around. And yet—

And yet, there was the car, still sitting in the driveway, with her dad's boat trailer resting on the hood. The boat itself was off the trailer, propped at a cockeyed angle against a palm tree, clear across the yard. Mallory blinked and looked again to where the house should be. A pile of rubbish had taken its place.

She struggled to her knees and spotted the heavy oak door at the end of the driveway, Diana lying next to it. Mallory wanted to run over, but her legs felt like jelly. She crawled instead. Diana seemed to be fast asleep, her right arm twisted away from her body at a scary angle, her wrist and hand wedged beneath the door. A wicked-looking triangle of glass was imbedded in the middle of her cheek. Mallory reached out, then withdrew her hand, afraid she would hurt Diana if she touched it.

"Diana?" she whispered. "Wake up! Please?" She touched her big sister's shoulder, lightly at first, then shaking it, but Diana's eyes remained closed. "Di? I'm sorry I sprayed you." There was no answer. Mallory watched Diana's still form until her own wobbly head grew too heavy for her neck to hold up.

Exhausted, she lay it down on her sister's shoulder, nestling close. She would sleep, too, she decided, and then they would get up and play with the kitten. "I'm sorry I broke your sand tower," she whispered as darkness fell once more.

Book One

Hope and Fear

1

Los Angeles, California
June 29, 1992

Mallory stood before the studio audience, acknowledging their cheers as the closing credits rolled on the television monitor that sat facing her on stage. On the small screen, her smiling face winked in and out of view as the long list of names streamed by—producers, researchers, technicians, and makeup, wardrobe and other specialists who labored each day to turn out "The Mallory Caine Show."

Nothing in her on-screen expression betrayed the sober thoughts running through her mind as she conducted what had become a habitual search of the faces before her. When the stalker had stepped into the light that previous September night, she thought she'd seen him before—on the fringes of the crowd at charity events, perhaps. Or outside the studio gates, staring at her as she waited to pull onto the busy street in Burbank. In the audience, maybe, his the only serious face amidst the smiles. Had she *really* seen him here? Or did it just seem that she had?

Mallory's eyes raked the crowd again, her mind recalling the dictionary definition of stalking: *To pursue an animal stealthily for the purpose of capturing or killing it.* That didn't capture the reality, she thought. What it didn't say was that merely *being* stalked, even without capture, created a kind of imprisonment and a slow dying of the soul. What it also didn't say was that there were many kinds of stalkers. Being pursued by the twin specters of fear and failure and by memories of the dead was almost worse than evading stalkers of the flesh-and-blood variety. You could face down and defeat a living menace, but the shadowy ones followed you every minute of every damn day. There was no escape from them.

Stalked and stalker: she was both. "America's Joan of Arc," *Time* magazine had called her, a crusading talk-show host you had to love or hate. Mallory Caine invited few neutral reactions. In photographs, she seemed almost ethereal: younger than her thirty-one years, with a halo of thick, wheat-blond hair, haunting brown eyes and a lean, fragile-looking body. In person or on-camera, however, the impression of fragility vanished, shoved aside by the energy that kept her in constant motion, stubborn perseverance flashing in her dark eyes. And when Mallory opened her mouth and gave way to impatience, even the most arrogant and self-assured trembled. She did not suffer fools gladly. It was a large part of her popular appeal.

In the studio now, the Applause sign had been lit and would stay on until the floor manager signaled "all clear," indicating that the credits were done and the taping was finished, but the prompt was unnecessary. The audience was on its feet, three hundred red-palmed fans whose affection and enthusiasm swept over Mallory like a warm ocean breeze. She waved, her eyes meeting theirs, one by one, row by row, searching for that telltale coldness. She found none. Not today.

Someone was out there, though, waiting, watching for the right moment. Not now, maybe, but soon. Inevitably. Today, however, these people were hers. Nothing lasts forever, she reminded herself—not fame, not security, not love. Certainly not the people she loved. Sooner or later, she always managed to lose them.

There were strangers everywhere, dressed in white and green, poking her, shining lights in her eyes, asking her if she knew her name and how old she was. "I'm Mallory and I'm eight," she should have told them. She knew that, but she was too scared to say anything.

There were nasty smells, strong and bitter—smells that she grew to hate ever after. Hospital smells, antiseptic and chalky.

There were policemen. Mommy and Daddy said that policemen were our friends and that we shouldn't be afraid of them.

That they would help. But these ones didn't help. They kept asking questions, over and over, questions she couldn't understand. What had she seen? Who had her parents spoken to that day? What were the names of their friends? Who came to their house? What did they look like?

She didn't know! All she knew was that she wanted her mommy and daddy! She cried and screamed, but no one would bring them or say where they were. Not at first....

"A-a-and . . . we're clear!" Solly Yablonski, the floor manager, gave Mallory the thumbs-up sign, then wearily pulled headphones and mike off his grizzled head.

The last live-to-tape program before the summer hiatus was in the can. The tape would be raced over to the Burbank communications center to be bounced by satellite to the syndicate's main production facilities in New York. Staff there would have a scant hour to review the program for technical glitches and insert space for ads and station breaks before sending it out again to local stations from coast to coast, as viewers from Maine to Hawaii turned on their television sets to see what America's favorite daytime talk-show host had brought into their living rooms that day.

"The Mallory Caine Show" was already a national institution and was fast becoming a global phenomenon. The program was taped at 11:00 a.m. most weekdays, usually in Burbank, unless they were doing a "remote week" in one of the cities where "Mallory Caine" was aired on local outlets. When they were on remote, Mallory and her crew were treated like visiting royalty by the local station and population, and she had already received the keys to nine cities across the country. But for the next four weeks, audiences would be treated to "The Best of Mallory Caine," reruns of the most popular and/or controversial episodes from the five seasons the show had been on air.

Mallory always winced to see herself in those early broadcasts, with her choppy monologues and nervous interviewing style, bad haircuts and the off-the-rack power suits that preceded the more relaxed American-designer originals she now favored and could afford. She tried not to spend too much time analyzing why the show had taken off the way it had. Certainly nothing in her early life had hinted at wild success. It was probably best not to look a gift horse in the mouth, she decided, just enjoy it while it lasted.

But even she could see that there was something appealing in those rough early shows. She'd been a junior *Los Angeles Chronicle* beat reporter, a twenty-five-year-old rookie still wet behind the ears, first thrust into national prominence when she'd unraveled a bribery scandal at a county sheriff's office and almost single-handedly brought down a long-reigning sheriff and eleven other officials. As a young and photogenic journalist with bulldog tenacity, Mallory had become almost as much a part of the story as the corrupt lawman, who publicly speculated which parts of her anatomy he would like to see skewered.

Not long after, she was offered a job hosting a summer-replacement show on the local NBC affiliate. Anxious for personal reasons to get out of the *Chronicle* newsroom, she'd leaped at the chance. "Uncommon Passions," with its high-profile interviews and offbeat features, had been snapped up for syndication in the fall and winter daytime-television lineup. In the second season, the program was renamed "The Mallory Caine Show." By her twenty-eighth birthday, it had gone into international syndication, was watched daily by twelve million viewers, and had garnered three Emmys, one for best show and two for best host. Now, at the end of the fifth season, Mallory's audience was estimated at over twenty million, the Emmy count stood at eight and she was in the process of establishing her own production company.

Despite her initial awkwardness in front of the camera, audiences had fallen in love with the self-deprecating young woman, who was gentle with guests who had suffered or were in pain, but who bristled visibly at the pompous, the vain and the overly powerful. From movie stars to politicians, mass murderers to Mother Teresa, Mallory posed the questions everyone wanted answered but wouldn't have had the nerve to ask. She was the defender of the little guy and the toppler of the self-important. Her mail and her ratings told her she was the sister, daughter, wife, lover and friend that millions wished they had. Funny, Mallory sometimes thought, that she should also be the real-life sister, daughter, wife, lover and friend of others who were decidedly less enthused about the idea.

Diana wasn't there, either. They said she was somewhere in the hospital, but she was very badly hurt. The doctors were trying to help her big sister get better, they told Mallory, and then maybe she could see her. "But later, Mallory. Diana's sleeping now. Be a big girl. Don't make a fuss."

Diana! Mommy! Daddy! Why wouldn't Mom and Dad come and take her home? Mallory was so mad at them. Where were they?

Everybody was mean. And she hurt inside. They said she had some broken ribs and a lot of bruises, and something about her head that was giving her this headache. Her stomach hurt, too, but the nurses said no, there was nothing wrong with her stomach. She was just frightened, was all.

No! It hurt! She wanted her daddy! She wanted her mommy! Somebody better bring them right now, or else!

Mallory bounded off the stage and over to the exit at the side of the studio. The big steel doors were propped open, and the audience began streaming down the steps of the bleachers. In the hall outside, the red No Entry—Taping in Session sign had been switched off. Mallory positioned herself underneath it, ready to shake hands with each and every member of the audience as they filed out. Her staff had urged her to forgo this farewell ritual, which took so much time out of what was already an insanely jammed schedule. Studio execs, too, after hearing grumbles from the maintenance staff, had hinted that she should drop the practice, since it slowed down the cleanup, but Mallory ignored their protests and went on doing it, show after show. The day she got too big for her britches to express her appreciation to her audience, she said, was the day she should be yanked off the air.

People wrote months in advance for tickets, and they started lining up outside the Burbank studios at 7:00 a.m. in order to get the best seats for the eleven o'clock taping. "You're the most important part of the show," she told them every morning during the warm-up, when she moved among them in jeans and sweatshirt, chatting informally before the lights and cameras were turned on and the program got under way. "I need you to ask questions and react to my guests. Help me out, *please,* or I'm going to die up there!''

No one believed it, but the audience loved her for her butterflies and her vulnerability. When Mallory came back out a while later, dressed and made up like the star she was, mugging and pirouetting for them like a little girl in a tutu looking for approval, they cheered and clapped and whistled. And when the cameras started to roll, they, too, became a part of the daily excitement that was ''The Mallory Caine Show.''

Thirty-five minutes after she had first planted herself in the hallway, Mallory looked over the head of the elderly woman whose hand was clasped in hers and caught the eye of Brenda Vasquez, her personal assistant. Brenda made a wiping motion across her forehead, signaling that the old couple in front of her was the end of the line. A subtle sigh of relief escaped Mallory's lips. She had shaken three hundred hands in the last thirty-five minutes. Three hundred greetings and thanks and congratulations graciously acknowledged.

''It was a wonderful show!''

Mallory shifted her gaze back to the silver-haired lady in front of her and smiled. ''I'm glad you could come.''

''Oh, I wouldn't have missed it for anything! I told Ben—this is Ben, my husband—I'm Doris. We're from Indiana,'' the woman added, pushing forward a balding man in a brilliant red-and-yellow-plaid shirt. Mallory smiled and shook his hand, too. ''I told Ben, we go to California, first thing we do is get tickets for 'Mallory Caine.' And he agreed, didn't you, Ben?'' Ben opened his mouth to reply, but his wife rolled right on. ''He watches every afternoon, too, now that he's retired. Come four o'clock, we sit down with a cup of tea, and if the phone rings or someone comes to the door, that's just too bad. When our daughter moved to Pasadena, we said, 'This is our chance to see Mallory!' ''

''Well, I'm really glad you came.''

''My hands are freezing, though,'' Doris said, examining them thoughtfully.

''I know. I'm sorry it's so cold in there. They have to keep it that way because of all the lights and equipment. Otherwise, the temperature would rise to about a hundred and sixty degrees and blow everything out."

"That's what Ben figured, didn't you, hon?" Her husband nodded, but Doris's gaze had already moved down to her feet, where painted toenails peeked out of strappy sandals. From the number of Band-Aids plastered on pressure points, Mallory guessed that the sandals were bought especially for the couple's California vacation. Doris's flesh was swollen over and around each thin strap. "I near to froze my feet off, but it was worth it."

Mallory gave her a hug. "You're a great sport."

"We loved it. You are just the smartest thing, and your show is so fine, not like those other trashy talk shows." Doris sniffed. "Women who love their daughters' boyfriends! Men who wear ladies' underwear! All those dippity-doos! Who needs to watch that stuff?"

"Well, we *do* try for something a little more uplifting."

"You surely do. That show you did on foster grandparents a few months back got everybody in Washburn—that's the town in Indiana where we live—got 'em thinking, and now we've got a foster-grandparents program of our own. And the way you took on those insurance companies who cut off medical benefits to people when they need them most!"

Doris was just warming up, Mallory realized with dismay. She had a plane to catch, and barely enough time to swing by the house to grab the suitcases she had packed the night before. Gridlock on the freeways kicked in early on Fridays. She'd never make it to the airport on time.

"That happened to my brother-in-law," Doris was saying, "and to three other people I know. After they'd paid their premiums for years and years! When her husband got Alzheimer's, they told Millie, my sister—"

"Doris," her husband interrupted, "I don't think Miss Caine needs to hear the whole story. She's probably got things to do."

God bless you, Ben, Mallory thought.

"Oh, for heaven's sake! What am I thinking of? Of course you do! But you just keep givin' 'em what for, okay, Miss Caine?"

"Call me Mallory. And I'll do my best, I promise. You two enjoy the rest of your vacation, okay?"

Doris and Ben wore broad smiles as they headed down the hallway toward the main doors, Doris shuffling painfully on her poor, swollen feet. "Wasn't she just so nice?" Mallory heard her whisper. "Just like on TV!" Her husband's head bobbed up and down.

Watching them go, Mallory felt a familiar stab of pain and rage in her solar plexus. Her mother would have turned sixty this year. Would she have been a sweet, rolling grandmotherly type like that? Probably not. She'd always had a slim, athletic build, and Mallory suspected she would have been one of those women who never looked her age. As it was, she was frozen forever in Mallory's memory as she had been that last afternoon: a laughing, auburn-haired, dark-eyed English beauty who, even as the thirty-six-year-old mother of two young daughters, had turned heads on the beach. "A Drop-Dead Gorgeous Junkie," some reporter had labeled her after she was killed.

Mallory was so scared. She promised not to be bad anymore. Please, please, won't you bring my mommy? What do you mean? Why can't she come?

No! Don't say that! I want my mommy! I want my daddy! They have to come! Mommymommymommymommy...!

2

As her new Indiana friends, Doris and Ben, disappeared down the hall, Mallory and her assistant walked back into the studio, deceptively small, despite its warehouse-style high ceilings. Heading for the stage, they passed tiered seats, half a dozen television monitors, row on row of extinguished arc lights, three main-floor cameras, stripped now of their big Panavision film cartridges and the TelePrompTer from which Mallory read the show's lead-in monologue. Remounting the stage, the two women crossed it and passed through the curtains at the back, coming out in the long hallway that led to the greenroom, where guests watched the show as they awaited their introductions, and which wasn't really green at all, but a putrid shade of yellow. They walked past Makeup, where Adele and Jonathon somehow managed to make everyone better-looking than they were in real life. Past storage rooms that held lights and cables and other equipment, plus a bizarre array of props that had been used on the program at one time or another.

As they walked through a set of soundproof doors, they emerged in yet another cavernous hallway leading to offices, dressing rooms and still more studios where the local news and various afternoon soaps were taped. A maintenance man on an approaching electric cart beeped a warning.

"Hey! Whoa!" Mallory called, waving. "How about a lift to my office?"

The man grinned as the cart pulled to a silent stop. "Sure thing, Miss Caine. Hop on."

Mallory reached to support Brenda's elbow, but her assistant climbed aboard without difficulty, despite her pudginess,

and despite being laden down with a clipboard, a cellular phone
and a variety of objects that had been shyly handed to Mallory
by members of the audience as they filed out. Mallory always
gave these mementos to Brenda for safekeeping until they could
get back to her offices. Today, Brenda was holding three bou-
quets of flowers, a glass knickknack in the shape of a boot, two
photos of someone's grandchildren, a box of Fanny May
chocolates from a Chicago fan and six letters that had been
anxiously pressed into Mallory's hand—invariably seeking
money or a job.

As usual, Mallory would give the flowers to some of the secretaries, runners, hairdressers, floor assistants or other grem-
lins who worked on the show for next to nothing except the
dubious—to Mallory's mind—thrill of being able to say that
they were on her staff. The photos would be added to a collage
that covered most of one wall of her dressing room: a growing
portrait of the cross section of people across the country who
felt close enough to the woman on their television screens to
send her their pictures and incredibly intimate stories of the joys
and tragedies in their lives.

The chocolates would go in the trash. It was a sad commentary on modern life in America, but she didn't dare let anyone
eat a food gift from a stranger, in case some nut out for twisted
fame had decided to poison her. The letters would be answered in Mallory's name by her public-relations staff, each
reply accompanied by an eight-by-ten machine-autographed
glossy, the employment and cash requests regretfully denied.
The glass boot—well, she wasn't sure what they'd do with the
glass boot.

"Here, let me help you with some of that stuff," Mallory
offered as they settled on the rear seat of the cart and it began
to roll.

"I'd be happy to," Brenda said, "but it's so carefully balanced that if you remove one thing, it'll tumble like a house of
cards."

"Let me get the flowers, at least." Brenda had all three
bunches clutched precariously in the fingers of one fist. Mallory pried them open and relieved her of the huge bouquet.

"Thanks," Brenda said, able now to get a better grip on the rest. "That helps. So! Last show's in the can. You all ready for your trip?"

Mallory sighed. "I guess. I feel like I'm running away, though. I should be staying."

"Baloney! It'll do you good to see your sister. How long has it been?"

"Almost a year."

"There, you see? You're overdue. And besides, you need a break."

"I need a new life."

"Wanna trade? You can have mine. On second thought, never mind. I wouldn't inflict my mother on my worst enemy, let alone you."

"Your mother's a hoot!"

"Yeah, sure. You say that 'cause she doesn't phone *you* every day to nag about when you're gonna get married and give her some *nietos.*"

"*Nietos?*"

"Grandchildren. I say, '*mamacita,* gimme a break here. I got a great job, a good life, terrific friends, a nice place to live, I pay my bills.' But of course, that's not enough for Carmen Maria Ramirez y de la Fuente de Vasquez, so she prays to the Virgin of Guadalupe every day to send me a husband."

Mallory grinned ruefully. "Think the Virgin of Guadalupe would work for me? Send mine back, I mean?"

Brenda's expression turned sober. She studied Mallory's face for a moment, then took a deep breath. "I was going to tell you."

"Tell me what?"

"Ian phoned."

Mallory's smile faded. "When?"

"While you were taping."

"While I was—"

"I told him. I said you'd call back just as soon—"

"No. He did that deliberately."

"Mallory, I don't think—"

"Of course he did! After five years, you think he doesn't know what my taping schedule is?"

''Maybe he forgot.''

Mallory glanced at the man driving the cart, but he seemed preoccupied. She leaned toward Brenda and lowered her voice to a whisper. ''The guy's a Pulitzer Prize–winning journalist with a photographic memory, Bren, and he only moved out ten days ago. He didn't forget.''

''No, I guess not.''

''Here you go, Miss Caine!'' the driver called. The cart swept to a stop in front of a door whose plaque read The Mallory Caine Show. As the two women jumped off, Mallory glanced at the oval name tag above the driver's breast pocket.

''Hey, Pete, are you married?''

''Yup. Two kids.''

''Well, here,'' Mallory said, handing him the bouquet of flowers. ''Take these home to your wife, why don't you?''

''Thanks! I will. She'll be real pleased.''

''Give her a big hug, too, okay?''

Pete laid the flowers on the vinyl seat beside him and grinned as he touched his finger to the peak of his baseball cap. ''You betcha, Miss Caine. Thanks again.''

''No problem. Thanks for the ride.''

The two women entered the suite of offices, where nine assistants were fielding phone calls, answering bags of mail and typing upcoming-program schedules. In cubicles around the room, research staff were poring over newspapers, magazines, wire services and tips from viewers, scouring for new program ideas. It was a cluttered, noisy, stressful, mad place to work, and not one of the people there wanted to be anywhere else.

Mallory composed her face into the broad, steady smile that she wore as armor around all but a very few, and gave her staff a wave. As if on cue, an inner-office door opened, and out strode Shawn McFee, her executive producer, closely followed by his senior coproducer, Sheena Delaney. Mallory wondered if they'd had their ears pressed to the door, waiting to pounce the moment she came in. Shawn and Sheena: the Anxiety Twins, she called them affectionately. Shawn was obviously having a bad day. His thick black hair had been tugged straight up, they way it always was when he started fretting. His hairline, Mallory noticed for the first time, was receding, and what little was left on top was getting very thin. Five years of tearing it out over production crises was finally taking its toll. Sheena was biting her cuticles.

"Michael Keaton canceled!" Shawn groaned. Mallory continued toward her own office, no longer thrown by Shawn's daily panic attacks. He and Sheena, in lockstep with each other, threaded their way around the desks and sacks of mail in the outer office and followed Mallory and Brenda through to her inner sanctum. "Spielberg has signed him to a new film that starts shooting up in Canada next week," he went on, "and Michael says he won't be able to make it, after all."

"Can we reschedule?"

"But he was going to be our first guest after the hiatus."

"Well, now he won't, I guess. Where in Canada is he shooting?"

Shawn looked perplexed and glanced at Sheena. "Somewhere in Ontario, I think," she said.

"Aren't we doing a remote in Toronto in September?" Mallory asked.

"Yes, but the lineup's already decided for that week."

"Now it's changed." Mallory picked up the telephone from her desk and buzzed her secretary. "Elise, could you see if you can get Michael Keaton on the phone for me?" Five minutes later, Keaton was rescheduled to appear on the Labor Day edition of "Mallory Caine" with a promise to try to drag Spielberg along as a surprise guest. "That just leaves August to straighten out," Mallory said, returning the phone to its cradle and starting to stuff her briefcase with the mass of papers from her desk. "Brenda's riding to the airport with me to go over all this bumpf. We'll see if we can come up with any ideas. You guys can work on it while I'm gone, too." She looked up and gave the Anxiety Twins a broad, winning smile.

Shawn opened his mouth as if to protest, then closed it again and slumped his shoulders. "Yeah, sure," he grumbled. "Don't worry about us. You just run off and eat truffles and sip Dom Perignon. We'll be *fine.*"

Mallory laughed as Brenda, standing out of sight behind him, drew one arm across another in imitation of a tragic violinist. "You'll do great!" she said.

She knew they would. For all their hand-wringing and complaining, Shawn and Sheena were two of the most creative minds in television. Shawn had been with Mallory from the start, when he was a young assistant producer on the old "Uncommon Passions." Sheena had joined them in the second season.

"But you know the rules," Mallory added, as she snapped shut the locks on her briefcase. "No sob sisters. No so-called experts on victimization. No whiners who blame everyone else for their screwed-up lives."

Brenda, Shawn and Sheena linked arms and raised fists, chanting the unofficial "Mallory Caine" chorus: "Give us your dreamers! Your fighters! Your hungry idealists yearning to do good!"

Mallory rolled her eyes. "I think I've overtrained you people."

They laughed, but they all had agreed early on that they were sick of the steady stream of losers and ne'er-do-wells who paraded every day across most television talk programs. Mallory had no objection to pure entertainment. She had produced her share of light themes and crazy stunts for the sheer, exuberant joy of it. But not for her was the modern-day equivalent of the circus freak show programs that titillated audiences with socially rather than physically deformed people, degrading subject and viewer alike. Gawking at problems did nothing to help solve them, she said. Audiences needed inspiration, not antiheroes who only fed a sense of helplessness and hopelessness. As her popularity grew and she acquired greater control as senior executive producer of her own show, Mallory had insisted on featuring people who made a difference in their chosen fields. The "take charge of your life" refrain was a large part of her program's success, offering a daily booster shot of self-confidence to a public weakened and disheartened by media defeatism.

All eight "Mallory Caine" Emmys were proudly encased in the show's front office, even the four that named Mallory as "best host." The awards were a shared achievement, she told her staff. If she looked good, it was because they worked their tails off to make her look good. If she seemed relaxed and in control in front of the camera, it was only because she went on air every day knowing that the Anxiety Twins had sat up late the night before, ensuring that every tedious little program detail had been taken care of before she stepped out on stage. All Mallory had to do was juggle unforeseeable glitches, like trained animals that pooped on air, or props that backfired, or cantankerous guests who tried to wriggle out of tough questions by going on the offensive against the host. She was quick on her feet and could handle those little problems. What was more, *she* got audience sympathy, fame and an eight-figure annual salary for her trouble. All the Anxiety Twins got were ulcer symptoms and a reserved spot in the studio parking lot.

"You guys make sure you take some time off while I'm gone and *relax*, you hear?" she said.

"Yeah, yeah," Shawn said. "Go on now, get outta here."

She punched him lightly in the shoulder. "I mean it, or you're fired."

"Yes, ma'am," he said, rubbing his shoulder and grinning ruefully.

"Have a great vacation, Mallory," Sheena said, giving her a hug.

"Thanks. Come on, Bren." She grabbed her briefcase. "Let's go sit in gridlock and suck exhaust fumes."

3

She had all the fringe benefits of celebrity, Mallory thought as she and Brenda climbed into the limo, heading for the airport via her home in Brentwood. But it wasn't as if fame and fortune cured everything. As a matter of fact, it didn't help at all with most problems. Some, like failed marriages, were only made worse by the lack of privacy that came with a high profile. There was no protection from the buffeting she would take when the tabloids and gossip columnists learned that she and Ian had split.

It was a miracle they hadn't found out yet, although Mallory had no doubt that Liz Smith or someone else would get wind of it any moment, especially after the date Ian had apparently had the night before with Caitlyn Allis, the high-powered, highly visible defense lawyer. At *Spago,* no less. Why not just take out a billboard, Gallagher? she thought bitterly. Or hire one of those advertising planes to fly over Dodger Stadium: *Beautiful women take note—Ian Gallagher has walked out on Mallory Caine. Free, free, free at last!* Maybe getting out of town wasn't such a bad idea, she decided, given the media circus that would erupt when word hit the streets.

One of Mallory's acquaintances from the studio, an afternoon-soap actress whose career was fading as fast as her looks, had bumped into her that morning. Season Garner had accidently stumbled on the news, and felt obliged to commiserate. "Mallory! Dear heart! How *are* you?" Season's pouty expression and hangdog look, Mallory guessed, was supposed to pass for warm sympathy.

"I'm fine, thanks. How are you, Season?"

"Well, fine, of course. But I've been *so* worried about you," she crooned.

"About me? Why?"

"Well, you've been going through such a rough time this past year or so. Personally, I mean, what with that stalker and the publicity and all. Though your show's doing just *so* well, isn't it?"

"The ratings look good," Mallory said noncommittally. What *was* this obnoxious woman driving at?

"Don't they? And I'm *so* glad that part of your life is happy, now that Ian—"

"What about Ian?"

"Well, Jason and I were at *Spago* last night—" Jason Frame was Season's current lover, a brooding, no-talent hunk from the soap who was half her age, but looking to turn his guest status into a full-time gig. No doubt he figured that sleeping with one of the stars was a good way to go about it. "—and we ran into Ian. He was there with that lawyer lady." Season's forehead wrinkled prettily in what apparently signaled deep concentration. "The one who defended the woman who shot her daughter's murderer?"

"Caitlyn Allis?"

"That's the one!"

"I see. Well, she's an old friend." Mallory wasn't about to volunteer the information, if Season didn't know it, that Caitlyn had also been Ian's first wife.

"Oh, dear, dear Mallory! They certainly *did* look friendly."

Screw you, Mallory thought. And screw you, too, Ian. "I have to be going, Season. I'm late for a wardrobe fitting."

"Of course. But Mallory? If there's anything I can do—anything at all—call me, won't you? We girls have to stick together in times like these."

Mallory had stiffened as Season threw her arms around her shoulders, nearly choking on the miasma of *Opium* that surrounded the woman. She had extricated herself from Season's grip and wheeled away, heels clicking on the corridor's polished tile floor.

* * *

"Hey, girl. Penny for your thoughts?" Brenda Vasquez poked Mallory with her elbow as they settled into the soft leather seats and the limo pulled out of the studio parking lot. In general, Mallory would have preferred to drive herself, but ever since the stalker had broken into her house several months earlier, Fleet Productions, the television syndicate that distributed "Mallory Caine," had insisted on providing a limo and burly driver for the woman who had become one of their major investments.

Mallory pulled out of her gloomy reverie and looked over at the sympathetic smile on her assistant's wide face. With one hundred and forty pounds of energy on a five-foot frame, Brenda was as plump and dark-haired as Mallory was lean and fair. She had been sent over by the network early in the second season to help with the influx of fan mail when the show took off into the stratosphere of the daytime ratings. But, although Brenda had started out in the typing pool, her sharp mind and total unflappability had became indispensable as she helped deal with office overload, booking problems and producer temper tantrums. Mallory had soon named Brenda as her personal assistant, at a salary no one in the working-class Vasquez family had ever dreamed of earning. Mallory's faith had never been disappointed. Brenda had quickly learned the ropes, handling program staff, network execs, guests and fans with the same even-handed humor and brilliant efficiency. She was also, Mallory knew, completely discreet. Nothing Mallory shared with Brenda ever went past the two of them, and as a result, the woman had earned a special place as Mallory's sounding board, her confidante and her friend.

"So," Mallory said with a sigh, "did Ian want me to call him back?"

"Actually, he just asked me to give you a message," Brenda looked as uncomfortable as anyone could be who gets caught between estranged spouses.

Mallory nodded. "I rest my case."

"Maybe he was just tied up."

"I'll bet. With Caitlyn Allis."

"Come on, Mal, don't say that. Season Garner's a first-class bitch. You can't believe anything she says."

"Why would she lie about them being at *Spago*?"

"So what if they were? It was probably perfectly innocent. Season's just trying to get your goat because you've never let her guest on the show."

"Yes, well, she succeeded."

"So I guess this means we won't be booking her real soon, huh?"

"Sure we will—when hell freezes over. Damn! How could I have messed things up so badly with him?"

"Don't do this to yourself, girl. Things will work out. Don't tell yourself horror stories."

"How can I not? Fact—he's moved out, which would naturally lead to the conclusion that he's on the prowl. And fact—his ex has the hots for him again."

"You don't know that."

"Oh, yes, I do. Caitlyn sat next to him at the Cedars-Sinai Hospital benefit last month. I can't prove it, but I'm almost certain she switched her place card before dinner so she'd end up beside him. I thought she was going to slide off her chair and into his lap by the time dessert was served. Plus, she fed him inside information during that murder trial she was working on, at considerable risk to the case and her professional reputation."

"*That's* who the *Chronicle's* source was?"

"Yeah, but don't tell anyone. So, you see, if it were anyone else that Season and Jason had seen at dinner with Ian, I wouldn't be so worried, but Caitlyn Allis..." Mallory slumped down in the seat and dropped her cheek onto her fist. "Damn!"

"Oh, Mal. It'll be okay, you'll see."

Mallory looked up wearily. "So what was Ian's message?"

"He wanted to make sure you don't change the security code on the house alarm before you go."

Mallory sat up straighter. "He wants to go back to the house?"

"He wants to get some stuff out while you're away—books and his bike or something."

"His bike? He hasn't ridden that thing in at least three years. But of course, he *would* want to get in shape, wouldn't he, with his ex-wife checking out his body again, comparing him to her Ian of old? Great. Just bloody great!"

"He's what, Mal—forty?"

"Forty-two."

"Well, that's it then. He's having a midlife crisis, is all. Guys do it all the time, but they come to their senses eventually. Ian will, too. Give him time. This is just some testosterone thing."

"No, it's not, Bren. I wish it were, but it's not. The problem isn't Ian, it's me. It's always been me."

"I don't believe that."

"Believe it, girl. I'm the Typhoid Mary of relationships."

Brenda laughed. "You think I'm kidding?" Mallory asked.

"Twenty million people would think you're kidding, Mallory."

"That's just because they've never lived with me." Or seen the wreckage of disastrous relationships that trailed in her wake, Mallory thought. It wasn't that she didn't *try* to take care of the people who meant the most to her. It's just that she seemed congenitally prone to self-destruction.

Congenitally prone: it was exactly the term the Reverend Harold Caine would have chosen. Well, maybe her adoptive father was right, after all. He'd always thought that she was the Bad Seed, spawned by common criminals. And if Mallory's sister had escaped the Rev's harangues for the most part, it was only because Diana had been given her own particular cross to bear.

Everything hurt, and still, they wouldn't bring her mommy and daddy. "I'll be good. Please let me see them," Mallory begged. But they wouldn't—said they couldn't. Mallory didn't want to hear that.

And then one day, Reverend Lennox, the minister from church, came to talk to her. He was a nice man, with white hair and a round face, like one of Santa's old elves. He sat with her for a long time, patting her hand, and telling her she must be a brave, brave girl. Mommy and Daddy had gone to heaven. It was hard, he knew, but they were with God now, and they wanted her to be brave.

Mallory nodded, but she didn't feel brave at all. "Why can't I see Diana?"

"You will, soon. Maybe even today. But she won't be able to see you yet, Mallory. She's asleep. She's been hurt very badly."

"What's wrong with her?"

"A lot of things. She'll get better, but it will take some time. She has internal injuries—she's hurt inside. And both of her legs and her right arm are broken. The legs will heal, but the doctors think her arm may not work very well anymore. They'll have to see."

"But that's the arm she writes and draws with. She's really good at it."

"She'll be taught to use her other arm instead."

Mallory knew that wouldn't work. She and Diana had practiced writing with their left hands once, but you could hardly read anything. Diana was practically an artist, even though she was just ten. How was she going to make her pictures now?

"You'll have to help Diana," *Reverend Lennox said.* "She's going to have a lot of work to do, getting better and learning to cope with one good arm. When it's time for her to leave the hospital, she'll need you to do some things for her, for a little while at least."

"You mean, like now I'm the big sister?"

"Something like that. Can you do that, Mallory? Can you help take care of Diana?"

"Yeah, I can. But I'm not allowed to use the stove."

Lennox smiled. "You won't have to cook her meals, honey."

"Who's going to come to our house to do the cooking?"

He hesitated, his smile fading. "Your house isn't there anymore, Mallory. Don't you remember? We talked about that. How there was—um—an accident, and that's why your mommy and daddy went to heaven, and you and Diana were hurt?"

Mallory looked away. That's right. She remembered, but she didn't want to think about it—about the light and the big noise, and then seeing just a pile of rock where their new house used to be. Mommy? Daddy? She turned back to him. "Are we gonna live in the hospital forever?"

"No. Only until you're feeling a little better. In fact, you yourself will be able to go ho—" he caught himself just in time *"—to leave the hospital in a few more days. There are some nice people, a foster family, who will take care of you until Diana is stronger."*

"Are they going to be my mommy and daddy now? Do I know them?"

"No, honey, but I think we've found a new mommy and daddy for you and Diana. A minister, just like me, and his wife—Reverend and Mrs. Caine. We should know in a few weeks. I'm working on it with the child welfare authorities."

"The who?"

"The people whose job it is to find new homes for children."

"Am I an orphan, like Pollyanna?"

"I guess you are."

"But I don't have an Aunt Polly."

"No, I know. Unfortunately, neither of your parents had any relatives who could take you in, I'm afraid. But the Caines seem like good people, and they have no children of their own. They'd love to have two nice little girls like you and Diana come to live with them. Would you like that?"

Mallory shrugged. *"I guess. Can I see Diana now?"*

"She's still sleeping most of the time, you know. She can't play with you."

"I know. I just want to stay with her. I'll help take care of her."

"I think that would be a very good idea, Mallory. Let's go talk to the head nurse."

Book Two

Rage and Envy

4

The Reverend Harold Caine and his wife, Frances, were living in a parish near Sacramento when Mallory and Diana's parents were killed. Hearing about the dead couple's orphaned girls, Frances Caine's sympathetic heart was moved. She would never have children of her own, she knew by now. She had often thought about trying to adopt a baby, but her husband showed no interest. Anyway, adoptive babies were in great demand, but no one wanted half-grown children who might come with a packet of personal problems.

"We should take in these little girls, Harold," Frances said one day. "It's what God wants us to do. I feel certain of it."

Caine was in his church office, preparing his homily for the following Sunday. He looked up at his wife over half-moon glasses. "That's all well and good to say, Frances, but we mustn't let good intentions blind us to reality. Those children saw their parents murdered. Who knows what else they might have been exposed to in their short lives? You know what the papers are saying about the murder—that it was a mob operation. I know Doug Lennox says the parents seemed all right, but they hadn't been in his parish long. We know next to nothing about them, except that they were mixed up with criminals."

"You don't know that for certain."

"Really, Frances, you're so naive. The police found drugs in the car, the papers said. What kind of people drive around with heroin in the trunk, I ask you? Heaven only knows what they had gone to the beach to do that day, and whom they had gone there to meet. It makes me shudder to think that they dragged the children along with them.''

Frances sighed deeply. ''You're right, dear, but the poor little girls... You can't blame them for the sins of the parents. What's to become of them?''

Harold Caine sat stiffly in his high-back chair. ''It's unrealistic to think that we could give them what they need. In all likelihood, these are disturbed children. They would be better off in a group home of some sort. In any event, we have no shortage of responsibilities here, to my parishioners.''

Frances moved around behind the desk. ''It would set an example,'' she said, placing a hand on his shoulder.

The clergyman flinched but eyed her curiously. ''An example?''

''Of brotherly love. For your parishioners. Taking in these children is the Christian thing to do. I imagine that even the bishop would be impressed.''

At the mention of his clerical superior, Caine leaned back in his chair and stared into space. ''It *would* take a noble sort of man, wouldn't it? To take on these children, who have lived amidst Lord knows what kind of corruption, and remold them into worthy creatures.''

''It would take a man like you, Harold.''

Maybe it wouldn't have mattered whom she was sent to live with, Mallory often thought. She would have probably hated any adoptive parents on principle. They were not her own, after all, and never for a moment would she pretend otherwise.

She hadn't done well with the foster parents who took care of her during the period when Diana remained in hospital and their adoption by the Caines was being arranged. Mallory had spent the entire four months on pins and needles. No matter how often they told her that she and Diana would soon be together, her childish trust had been ripped apart in the blast that took her mother and father. What if something happened to Diana? She would be all alone.

If they had let her, Mallory would have spent every waking minute sitting on that hard chair next to Diana's hospital bed, just to make sure that God didn't try to steal her sister, the way he had stolen her mommy and daddy. At first, she cried and clung to the bed rails when visiting hours were over, but when the nurse told her that she would have to stay away if she continued to make such a racket, Mallory saved her tears and her frightened rage for outside the hospital.

Her foster family were kindly souls, with two good-hearted teenage boys who tolerated her black moods because they felt sorry for her. Under any other circumstances, Mallory would have adored those big boys—they took her for ice cream and lifted her onto their shoulders to shoot baskets in the driveway. But when the day came to leave her foster family for the last time to get Diana from the hospital and take her to their new home, Mallory had leaped into Frances and Harold Caine's car without a backward glance.

Frances Caine had a kind heart and a love for children. Even when Mallory, the younger of her two adoptive charges, turned out to be a rambunctious handful, Frances waited out the angry little girl's temper tantrums with such forbearance that the two of them eventually came to a kind of truce. Frances would not insist that Mallory call her Mother, and Mallory would not remind Frances at every opportunity that she would never be more than a pitiful second best in the parenting department. For Frances, it was a fair deal, more than she ever would have dared to hope. Having these pretty little girls to love and fuss over went a long way toward compensating for all the other gaps in her life.

She could hardly believe that she had managed to convince her husband to pursue the adoption. He was not comfortable with children. The only ones he resigned himself to dealing with were his acolytes, who assisted him at Sunday services. Nor would Frances and Harold Caine ever have children of their own, as she had once hoped. Frances had been thirty-seven when Harold proposed—three years older than he, although she was too embarrassed about their age difference to ever admit it out loud. In the early years of their marriage, she had harbored a secret hope that it wasn't too late for a baby, but it never happened. Now, of course, she *was* too old, her body well into the change and holding little interest for her husband.

It would be a gross understatement to say that Frances was no beauty. Still, the middle-aged Frances Caine who adopted Mallory and Diana was an improvement over the Frances Parker of her youth. At least, by the time she reached her late forties, Frances suffered less by comparison with her contemporaries, whose jowls and eyelids now sagged, and whose bodies had gone broad and flaccid from childbearing. But in her youth, compared to sparkling girls with permanent-waved hair and voluptuous figures, Frances had been so plain she was almost invisible.

Back in Enfield, Massachusetts, where she was born and raised, Frances had never been considered a catch. She had wispy, mouse-colored hair that refused to hold a wave and slid out of every effort to roll it into a respectable mass with the help of hairpins. When she made the mistake of having it bobbed, to her mother's horror, all she accomplished was to emphasize its thinness as it lay flat against her head, flaky scalp peeking out between the strands. Behind thick spectacles, her hazel eyes appeared crossed. Even from a distance, she wasn't one of those girls to invite admiring glances, her small-breasted, wide-hipped figure giving her the appearance of a walking pear never quite ripe for picking. In her narrow bed at night, the young Frances, lips pressed to her down-filled pillow, dreamed of romance with Tyrone Guthrie look-alikes. But when she rose in the morning and looked in the cruel mirror, picking loose feathers out of her hair, it was only too obvious why young men never gave her a second look.

Once, after reading an advertisement in *Collier's Weekly* in which Ironized Yeast promised to give wallflowers "new pep and ginger that often bring instant popularity," Frances slipped out to the drugstore and bought a bottle. Desperate for results, she gulped half the awful-tasting concoction right away, washing it down with glass after glass of water, then sat back and waited to be pepped and gingered. Unfortunately, all she got was a severe case of flatulence, which mortified her mother during Sunday church services and left Frances resigned to a life of permanent peplessness.

The fact was, she often told herself later as she brushed Diana's pretty dark curls and ironed Mallory's favorite blue jeans, motherhood at this late stage in her life, even second-rate motherhood, was no less miraculous than the fact that she had managed to avoid the stigma of spinsterhood, and had even become a pillar of the community as a minister's wife—proof positive there was a God in heaven, for which she gave fervent thanks every day.

Before Harold Caine, Frances had had no experience of men, much less of the things that went on between men and women. After high school, when her father had died, she took a job in Finney's Dry Goods Store. Her only social outings were Sunday services at St. John's Episcopal Church and the women's-auxiliary meetings that she attended with her mother, where she became such a reliable, hardworking fixture that everyone soon forgot that she wasn't just another middle-aged housewife. World War II came and went, but neither the young sailors who passed through the nearby ports nor returning veterans eager for mates took any notice of the pear-shaped young woman with slightly crossed eyes. Frances went on measuring cloth and dusting the shelves at Finney's, and nothing really changed in her life until 1954, when a young minister right out of divinity school arrived in Enfield.

By this time, Frances was thirty-two, plain as old linoleum and just about as faded. Her mother had grown sickly and fussy, but Mrs. Parker wasn't beyond rousing herself from her bed long enough to invite the new minister to tea. Frances, out of deference to his position, wore her best flowered dress when Reverend Caine came to call, but she could see that the young cleric's eyes slid over her without interest, just as other men's did. For the next five years, in the course of his duties and their involvement with the women's auxiliary, the Parker ladies saw a good deal of him. When old Mrs. Parker developed cancer, finally vindicated after years of complaining about her health, Reverend Caine began calling once or twice a week. But even then, no one, least of all Frances, would have said he had anything in mind except good works. In a denomination whose liturgy was vaguely Catholic but which never demanded mari-

tal abstinence from its clergy, Harold Caine seemed to be that
odd breed: a Protestant minister called to a life of celibacy.

As it happened, Caine was not there to conduct the funeral
when Mrs. Parker finally passed on. A few weeks earlier, one
of the altar boys had committed suicide by locking himself in
the family garage and blowing his head off with his father's
hunting rifle. Devastated by the death and his own inability to
recognize the boy's signs of distress, Harold Caine had withdrawn to a religious retreat. Mrs. Parker's funeral had had to
be conducted by a stranger, a minister sent in by the diocese. No
one knew Harold had returned to Enfield until the day Caine
showed up at Frances's door.

"Reverend Caine! I didn't know you were back."

"I just got in. I heard about your mother, Miss Parker. I
wanted to tell you how terribly sorry I am that I wasn't here for
her at the end."

"Oh, that's all right. She wasn't really there with us these last
months, anyway, you know. Mentally, I mean. But you always
were a great comfort to her before." Frances felt herself becoming flustered. She picked up Fergus, her fat old tomcat,
who was circling between her legs. Clutching him close like a
shield, she scratched his ears and bent her head to study his
face, as if he had been lost for ages and had only just reappeared. He hadn't, of course, but studying the cat was easier
than raising her gaze to the man in the doorway and letting him
see how flummoxed he made her. Only on Sundays, when she
pretended to be intent upon the words of the sermon, did she
permit herself to look at him.

She wouldn't have said he was handsome. He had thick eyebrows, a receding hairline on a bullet-shaped head, and cautious eyes—hooded, as if a curtain would drop if you tried to
look too closely. And, of course, he was younger than she, although his reticence and authority made him seem mature beyond his years. From the safety of her Sunday pew, Frances
would often imagine scenarios of confessed mutual love and
unexpected passion. Scenarios where loneliness and fear were
understood and kissed away. Scenarios that ended with Frances
and several little Caines, like baby ducklings, lined up on the

front pew, the reverend smiling down on his family from the lofty pulpit. How ridiculous! she thought. How impossible.

Suddenly remembering her manners, Frances stepped back into the vestibule of the big house in which she now rattled around all alone. "Won't you come in?"

"I don't want to bother you, if this is not a good time."

"No! I mean no, not at all. I was just going to make coffee, if you'd like some. Or tea—I could make tea. Mother always used to drink tea. I prefer coffee, but it didn't seem worthwhile to make both. Unless you'd prefer," she added hastily. "I *could* make tea. It wouldn't be any trouble at all, really."

"Coffee would be fine."

She considered having him wait in the front room, but before she could say anything, he headed down the long, narrow hall toward the kitchen. It didn't seem right, the minister in there. Her mother would be appalled, but he had already made the decision for her, so Frances followed him into the kitchen. Caine settled himself on a wooden ladderback chair next to the table while she measured coffee into the percolator basket. She set the pot on the stove, trying to ignore his watchful eyes as she collected the cream and sugar and teaspoons.

"I'm sorry, I don't have any biscuits on hand," she said, keeping her back to him. He had always said he liked her macaroons and tollhouse cookies.

"It's all right."

"Since Mother died, I haven't been baking much. She always liked a sweet with her tea, but they go straight to my hips." She felt her face go hot. What a thing to say to the minister.

"It's quite all right, Frances."

Frances—had he ever called her by her Christian name before? Frances couldn't recall. The cups clattered as she set them down on a tray. "You'd be more comfortable in the front room. We'll go and sit in there."

"No, this is fine. I like to watch you in the kitchen."

She stopped and looked at him at last. "You do?"

"Yes. You seem so comfortable in here. Familiar."

"Familiar?"

"Yes. You have an air of domesticity about you." Caine glanced around the spotless kitchen. "You like taking care of your home, don't you, Frances? Taking care of others, too."

"I like to keep busy and look after my cat and my mother—before she passed on, that is. Make things nice."

"And so you do, Frances, so you do."

The percolator began chirping on the stove. Frances poured their coffee, and for a while, only the sound of Caine's spoon tinkling against the side of the cup broke the silence. After a few moments, he raised his head. "Do you ever feel lonely, Frances?"

She glanced up sharply, then away. "Oh, I don't know. Sometimes, maybe. But I see people all day at Finney's, and then at the church and the auxiliary and all."

"But you don't wish for someone to be there at other times? Someone to take care of? Someone to take care of you?"

Frances hesitated, then sat back, sighing. "What's the point of wishing for something that can never be?"

"Why do you say that?"

"Look at me. I know what I look like. What I am. Good old Frances. Hardworking, reliable, plain, boring old Frances. The one people call on for the bake sales and cleanup committees and the altar guild. The one who fills in when someone's sick. Who'll always be available in a pinch. Goodness knows, she has nothing else to do."

"Frances! Are you feeling sorry for yourself? People depend on you, I'm sure, but there's no shame in that. They do the same to me, you know."

"Oh, yes, I'm sure they must. Forgive me. I didn't mean to complain. It's just that . . ."

"You're lonely."

"Yes," she whispered.

"So am I, Frances."

When she dared to look at him again, his half-curtained eyes were intent upon her, and she felt mesmerized by their unblinking regard. She scarcely breathed as he slid his chair closer and took her hand in his, but she felt certain he must be able to hear the pounding that was reverberating in her ears.

"I've spent a lot of time thinking and praying in the past few weeks, Frances," he said. "I've always been a solitary person. I suppose I felt rather odd for much of my life, until I was called to serve God. I thought if I did that, and carried out my duties with all my heart, that it would be enough to make up for other things that I lacked, like love and close companionship. But now, I don't know if I'm strong enough to go on this way. To resist temptations and..." He turned in his chair to face her full on, grasping both of her hands. "Man was not meant to live alone, Frances. That's why God created Eve. To take care of Adam."

"What are you saying, Reverend?"

"Harold."

"Harold," she whispered.

"I'm saying, I've been thinking that someone like you and someone like me, perhaps we belong together. To take care of each other in this world of trials."

"Together?"

"Yes. If you would have me."

"Have you? You mean . . ."

"Would you be my wife, Frances? I am not always an easy man, but I would be grateful if you would give your consent. You wouldn't be lonely anymore, you would have me to take care of. I could use your help, and—"

"Yes," she said.

"You would?"

She leaned forward and laid her cheek against the stiff fabric of his black shirt. "Yes. I will be your wife, Rev—Harold."

One of his hands began to stroke her head, his touch tentative. His hand, she realized, was trembling. He was as terrified as she was. "Thank you, Frances."

"You're welcome. Thank *you*."

Only later did Frances realize that he had never said he loved her. She didn't mind. She had enough love for both of them, and she would care for him so tenderly that his affection would eventually bloom into love.

5

Mallory fidgeted in the pew, her tailbone sore from sitting more than an hour on hard, uncushioned wood. Her skin itched from the acetate lining of the stiff velveteen dress she wore, and her legs were hot in the thick knit tights and winter boots. She could have left the boots in the cloakroom with her coat, but she had forgotten her shoes again.

She was almost eleven, and it was two years since the Caines had moved from Rosemont, California, to Ferry Falls, Minnesota. There had been some kind of argument back in Rosemont between Reverend Caine and his congregation, and the vestry had asked that he be replaced. After several weeks of tension in the household, the Rev had announced at dinner one night that he was taking over a parish in Minnesota. The next thing Mallory knew, they were driving through a late-April blizzard to reach Ferry Falls. Now, after two years, she still hadn't gotten used to the bitterly cold winters and the layers of extra clothing that were required to survive them. Back home in California, the most she'd ever worn was a light jacket, except those few times her parents had taken her and Diana up to Big Bear to go winter sledding. It had been fun back then to spend an afternoon jumping in the snow, but out here on the prairie, after five months of snowdrifts and slush, the whole thing got to be a colossal pain.

Squirming restlessly again, she felt a hand on her arm, and looked up to see Frances's head shake, her forefinger moving to her lips. The Rev was in the middle of his sermon, and Mallory knew how much it annoyed him to see his young charges jittering in the front row. Big deal, she thought. It's not like everyone else in the church isn't wishing he'd finish so they could get out of there. One time, Mallory had heard two men grumbling about the long Sunday service on their way out the door. "Sure likes to hear himself talk, don't he?" one of them had said.

Mallory had also noticed that in all the Rev's sermons, whenever he drew on some experience from life to back up the scripture he was pushing that week, he always seemed to emerge as the hero of his own little tales. He'd act a little sheepish when he told these stories, as if he didn't really want to blow his own horn, *but....* How convenient, Mallory thought, that none of these people were ever around to confirm that the Rev had performed his little miracles. Still, he seemed to have *most* people convinced he was a saint, especially the old people with their fat wallets, come collection time. It embarrassed Mallory to see how white-haired ladies twittered whenever he gave them a naughty wink.

As the sermon droned on, the rustling and coughing grew, and at the back of the church, a baby began to fuss. Glancing over Frances's shoulder, Mallory caught sight of Wiley Dixon a few rows behind them, and he grinned at her, then crossed his eyes and dangled his tongue. She giggled, just as he knew she would, the rat. Both Frances and Diana, sitting on Mallory's other side, poked her hard. Mallory turned back and stared at the altar, pressing her lips together to squelch her laughter. Wiley was a year older. They had met not long after the Caines arrived in Ferry Falls, and he was her very best friend. Pretty much the *only* friend she had, when it came right down to it.

When they'd moved here, Frances had said that maybe leaving California would be a blessing, taking Mallory and Diana away from the bad memories the place held for them. Mallory could have told her that the memories had travelled with them, along with the furniture and cutlery and household linens packed tight in the U-Haul. On top of that, she had soon decided that she hated this ugly, weather-beaten little town and everyone in it, except Wiley. And Diana, of course. She hated

the freezing cold in winter and the hot, dusty wind that whipped
the prairie dry in summer. She hated it when grown-ups met the
Caines and found out that Diana and Mallory were not their
natural daughters—the way they whispered and clucked over
the story of what had happened to the girls' birth parents.

Why did the Rev always have to *tell?* She hated the way people stared at Diana's withered arm, paralyzed by nerve damage, and the way their lips pursed as they mouthed "poor
thing!" heads shaking as they walked away. She hated the pity
and smug superiority that oozed from all of them. And she
positively *despised* the stupid, moronic kids who teased Diana
and called her a cripple. In the first two weeks after they'd arrived, Mallory had been sent home from school four times for
punching out the lights of one smart aleck or another.

Diana was thirteen now and attending junior high, while
Mallory was still stuck in Ferry Falls Elementary in sixth grade.
She had worried about Diana when they were first separated,
but her sister told her not to. "The kids are used to me now,"
Diana murmured. "They don't tease much anymore."

Or maybe, Mallory thought, it was just that Diana was so shy
the other kids forgot she was there. Her older sister slipped
from home to school and back again, spending hours up in her
room in the rectory, drawing. Although her right arm was useless, she had regained some movement in the fingers of that
hand. With her arm propped on a desk, Diana made pen-and-
ink drawings with such fine detail that Mallory could look for
hours and still not notice all the things going on in them. They
were dark, fantastic things, with fairies and goblins and dragons breathing fire. It was as if soft-spoken, auburn-haired Diana, who looked so much like their poor, dead mother, spilled
all her fears, all her rage onto the pages of her art pad.

Mallory had no such quiet way of releasing her own furies,
and so, periodically, her rage would vent loudly. Long hours
spent in detention at school, being locked in her room at home
or doing penance in front of the altar at the church only added
to her anger. With Diana preoccupied and no longer needing
her sister's skills as a pugilist, Mallory might have been even
more lonely and frustrated, had it not been for Wiley Dixon.

Wiley's real name was William, but although his mother called him that, Wiley would have decked anyone else who tried to do the same. Way back in second grade, he told Mallory, he had renamed himself after Wile E. Coyote of "Roadrunner"-cartoon fame. The name suited him, with his wicked grin, floppy dark hair and long, pointed wolverine face. They'd met in summer church camp, and Mallory soon found out that Wiley was an orphan like her—or half an orphan, anyway.

"My dad croaked when I was a baby," he told her. "He was a mechanic, and a car he was working on fell off its blocks and crushed him dead like a bug." Mallory winced. "My mom remarried. My stepdad's a state trooper."

"Do you like him?" Mallory asked.

"He's okay, except when he drinks. Then he beats the crap outta me. Used to, anyway. Now he's gotta catch me first."

Mallory nodded in understanding. Not that the Rev often hit her. Most of the time, it was a tongue-lashing he used to keep her in check. Once or twice, though, when she'd provoked him into a real fury, his face had turned red and he'd leaped to give her a smack. After the first couple of times, Mallory had learned to duck. Now, as in Wiley's case, the Rev had to catch her first. He soon abandoned that approach, anyway, preferring to lock her in her room without meals, or force her to kneel at the church altar until she was ready to confess her sins and seek forgiveness. When finally, bored and hungry, she would pretend to give in to him, he never failed to round off the punishment by reminding her of the Christian charity he had shown, taking in her and Diana when no one else wanted them.

"I wonder that you are not more grateful, Mallory. One day, you will look back in shame on this behavior of yours."

Diana rarely drew this kind of attention from the Rev, but Mallory was on the receiving end of it with depressing regularity. Only when the two little girls were alone together did they allow themselves to speak of and mourn their lost mother and father, who had never spanked them, and who had always seemed to find a way to divert Mallory's excess energy. When the day came that the Rev began to speak openly about corruption, about how their parents had brought their fate on themselves, Mallory was enraged and refused to believe him. It was just one more nail in the coffin of their stillborn relationship. Only later, when Frances reluctantly confirmed what her husband had said, did Mallory's bright memories of her mother and father begin to tarnish.

In the meantime, she and Wiley became staunch allies. But the day they were caught setting off a stink bomb in chapel, Wiley was expelled from church camp, and it was almost the end of a beautiful friendship. Mallory wished *she* could be expelled, too, but she was too well connected, what with the Rev and all, to be so lucky. Instead, after spending a full day on her knees, she was forced to go around and ask every single camper for forgiveness. She was also forbidden to see or speak to Wiley again.

Fat chance.

Mallory took to sneaking off on her bike at every chance, meeting Wiley at the tiny waterfall that gave Ferry Falls its name. After the third time she was caught and punished by the Rev, Frances stepped in. Mallory pressed her ear to the heat register on the floor of her room, listening to their conversation as it wafted up from the kitchen.

"Harold, we *can't* keep the child locked in her room forever!"

"What do you suggest? Let her associate with the Dixon boy and become a complete juvenile delinquent?"

"He's not *so* bad. Maybe if we loosen the rules a little, she'll eventually outgrow his influence and move on to other friends. Or maybe they'll be good for each other."

"Hmmph! I highly doubt that. Giving in to that willful child is not the way to pull her into line, Frances. Mallory needs a firm hand. I can't be here every minute of the day to ride herd on her. But I warn you, if you go behind my back on this, you'll have only yourself to blame when she gets into serious trouble."

Frances said nothing, but after a while, Mallory and Wiley's friendship slipped into a no-man's-land, a "don't ask, don't tell" period, where Frances didn't inquire who Mallory saw when she left the house and Mallory didn't volunteer the information.

She and Wiley passed long afternoons at the Ferry River, scrambling over rocks, playing *Star Wars,* or King Arthur's knights, or *The Lost Voyage of Sinbad.* Wiley taught her how to tie a clove hitch and make a hangman's noose. He showed her how to wrap her legs around a knot in a rope and swing from a branch that hung over a narrow stretch of the river, letting go at precisely the right moment to land on the soft bank on the other side. He taught her how to search the base of trees for disgorged owl pellets, how to soak them and take them apart, looking for the tiny jawbones and femurs of mice the owls had eaten. When Mallory told him he was disgusting, he made her look even closer.

"Remember this little mouse, Mal. It's all about the great ladder of life." Wiley picked up a delicate triangle of bone lined with minuscule rodent teeth. "This little mouse was low down on the ladder, see, so he got eaten. We're high up, but that doesn't mean there aren't enemies out there. The trick is to move fast, and don't ever let 'em get their claws into you. That way, you'll never get eaten."

Mallory stared at him for a moment, then burst out laughing. "You're a real weirdo, Wiley, you know that?"

"Yeah, but I'm not as dumb as I look."

"Good thing!" Mallory hooted, giving him a shove that sent him rolling down the hill.

She always returned home from the riverbank filthy—the knees of her Lee jeans worn white and tissue-thin from crawling over stones, rubber soles flapping on her soaked, ruined sneakers. Inevitably, she was late for dinner, provoking glares and lectures from the head of the table. But she was so uncharacteristically cheerful that after the third or fourth time, even the Rev, who wasn't fooled for a minute, was forced to concede that Wiley might not be a totally negative influence after all.

"As long," he emphasized sternly, "as you keep up your grades, your church activities and your household chores."

Mallory nodded, keeping her eyes on her reheated dinner plate, determined not to let out the whoop of joy that was

6

For the life of her, eighteen-year-old Mallory could never remember why she had been at Patty Lintz's party the night she met Gunnar Anderson that Easter weekend.

It had been a Saturday night, but Saturdays usually found her cruising with Wiley on his Harley-Davidson, stopping for coffee at the greasy Polar Star Café, or maybe smoking a joint on the banks of the Ferry River, watching the stars come out while Wiley spun one of his fantastic tales of Avaron and Sagramor, futuristic space warriors. Maybe Wiley was at the Moto-Rite that night, working on the motorcycle after one of its frequent breakdowns. That might explain it. When he'd first bought the old bike, Mallory would go with him to the garage where the owner, who'd known Wiley's dad, let Wiley use his tools for free. But after having her bottom pinched and her breasts "accidentally" brushed one too many times by the grease monkeys who hung out there, Mallory had decided to let Wiley do repairs on his own.

Patty Lintz's bash was one of those parents-are-away, open-house affairs that anyone could attend—even Mallory, with her black-and-denim contempt for the trendy styles and arbitrary rules of the rat pack, Ferry Falls's in-crowd. And she would have gone anywhere rather than hang around the rectory on a Saturday night, putting up with the Rev's stern glare of disapproval and his deep, martyred sighs.

Although she had long since quit attending All Saints' Church, Mallory knew that he still mentioned his rebellious ward's name each week when it came to the "prayers for the people" part of the service, when everyone in the congregation spoke up to let everyone else know how stuffed full of Christian concern they were for those who had strayed or were in torment. If she had been inclined to talk to him about it, Mallory could have told the Rev that he and Ferry Falls made her so crazy that she had no choice but to stray from the narrow path he tried to force her to follow. That her torment came from living in the rectory, its air untainted by the sound of laughter, and from this narrow-minded little town, where whispered stories about her birth parents had multiplied until they'd turned into a latter-day Bonnie and Clyde. Mallory knew that she and Diana were scrutinized constantly for signs of inherited mayhem.

But Mallory had no use for heart-to-hearts with the Rev, not since the first time he had hinted that her parents' deaths might have been their own fault. "We make our beds, Mallory, and then we must lie in them. And although the sins of the father should not be borne by the child, you can atone for mistakes of the past by living a good, pure life." It was more in sorrow than in anger, the Rev used to say when he forced her to remain for hours on her knees in front of the altar, searching her heart and seeking forgiveness for some misdeed or another. "You are *nothing*, Mallory. Only when you realize that will you find humility and salvation."

The first time it had happened, she'd been just eight and a half, but the Rev had said he was determined to correct the errors in her upbringing before it was too late. That was back when he still pretended to care about her. The day he dropped all pretense of fatherly concern was when he caught Mallory and one of his altar boys kissing in the sacristy. She'd been thirteen at the time. The Rev had turned purple with rage, accusing her of corrupting the youth, even though the older boy had tried to explain that he himself had made the first move. It was no use.

The lectures and punishments went on for a few more years, but by the time Mallory reached her senior year of high school, all she got from the Rev was a sniff and a pained look whenever she miscalculated and their paths crossed in the rectory.

And so, as much as she despised the rat pack mentality that prevailed among the offspring of the town's leading citizens, Patty Lintz's party would have been preferable that Easter weekend to listening to the Rev's complaints, or watching Frances jump and Diana tremble whenever he crooked his little finger.

By the time she met Gunnar Anderson, Mallory was desperate to escape.

She remembered that she was bored silly at the party and was getting ready to leave, when Gunnar asked her to dance. She knew who he was, of course. He had graduated a year earlier and was attending college in Moorehead, but at Ferry Falls High, he had been captain of the football team and the not-so-secret crush of every girl in the school—Mallory included, although bamboo under her fingernails wouldn't have dragged the information out of her. Gunnar had come to the party with someone else, but Mallory later learned that he and the girl had had a fight. All she knew was that he'd left with *her* that night, and that he had come back to Ferry Falls every weekend since to be with her.

After two months of steaming up the windows of Gunnar's fire-engine-red '67 T-Bird, they had reached a kind of crossroads. Never before, on any of the groping dates she'd had with other boys—and certainly not with Wiley, who remained her best, but strictly platonic, friend—had Mallory ever felt so out of control of her own body and emotions.

Despite her prickly aloofness, she had attracted plenty of male attention growing up in Ferry Falls. Mallory suspected that many of the boys in town, misled by her disdain for the unspoken rules of femininity, thought she would be an easy lay if they could just get her alone. They also thought she was Wiley's girlfriend, but that didn't stop them from sniffing around. Most were too timid to approach her, or, if they did, for Mallory to take them seriously. The couple of guys she *did* go out with soon discovered that her "easy" reputation was baseless. Winking and snickering with their friends later, however, they never admitted that they had struck out.

The truth was, there was nothing easy about Mallory Caine. It wasn't that she set out to tease and torture. It was just that every time she thought she had found the kind of strong cohort that she knew she needed, they just turned out to be egocentric bullies, trying to force her to their will. At eighteen, Mallory craved loving hands. But she would *not* be told what to do, how to act or when it was time to hand over self-control. Not by some boy, not by the Rev, not by anyone.

And then, along came Gunnar Anderson. He was studying hotel and restaurant management at Moorehead University so that he could come back and take over the Two Loons Motel when his parents retired. Mallory couldn't quite see why it required a college degree to keep the Two Loons' thirty-four units clean and stocked with paper-wrapped glasses, but Gunnar said he had an idea to expand the operation, adding a restaurant and a lounge, and maybe a miniature golf course. He looked adorable when he talked about those plans—six feet of blond, blue-eyed, soft-spoken sincerity. Not a rocket scientist, Mallory knew, but awfully appealing, just the same. His wide forehead would wrinkle when he described how Tex-Mex food was going to be the next big trend, and how he would make the Two Loons into *the* hot night spot in Ferry Falls. He was irresistible when he got all excited like that.

Gunnar was trying to convince Mallory to sign up for the hotel course so that she could manage the books at the Two Loons. Paperwork was not his strong suit. Implicit in all this was that the two of them were a permanent item, and that marriage was on the horizon. It was an assumption now held by everyone in Ferry Falls, even the rat packers, who had previously regarded Mallory with snide curiosity and condescension. But if Gunnar Anderson had given her his stamp of approval, who were they to question? All they could do was shake their heads at how Mallory had snagged the best catch in town, and how Gunnar had tamed Ferry Falls's own young shrew.

Mallory always skirted Gunnar's questions about the future, repelled by a mental picture of herself in Mrs. Anderson's bib apron and yellow Playtex gloves, lugging around an institutional-size bottle of Lysol. And yet, when Gunnar held her close and called her his baby, all her pent-up rage, all thoughts of escape from Ferry Falls faded. Back at the rectory, they would come rushing back, but as soon as she saw Gunnar's sweet face again, she wanted only to be with him.

He never mentioned the girls who had preceded her, but it was part of Gunnar lore among the rat packers that he'd had his first sexual encounter at the age of thirteen, when a divorced lady passing through Ferry Falls had spotted him vacuuming the Two Loons pool and invited him to her room. Mallory knew that any female in town would have dropped for him at the blink of his blue eyes—and some had—and yet Gunnar never tried to force her to go farther or faster than she was ready. For that alone, Mallory loved him. Was *in* love with him. So how could she even *think* about leaving Ferry Falls, she decided, without giving him back some of the comfort he had given her? She was curious to know, as well, how much forgetfulness could be found in a touch. Because what if, like Dorothy in *The Wizard of Oz*, she ran off to find her heart's desire and it was here all along, in Gunnar's arms?

Half the couples they hung out with had already taken the plunge, so to speak. A few of them had been obliged to take a quick hike down the aisle, too. Mallory couldn't let that happen to herself, not until she was sure about everything. Just the same, she had told Gunnar a couple of weeks before the senior prom, when he phoned from Moorehead one night, that she would go to bed with him.

"You mean it?" he asked.

"Yes, I do. I really want to."

"Ah, Mal, that's so great. I was scared."

"Scared?"

"That you'd run off. But you're not going to, are you? That's what this means."

"Gunnar, I'm not sure—"

"We can get married over the summer."

Mallory felt the room begin to spin. "Married?"

"Yeah. They've got apartments for married students up here. It'll be great, having you here, doing the course with me."

"Hey, Gunnar? Maybe we should talk about this. I mean, I'm only eighteen, and—"

7

Ferry Falls, Minnesota
June 19, 1979

They had agreed that it would happen on prom night, and in a real bed—no contortionist maneuvers on the custom leather bucket seats of his T-Bird. Finding a bed, of course, wasn't all that hard. Gunnar had access to sixty-eight double beds at the Two Loons Motel, some with Magic Fingers vibrators. Since the summer rush of tourists hadn't started yet at Minnesota's famous sights—like the headwaters of the Mississippi, or the giant statues of Paul Bunyan and his blue ox, Babe—there would be plenty of vacancies at the motel. Once Gunnar found out that his older brother, Lars, rather than one of his parents, was going to be on duty in the office that night, they were home free.

"Hey, guys, no problem," twenty-three-year-old Lars Anderson had said. "I was a kid once, too. I know how it is."

Three babies later, he certainly must, Mallory thought, standing in front of the mirror the night of the prom. Her mouth was full of bobby pins as she struggled to get her wheaty hair to stay up on her head like the picture in *Glamor* magazine that lay open on the dressing table in front of her. Half a can of hair spray later, she almost had it. "A sophisticated 'do' for a hot night on the town" was what the magazine had promised. If it could turn an eighteen-year-old tomboy into Gunnar Anderson's dream lover, then a miracle is what Mallory would call it.

She stood back and surveyed herself with a critical eye, debating whether to forget the whole idea. Who was she trying to kid? He knew what she really looked like, and he wanted her, anyway. So why was she doing this? Dumb, dumb, dumb. Her hand reached up to start pulling out the pins, but just then the front doorbell rang. She froze as the sound of Frances's cheerful greeting drifted up the stairs, followed by Gunnar's deep murmur. A jolt like an electric current shot through her body.

Her arms dropped to her sides and she stared at the stranger in the mirror. Where was the skinny, tumble-haired girl in jeans and T-shirt, the girl with the fierce dark eyes who tore around town on the back of Wiley Dixon's Harley? The girl who always trailed everyone else into class at Ferry Falls High, arriving just before the door was shut so she wouldn't have to sit in painful solitude while laughing voices all around her made weekend plans that had never, before Gunnar, included her? The girl whose senior yearbook entry called her *"Lady James Dean, who keeps her future plans to herself, but has the smarts to go wherever she wants?"*

That girl was gone for the moment, it seemed. Staring back from the mirror was a disco Cinderella in a peach-colored, strapless dress of satin moiré. Its full skirt stopped well above her knees, revealing long legs in sheer hose that ended in two-inch heels. There had been raised eyebrows when she brought the outfit home from a shopping excursion to Minneapolis, although no one had actually fainted or ordered her to take it back. Not that it would have mattered. Laying down the law to Mallory was a surefire guarantee that she would stomp right over it. Particularly in this case. She had chosen the dress carefully, with one special evening and one special person in mind.

Tonight, she was a satin-wrapped gift to Gunnar Anderson.

Diana hung back on the staircase, hugging the banister. Her lips were set in a fixed smile as her eyes skirted the pattern in the worn stair-runner. Only occasionally did she venture to look up through dark lashes at her sister's date, who was standing in the front hall. Gunnar had arrived a few minutes earlier, and he and Frances were making small talk while they waited for Mallory. He had the quiet ease of a young man who knows he is every mother's dream for her daughter—if not for herself, Diana thought, watching Frances's eager smile. Diana felt a quiver run from her solar plexus to her toes. She knew something their mother didn't. In a few hours, Gunnar and Mallory would become lovers.

She clutched her useless right arm protectively against her ribs, desperate to hide how ugly and ill at ease she felt. Tongue-tied, as always. Hating herself for it, as always. You're twenty years old, she told herself sternly. Grow up. But despite the self-lecture, she felt as heart-thumpingly awestruck as a child at a candy-store window. A store she could never enter. Well, who wouldn't feel overawed? she reasoned. Gunnar was a year younger than she, but that didn't change the fact that he was beautiful. He was also nice and hardworking, and less conceited than he had a perfect right to be. No wonder her sister had fallen so hard for him. Not that Mallory would admit it.

"He's not all that smart, you know," Mallory had told her. "I mean, he hardly ever talks about anything except football and building his miniature-golf course."

Diana could never understand why her sister pretended to be critical of Gunnar. Probably to hide how crazy she was about him. Mallory never wanted anyone to think they had the upper hand with her.

In her sister's shoes, Diana would not have gone around pretending she could take him or leave him. It wasn't that she was especially fixated on Gunnar himself. It just would have been nice to have someone half as wonderful show an interest in *her,* too. Oh, sure, she thought. You'd faint dead away if anyone like that said boo to you. Not Mallory, though. She just accepted it as her right. But then, why not? She was energetic and funny, with a blond self-confidence that boys seemed to find irresistible. Mallory never even seemed to notice the way their eyes trailed her down the street, but Diana did. Mallory would rather hang out with Wiley, never dating anyone else more than once or twice. "Love 'em and leave 'em," that's what she said—at least, until Gunnar came along.

Diana glanced at him again, feeling her cheeks burn as she watched his big hands play with the plastic corsage box. It was a wrist corsage, an orchid, of course. Mallory would probably take *that* for granted, too, giving it no more notice than if it were a ten-cent carnation. Everything came so easy to Mallory.

Diana had graduated from Ferry Falls High two years earlier, but hadn't attended her own senior prom—although she *could* have, she reminded herself. Arvid Dolk and she had become biology-lab partners on the first day of fall semester, after everyone else in the class had paired off. Even before he'd worked up the nerve to invite her to the prom, Diana had noticed that Arvid seemed to look for reasons to meet outside the lab, and that he blushed deeply every time she sat on the stool next to his. She had tried to be nice to him. Beggars can't be choosers, after all, and Arvid was nice enough. With his deep green eyes and tousled brown hair, he wasn't even bad-looking. But he always wore wrinkled, grass-stained overalls and had a permanent dark line under his fingernails. He wiped his mouth on the sleeve of his checked flannel shirt, and he drove a Ford pickup so rusted it was impossible to tell what color it was when it was new, which had to have been at least a century ago.

Diana felt snobbish and uncharitable for even noticing these things, especially when it was obvious that Arvid was infatuated, despite the handicap of her paralysis. She might have been able to overlook his minor defects, though, if it hadn't been for Arvid's fatal flaw. When they sat next to each other in lab class, she couldn't help noticing that he smelled distinctly cheesy—an unfortunate side effect, she supposed, of living and working on his family's dairy farm outside of town. Whatever the reason, his mozzarella-like odor, ripe and a little sour, was the coup de grace for the amorous intentions of Arvid Dolk.

"How can I dance all night with someone who makes me hungry for pizza?" Diana argued when Mallory had tried to convince her to go with him to their prom.

Mallory laughed. "Good thing his dad doesn't have a pig farm. Phew! Come on, Di, say yes. Arvid's not so bad."

Easy for Mallory to say, when she could get a Gunnar Anderson. If she didn't love her so much, Diana could actually have hated her younger sister. But she didn't. How could she, after what they had been through together, and all the battles that Mallory had fought on her behalf, even when Diana wished she wouldn't? Just the same, only Mallory could be so nonchalant as to casually mention, right in the middle of Kinney Shoes, while she and Diana were waiting for the clerk to bring them some Adidas to try on, that she was planning to lose her virginity on prom night. Diana had spun around open-mouthed, failing in her determination to never look shocked at anything Mallory said. Her sister liked nothing better than to shock.

"You *are?*"

"Yup. I think it's about time."

"You're kidding, aren't you, Mallory?"

"Would I kid about a thing like that?"

"But . . . but . . . *how?* Where?"

"In the usual way, I guess. At the motel, probably."

"Oh, Mal, Father will have an apoplectic fit when he finds out!"

"The Rev's *not* our father, Diana, and he won't find out. Not that I care. Gunnar's got everything arranged for us to get a room. Everybody stays out all night for senior prom. Screw the Rev if he thinks I'm going to be in for an eleven o'clock curfew."

Diana glanced around the store. "Don't swear," she whispered.

"Yes, big sister."

"But what about . . . um . . . you know? If you get into trouble."

"Taken care of."

"It is?"

"Yup. Remember when Wiley and I drove down to Minneapolis last month? I went to a clinic."

"You went all the way to Minneapolis to see a doctor?"

"You don't think I'd go to old Doc Norquay, do you? Wouldn't *that* have given him something to raise at the next church-vestry meeting!" Mallory puffed up her chest and dropped her voice in her best imitation of the aging GP who, like the Rev, was one of Ferry Falls's most pompous self-appointed leading citizens. "'Well, Reverend Caine,'" she droned, "'we have two hundred dollars in the Widows and Orphans Fund, contributions of six hundred and thirty-seven dollars toward the new church roof, and, oh, yes! I prescribed birth control pills for Mallory so that she and the Anderson boy can screw their brains out at the Two Loons Motel.'"

"Mallory!"

"You see my point?"

"I guess. Still, are you sure?" Her sister nodded and Diana sighed. "I wish I had your nerve."

"You could, Di. You could do anything you want, but you have to fight for it sometimes."

Diana had just shaken her head. She didn't have her sister's courage and never would. She had always been shy, but after the accident, when she had lost the use of her right arm, she found she couldn't bear to look people in the eye and see them staring at the withered limb. Instead, she had withdrawn deep inside herself, panicked by strangers and strange situations. Except with Mallory and Frances, Diana could never speak up and say what she felt, because most of the time, all she felt was fear. Her retreat from the world was so complete that some people thought she was mentally slow, Diana knew. She couldn't help that. Better to be thought slow than risk pity or ridicule.

No one even noticed her anymore. But back in the beginning, after the explosion and when they were adopted by the Caines and moved to Ferry Falls, the comments had been relentless. Oh, how she remembered the voices! Crooning adults: *"Poor thing! A shame! Negligence! A crime! Pitiful!"* Nasty, childish voices: *"Rag doll! Floppy arm! Scarecrow, lost her stuffin'!"* And, above all, one ugly, hurtful refrain: *"Cripple, cripple, cripple!"*

"Ready or not, here I come!"

Mallory's step reverberated on the landing above. Frances looked up and broke into a broad smile. Her thick glasses magnified the deep crinkles around her eyes, and she clapped her hands in delight. "Don't you look pretty!"

Gunnar was wide-eyed and wondrous, Diana noticed, like the Archangel Gabriel viewing the approach of his God. His Adam's apple was bobbing, but he seemed incapable of speech.

Diana turned to watch her sister's descent, one satin-pumped shoe following the other, dyed to match the peach dress that clung to her like a peel. Without her uniform of baggy T-shirt and Levi's, Mallory had suddenly, like Cinderella, turned into a beautiful young woman, with long legs and a figure to die for. She had done something different with her hair, too, piling it on her head. Wispy blond tendrils escaped at the sides, caressing flushed cheeks. Mallory's eyes, bright and shining, were locked on Gunnar as if he, and he alone, were the cure for the fever that seemed to have her in its grip. He probably was, too. When she reached Diana on the staircase, Mallory tore her gaze from Gunnar and gave her sister a nervous grimace, as if seeking reassurance.

Diana squeezed her arm. "You look fabulous!"

"Are you sure?" Mallory whispered, running her hands over the brief skirt. "I feel kind of stupid."

"Honestly. I can't believe that this is my baby sister. You look like . . . like a movie star. Like Farah Fawcett. No, better."

"Baloney." Mallory screwed up her face, the old tomboy returning in a flash.

"Really! Doesn't she, Gunnar?"

They all turned to the young man at the bottom of the stairs, who still hadn't managed to lift his fallen jaw. "Oh, yeah," he breathed finally. "Unbelievable."

Diana felt her stomach flip again. What must it be like to have someone as drop-dead gorgeous as Gunnar Anderson look at you that way?

"Let me get my camera and take a picture of you two," Frances said. She bustled down the hall, returning just as Gunnar's trembling fingers were slipping the orchid over Mallory's wrist. The lenses of Frances's glasses clattered against the viewfinder as she snapped away, the young couple posing self-consciously until she ran out of film. "Oh, wait," she said as they turned to leave. "I'll call Father. He should see how wonderful you look."

"No!" Mallory said too quickly. "Don't bother him, Franny. He doesn't like to be disturbed when he's working, you know that."

"But . . ."

"He'll see the pictures. It's not important." Mallory kissed her cheek. "We're late. Gotta run. Don't wait up, okay?"

"All right," Frances said, resigned. "You two have fun now, and drive carefully."

"We will. 'Bye, Franny! 'Bye, Di!"

Frances and Diana followed them onto the front porch, waving as the red Thunderbird drove off. When the roar of the engine had faded to silence, Frances snapped out of her reverie and seemed to remember that Diana was standing next to her. "How about if you and I make up a nice big batch of peanut brittle before 'Mork and Mindy' comes on?"

"Oh . . . maybe not tonight. I'm a little tired."

"I'll do it. You just go in the front room and put up your feet. I'll make some hot chocolate, too. Would you like that?"

"No, thanks, Mother. I think I'll just go up to my room, if you don't mind."

"We could play Scrabble, if you'd rather not watch television. Or cribbage, maybe?"

"No, really. I thought I'd draw for a while."

"Are you sure?"

"I am. I'll probably turn in early."

"All right, dear. Isn't there *something* I can get for you?"

"No, nothing." Diana smiled, then glanced down the driveway one last time. "She looked fabulous, didn't she?"

"Yes, she did." Frances's owlish eyes turned moist behind her glasses, and she took Diana's hand in hers. "I can't believe you girls are grown-up already. Where did the time go? Soon, you'll be itching to get away from this boring old place."

"I don't know about that," Diana said, giving her hand a squeeze. "I'd miss you too much, I think."

"I'd miss you, too. This is your home, after all. I hope you'll stay here with me for a long, long time."

"I'm not rushing off anywhere."

"Good. I hope you never do." Frances peered out into the night and sighed. "I don't think we'll be able to hold on to Mallory much longer, though, do you?"

Diana shook her head slowly. "Maybe not." She kissed Frances, then went back into the house and up the stairs. When she heard Reverend Caine's study door open and his heavy tread in the hall below, Diana paused, listening.

"They've gone, have they?"

"Just now. I wanted you to see Mallory. She looked beautiful, Harold."

"Hmmph! I saw the dress when she brought it home. I'm amazed you would let her go out in such a thing."

"It's what all the young girls are wearing."

"That doesn't make it decent. Prancing around like that is just an invitation to trouble. I suppose you didn't remind her about curfew."

"Oh, no, I didn't, dear. Not on prom night."

"I don't see that it should make any difference."

"But this is the biggest night of the year for them, and the dance is chaperoned."

"The dance, perhaps, but what about afterward?"

"Gunnar Anderson is a fine young man. I don't think we have to worry."

"He's a healthy male. Young men can't be expected to behave like gentlemen when females prance before them half-naked, like Jezebel."

"Harold! What a thing to say about our daughter!"

"If she had one ounce of your sensible blood in her, Frances, I would have no concern about the girl. As it is, living the sheltered life you have, you simply can't imagine the kind of wickedness from which that child has sprung. They say the apple doesn't fall far from the tree, and I fear Mallory is walking proof of that."

"You can't really believe that. And anyway, if it were true, what about Diana?"

"Diana is an example of God's mysterious wisdom. He made her a cripple in retribution for the sins of the parents, but also, I think, in order to save her soul. There is a reason she was sent to us, a reason she was made unfit for a worldly life. We've been given the lifelong responsibility of watching over her, to keep her pure and prevent her from slipping back into the kind of degradation into which she was born."

"Do you really think so?"

"It's self-evident. And now, if you don't mind, I'd like some tea."

"I'll make it right away. How is your sermon coming?"

"Not well. I've been grappling for a theme." Caine paused. "Perhaps St. Paul on the spiritual dangers of carnal sin would be appropriate this week, given the revelries of our young people. Hmm... I can work with that."

"I knew you'd think of something. You always do."

"You'll bring that tea in, won't you, Frances?" Caine said, his step heading toward his study.

"Right away, dear."

Diana closed her bedroom door, holding the knob until the last minute so the latch wouldn't click. At her small desk, she began tidying, her movements mechanical, returning pastels and conté crayons to their boxes, wiping charcoal dust off the laminated work surface, sorting pencils and arranging them in a drawer, from soft lead to hard, alongside art gums, pen nibs and India ink.

When she had finished that and tucked in all the straggling art books and periodicals on a nearby shelf, she withdrew the top coil-bound sketch pad from a pile and began flipping through the pages. Through wildlife studies of birds and animals. Through fantasy scenes of dragons and fairies. Through sketches of the view outside her bedroom window: church spire over clapboard houses, the Minnesota prairie rolling off in the distance. She flipped past sketches of Frances, which flattered her adoptive mother by deemphasizing her skewed eyes. Past others of Mallory that reproduced faithfully her arresting dark eyes and fine bone structure, but failed utterly, in Diana's view, to capture her sister's vibrant personality.

Dissatisfaction growing, she turned to a series of penciled self-portraits—pathetic efforts, she decided, that showed a young woman with her sister's piercing eyes and their mother's masses of dark hair. This isn't me, Diana thought. If I didn't know I was the model, I might have said this was some legendary heroine, a raven-haired Guinevere, maybe, with the beauty to drive a fatal wedge between good King Arthur and his loyal Lancelot. Pathetic lies! Securing the sketchbook cover under her dead arm, she grabbed the corner of the first self-portrait, ripped the drawing from the notebook with her good hand, wadded it into a ball and flung it across the room. *Lies!*

She ripped out the next, and the next. *Lies! Lies!*

Finally, she tossed the pad itself into the wastebasket. The basket tipped over, spilling pencil shavings and charcoal-smudged tissues onto the threadbare brown carpet. Diana stared at the mess, then sank to her knees and began to cry softly. Pressing her lips together, she reached with her left hand to right the basket and began gathering up the litter. When she finished, she rocked back and forth on her knees until the tears subsided.

Feeling hollow and miserable, she looked around the room, with its faded lilac wallpaper and limp white lace curtains. The mismatched furniture had been donated by various parishioners over the years. There was an ancient, balding chenille bedspread on her narrow bed, over which hung a cheaply framed reprint of an inspirational painting—Christ healing the sick.

Heal *me!* she pleaded silently.

8

Climbing out of Gunnar's T-Bird at Ferry Falls High, Mallory was a little annoyed to discover that his brother Lars wasn't the only one clued in to their late-night plans. A group of guys were congregated around somebody's tailgate, passing around a quart of Jack Daniel's in a brown paper bag. When the two of them walked over, she would have had to be deaf, dumb and blind not to notice the winks and nudges they were giving Gunnar. The looks *she* was getting left Mallory feeling like a juicy ham bone dangled before a kennel of slobbering mutts. The girlfriends, none of whom she had ever had a thing in common with, kept squeezing her upper arm and cooing—as if screwing Gunnar Anderson turned Mallory into Queen For A Day.

This had to be Gunnar's doing, she thought. Mallory had only discussed her soon-to-be-enriched love life with Diana, but her sister wouldn't have told these clowns, and Mallory hadn't mentioned it to anyone else—well, hardly anyone else. As the crowd headed up the front steps of the school, Mallory thought she heard the growl of a Harley-Davidson engine, but when she turned around and looked out into the night, no one was there. She frowned, then shrugged and walked into the school on Gunnar's arm.

Someone on the decorations committee had had the brilliant idea to make this year's prom theme "Peach Blossom Rhapsody," despite the fact that peach trees were not exactly part of the Minnesota landscape. Maybe the inspiration for the theme had been the recent revival of *Gone With The Wind* at the Rialto. Or maybe it was just that "Crab-Apple Blossom Rhapsody" didn't have quite the same ring. Whatever the case, the high school gym had been transformed into a jungle of paper peach blossoms.

Mallory and Gunnar paused under an arbor of blossoms just inside the big double doors. Peach-blossom garlands draped the bleachers and basketball hoops. Giant construction-paper peach trees marched in neat, orchardlike rows along the walls. Helium-filled, peach-colored balloons festooned every corner, like floating bunches of ripe fruit. It was some decorating job, Mallory had to admit, even if the place *did* still smell like stale sweat and old sneakers.

Gunnar wrapped his arms around her and nuzzled her neck, just under her ear and *Glamor* magazine hairdo. The sight of her bare shoulders seemed to be working him up into an early lather. The Jack Daniel's probably helped, too. "You fit right in, with that peach-colored dress," he murmured. "I know I said it before, but you look incredible."

Mallory smoothed the skimpy, flaring skirt, then moved her hand to her chest to make sure she wasn't falling out of the strapless, disco-queen number. Reassured that everything was where it should be, she slipped her arms around Gunnar. "You look pretty luscious yourself."

He did, too, in his rented tux and cummerbund. But then, he always did, even in faded old cutoffs. Gunnar Anderson was as close to a Norse god as Mallory had ever seen—like Thor, shooting thunderbolts, or something.

He pulled her closer and they kissed under the arbor, a long, slow, wet one that made her wonder how they were ever going to make it through the prom without ripping off each other's clothes in the middle of the dance floor. Obviously, she wasn't the only one thinking that. She felt a jostle, as one of Gunnar's buddies punched him in the shoulder.

"Yo! Guys! Later, huh? The night is still young."

Gunnar pulled back and gave her a kind of sleepy-puppy gaze before raising his head and breaking into a grin. He loosened his grip and took her hand, leading her onto the dance floor where the crowd was working itself into a frenzied heat to the beat of Donna Summer's "I Will Survive."

As the night wore on, the gym grew stuffy and hot from two hundred writhing bodies, but Mallory and Gunnar made frequent escapes to the parking lot for fresh air and cold sodas, spiked with liberal doses of the old J.D. She declined the alcohol after the first couple of times the bottle came around; she wanted to remember this night.

It was nearing midnight when Gunnar left her on the dance floor and went to talk to the disc jockey. Mallory saw the deejay nod, and then Gunnar sashayed back with a dopey grin on his face. "What are you up to?" she asked.

"I asked him to play our song."

"We have a song?"

"Yup. It was the first song we ever danced to. At Patty Lintz's party, remember?"

Mallory pursed her lips. She remembered the party, but what music had they danced to? As the music died away and the first chords of the next number echoed through the gym, she grinned. The BeeGees' "How Deep is Your Love?" She slipped her arms up around Gunnar's neck. He smelled, not unpleasantly, of exertion, Brut and Jack Daniel's.

"You remember now?" he asked.

"Yeah, I remember."

"So do I, Mal. So do I."

There were no fancy disco steps this time. He pulled her tight against him and their feet barely moved as they swayed on the floor. Her head rested on his shoulder, fingers stroking the blond curls that trailed over the back of his shirt collar. One of his big hands held her close at the curve of her spine, while his other arm wrapped around her, caressing her bare shoulders, his lips brushing her neck. Mallory lifted her head and they kissed, tongues exploring, little shivers running through her. She could feel Gunnar up against her midsection, getting very hard. Her stomach was doing somersaults, and lower down, a hot, sweet ache was growing. When they pulled out of a long kiss and rested their foreheads together, Gunnar's voice was low and hoarse. "Let's go now, please, Mal?"

She could only nod. Her legs felt like rubber, and Gunnar was none too steady, either, as they slipped away from the dance floor and out the nearest exit. She doubted that anyone noticed them leave. From the clinches she saw in that gym, she knew she and Gunnar wouldn't be the only ones going all the way that night. Even Mrs. Beck and Mr. Gerber, the staff chaperons, had disappeared after eyeing each other all night across the floor, apparently infected by the naked lust permeating the gym.

When Mallory and Gunnar reached the T-Bird, he opened her door. She started to get in, but he pulled her back and pressed her up against the car. As they kissed, Mallory felt his hands slip under her dress, and inside her panty hose and panties. First one hand and then the another wrapped themselves around her buttocks as he kissed her face, her neck, the tops of her breasts. When she felt him start to tug down her panties over her hips, Mallory grabbed his arms.

"No!" she whispered. "Not here!"

"I can't wait, Mal. I want you so bad."

"I know. I want you, too. But not this way. Not the first time."

"Mal—"

"Please, Gunnar? You promised."

He pulled up short. He was breathing hard, but his eyes, as they watched her, seemed to come back into focus. He nodded abruptly and pulled up her panties. He stepped back and Mallory slipped into the front seat of the car. A moment later, Gunnar's hand was shaking as he tried to get the key into the ignition.

"Do you want me to drive?" Mallory asked.

The key found its slot and the big V-8 roared to life. "No, it's okay."

The tires squealed as the T-Bird careened out of the Ferry Falls High parking lot. When they got to the Two Loons, Gunnar pulled his car around the back, out of sight of the main road, next to the last unit in line. As he fumbled in his pocket for the room key, Mallory saw the silhouette of his brother appear at the screen door of the motel office. Lars raised his hand in a wave, but by that time, the room door was open and Gunnar was nudging her in. He shut the door behind them, and they were alone.

They stood for a moment, not touching or speaking. Then Gunnar drew the curtains and reached for the nearest bedside lamp to turn on. Mallory put her hand on his arm. "Don't."

"I want to see you," he said, his voice husky.

Mallory hesitated, then nodded and withdrew her hand, squinting as the light came on. When her eyes adjusted, she saw that Gunnar was standing next to the bed, arms limp at his sides, staring at her. "God, Mal. You're so—you're so—" Whatever she was, he didn't seem to be able to spit it out. Tearing his gaze away, he reached back and pulled the bedspread off the bed, then grabbed the starched sheet folded over a fuzzy green polyester blanket and yanked that down, as well. When he turned to her again, they stood awkwardly, staring at each other.

"Maybe you should take off that jacket so it doesn't get all wrinkled?" Mallory suggested.

He nodded, but didn't move. She stepped forward, slipped it off his shoulders and folded it over an armchair. He reached out and his fingers ran lightly up her arm, across her clavicle and down inside her dress. Mallory shivered. Gunnar began to play with her nipples, holding himself away from her, letting his fingertips tease and entice. She closed her eyes, her breath coming shallow and rapid until a gasp slipped past her parted lips. When she looked at him again, Gunnar was watching her intently, a smile on his face. He was enjoying driving her crazy.

He leaned forward and kissed her lightly, then raised his hands in front of her face, holding them there expectantly. Confused, Mallory stared at them until she noticed the cuff links. She removed one, then the other, laying them on the bedside table. Gunnar tossed his tie beside them.

Mallory stepped closer, reaching her hands around his back to undo his cummerbund. While her fingers struggled to find the hooks, he reached behind her back to find the zipper of her dress. Their eyes were locked onto each other, and the cummerbund and dress hit the floor at the same moment. Mallory kicked them away and went to work on the buttons of Gunnar's shirt. He went to work on her breasts, propped up in a strapless half-bra. He covered each globe with one hand and stroked, his eyes shifting back and forth between them. Finished with the buttons of his shirt, Mallory tugged to free it from his pants. Gunnar dropped his arms and gave up the shirt, then unsnapped her bra and tossed that aside, too. He pulled her to him, swaying from side to side, watching her breasts rub against the pale hair of his chest. Mallory looked down, seeing as well as feeling her nipples get hard as he moved back and forth against her.

When he lifted her head, they kissed so deeply that it seemed to Mallory they would swallow each other whole. Gunnar's hand reached up to her hair, but when his fingers got caught, Mallory pulled out the bobby pins and it tumbled down around her shoulders. He groaned and held her tighter, his mouth wide over hers, his tongue deep inside, probing hungrily. Then his legs bent, and his mouth worked its way slowly down her face and neck until he reached her breasts. He paused there, taking them in, one by one, tasting and comparing. Mallory felt a flicker of embarrassment, standing exposed and almost naked like this, letting him do whatever he wanted.

She felt something else, too—out of control, the one place she struggled never to be. A panicky voice rose in the back of her mind. Mallory heard its reflexive warning, but then she pushed it away, ignoring her anxiety as she cupped Gunnar's head and gave herself over completely to him and her own yearning.

His hands moved down her back to her hips, yanking her panties and hose with one tug. Mallory kicked off her shoes. Gunnar dropped to his knees to slip her hose and panties over her heels and toes, and she stepped out of them. Then he moved his lips up her thighs, covering them with kisses. Reaching the top, he spread them a little. Mallory froze. "It's okay, Mal," he whispered, looking up at her. "Just relax. I'll make this real good for you."

He went back to what he was doing, and after a moment, Mallory felt herself opening to him. She held his head in her hands and closed her eyes as the sensation grew more and more pleasurable. Suddenly, without warning, a flash of electricity shot through her body, frying it to her very fingertips, and a guttural cry rose from deep in her sternum. Gunnar slowed, then stopped, and Mallory looked down, disoriented, worried that she had done something wrong. But his lips formed a smile, and he got to his feet, kissing her over and over as he walked her slowly backward to the bed. When the backs of her knees touched the mattress, he picked her up and lay her in the middle of it, giving her legs a gentle push to spread them apart before he straightened again.

Mallory lay on the sheets, watching him watch her as he unbuttoned his tuxedo pants and let them drop to the floor. Then he crouched low at the side of the bed, like a tiger ready to spring. Mallory held herself still, ready and willing to accept him, intimidated by the prospect just the same. But instead of pouncing, Gunnar uncoiled himself over her legs, his fingers traveling from the arches of her feet all the way up her legs in a slow, sensuous flow, lips and tongue joining them on their trail of exploration. Even as she squirmed and moaned, it occurred to Mallory that this wasn't at all the way she had imagined it— which only goes to show, she decided, that there are some experiences that just *can't* be imagined.

Another bolt shot through her before Gunnar finally brought his head level with hers and lifted himself, push-up–style, over her. But when she opened her eyes to look at his incredible, wonderful face, his expression was odd. As a matter of fact, he looked decidedly green around the gills.

"Gunnar? Honey? What's wrong?"

"I'm going—I'm going—"

"Going? You mean coming? You want to come inside, quick?"

"No, I'm going—"

She heard a gurgle rise from somewhere around his Adam's apple. "Oh, shit! You're going to throw up?"

He nodded frantically, lips pressed tight. Mallory pushed him aside, scrambled out from under him and off the bed. She glanced around and spotted a wastebasket, which she grabbed and shoved in his face. "Here! Do it in here!"

Gunnar rolled to the side of the bed and just managed to get his face over the plastic basket before he spewed. Mallory sat down beside him and rubbed his heaving back—not that he was in any shape to notice or care. When he was quiet again, she got up and padded to the bathroom, soaked a washcloth in cold water and wrung it out. She came and sat next to him, and he took it from her, pressing it against his face.

"Better?" she asked, pushing away his sticky hair.

He nodded behind the cloth, his voice muffled. "I'm sorry."

"It happens." That just elicited a groan. "Don't worry about it. Maybe you should lie down for a bit."

He tumbled over onto the pillow. Mallory stood and lifted his feet to the bed, then pulled the sheet and blanket over him. Only then did he lower the cloth from his face. "Christ, Mal, I'm sorry. I was okay as long as I was vertical, but as soon as I, you know, got down, everything started spinning."

Yeah, sure, Mallory thought. Doing that to me made you sick. Thanks a lot.

"It wasn't you," Gunnar said, as if he could read her mind. He gripped her wrist. "I drank too much J.D., that's all. You were—" He tried to sit up, but that seemed to be a bad idea. He groaned, and Mallory urged him back down.

"Don't talk now. Just sleep it off, okay?"

"Don't be mad at me. I don't want you to be mad at me. I love you. You're incredible. You're so beautiful, Mal. Don't be mad at me, okay?"

"You're blathering, Anderson." He really was. However much he'd chugged into that wastebasket, there was obviously a heap of Jack Daniel's still left in his system. Mallory was tempted to kill the big jerk, but it was hard to think lethal thoughts about someone who looked as if he was already dying—especially when that someone had been doing such incredible things to you just a few minutes earlier. "I'm not mad at you, Gunnar, I promise."

"Yes, you are. I ruined your big night."

"No, I'm not, and you didn't."

"Really?"

"Really."

"Kiss me?"

"You've got vomit breath, Gunnar!"

"Okay, no kiss. But Mal?"

"What?"

"You really are hot stuff, you know. And you're gorgeous," he added, giving her a bleary once-over.

Only then did Mallory realize that she was still naked. She sat down beside him and stroked his chest. "You're hot stuff yourself, Mr. A. Pretty gorgeous, too."

"C'mon in here beside me, okay? We can try again in a little while."

She shook her head reluctantly. "I'd better get going. But I'll tell you what—I'll take a rain check on that invitation."

"You mean that?"

"Oh, yes, I do. I surely do."

Gunnar leaned back on the pillow and smiled. His eyes were looking heavy.

"Gunnar?"

"Mmm?"

"Can I take your car? I'll come back and get you in the morning."

"S'okay. Lars'll give me a lift home." His eyes were closed now, and he was almost gone.

"Okay," Mallory said. "I'll bring the T-Bird to your house tomorrow. Deal?"

"Mmmfff." She took that for a yes.

Mallory rose from the bed and began gathering her things. It took her a full five minutes to figure out where her bra had landed when Gunnar tossed it. She finally found it caught between the mattress and the Magic Fingers coin box on the next bed. With her clothing under one arm and the wastebasket held at arm's length in her other hand, she headed for the bathroom. She dumped the contents of the basket in the toilet and flushed, swallowing a gag, then parked the basket under the bathtub faucet, turned on full. Leaving that to soak, she shimmied back into her underthings and dress.

Her face stared out at her from the bathroom mirror. Mascara had settled under her dark brown eyes, giving them a smoky, Garboesque appearance. Bright flushes of color stained her cheeks. Her lips were swollen and bruised-looking. At the base of her neck, just above the left side of her collarbone, she was distressed to see a small but distinct hickey. All in all, Mallory thought, she looked like a girl who had been well and truly laid. And she almost had been, too. Damn!

She made one or two halfhearted attempts to pile her hair back up, but the steamy evening had taken out all the body and it wouldn't stay. The hairstyle instructions in *Glamor* hadn't covered how to repair your "do" after that hot night on the town. It was just as well. Mallory doubted that anyone at home would be waiting up for her—they had given that up long ago. In the event that somebody did see her come in, though, fallen hair would provoke less hand-wringing than a hickey. She pulled a folding brush out of her clutch bag and gave her hair a few perfunctory swipes, draping it over her collarbone.

She walked out of the bathroom carrying the clean wastebasket and was greeted by deep, snorkel-like sounds. Tiptoeing over to the bed, she placed it next to Gunnar, just in case. He was sprawled on his back at an angle, his mouth open, a wafting alcoholic ether rising from his pores. Yet for all that, Mallory noted with wonder, he was still beautiful. Maybe when he was forty, when he had a bald patch, a sagging belly and pouches under his eyes like his father, maybe *then* Gunnar Anderson would be resistible. But here, at nineteen, he looked good enough to convince her that life as assistant manager of the Two Loons Motel might not be such a bad thing.

She leaned over and kissed him on the cheek, but he never stirred.

9

The next day, it was past noon when Mallory staggered out of bed. Wearing just panties and the ripped, shrunken T-shirt she always slept in, she leaned against the wall next to her closet, staring at the jumbled mess inside. She had a splitting headache, and her eyes felt gritty and unfocused, as if mice were gnawing on her optic nerves. At the sound of a voice, she nearly leaped out of her skin.

"Are you sleeping standing up?"

Mallory turned to see Diana peering around her bedroom door, thick auburn hair frizzed around a Botticelli face. "No. I was just trying to decide if I could get away with wearing a turtleneck."

Diana stepped in and shut the door, then walked over and examined the small, purple patch on Mallory's neck. She stood back and shook her head, struggling unsuccessfully against a grin. "I don't know, Mal. It's going up to ninety-three today."

"Shit." Mallory turned back to her closet and stared at it again.

Diana reached past with her good arm and flicked the hangers until she found a sleeveless cotton navy crewneck. "Here," she said, handing it to her. "This should cover."

Mallory pulled off her torn shirt and tugged the other over her head, then fished around the floor of the closet until she found a pair of cutoffs that were reasonably clean. No sooner had she wriggled into them than she was startled again by a sharp rap on the door. What a nervous Nellie, she thought as her heart launched into a pounding beat. No more Jack Daniel's for her. Or maybe it wasn't just the J.D. Everything seemed speeded up, as if she'd stepped over the edge of a cliff with

Gunnar last night and was hurtling toward some inevitable fate.

"It's open!" she called.

In the mirror, she saw the door swing wide and the broad girth of the Reverend Harold Caine emerge. In his dark shirt and cleric's collar, he was a black-and-white portrait of chronic disapproval. Out of the corner of her eye, Mallory spotted the lacy, strapless bra she had tossed on the dresser when she'd come in from the Two Loons in the wee hours of the morning. Grabbing and wadding it into a ball, she stuffed it in a drawer, then took up a hairbrush and went to work on her hair. When she ventured another glance in the mirror, she saw the Rev's gaze probing every corner of the room, his fingers gripping the pectoral cross strung around his neck, as if invoking its protection. His fleshy lower lip pushed against the upper one and rolled back down over itself, an expression of obvious disdain for everything his half-shuttered eyes perceived.

His head had become more bulletlike with each passing year as his hairline kept receding. He had taken to wearing his stone gray hair longish in the back, the wisp hanging over his stiff collar either an effort to compensate for the loss on top, or an attempt at trendiness—Mallory wasn't sure which. Church attendance had plummeted, and the current diocesan bishop was a big one on "making the church relevant to today's young." The Rev had little use for today's young, but he was big on making himself relevant to the bishop.

"What's up?" she asked as his eyes continued to rake the room.

He shifted his gaze to her. "Well, *you* are, at long last, I see."

"It was a late night."

"Hmm, indeed. Is that Mr. Anderson's car blocking the driveway?" The Rev, she realized, thought she had Gunnar hidden in the bedroom. Under the bed, maybe, or in the laundry basket. As if they had defiled the rectory with a night of illicit passion.

"I drove myself home. I'm taking the car back to his parents' in a little while. I'll move it, if it's in the way."

"Don't bother now. Mother ended up walking to her Saint Helena's Guild meeting." Frances walked to her meeting *every*

Saturday, Mallory thought, but the Rev would never let mere facts get in the way of an opportunity to instill guilt. "Why couldn't Gunnar drive?" he asked.

"He was tired. He drove down from Moorehead yesterday."

"Was he drinking?"

"He was tired."

"Did the two of you have a fight?"

Mallory slammed the brush down on the dresser. "No! He was tired, that's all, so I drove! Is that all right?"

"If Gunnar was unfit to drive and you took away his keys, Mallory, of course that's all right. I just hope you weren't drinking, as well. Goodness knows, I've spoken often enough about the dangers of drinking and driving. I don't know why you persist in being so reckless. If it's not Gunnar Anderson, it's young Will Dixon and that blessed motorcycle."

Mallory ignored the comment about Wiley's bike. If there was one thing that made the Rev antsier than Mallory's heavy-breathing relationship with Gunnar and the fear that she would scandalize his parish by showing up pregnant one day, it was the roar of Wiley's Harley coming up the driveway. "I'm not reckless. I drove, and I was stone-cold sober." It was near enough to the truth.

"Well, if that's true, then I am of course pleased that you are finally showing faint signs of maturity."

Mallory jammed her balled fists into the pockets of her cutoffs. "Was there something else?"

"No." The two gray bristles over his eyes tangled together as he gave Mallory one of his piercing stares. He started to turn, then stopped. "Oh, yes, there *was*. Mother asked if you want to invite Gunnar for dinner tonight."

"For dinner? I . . . I'm not sure. He might be heading back to Moorehead."

"*You'll* be here, though, won't you?"

"I'm not—"

"I hope you haven't forgotten that Bishop Lennox is passing through town. He's saying the Eucharist tomorrow, and I'd like you at the service, too, please."

Right, Mallory thought. Best foot forward. One big, happy family, especially for Bishop Lennox who, as the Reverend Lennox back in California, had arranged for the sisters to be placed with the Caines.

"I don't ask for much from you, Mallory, but the bishop always asks after you and Diana, and I like to reassure him that we have done well by you girls. It's not that I'm looking for praise or gratitude. The sacrifices I have made, the burdens I have borne, I have taken on willingly. But I think he would like to see you, and I know it would please Mother to have you there. Assuming," he added, "that you would be on your best behavior. You might also try to wear something decent."

Frances would be pleased, Mallory thought. Sure. She ignored his dig about her appearance, but pulled up sharp at his next comment.

"The Bishop and Mrs. Lennox will be here for dinner tonight."

"You're inviting Gunnar and the Lennoxes to the same meal?"

"It was Mother's idea, not mine. She ran into Mrs. Anderson at the ShopEasy yesterday, and they seem to think you and Gunnar have an announcement to make. Do you, Mallory?"

"I don't—"

"Never mind, you don't have to tell me. I'm sure I'll be the last to know, as always. But the Andersons are a good local family, and if that's your decision, you'll have our blessing and the bishop's, I'm sure." He looked down his nose and pursed his lips. "It has occurred to me, in fact, that marriage might be the best thing for you. Perhaps you could take a course or two up at Moorehead later, as long as Gunnar is there."

Mallory's stomach rose to a boiling pitch. The Rev had been dropping hints for some time now that she should be thinking about a job after graduation. He had never even bothered to ask whether she might like to attend college. Her grades at Ferry Falls had been reasonably good, as a matter of fact, despite a few too many hung-over mornings and cut classes. The Rev, however, had little use for educated women, and, in her case in particular, had already written her off as unlikely to amount to much. An early marriage would probably suit him just fine.

"It would get me out of your hair, anyway," she said.

"You read too much into my words, Mallory. Despite the fact that my legal responsibility ended eight weeks ago on your eighteenth birthday, my spiritual responsibility continues. I'm not one to abandon a burden, however little you think of my efforts."

Mallory looked away from him, furious at the lump that had formed in her throat. Why did he have the power to do this to her—make her feel like a piece of crap?

"In any event, let Mother know about Gunnar, will you?" Caine rotated his girth to address her sister, who had been sitting quietly on the bed. "Diana, I'll be in my office all afternoon, working on my homily for tomorrow's service. Get the phone if it rings, please. I don't want to be disturbed unless it's an emergency or the bishop."

Diana nodded, gaze fixed on the carpet, her left arm gripping the paralyzed right, her expression uncomfortable, just as it always was when she got caught in the middle of their arguments.

As the Rev disappeared down the hall, Mallory reached with her foot and shoved the door closed behind him. When she looked back at Diana, her sister had raised her head and was watching her. "Don't say it, Diana."

"I didn't say a thing."

"You were thinking it."

"You don't know what I was thinking."

"You were thinking I shouldn't let him get on my nerves. Well, I'm sorry, but he drives me crazy when he stands there with that all-seeing look on his face, like I'm one of those plastic models of the Invisible Woman and he can see right through me. You were also thinking that I should try harder to be nice to him, because even though he never fails to remind anyone who will listen that he and Franny took in two orphans—one of whom turned out to be a royal pain in the ass, in case anyone doubts what an absolute saint he is—that he's really a peachy guy and I should lighten up. Well, screw that,

Di! He treats you and Franny like servants, and to me, he's a f—''

"Actually, I was thinking how terrific you looked with Gunnar last night, and I was wondering if Father guessed right—that you finally broke down and agreed to marry Gunnar and live in wedded bliss behind the Two Loons, only maybe you're having second thoughts, and that's why you're in such a pissy mood."

The lump in Mallory's throat melted away in the warmth of a rising laugh. "Pissy? Excuse me, is this my sister Diana speaking? *Pissy?*"

Diana returned her grin, and Mallory motioned for her to sit in front of the dressing table. "Come here and let me tie back your hair. I'm hot just looking at you."

Diana settled on a stool, placing her right arm with her left in her lap. Mallory set to work gathering up the auburn waves into a ponytail high off Diana's neck. When she looked up again, Diana was watching her intently in the mirror.

"So?"

"What?"

"*Are* you and Gunnar getting married?"

"We didn't talk about it," Mallory said, hedging.

"Well, are you going to say yes when you *do* talk about it? And you *know* you will. Apparently, Gunnar's told half the town he's going to marry you, Mother says."

"Gunnar talks too much." Mallory rested her hands on her sister's shoulders and let out an explosive exhale. "Honestly, Di, I don't know what to do. I've spent half my life waiting for the day when I could blow this crummy pop stand. I was almost home free. Graduate, then gonzo. Next bus out of here. And then I had to go and get tied up with bloody Gunnar Anderson. *Arghhh!* I want to go away, but he's so—God! He's so..." She flopped onto the bed and propped her aching head in her hands. "I don't know what to do," she moaned. "And I've got one hell of a hangover, to boot, which isn't helping at all. Where's Wiley when I need him?"

The first time she had gotten drunk with Wiley on a pint of Johnnie Walker Red down at the Ferry River, the night had slipped away under the disconcerting spin of a starlit sky. The next morning, their heads threatening to explode, Wiley had taught Mallory a quick hangover cure. The two of them had crept into the back of the Ferry Falls emergency-rescue truck, parked in his stepfather's driveway. A couple of hits from the oxygen tank, and they were both right as rain, except for the beating Wiley took from his stepfather and the grounding Mallory earned for staying out all night.

"He didn't go to the prom, I gather?" Diana asked.

"Wiley? No. He doesn't do dances."

"Especially not when you're there with someone else."

"That's got nothing to do with it. We're best buds. That doesn't mean we don't go out with other people."

"So how many girls has Wiley dated?"

"I don't know. I don't keep track of his love life."

Diana shook her head. "You know, Mal, for a smart girl, you're awfully dumb about some things."

"Go on!"

"Hmmph! Anyway," Diana said, "how was it? Your evening and everything. Was it—you know—wonderful?"

Two points of vermilion had risen on Diana's cheeks, Mallory noticed. She was annoyed to see in the mirror across the room her own face had turned a deep shade of red, which left her looking like an overboiled lobster in a blond wig. "Let's just say it didn't quite turn out the way I expected."

"How so?"

"Our big party was crashed by a guy named Jack Daniel's."

"Oh, no. So *that's* why you drove."

"Yeah. And so technically, I guess, I'm still as pure as the driven snow."

"Technically?"

"Well, let's just say that I'd be surprised if my neck is the only place on my body with a hickey. Unfortunately, the big dope tossed his cookies before the main event."

Diana giggled. "Oh."

"Right. Oh."

"But it was enough to convince you to stay with him?"

Mallory was silent for a while. "Yeah, I think so. Maybe. I don't know." She sighed. "I love the guy, Di, but I hate this town, and he'll never live anywhere else."

"Well, I guess that makes two of us who are here for life. Oh, Mal, I know how unhappy you've been, and I've always known that you'd leave eventually, one way or another. But I'd miss you so much if you weren't close by."

Diana's voice had sunk to a low, strained whisper, and when Mallory glanced up, she saw that her sister's eyes were glistening. She scrambled off the bed and over to her side, kneeling in front of her. "Why don't we go away together, Di?"

"Away? Where? And what about Gunnar?"

"How can I make a decision about Gunnar when I haven't seen anywhere else, to know if marrying him and staying here is what I really want?"

"Where would you go?"

"I've been thinking about it, and you know where . . . ? California. Back home."

Diana stiffened. "No, I can't. I couldn't manage."

"Sure you could! We'd be together. I'd help you. You don't want to spend the rest of your life in Ferry Falls, do you? You're an artist. You should be in a big city." Mallory took Diana's hands in hers, examining them. Bright pigment—yellow, red, cerulean blue—was caught under the nails and in the cuticles. "You started a new canvas, didn't you?"

"Last night, after you left."

Diana's artistic talents had always been obvious, but more recently, her injuries had had a curious effect on her work. Although she still drew with her right hand, she had been retrained after the explosion to use her left hand and arm for most other functions. When she took up painting in her late teens, she'd had to use the left, but she was never able to master the same precise control and minute detail in her left-handed paintings as in her right-handed drawings. Instead, she turned out huge landscape canvases, whose shimmering shapes and colors gave the impression of a world illuminated by candles. It was as if two different artists lived in her beautiful, ravaged body.

Mallory had often tried to understand what it was that motivated her sister to sometimes turn to canvas, sometimes to the tiny format of her pen-and-ink drawings. She was so self-contained that her moods were difficult to read, but Mallory had finally concluded that Diana relied upon the broad strokes of the paintbrush in times of stress, as if she could sweep away her fears. That was the difference between them, Mallory thought. If *she'd* had any artistic ability, the canvases that she'd create of her own anxieties would have been dark, monstrous things. Rage incarnate. But Diana only produced things of beauty.

What was going to happen to her sister if—*when*—she moved out? Diana would spend the rest of her life locked away in this house, growing more and more afraid of the world. She would end up like Frances, the Rev's unpaid secretary and handmaiden, forever subjected to his tirades. The brightest note in her life would be Frances's endless stream of perky chatter, the determined cheeriness with which their adoptive mother tried so hard to sand the razorsharp edges of life with Harold Caine.

Mallory squeezed her sister's paint-stained fingers. "I would kill to have your talent, Di, but you need to get out and do something with it. Go someplace where there are other artists, and schools, and galleries and stuff. People who can appreciate your work."

"My 'work,'" Diana sniffed. "It's just a hobby. Anyway, I couldn't go away. Mother's getting on, you know, and she needs me here."

"Diana, wake up! You're twenty years old. You have no life!"

"I'm not like you, Mallory. You like all that partying and socializing, and guys like *you*. You can do whatever you want, go wherever you want, and that's good. But I can't."

"I *hate* partying, and that's not what I'm talking about, anyway. But while we're on the subject, there are plenty of guys who would love to go out with you."

"Oh, sure. Like Arvid Dolk."

"Well, yeah, Arvid, for one. But there are others."

"Not that I've noticed."

"You would, if you'd look up once in a while."

"Who are we talking about here? Zippy, the ShopEasy bag boy? Ernie Spivak, the washing-machine repairman?"

"See? You *have* noticed. They both have the hots for you, as a matter of fact."

"Wonderful."

"There are others, I bet, but that's not the point. There's no one in this town good enough for you, Di, because you're an artist, and you're beautiful, and you're brilliant—"

"You're *so* good for my ego, Mallory."

"And you need to be around people who can understand and appreciate what you do."

"I don't know."

"Yes, you do, dammit! You hate it here as much as I do. Let's do it, Di! Let's go to California! We were happy there once. There's lots going on, and they say the light is great for artists, and—"

"No."

"Diana—"

"No, Mallory."

"You could—"

"No! I can't go there. I can't!" Diana's face had gone sheet-white. The crease in her left cheek that most people thought was a dimple showed itself for what Mallory knew it to be—a small, deep scar left by a wicked shard of glass, imbedded there in the explosion that had destroyed their home, killed their parents and left Diana with a useless right arm.

Mallory wrapped her arms around her sister's trembling shoulders. "Shh. It's all right."

"I'm sorry, Mal. I just—"

"I know," she whispered. "I know." They rocked, silent for a while, and then Mallory straightened. "Hey! How about something to eat? If Wiley's not going to help me out with this hangover, I've *got* to have some food."

Diana took a deep breath and stood, a smile and a hint of color returning to her face. "Come on. Mother left some fresh cinnamon rolls in the oven for you."

"Hallelujah, and God bless Franny! You know, I've never understood how a nice lady like that got herself condemned to being the wife of the Reverend Windbag. You think maybe she was an ax murderer or something in a previous life?"

"Mallory!"

Mallory laughed, draping an arm across Diana's shoulders as they headed for the kitchen. "Yeah, yeah, I'll be good. I'll try, anyway."

10

When Mallory pulled up to the front of the Anderson house that afternoon, a Ford Fairlane with North Dakota plates sat blocking the driveway. She parked Gunnar's T-Bird on the street and was coming up the walk when Gunnar burst out of the front screen door, head down, his father's bellowing voice following him. "Gunnar! Get back here! Now!"

"Leave me alone!" Gunnar stomped across the porch and down the steps. He had almost bowled Mallory over before he noticed her. "Mal," he gasped. "Oh, Jesus—Mallory."

He glanced back at the house, pushing damp hair out of his eyes. Mallory guessed he had showered before leaving the Two Loons, because he smelled like the little bars of Palmolive soap they put in the rooms. He still wore his tux pants, bare toes peeking out from under the cuffs. His pleated dress shirt was wrinkled, tieless and open at the neck. He grabbed her arm and started toward the street. "C'mon, let's go."

"What's wrong?"

"Let's just get the hell out of here, okay?"

"You've got no shoes on. Where are we going?"

"Doesn't matter."

"Did your parents find out about us and the motel room?"

"No."

Mallory ran to keep up with his long strides as he pulled her toward the car. He had his hand on the door handle, when the rusty hinge on the Andersons' screen door screeched again. "Gunnar! You come back!"

Mallory turned to see Mr. Anderson on the front porch, his face a brilliant shade somewhere between red and purple. Di-

ana would know what that color was called. Magenta, maybe?
"What happened?" she said, looking back at Gunnar.

"Nothing. Just get in."

"Wait a minute—"

"Get in the fucking car!"

She yanked her arm away. "No!"

He took a deep breath. "Oh, hell, Mal, I'm sorry. I didn't
mean it. Just get in, please?"

"Tell me what's wrong."

Gunnar stared at her, then took a step toward the T-Bird.
Mallory flinched as his fist smashed down, leaving a deep dent
in the gleaming red hood. He glanced up at the house, then at
Mallory, his shoulders rising and falling with each labored
breath. "I love you, Mal, more than anything in the world. I
want to marry you. You know that, don't you?"

"Yes, but—"

"And you want to marry me, too, right? That's what last
night was all about. I mean, I messed up, I know that, but I'll
make it up to you, I promise."

"Gunnar, for God's sake, what happened? Why is your dad
so upset?" Knut Anderson was one of the most easygoing men
in Ferry Falls. Even when he staggered out of the Legion Hall
every Saturday afternoon, he was only more gregarious, never
a mean drunk. Mallory's gaze shifted to the Fairlane with the
North Dakota plates sitting in the driveway. "Whose car is
that?"

"Some people I know from up near Moorehead. They were
waiting here when Lars drove me home a little while ago."

"Friends of yours?"

"No. Sort of. Not really."

"You're not making any sense, Gunnar. What's going on?"

Just then the screen door creaked yet again, and a person
Mallory had never seen before emerged from behind Mr. Anderson's bulk. The girl looked about her age. Her fair hair was
shoulder-length and her eyes were ringed with black liner, some
of which appeared to be running. That was the first thing that
caught Mallory's attention. The second was the melon-shaped
bulge at the girl's middle. An oversize green T-shirt from Molly
Maguire's Pub in Minneapolis was pulled taut across the bulge.

The shirt was identical to one that Gunnar had bought shortly after Easter, when Mallory had gotten herself a fake ID and they had driven down to the city with a bunch of his friends. She couldn't remember the last time she had seen Gunnar wear it. Until that moment, it had also never occurred to her that Levi's might come in maternity styles.

"Mallory, listen to me," Gunnar pleaded. "It's not what you think. I mean it is, but it's not—"

He took a step toward her, his arms out, but she held up her hand. "Don't."

"Please, Mal, you've got to listen. When we first met, I didn't plan for this to happen. I just thought it would be nice to get to know you. I'd seen you around town, but everyone said you were Wiley Dixon's girl and you weren't interested in anyone else. Then, when we got talking that night at Patty Lintz's, I saw how different you were from all the other girls. You were such a funny little wiseass and so full of fire, I was hooked. I had to see you again, no matter what it meant for Wiley or—or anyone. Before I knew it, I was so crazy about you, it was scary. I knew it was wrong. I told myself, 'Anderson, you can't have this girl.' But I couldn't give you up. Every weekend, I came home to be with you and try to figure out how to hold on."

"Gunnar, don't."

"And then, when I phoned you that night, and we talked about—you know, after prom night and everything—I thought, holy smoke, she loves *me,* too! It'll work out, somehow."

The flood of his words seemed to be coming to Mallory from down a long tunnel, echoing low and indistinct. Meanwhile, the girl was walking toward them. Mallory was mesmerized by the shape under her T-shirt, which made the Molly Maguire leprechaun stand out like a 3-D image, bouncing with every step, as if he were dancing for joy at having found his pot of gold. Mallory wondered if the baby inside the bulge would be about the same size as that green elf.

The girl pulled up in front of them, and she and Mallory stared at each other. It was the girl who finally broke the silence.

"So—you're Mallory."

Mallory nodded. What does a person say at a time like this? The Rev, she suspected, had a book somewhere with a long list of inane things to say at funerals, weddings, baptisms, confirmations and those boring times when the service was over and everyone stood around the front of the church, shaking hands and trying not to show that all they really wanted was to get out of there. Mallory had never found that book, but it probably wouldn't have had anything to cover this situation, anyway. Not unless there was a chapter entitled What To Say When You Meet Some Girl Who's Been Knocked Up By Your Boyfriend, A Supposedly Great Guy Who Supposedly Is Madly In Love With You. Even the Rev, Mallory guessed, would have been at a loss for words.

She looked at Gunnar, who appeared to be suffering the hangover from hell. This experience would probably make teetotalers of them both. He leaned against the Thunderbird, propping his elbow on the roof and resting his forehead in his hand. "This is Janice Kazminski," he muttered, waving his other hand in her general direction. "Janice, Mallory Caine."

"Pleased to meet you," Mallory said. Ten years of the Rev's drilling on etiquette had left its mark, after all.

"I'll bet."

"Well, about as pleased as you are to meet me, I guess."

Janice nodded, then looked at Gunnar. "You told me you had to work for your parents." Her gaze traveled up and down his rumpled formal wear. She snorted, then turned to Mallory. "Every damn weekend for the last two months, he said he had to come home to work for his parents. But it was *you* he kept coming back to, wasn't it?"

"Janice," Gunnar said, "I told you about Mallory."

"Shut up! You told me, all right, when you dumped me." She looked again at Mallory. "I bet you think I'm a real dope, don't you?"

"I don't—no—I mean . . ."

At the sound of the screen door, they all looked up. Gunnar's mother appeared on the porch, accompanied by a gray-haired, angry-looking man and a short, overweight woman with fried blond hair. Gunnar slumped against the car, and Janice groaned.

"Great!" she said to Mallory. "I knew this was a stupid idea, coming down here. Last Tuesday night, Gunnar shows up at my place, after avoiding me for, like, two weeks. All this time, I'm telling my folks we're gonna get married, soon as his finals are over. I thought he would marry me, I really did. Then, all of a sudden, he shows up, says he's sorry, he can't, but he'll send money for the baby." Janice shot a malevolent look at Gunnar. "Thanks a lot, shithead!" She turned to Mallory once more. "After he left, I guess I kind of fell apart, so my dad says, 'No way that jerk's walkin' out on my little girl, we'll just see about that,' and next thing I know, they're dragging me down here. Don't you wish your folks'd keep their nose out of your business?"

Mallory shrugged. "I don't know. My parents are dead."

"Yeah? Well, maybe you're better off. I wish they'd just leave me alone, you know?"

"Yeah, I know." Shared anger at Gunnar and the meddling of parents managed to dissolve hostility between the two girls. They stood and commiserated, like this was some kind of female gab fest, Mallory thought, and all she and Janice had to worry about was bossy parents, boyfriends and whether disco was killing rock and roll.

"I feel so stupid," Janice said finally.

"You shouldn't."

"Mallory—"

"Shut up, Gunnar." Mallory snapped. She turned back to Janice. "I'm really sorry. This is awful. I didn't have a clue."

"Yeah, well, I guess neither of us did, huh?"

Janice took her turn glaring at Gunnar. Mallory racked her brain for an exit line. She had to get out of there, fast. So far, she had managed to stay calm, but inside she could feel the old rage awakening, clawing, threatening to burst out—only this time, Gunnar wouldn't be there to help her put it back in its cage. He couldn't help *himself,* so how had she ever thought he could help her?

When she looked up again, she saw that the other girl was studying her. "He didn't tell me how pretty you are," Janice said, "but I should've known."

Mallory didn't want to hear this. "Listen, I should be off. You guys need to talk and—"

Suddenly, Gunnar stood upright. "Mallory, no! Don't go!"

"I can't stay *here,* Gunnar!" Mallory said, waving her hand at the porch. "Are you nuts?"

"All right," he conceded. "But I'll see you later, okay?"

"I don't think so."

"Mallory, please—"

"No! No," she repeated, softer this time. "Look, you should have been honest with me, Gunnar. I don't hate you, but this hurts *so* bad."

Gunnar glanced at Janice, then stepped closer to Mallory. "I want us to get married," he whispered. "You and me, I mean."

"I can't. *You* can't. You know that."

He stared at her blankly, then looked for a moment at Janice, she of the bulging leprechaun T-shirt. When he spoke, his voice came out sounding strangled. "Yeah, I guess. I mean, I don't know. God, Mal! There must be some way."

He looked so terrified that Mallory felt an overwhelming urge, in spite of everything, to put her arms around him, or do *something* to help him. "It wouldn't have worked," she said softly. "Not just because of this. I want to go away for a while. To California. I don't think I can ever be happy until I see it again and understand what happened there. Why my parents died. Why Diana got hurt."

"I'd go with you. We could find what you need, and then come back home together. We could be happy."

"I'm not sure I can go on living in Ferry Falls, Gunnar."

He paused. "Okay. Someplace else, then."

"I don't think so."

Gunnar's forehead creased, and he studied her face as if he were seeing it for the first time. "Don't you love me, Mallory?"

"I do, but—"

"But what?"

"But not enough, I guess, to pretend that nothing else matters." That was it, Mallory suddenly understood. It wasn't only this other girl. Hiding in Gunnar's arms would never have been enough. Sooner or later, her rage and frustration would have returned, and she'd have ended up lashing out at him, hurting him. Gunnar looked as if he had been punched in the gut, and Mallory herself felt as if she had been kicked by a horse. "I have to go." She turned to Janice. "I hope everything works out for you, with the baby and everything . . ."

Her voice trailing off, Mallory turned away and broke into a run. The last thing she heard as she rounded the corner at the end of the block was Gunnar's voice, bellowing her name. She ran for several blocks, her feet thumping over the cracked, uneven sidewalk, her breathing pained and raspy in the dry prairie air. Finally, she forced herself to slow down, but she trudged on, looking neither to the left nor right. In the hot wind, her tears dried quickly, but she could feel the salty trail they left on her cheeks.

She had no idea how long the motorcycle had been following her, but when she looked up at last, there was Wiley Dixon on his Harley, clutch in, revving the engine to get her attention as his feet dragged along the ground on either side of the big machine. His smile was slightly bucktoothed, and the long, lean angles of his face and deep hollows under his cheekbones reinforced the impression of Wiley as wolverine. His pale complexion and lanky frame, Mallory always thought, made him look malnourished, like the "before" pictures in those body-building ads on the inside pages of Superman comics.

Wiley's smile faded when he saw Mallory's expression. "How ya doin'?"

She glanced around the deserted street, then back at him. "Like hell, to tell the truth."

"You want to talk about it?" Mallory just waved her hand. "Where are you headed?" he asked.

"I don't know."

"You want a ride?"

Mallory hesitated, kicking stones, then looked up. "Yeah, I do."

11

It's pretty hard to keep your perspective, Mallory decided, when someone has one hand under your T-shirt and is desperately trying to undo your shorts with the other. It's even harder when you can't make up your mind whether you want him to succeed or not.

She and Wiley were lying under the stars next to the Ferry River, just above the falls. Half the babies in town, she thought, could probably trace their beginnings to these grassy banks. Except, she amended, the one over at the Andersons' house, inside Janice Kazminski, waiting to be born.

All around her and Wiley, the bushes were alive with the rustles and moans of young couples caught up in the oldest rite of spring. Beneath Mallory's left shoulder blade, a stone drove itself into her flesh. She shifted her weight a little, and the movement made Wiley lose his grip on the brass button of her cutoffs, giving her time to think, and get the situation under control.

After she had run away from Gunnar and his pregnant girlfriend, she and Wiley had headed out of town on the Harley. As usual, Wiley seemed to know what she needed—just as he knew that what she *didn't* need was questions. Wiley had always understood about things. Ever since their first days together as rebellious church campers, the two of them had shared a frustrated, restless energy that neither parents nor teachers could comprehend nor cure. For eight years, Mallory had shared all her secrets, all her hopes, all her fears with Wiley. As they grew older, they had learned together how to drink coffee and whiskey, how to roll and smoke a joint, how to drive his Harley, how to forge an absentee excuse slip, how to get not-quite-falling-down drunk, and, of course, how many oxygen hits from the rescue truck it took to cure their hangovers.

She and Wiley had snuck into movies at the Rialto, sitting through two and three showings of the same adventure, feet up on the seats in front of them. Afterward, they would hang out at the Polar Star Café, where no one else they knew would be caught dead, but whose stubble-faced owner never bothered them. Over endless cups of coffee, Wiley would wax enthusiastic about the animation of Ray Harryhausen, or the films of Lucas and Spielberg, or the novels of Bradbury and Heinlein. Often, he would weave fantastic tales of his own about his mythical Avaron and Sagramor, his malleable face shifting and reforming into the bizarre fictional characters that sprang to life in his mind, voice rising and falling as Mallory posed questions to each in turn, interviewing them, drawing out their amazing, fabricated histories. Long past their curfews, heedless of parental harangues and punishments that were sure to follow, they stayed glued to the chrome-and-vinyl chairs of the Polar Star, pretending it was a writers' coffeehouse in some place like New York or L.A. where they would go one day soon—hell, even Minneapolis. *Anyplace* but Ferry Falls. They agreed on that, as on so many other things.

They were so close that Mallory suspected Wiley had flunked out deliberately in his senior year so he wouldn't graduate ahead of her. If he had wanted to, he could have sailed through—although Mr. Jaworski, the Ferry Falls High principal, said Wiley needed a serious attitude adjustment. Mallory had always thought Wiley's attitude was just fine.

Lying on the riverbank now, she shifted her weight once more, but the stone under her shoulder rolled along with her. Wiley moaned as he repositioned himself on top of her, then pressed his mouth hard against hers. Mallory returned his kiss, accepting his probing tongue and giving it a friendly caress, determined not to hurt his feelings, no matter what. Just the same, she was beginning to think maybe Diana was right, and she *had* been a little dense about Wiley.

Even before Gunnar had come along, Mallory and Wiley had dated other people. Well, she had, anyway. With his pallid, so-so skin and pigeon chest, Wiley was not exactly a classic heart-throb, although he *did* do a terrific Steve McQueen impression. After Mallory got involved with Gunnar, it was harder for them to be together on weekends, but Wiley never seemed to mind, making himself scarce while Gunnar was in town, reappearing each Sunday evening just as the red T-Bird roared off, helping her to get through the tedious week.

If Wiley were dying of kidney disease and needed one of hers, Mallory thought, she would gladly give it to him. She just hadn't planned on having sex with him. It wasn't that kind of relationship. At least, *she'd* never thought it was, and she'd assumed Wiley felt the same way.

That afternoon, after she'd climbed onto the back of his Harley, they'd driven for hours, exploring back roads, outracing yapping dogs, waving to farmers seeding fields. They stopped for a six-pack of cold Pabst at a crossroads grocery store with faded Dr. Pepper signs on its clapboard sides, then chugged the beer down in a farmer's field, tossing the cans. Afterward, they flew like the wind again, down one dirt road after another, yelling and hooting like lunatics until they were hoarse. Wiley switched seats with her at one point, and never said a word when Mallory opened the throttle and took the bike up to eighty-five miles an hour, even though a gopher hole would have made mincemeat of them both.

In all those hours, he never once asked what had happened, or why she had been running away from Gunnar's house, alone and miserable. Finally, on the banks of the river above the falls, watching the stars come out, Mallory told him. Then she did something she had never before done in front of Wiley—she cried, hard and long, for almost an hour, hating herself for being stupid and weak, but incapable of doing anything about it. Wiley put his arms around her—which *he* had never done before—and rocked her against his ropy shoulders, stroking her hair. When she was drained and exhausted, Wiley wiped her tears and gave him his old bandanna to blow her nose. Mallory finally managed to look up and give him a faint smile, and it was then that Wiley did one more thing he'd never done before. He kissed her. Then he kissed her again, and the next thing Mallory knew, they were sprawled on the riverbank, him half on top of her, his hands inside her clothing, working mightily to get it off.

"Wiley?" Mallory mumbled, wincing as their front teeth knocked together. "Hold up a little, okay?"

He lifted his head, breathing fast and hard. "What's wrong?"

"I don't think we should do this."

"I do. I think we should, Mal. I really do."

He dropped his head again, but she slipped her hand up against his chest, feeling the ridge of his breastbone against her fingers. "Wiley, please! I'm bummed out and it's hard to think straight, but I don't think this is a good idea."

He watched her for a moment, then sighed and rolled off. Sitting up, he turned his attention to the falls, and after a moment, he began pitching stones into the water. Mallory sat up, as well, the silence between them as loud as the roar of the waterfall. "Are you mad at me?" she asked. Wiley said nothing. She put her hand on his arm. "Don't be mad. You're my best friend."

"Yeah, but I'm no Stud Anderson, am I?"

Mallory snorted. "Thank God! The big shit!" Wiley flung another rock, but it pinged off a tree and ricocheted into the bushes. "Come on, Wiley, give us a break, will you? You and me, both? You're a better person than he is."

"I'm a great guy, all right."

"You are."

"Yeah? So how come *he's* the one you cry over? How come he's the one you wanted to give yourself to, when he's such a jerk? What is it with guys like that, that they can be total assholes and get away with it?" Wiley flung yet another stone into the river, his profile grim and set.

"I don't know. Hormones or something, I guess."

"I got hormones, too, you know."

Damn, Mallory thought, she really *was* dense. But who knew he was thinking this way? If she'd known, she certainly wouldn't have asked him to drive her to the Planned Parenthood clinic in Minneapolis last month to get those birth control pills. "I know you do, but we're best friends, Wiley.

There's more than hormones between us. Hormones come and go, but our friendship is forever."

He looked over at her, all the laughter and spark and mischief gone from his face. For the first time, she saw the young man who had, somewhere along the way, slipped into the shoes of her childhood friend. "Don't you know I'm in love with you, Mal?"

"Oh, no," she breathed, truly horrified. "Don't say that, Wiley."

"I can't help it."

"But it'll spoil everything!"

"It wouldn't if you loved me back."

"I *do* love you."

"No, you don't."

"Yes, I do, dammit!"

"Not like you love Gunnar."

"*Better* than him. Just not—"

"Just not enough, right?"

Not enough. There it was again. Mallory jumped up, fists clenched at her sides. "How the hell should *I* know, Wiley? Damn you, and damn Gunnar! Damn both of you!" She spun away from him and kicked viciously at a tree trunk, sending chips flying from the toe of her sneaker and a sharp pain up her foot. "Everybody wants me to be something I'm not. The Rev wants me to be Miss Goody Two-Shoes. Frances wants me to be her loving, sweet homebody. Gunnar wanted me to be his forgiving little wife and help him run the stupid Two Loons Motel. And now you! How can I be what *any* of you want me to be when I don't know what I want myself? How am I supposed to love anybody when I don't even know who I am?"

She turned to face him.

"I don't know who I am, Wiley. I don't know what the fuck I'm doing here! I don't belong. I never have. This wasn't supposed to be my life, only I don't know what it was supposed to be. My parents were killed, and everybody says it was their own fault that it happened, and they treat me like I'm damaged goods, or something. What if they're right? What if I'm just basically rotten inside, and that's why I can never do anything right? What if I come from a long line of terrible people? How can you love someone like that? Why would anyone want to have anything to do with me?"

"You're not a monster, Mal, you're just mixed up."

"Damn straight I'm mixed up." She slumped down on the riverbank again. "I want to know who I am. I want to know where I came from. My mother and father can't have been *all* bad, not when the only memories I have of them are good ones. And even if they were screwups, I want to know how they got that way. Once and for all, I want it out in the open. I want the whispers to stop, not just around me, but in my head, too—the whispers that tell me I'll never be any good."

They were silent for a long time, listening to the roar of the falls. "You're going to go away, aren't you?" Wiley said at last.

"I have to."

"Back to California?" She nodded. "Okay," he said. "We'll go together. We can take the bike, drive cross-country."

Mallory hesitated, then shook her head slowly. "No. I have to go alone."

"Don't walk away from me, Mal. I'm sorry I pushed. It's okay. We can leave things just the way they are."

"It's not that."

"Then let me come with you."

"I have to be by myself for a while, Wiley."

"You want to get rid of me."

"No," she said, twisting to face him. "Never. Leaving you is like leaving a leg behind. But I can't learn to stand on my own two feet unless I figure out who I am."

His expression was dubious. "I'll never see you again."

"That's bull, Wiley. We're kindred spirits, twin siblings of different mothers. You'll always be part of my life. I just need to do this on my own."

"When will you go?"

"I'm not sure. As soon as possible. I just don't know what to do about Diana."

"What about her?"

"I asked her to go with me, but she's dead set against it. She still has nightmares about the explosion—has had for years. I think she figures seeing California again would completely unhinge her. I know she's wrong, but I can't convince her.

Whether or not she goes back, though, she has to get out of that house.''

''Maybe she's happy there.''

''No, she's not. I know she's not, even though she won't admit it. Diana's buried alive, Wiley. Frances is a good person, but she coddles and protects Diana like she's brain-damaged, instead of just having a paralyzed arm. And the Rev treats her like his personal servant, the way he does Frances. Diana's afraid of him. She'll never have any kind of a life if she doesn't get out of there.''

''But what can you do, Mal? You can't live her life for her. She has to make her own decisions.''

''I can't leave her there.''

''You're not her keeper.''

''Yes, I am. My parents always told us to look out for each other. After they were killed and Diana was hurt, Reverend Lennox—he was the one who watched over us and found us a new home—he said I had to help take care of her. So I did. I dressed her until she was able to do it herself, and I did her hair, and tied her shoes, and carried stuff for her, and fought the bullies for her. *She's* the reason I didn't run away long ago. You helped me survive living in this town, Wiley, but if it weren't for Diana, I wouldn't even *be* here. She's my sister and my responsibility, and nothing will ever change that.''

12

Ferry Falls, Minnesota
June 21, 1979

It was after midnight when Mallory arrived back at the rectory to find all the downstairs lights on and a strange car sitting in the driveway. "Oh, no," she breathed, climbing off the back of Wiley's bike. "I forgot."

"What?"

"Bishop Lennox. He and his wife are in town. I was supposed to be here for dinner with them."

"You want me to come in and face the music with you?"

"No, you'd better go."

The front door opened at that moment and Reverend Caine stepped out. Under the porch lights, his face looked pinched and hard with fury.

"Go on, Wiley," Mallory said quietly, watching the dark figure on the front step. "I'll talk to you tomorrow."

"You sure?"

"Yeah. You'd better head off."

Wiley jumped on the kick starter, twisted the throttle and the Harley screamed to life. Rolling down the driveway, he angled the bike toward the street, then roared off into the night. Mallory's ears rang with the echo as she and the Rev stared at each other across a vast, unbridgeable chasm.

"I hope you realize," Caine said finally, his voice a glacier, "that Mother has been sick with worry."

"I'm sorry."

"You're always sorry, Mallory, but it's not enough."

"I forgot about dinner."

"*And* about your responsibility to others, for the ump-teenth time. About Bishop Lennox and Mrs. Lennox. Mother held dinner for hours, until it was ruined. We were half expecting state troopers to arrive with news that you were dead on the highway somewhere. The Lennoxes decided to stay over at the house until there was word. The ladies and Diana finally went to bed, but not before Mother had roused half the town trying to discover where you could have gotten to. Have you no consideration?"

"I said I'm sorry. I don't know what else I can say."

"Nor do I. Quite frankly, Mallory, I give up. The Lord knows, I've tried to do my best by you, but obviously, it hasn't been sufficient. I devoted my life to making a better life than you had in the past, but it seems a poor clergyman's efforts were not enough to lift *you*, at least, very far from your roots. I prayed for guidance, but I have been tested and found wanting."

"Oh, for Pete's sake," Mallory cried, "it's not about *you!* Can't you see that? Everything isn't always about you. This is about *me*. I can't be what you want me to be."

"What I want is unimportant. What does God want you to be, Mallory? That's the question you should be asking yourself."

She shook her head and laughed bitterly. "Damned if I know, Rev. He may talk to you, but he sure as hell doesn't talk to me."

He reared back. "Must you work so *hard* at being offensive?"

"I don't work at it at all. It just seems to come naturally." Mallory exhaled deeply. "Look, there's something I should tell you, and I guess now's as good a time as any. I've decided to go away. Out west. I have enough money from my parents' trust to last for a while, until I can get a job. I'll leave in a couple of weeks, as soon as exams are over. Assuming," she added, "that it's all right for me to stay here that long?"

Caine watched her for some time before answering. "You may stay on the understanding that you cause no more disruptions in your remaining time. Mother may be upset by your leaving, but I think in the long run, it will be for the best.''

"Fine. I'll make my arrangements and be out of your hair as soon as I can.''

Caine nodded and turned away, his hand on the door. "Are you coming in now?''

"In a while. I want to sit out here and think.''

"You might try praying for some guidance, Mallory.'' He pulled open the screen. "Lock the doors and turn off the lights when you come in.''

When he had gone into the house, Mallory slumped down on the front step, breathing a deep sigh of—what? Relief? Maybe. The die was cast and there was no going back. She was finally going to get out of this house and out of this town that she had always hated. So why didn't she feel good about it? Because, she thought, wrapping her arms around her knees, trying to soothe a gnawing feeling that had nothing to do with hunger or a headache from the beer she and Wiley had consumed, she was leaving behind a life that was familiar, despite its trials. The future held nothing but uncertainty, and there would be no Gunnar, no Wiley, no Diana to smooth out the bumps.

Diana. She was abandoning Diana, running out on her. Leaving her a prisoner of her shyness and her handicap, of Frances's overprotectiveness and the Rev's domineering arrogance. Between them, they would crush her, and Mallory wouldn't be there to help. She was breaking the silent vow she had made long ago to her father's and mother's memories, the promise to watch over her sister. But Diana would never go back to California. What would happen to her now?

From the murmur of deep voices inside the house, Mallory presumed the Rev was telling Bishop Lennox she'd finally shown up. The living room lights snapped off, and a moment later, she heard the familiar creak of the third step in the stairs off the front hall, the one she'd long ago learned to step over when she snuck in late. She waited for the second creak, announcing that both men had retired for the night. Instead, the front door opened and Bishop Lennox stepped out. Mallory sprang to her feet.

He held up his hand. "Don't get up. I thought I'd come out for a breath of fresh air. I didn't mean to disturb you."

"You're not disturbing me."

"Can I join you?" he asked, indicating the wooden step.

"Wouldn't you be more comfortable on the porch swing?"

"Oh, no," the bishop said, knees cracking as he settled. "This will do fine."

Mallory sat down, examining him out of the corner of her eye. He still reminded her of an elf, she decided, with his small frame, round face and smiling eyes under that shiny dome fringed with snow-white hair. The fringe had been a little fuller, the circumference of the dome a little smaller when she had first met him eleven years earlier. But after all, she thought, he must be pushing seventy by now.

When her family had begun attending church in Newport Beach, California, Mallory recalled the then–Reverend Lennox as being warm, funny and welcoming. They had been parishioners for a little over a year when the explosion happened, but Reverend Lennox had been there for her and Diana as if he had known them all their lives, stepping into the breach when no relatives had been available to take on two half-grown children. She might have resented him for sticking them with Harold Caine, except that in her most reasonable moments, Mallory knew that Reverend Lennox had done the best he could by them. Frances was a kind, loving woman, and few others would have been willing to adopt two girls, what with Diana's handicap and Mallory's rambunctious nature, especially given their troubled background. Lennox had been made a bishop several years ago, but he'd remained in contact with the Caines and the girls, writing and telephoning, visiting when his travels brought him to the northern states.

"I'm sorry I spoiled everyone's evening," Mallory told him.

He shrugged. "I'm just relieved that you're safe. You gave us a bit of a scare, you know."

"I know. I'm sorry. I should have called. I just…" Her voice drifted off. It was too hard to explain.

"Frances spoke to the young man's mother—Mrs. Andrews?"

"Anderson."

"Anderson. She told Frances what happened. About your young man and the difficulty he's gotten himself into." Mallory closed her eyes and turned away, feeling sick and betrayed all over again. Bishop Lennox put a hand on her shoulder. "I'm so sorry, Mallory. It must have been a terrible shock for you."

She nodded, distressed to feel tears streaming down her face once more. She patted the pockets of her cutoffs, searching in vain for a Kleenex. Bishop Lennox extended a clean, white handkerchief. "Thanks," she said. She wiped her eyes, blew her nose, then wadded the hankie into a ball and held it clenched against her chin, willing herself to stop blubbering. "I thought Gunnar loved me."

"I'm sure he does. Apparently, he lacks self-control and strength of character, but his mother says he's very upset that he's lost you."

"Well, what does he expect, the big shit?" Mallory snapped. She winced, then peered up sheepishly. "Pardon my language."

The bishop went on as if he hadn't heard. "I can't imagine what he expected, but I know what his family expects. That he will do the right thing by the other young lady. Is that what you think should happen, too?" She nodded. "I'm proud of you, Mallory. You have a strong sense of decency and kindness. His parents believe that Gunnar would abandon her, if you wanted him to. I know how hard this is for you, but I'm very impressed to see you thinking of the other girl, who, after all, has also been badly hurt in all this."

Mallory felt ready to burst into tears again—but tears of gratitude this time. In all her life, few adults except Frances had found anything in her that was worthy of praise. But Franny saw good in *everyone,* including the Rev, which tended to devalue the currency of her approval, as far as Mallory was concerned. Teachers had been impressed by Mallory's schoolwork, almost surprised to discover evidence of a brain behind those stubborn dark eyes. But they always despaired of her distrustful, rebellious attitude—her "fatal flaws," the guidance counselor had felt obliged to inform her, offering his learned opinion that she wasn't advancement material. No one in Ferry Falls had ever told Mallory they were proud of her. In this case, however, she wasn't sure she was worthy of the bishop's kind words.

"I debated about it," she confessed.

"About what?"

"Going back to Gunnar's house. Fighting to hold on to him. Two or three times this afternoon, I wanted to tell Wiley to drive me back."

"But you didn't."

"No."

"Why not?"

"Partly because of Janice, the other girl. But partly because I was never sure about Gunnar. Whether I wanted to stay with him. He kept pushing for a commitment, and I kept stalling. Maybe I was stringing him along. Maybe it was my fault he got so mixed up about everything."

"No," the bishop said sternly, taking her by the chin. "Look at me. That's no excuse for the way he treated you or that girl. Did you know about her before today?"

"No."

"Then there's no blame on your head. You're young, Mallory, too young to be pressured into marriage when you're not ready. But Gunnar knew what he was doing, and he knew he didn't have the right even to ask you. Not when he had already made a promise to a young woman who was carrying his child. You did nothing wrong here."

Mallory shook her head dubiously. "I always mess up. The Rev thinks it's because I come from a bad line."

The bishop's head snapped back and he stared at her, his expression shocked and angry. Then his shoulders slumped and he sighed. "Oh, Mallory, I'm so sorry. I knew you and Reverend Caine didn't always see eye to eye, but I never realized you were so unhappy."

"Is it true?"

"What?"

"What he says? About my parents?"

"What exactly has he told you?"

"Not much, except that they were involved in some kind of illegal stuff involving drugs. That the explosion wasn't an accident. That they were killed by other criminals."

Lennox studied his hands for a long time, as if deciding what to tell her. Finally, he looked up. ''It's true that the explosion wasn't an accident, but the person or persons responsible were never found, as far as I know.''

''And my parents?''

''There were allegations about drug dealing.''

''Oh, God, it *is* true,'' Mallory groaned.

''They never had a chance to defend themselves,'' Lennox said. ''And frankly, I've always found it hard to fathom. I didn't know your mother and father very long or very well, Mallory, but they seemed like intelligent people, who loved you and Diana very much. When those stories came out, I couldn't picture the couple I had met as the same people the police and press were talking about.''

''Maybe that's not so surprising.''

''What do you mean?''

''Most people aren't what they seem. You think you know them, and then they go and do things you never expected. How can you trust anyone?''

''Oh, Mallory, you mustn't believe that. The world is full of good and decent people, and you're one of them. We all make mistakes occasionally. Some people make terrible mistakes, but you have to forgive them and then get on with your life. Don't carry anger around inside of you, because in the end, the only one you hurt is yourself.''

Mallory stared out into the dark street. ''I'm trying to get on with my life,'' she said, ''except . . .''

''What?''

''I want to go back to California.''

''Reverend Caine just told me about your plans.''

''I'm worried about my sister.''

''Why is that?''

''I don't want to leave her behind. She won't come with me, but she's miserable here. She has no friends, no life. Her art is wonderful, but she has no chance to do anything with it, no chance to develop her talent. And even though she gets along with Frances and the Rev, they don't understand her or what she needs. They'd be quite content to keep her hidden away forever in this old house. Diana needs to leave as much as I do, but it'll never happen if I abandon her.''

Lennox watched her closely. ''I think you're right, Mallory. As a matter of fact, it was a thought just along those lines that brought my wife and me to Ferry Falls this week, although I hadn't realized until now how necessary it was for you girls to move on.''

''What do you mean?''

''Let me run an idea past you, to see what you think.''

''An idea?''

''Yes. You see, Mallory, this old preacher has finally decided to hang up his cassock.''

''You're retiring?''

''More or less. As a farewell gift, the church has given my wife and me a year's sabbatical in Paris. A friend has arranged an apartment for us. I'll be handling some light clerical duties with the small American community there, but mostly, we'll just be enjoying the city.''

''That's great.''

''Yes, we're thrilled. In any case, Mary and I thought perhaps you girls could come and stay with us. The apartment has extra space, and we would love to have you. I mentioned it quietly to Diana this evening.''

Mallory felt a sudden cool breeze through the hot night air. ''And? What did she say?''

''She didn't give me an answer. She seemed intrigued, but she was too worried about you to give it much thought.''

''It's just what she needs! All those museums and art galleries.''

''She could take classes, if she wanted to.''

''Oh, yes, yes! It would be perfect.''

''Good. I'm glad you think so. We'll discuss it with her in the morning then, shall we?'' Mallory nodded eagerly. ''What about you? Will you come, too?''

She hesitated. ''I—I don't know. I hope Diana will say yes, but—''

''But you're not sure it's for you.''

''No, I'm not. I don't know why, but I think I have to see California first. Like I'll never know peace unless I go back there, for a little while at least, and find out the truth about my mother and father.''

"What if the truth turns out to be bad news? Will that still give you peace?"

"I'm not sure. I only know that I can't go on for the rest of my life without figuring out who I really am. One way or the other, I have to know."

"I can't promise that your journey of discovery will be easy, Mallory. You could hope for a miracle, but to be honest, I wouldn't advise you to count on finding another interpretation of what went wrong out there."

"I know, but it's what I want to do."

Lennox sighed. "I wish you would come with us, but if you really think you need to do this, then you must. I can only pray that you find your peace at last." He placed the palm of his hand on top of her head, and with his thumb, he traced a cross on her forehead, invoking a traditional benediction. "The peace of God, Mallory, which passes all understanding."

"Amen," she whispered.

Book Three

Joy and Avarice

13

They called it the City of Angels, but from the moment Mallory stepped off the Greyhound bus that morning in early July, she sensed that the city held more ghosts and demons than angels. Ghosts from her childhood. Demons from her nightmares. She might have lost her nerve and caught the next bus out, except that there was nowhere else to go, and no one to go to. She had spent over half her young life wishing she were somewhere else, preferably as far away as possible from Ferry Falls and the Reverend Harold Caine. Southern California was the last and only place she could remember being happy, and so she felt drawn to return there.

Gunnar Anderson's betrayal, and the smug satisfaction of the Ferry Falls rat packers, who'd thought Gunnar was crazy to go with her in the first place, ensured that the little town was thoroughly unlivable for her—even if she had wanted to stay. Gunnar had married Janice Kazminski at the end of June and the two of them were working at the Two Loons until it was time for him to return to college. Mallory knew that they were living in the same unit that she and Gunnar had used the night of the senior prom. She'd spotted the newlyweds one evening as she and Wiley were driving past, Gunnar following a round-bellied Janice into the room. When his eyes caught Mallory's, a powerful surge had passed between them, until she'd forced herself to look away and break the current.

It was finished. Not just Gunnar—everything. Ten years of Ferry Falls, more than half her eighteen-year-old life. She'd fought and rebelled every step of the way, until finally, she had gotten what she wanted. Her personal Berlin Wall had tumbled with an unexpected crash. But freedom, Mallory discovered, was an intimidating prospect.

Wiley had offered again to go away with her, to California or anywhere else. After she'd refused him several times, Mallory woke one morning to a call from his mother, telling her that Wiley had left during the night, following yet another battle with his stepfather. Before he took off, Wiley had asked his mother to give Mallory a package. Opening it, Mallory had found a battered notebook containing all the "Avaron and Sagramor" stories he'd ever written.

Two days later, Mallory had driven to the Greyhound Bus station in Minneapolis with the Lennoxes and Diana. When Mallory's westbound bus pulled in and her gear was stowed in its belly, both sisters had struggled to hold back tears, Diana clutching Mallory's sleeve as if she would never let go. "I wish you were coming with us. It's not too late. You could still change your mind."

"I'm not a Paris kind of girl, Di. But you're going to have a fabulous time."

"We've never been apart."

"You won't have time to miss me."

"Yes, I will. And I'll be worried about you, all alone in California. What will you *do* there?"

"I'm not sure. Get a tan, a room and a job, I guess, not necessarily in that order. Scout around." It sounded convincing. One thing she could say for herself, Mallory thought, she'd always had the ability to talk a good line. No one would ever believe what a lump of terrified mush lay under that tough shell she'd worked so hard to cultivate.

"Oh, Mal! It's such a big place."

"It's home."

"You'll never come back to Minnesota! I know you won't. I can't blame you, but I'm afraid I'll never see you again."

"That's not going to happen. We're the only family we've got, Di."

Diana shook her head. "You've fought my battles long enough. You need to get on with your own life."

"I'll always be there for you. And if anyone, anywhere, tries to give you a hard time, they'll have me to deal with." Somehow, Mallory thought. But as her bus pulled away from the station and she'd watched Diana's shrinking form, flanked by Bishop Lennox and his wife, she'd experienced a wave of guilt at handing over the protective role that her little eight-year-old shoulders had willingly assumed. The accusing finger of her conscience thrust itself in her face, denouncing her for abandoning her responsibility.

And above that, another frightened little voice in her head kept asking, over and over, "Who are *you?*" To that question, Mallory had no answer.

Arriving in afternoon rush-hour traffic, it took three hours for the Greyhound to negotiate its way from the northeastern desert rim of Los Angeles to the central terminal. When it finally arrived, Mallory stepped out of the bus's stale, smoky air into bright sunshine and took her first breath of the sprawling city's distinctive odor, vaguely familiar from childhood—a subtle blend of sea air, eucalyptus and smog. Somewhere in her backpack, she had some names and addresses and telephone numbers given to her by the Lennoxes, friends of theirs she could contact who were standing by to offer assistance to a young girl arriving on her own in the big city. Mallory knew she would never call. She was through with charity, through with whispers of curiosity and pity, through with playing Child of the Damned.

Instead, she made her own way. The first few weeks passed in a blur, as she took a room at the YWCA and struggled to orient herself in a city without a core. She picked up a part-time job right away at the Weenie On a Stick franchise down the street from the Y. She hated the garish, skimpy uniform she was forced to wear and the greasy smell that burrowed its way into her skin so that she had to scrub herself raw before she could collapse on her bed at night. And then there were the wise guys. After one too many customers, staring at her short-shorts, made what he thought was a terribly witty comment about weenies and sticks, she was ready to run them all through with

a skewer. But she gritted her teeth and carried on, wanting to
conserve her limited funds until she could figure out where she
was going to live and what she would do in the long run.

When she realized that public transport was hopelessly in-
efficient, Mallory withdrew three hundred dollars from her
carefully hoarded savings, found a motorcycle dealership on
Sunset Boulevard and bought a used Yamaha 125 and a
Thomas street guide. On her days off she explored, gawking at
the opulent, manicured estates of Bel Air and Beverly Hills, the
disappointing Hollywood strips, the drugged-out wanderers in
Griffith Park and the sprawling movie and television facilities
in Culver and Burbank and Studio City. It took over a month
to work up her courage, but finally, Mallory made up her mind
that on her next full day off from the weenie-biz, she would go
and take a look at her past.

Paris, France
July 28, 1979

Hemingway said that Paris was a movable feast, and when
she arrived with the Lennoxes in the City of Lights, Diana discovered a veritable banquet of rich sensations—sounds and
sights and odors that fed her long-starved soul and brought it
into delayed and unexpected vigor. Confined for years to the
drab and antiseptic environment of the rectory in Ferry Falls,
her heart quickened at smells of soft perfume, good bread and
pungent *Gaulloises*. Soft, dappled light on tree-lined boule-
vards made her want to skip with pleasure. Tires rumbling over
cobblestones, and impatient drivers sounding tinny *claxons*
infused her with an energy she had never known.

When they first arrived at the Rue Clément Maroi, where
they were to live for the year, Diana discovered that the ''little
flat'' the Lennoxes had spoken of was actually an American
Embassy–owned apartment, just two blocks from the Champs-
Elysées. Currently unoccupied, the flat was on loan from the
ambassador, an old schoolmate of the bishop's. The Empire-
style apartment building, with its double-pitched mansard roof,
featured an impressive portico and wrought-iron gate at the
front, watched over by a wizened concierge in a black beret.

Diana soon discovered that the little old man was there virtually twenty-four hours a day, seven days a week.

After the concierge had greeted them and assured himself that they were indeed the new tenants, she and the Lennoxes walked down a short passageway to a tiled center courtyard. Hidden from the street, it was a secret little enclave onto which opened the six apartments: three in front, three in back. Shaded by its surrounding walls, the courtyard was cool and comfortable, with green wooden benches around a babbling fountain, and hanging baskets of red geraniums that lent splashes of bright color to the monochrome background of stone and tile. As soon as she saw it, Diana knew she would paint this scene.

The embassy aide who had met them at the airport with the keys to the flat preceded them now to its front door. "The ambassador said to tell you that his wife had a few groceries stocked in the kitchen, and that the cleaning lady comes every Thursday morning. Oh, and Ambassador and Mrs. Pannet hope you'll join them for dinner this evening. He'll send his car around six, if that's all right. Casual—there'll just be you and the Pannets. And Miss Caine, of course," he added, giving Diana another in a series of curious, smiling glances that had started as soon as they came through the gate at Charles de Gaulle. Diana looked away, flustered as usual by any kind of attention, certain it was prompted by morbid curiosity.

The young man left soon after, and Diana and the Lennoxes explored the apartment, exclaiming over its large, comfortable sitting room and dining room and laughing at the tiny galley kitchen, hardly wide enough for the portly bishop and his round wife to get by each other. The den overlooking the courtyard held a big cherry desk and chair, and two deep leather armchairs, perfect for curling up with a good book. The tiled bathroom was about three times the size of the kitchen and held an enormous, claw-footed tub—an odd use of space, they decided, given the French reputation for loving food but having little affection for long baths. The Lennoxes' bedroom, Diana discovered when she peeked in shyly, was a big, ridiculously high-ceilinged affair, its walls and ceilings a Rococo splendor of gilt moldings. Her own room was much tinier and less ostentatious but bright and cheerfully painted in yellow and white, with a view to die for and a corner just begging for an easel.

It took no time at all for Mary and Doug—as the Lennoxes insisted she call them—to lead Diana into the thrill of discovering the city around them. Inspired by animated faces and dramatic styles of dress, Diana soon found richly colored scarves and flowing skirts in the Paris flea market, where Mary Lennox loved to poke around, and she added them to her wardrobe. The costumes would have seemed wildly eccentric in All Saints parish, but they suited Diana's artistic sensibilities and the city perfectly.

At first, she let herself be guided by the Lennoxes in her wanderings, but as her fascination and confidence grew, Diana began to venture out on her own. Elaborate buildings, like tiered cakes, and frothy Gothic cathedrals reflected in the Seine drew her into the city's colorful quarters, sketchbook in hand. Using her mornings to brush up on her high school French at classes at the Alliance Française, she spent her afternoons wandering farther and farther afield, relishing a freedom and sense of adventure that, up to then, she had only experienced wistfully and secondhand through her sister.

For the first time in her life, she experienced the joyous freedom of anonymity. If her handicap was apparent, its cause was not. In Paris, her past was unknown and she was free to present herself, or reinvent herself, as she saw fit. Mary and Doug Lennox introduced her to fellow Americans as the daughter of old family friends, and any mention of Diana's arm was passed off with a casual reference to a childhood injury, nothing more.

"No one knows?" she ventured to ask the bishop one day. "About my parents? What they were and what happened to them?"

He shrugged. "We've never mentioned it. Not that *you* have anything to be ashamed of, Diana. If you want to bring up the subject, that's fine, but the decision is yours."

"No! No," she repeated, more softly. "I'm not ashamed. It's just that I hate—" She fumbled, looking for the words.

"Pity?"

"Yes. That's it. I *hate* it when people find out, and they look at me with stupid, cow eyes, as if to say, 'Oh, the poor, pathetic thing!' It's a good thing I can't throw a punch with this right arm because I really feel like it when I see that look in their eyes." Breathing hard, Diana stopped short and clamped a hand over her mouth. "Listen to me," she said, her face hot. "I sound like Mallory."

Lennox, too, seemed taken aback by the unexpected vehemence of her words, but he burst out laughing. "That may be, Diana, but I agree with you. Pity's a worthless, deadly sentiment, as far as I'm concerned. I'm glad you don't give in to it."

14

Riding a street bike on the freeway was a suicide bid, Mallory decided, so when she started out one Saturday to retrace her family's final days together, she took a long, slow route along surface streets to get from downtown Los Angeles to the ocean. There she planned to pick up the Pacific Coast Highway and follow it south in search of the last place she had seen her mother and father alive, long ago, in another lifetime.

Passing through neighborhoods where faces tended toward darker hues and whose small houses featured barred windows and steel-caged doors, she sensed for the first time the kind of concrete segregation enforced by the city's freeway system. Without cars to access the freeway, there wasn't much chance poorer people would accidentally wander into the comfortable enclaves of Bel Air and Beverly Hills. And if the good citizens of those lush, palm-studded neighborhoods avoided exiting the wrong freeway off-ramp, they didn't have to think about kids growing up in poverty and violence within crying distance of careless opulence. People called the city La-La Land, an urban crazy quilt designed by people with sun-fried brains. Mallory suspected the city fathers knew exactly what they were doing when they laid out its walled freeways.

Arriving at the Pacific Coast Highway just as the morning fog was burning off, she headed the Yamaha south, reveling in the freedom the bike offered. Despite its name, the PCH was miles from the ocean at the point where she picked it up at Palos Verdes. Only an hour later, near the Orange County line, did the highway finally swerve out to meet the Pacific, embracing miles of sandy beaches and windswept cliffs as it rolled on southward. Onshore breezes pushed away the city's cloak of brown smog. The air near the water was clean and cool, and the sun glinted off the waves.

Mallory inhaled deeply, rediscovering a salty odor as primal as the womb. In doing so, bits of long-shelved memories began to shake loose and tumble into her thoughts. Her father's infectious laugh as he raced his little girls into the surf. The way the sun coaxed auburn highlights from her mother's dark curls, so like Diana's. A gray kitten with blueberry eyes, trying unsuccessfully to catch a small, skittling lizard.

She drove toward Newport Beach, tracing a route memorized from her Thomas Guide to the address where her family's brand-new home had been destroyed in a mysterious explosion—a place called Esmerelda Canyon. The Yamaha hummed between her knees, its steady throb resonating through her bones. An ache was growing inside her as she remembered Bishop Lennox's words the night they had sat on the front step. Her parents' murders had gone unsolved, he'd said. Only they might have understood why it had happened, if the rumors about their drug dealing were true. Mallory pushed the thought away as she entered the wealthy, picturesque community of Newport Beach and started watching for Esmerelda Canyon Road. When she found it, she gunned the motorcycle up the steep, winding incline that switched back several times over the course of a mile and a half until it finally came to an end on a bluff high over the ocean.

She didn't need the map to tell her where the house had stood. She remembered the celebration the day her parents had gained title to the best half acre at the end of the road, a promontory lot overlooking the blue-gray Pacific. Her mother and father had danced out of the lawyer's office, and the family had had a picnic, right on the vacant site. Mallory and Diana had shared in their parents' celebration, toasting with apple juice poured into her mother's best stemmed glasses, brought along in a wicker picnic basket, to mark the occasion.

Theirs had been the first house to be built on the upper reaches of the canyon road, she remembered. But climbing now, she counted a dozen or more homes, all obviously expensive, most with Mercedeses, Jags or BMWs parked in the driveways. Twenty-foot palm, eucalyptus and sycamore trees stood where eleven years earlier there had been only scrub brush. Like much of southern California, Esmerelda Canyon had been transformed from arid desert to tropical garden on borrowed water, diverted from northern rivers.

Reaching the dead end of the road, Mallory came upon the wide driveway that she'd watched bulldozers carve out of the hillside. She pulled the motorcycle to a stop as her mind's eye pictured the Kool-Aid stand she and Diana had set up that day for the thirsty construction workers while their mother was busy measuring and plotting the landscape design. At five cents a glass, the little girls had raked in a child's fortune.

Now, a huge wrought-iron gate barred entry to the driveway. Nearby stood two Queen Palms. Mallory stared at them, remembering the day she and Diana had helped their mother choose those palms at a nursery. When they were planted, the sisters had watered them, christening the trees after themselves—the Queen Mallory palm and the Queen Diana palm. The trees had seemed tall even then, higher than the top of her father's head, but now they towered forty feet above the driveway, their fronds undulating in the breeze. Mallory's stomach contracted as another memory pushed itself to the front of her mind—her father's speedboat, cocked at a weird angle against the Queen Diana palm, dust and debris from the explosion swirling and settling around it.

Blinking back tears, she looked down the canyon road that was so changed and yet still familiar. Finally, when she could avoid it no longer, Mallory forced herself to look up the long driveway, to the spot where she had seen her parents disappear through the front door of a house that, a few seconds later, had ceased to exist.

Their home had been designed by her father. It had been a stepped cedar and stone residence—a homage, he had said, to Frank Lloyd Wright and to the beauty of the setting. The house had blended into the surrounding scenery, its cascading levels hugging the terrain, its subdued colors echoing the browns and khakis of the native California grasses and shrubs that her mother had chosen for the landscaping.

In its place, now, stood a massive, pseudo-Tudor number with two pretentious, circular turrets, a four-car garage, blinding white stucco and fake half-timbers painted black. Around the house, in-ground sprinklers were chuck-chucking away on rolling, thickly green lawns, working desperately to hold the surrounding desert at bay. The place was a giant wart on the hilltop, Mallory thought. Huge and overweening, it would be visible from far below, probably even from the beach and the ocean. It looked about as natural in this setting as boobs on a bullfrog.

As Mallory stared at the monstrosity, one of the garage doors began to rise, revealing a silver gray Mercedes sedan. A woman in tennis whites appeared and tossed a racket and bag into the back seat, her blond ponytail bobbing coquettishly with her movements. Her figure was thin, her legs hard-muscled and deeply tanned. Little pom-poms peeked over the backs of her white leather tennis shoes. Mallory guessed her to be about thirty. The woman slammed the car's rear door, glanced down the driveway, then did a double take and froze, obviously startled to see Mallory there, astride her motorcycle. She hesitated a moment, then started walking toward the gate, shading her eyes with her hand. "Can I help you?" she called.

"No. Not really. I just..." Mallory shrugged, not sure what to say.

"Are you lost?"

"No."

The woman drew closer, her eyes casting around, checking, no doubt, to see if Mallory was alone or rather the advance for some gang of thieves. Or worse. Although wealth was a shield against many dangers, the memory of Charlie Manson and his band of psychos had to prey on the minds of people who lived in isolated enclaves like this.

"What exactly is it you're doing here?" the woman demanded.

"Just exploring, I guess."

The woman took up an aggressive, hands-on-hips stance, her mouth pressed into a line that was obviously meant to intimidate. There was a hard-edged beauty about her, but close up, Mallory could see the crepey lines of her neck and the taut stretching of skin over cheekbone that told of surgical efforts to cheat the calendar. She was clearly older than Mallory had originally thought. The roots of her perky blond hair also told Mallory that the woman was overdue at her hairdresser's.

"'Exploring,'" she sniffed. "Well, there's nothing more beyond this point. This is the end of the road and it's private property. You'll have to go back down the way you came."

"There used to be another house here."

"What?"

"There was another house. Before."

The woman looked perplexed. "Well—yes, there was, but it was destroyed."

"You bought the land?"

"Of course. Seven years ago. My husband snapped it up as soon as it came back on the market. How do you know about that?"

"I—I was reading about the architect who designed that other house. I saw a picture of it."

"I remember. Kind of rustic, wasn't it? Inconspicuous. Not much of a house for a setting like this."

"I thought it was beautiful."

"Well, I suppose, if you like that sort of thing. We wanted something nicer, though."

"Do you know anything about the previous owners?"

"Not really, except that it was the architect and his family. They had only been in the house a few days when it was destroyed. The fellow was dealing drugs on the side. Something like that. Got on the wrong side of his suppliers, if I remember correctly. The place was blown to kingdom come. It was propane that did it. California Gas ran a line up here after that. I think my husband said the whole family was killed."

"Not all of them," Mallory whispered, her gaze dropping to her feet. This was the very spot, she suddenly realized, where she had regained consciousness after the blast.

"What did you say?"

Mallory turned to the woman. "Nothing. Doesn't it bother you to live where people were murdered?"

The woman snorted. "Not at all. They got what they deserved, I'm sure. And anyway, the view is fabulous. Properties like this don't come along every day, you know. My husband had wanted this property for a long time, but when it finally came available, that architect beat him to it. After the papers reported what happened to the people and my husband realized it was this same property they were talking about, he called his lawyer right away to put in a bid for the land. We had to wait two years while police investigated and the dead couple's estate went through probate and whatnot. There were others who wanted to get their hands on the lot, too, but we never gave up," she added smugly, "until finally, we got it."

Vultures, Mallory thought in disgust.

"Anyway, you'll have to excuse me now," the woman said. "I've got a tennis game."

Mallory nodded but made no move to leave. The owner obviously wasn't going to drive away before this interloper did. The woman glared at Mallory until she had no choice but to jump on the Yamaha's starter. After the engine kicked in, Mallory glanced around one last time, but there was nothing more to see.

What had she expected? Answers? An explanation? Comfort? She wasn't going to find it where there were only strangers in an ugly house, people with no memory of her family and even less sympathy for the tragedy that had torn it apart.

15

Outside, it was a cold, rainy autumn afternoon in Paris. Inside the studio at the Institut Lautrec, the Left Bank art college where Diana took life-painting classes every Tuesday and Thursday, the air was not much warmer, but the fair-haired Adonis who posed for the class was evidently immune to goose bumps. Still, he seemed to delight in the shivers his naked body elicited from some of the lustier young women in the group, not to mention one or two of the young men. After the first embarrassing half hour or so, Diana, too, had found herself fascinated. He was, after all, the only naked man she had ever seen outside a book or painting. She could be forgiven, she supposed, if her mind wandered while her brush caressed his image on her canvas.

But on this particular afternoon, the class would have only a half hour to work on their paintings. Monsieur Jean Grenier, the instructor, had invited a special guest to speak to them. When his time was up, the model stepped off the platform in the center of the room, clearly happy to be done early, taking his time nonetheless to slither back into his tight jeans—a reverse striptease that he obviously enjoyed prolonging. Diana tried not to watch, but it wasn't easy. When she heard the old hinges on the door of the studio squeak, she dragged her gaze away, but as she caught sight of the man coming into the room, her heart sank.

A while earlier, before the start of class, she had slipped into the *brasserie* across the street from the institute to warm up with a café au lait. As she'd sat hunched at a corner table, hands cupped around the warm bowl, she'd noticed a very striking white-haired man leaning against the black anthracite bar. He was reflected in the mirror behind the counter, sipping a glass of red wine, his finely sculpted face set in a weary, distracted expression.

Diana hadn't planned to pull out her sketchbook in such close quarters, but she'd been fascinated by the contrast of his snowy hair tumbling over the collar of his black leather coat and by his face, so full of character. She'd thought she was being clever, studying him surreptitiously, sketching in quick, short lines that she would go over later, refining and correcting. Suddenly, she'd glanced up and realized that he was staring back at her, his forehead etched with annoyance as he evidently realized what she was doing. Mortified, Diana had stuffed her art pad into her tote bag and slipped away as fast as she could.

And now, here he was being introduced by Monsieur Grenier as none other than Marcus Desloges, owner of the small but well-respected Galerie Desloges in the Latin Quarter, near Rue St-Germain-des-Prés. Diana shuffled her stool farther back into the corner until she was almost hidden by her easel.

Desloges strode behind Grenier to the center platform, where the art dealer shrugged out of his leather coat, tossed it over a table and settled himself on the stool the model had vacated. Dressed casually in a navy turtleneck and slacks, Desloges was lean and spare, giving the illusion of height, although he was probably not much taller than five-ten or so. Under the full head of white hair, he had blue-gray eyes that were starred with lines at their outer corners. The creases around his mouth, likewise, hinted at a tendency to laughter, but his expression at the moment was reserved. He barely glanced at the hopeful faces in front of him, giving their instructor a brief nod as if to say he would endure the next sixty minutes like a good sport, but then had other more important places to be.

Grenier clamped a hand on the man's shoulder. "My friend Marcus Desloges," he said, "has been coming to this class for several years now to speak to young artists such as yourselves. He will tell you about the difficulty of making a living in today's marketplace. He pulls no punches.

"But what he will not tell you about is the thousands of hours he himself puts in, finding new talent, hand-holding and wet-nursing, finding backers, fighting critics, arranging exhibits and exchanges with other galleries—doing whatever is necessary, in short, to see that vision is not stifled for lack of opportunity and that artistic souls do not wither for lack of encouragement. I hear many artists grumble and complain about the crass commercialism of gallery owners who want only to line their pockets at the expense of starving artists. This description does not apply to Marcus Desloges, and so I ask you to be kind to him."

Desloges almost smiled, the fissures at the sides of his mouth lifting and deepening when he finally looked up at the class. Diana retreated farther behind her easel, terrified he would see her. But as his eyes flickered across the front rows, she knew he hadn't noticed her huddled in the corner and wasn't likely to.

"Almost twenty-five years ago, when we first decided to open a gallery," Desloges began, "my wife and I had many dreams and illusions. These did not, however, include the delusion that it would bring personal glory for us. It is the artist, after all, whose work is on exhibit. Gallery owners are simply purveyors of other people's genius. But Marie-France and I had the idea, arrogant perhaps, that we could project vision and energy into a marketplace that had, we decided, grown stale and jaded. As I said," Desloges added wryly, "we were young and naive." The class laughed.

He went on to describe the serendipitous business of discovering and developing talent, the mechanics of exhibition and promotion, the frustrations of a fickle marketplace and narrow-minded critics and the roller-coaster economics of the art world.

Diana found herself mesmerized by his voice, even if she missed half of what he said in his rapid-fire French. No matter, she thought, letting her mind wander. The subject matter didn't apply to her. She was a hobbyist—an untrained, unskilled dabbler. As much as she loved to paint and draw, she had no illusions about her talent. Some of these other students might have dreams of making a living at art, but Diana knew that when this magical year was over, she would have to return to Ferry Falls and get some sort of job to contribute to her up-keep. The Caines had never so much as hinted that she should work, and when Diana had offered to pay rent after high school, Frances wouldn't hear of it. Reverend Caine had been content to have her simply continue keeping his office in order.

Still, they couldn't be expected to support her forever, Diana thought. Although her share of the trust fund from her parents' small estate met whatever modest needs she had for spending money, it wouldn't provide enough income for her to live on for the rest of her life. She really *would* need to think about a job, especially since she'd begun to dream about renting a little apartment of her own when she got back. Her mother would be unhappy about it, of course. She knew from her letters that Frances was already counting the days until her return. But fond as she was of her adoptive mother, the very idea of going back made Diana shudder. How strange, she thought, when only a few months earlier she'd been terrified to set foot outside the rectory.

She put thoughts of Minnesota behind her and drifted along on the wave of Desloges's voice, lilting and impassioned as he warmed to his subject. The blue-gray eyes that she'd guessed were accustomed to smiling proved her right now, their weathered corners giving them a look of kindness. She inched out her stool to see him better, and watched his hands moving and gesticulating, the fingers long, fluid and expressive. He made such an interesting subject that, despite the embarrassing scene in the *brasserie*, Diana began thinking once again of trying to capture his image on paper.

Lost in thoughts of light and shadow, she was startled when the class burst into applause, and she realized that his talk was done. Desloges agreed to stay for a few minutes to answer questions, and there was a bustle of activity as students pressed to the front to catch the dealer's attention—all of them hoping, no doubt, that they would be his next discovery.

Diana sighed and went to work cleaning her brushes, wrapping and packing them in her tote bag along with her paint tubes, pencils and sketchbook. Tucking her easel against the wall for safekeeping until the next class, she lifted her cape off a hook at the back of the room and flipped it one-handed over her shoulders, then buttoned the throat catch. She was getting quite good at this, she thought, congratulating herself again on having found the cloak in a sidewalk rack on the Rue Mouffetard. It was so much easier to handle than a coat with sleeves.

When she turned to gather up her things, she saw that Marcus Desloges, coat on, was making an effort to detach himself from the crush of students and work his way toward the door on the far side of the room. Diana held back. She had been lucky so far not to have been spotted; she would wait and leave behind him. She put down the tote bag and sat on her stool, watching him patiently answer questions even as he pressed to make his escape. He had almost made it to the door, when a young man at his side tapped Desloges on the shoulder, and as the dealer's gaze swung around, it landed on Diana.

Groaning inwardly, she prayed for the power to make herself invisible. She bent over her bag and pretended to be arranging it, but a moment later, a pair of fine leather-clad feet appeared next to her easel, and Diana peered up to see Desloges standing next to her. Thankfully, he was not looking at her.

Oh, God, no! He was looking at her painting. Oh please, Diana thought, just let me die right now.

Desloges studied the half-finished oil sketch, frowning. Then, pursing his lips, he turned, giving her barely a glance before reaching into the tote bag where her sketchbook was poking out. "May I?" he asked. Not waiting for a reply, he picked it up and began flipping through the pages.

"No, it's not—" But her good arm was caught in the folds of her cape, and she couldn't untangle it before he came to the sketch from the *brasserie*. He pursed his lips and studied it for a moment, then looked through the rest of the pad, page by page. Humiliated, Diana felt as if he were trampling over the evidence of her meager little life. "Please, could I have it?" she finally blurted out, growing angry at his arrogance, but terrified that she would make a complete fool of herself by bursting into tears.

"Yes, of course." Desloges nodded, but continued flipping until he had examined every page. Only then did he hand it back. Diana dropped the book into her bag and slipped the strap over her shoulder. When she tried to flee, he stood in front of her, blocking her path so that she had no choice but to look up at him. He was staring at her, still frowning.

"Excuse me, please," she hissed, panicked that she was about to lose whatever shred of composure she had left. He hesitated, then stepped aside. A small crowd of curious students had gathered, which parted like the Red Sea as Diana headed for the door.

"Mademoiselle?" he called. Diana turned around. Desloges glanced at the others, then approached and leaned toward her, his voice low. "I feel I should tell you."

"What?"

"You don't belong here."

"Pardon me?"

"In this class. In this school. You're wasting your time."

Diana nodded. "I know that." She wheeled away and hurried out the door, making it all the way to the Métro station before the tears started to fall.

Los Angeles, California
October 10, 1979

Mallory had registered for a full course load at Los Angeles Westside College, disillusioned after two months of life in the working world, as an eighteen-year-old out-of-towner with no experience or training except a Minnesota high school diploma. In September, she'd found a tiny, furnished bachelor apartment in Westwood, which had a parking spot for her Yamaha and which suited her needs—except for the fact that it was periodically overrun by tiny ants and not-so-tiny spiders, forcing her to suck more Raid fumes than a body ought. She got a part-time job waiting tables in a nearby fern bar called Truffles, which featured folk music, chess boards and backgammon tables, and more greenery than an Amazon rain for-

est. As fall settled over California, a peculiar season of bone-
dry winds and temperatures that rose instead of fell, Mallory
hunkered down to her books, intent on her solitude.

Letters came from Diana and Wiley and Frances—excited,
wacky and plaintive, respectively. Diana had fallen in love with
Paris, and was taking a life-painting class at an art institute
there—with *naked* models, she had written mischievously.
Mallory had shaken her head in wonder at the leaps of courage that Diana seemed to be taking, and once more said a silent prayer of thanks for the Lennoxes, who were helping Diana
in ways that Mallory never could have. Maybe, when her year
in Paris was over, Diana might feel brave enough to try Los
Angeles with her sister. In the meantime, she was happy, and
for that, Mallory was grateful.

Wiley's letters were a combination of bizarre travelogue and
fantasy adventure. He had been bumming around on the Harley since July. In his most recent letter, posted from Stock-
bridge, Massachusetts, Wiley reported that he was staying with
some people on a communal farm. From the whiff of pot that
hit her when she opened the envelope, and the loose, ram-
bling—even for Wiley—style of his prose, Mallory had a pretty
good idea what kind of farm it was. Wiley also made too-casual
mention of someone named Moonbeam—not her original
name but her own choice of "rebirth name," he said, as if it
weren't obvious—and Mallory decided that old Wiley had finally managed to get himself laid. *I hope Moonbeam's good to
him,* she thought, feeling a twinge of guilt and envy.

Frances wrote to her every week, sending Ferry Falls news
that Mallory had no desire to know, her chirpy tone never quite
hiding her desperate loneliness.

I'm keeping Diana's and your rooms just as you left them,
so you'll feel right at home when you come back. Father
and I miss you terribly. We're both proud of you girls, of
course, but the house is much too quiet, and it will be
wonderful when we can all be together as a family again.

Mallory knew that the Rev didn't miss her in the least. She
would never, ever, go back to that house. Nor would Diana, if

Mallory had anything to say about it. Just the same, she was sorry for abandoning Franny.

Mallory missed them all—Diana, Wiley and Frances. She missed having someone to talk to, but sought no replacements. She held friendly neighbors and Truffles co-workers at arm's length. Turning away from every pair of eager male eyes that fell on her, she buried herself in introductory courses in English literature, political science, journalism, history and psychology. She knew she was earning a reputation as being aloof and unfriendly, but she didn't care. Books were safer than people. They didn't demand. They didn't wound. They didn't betray.

16

It was late afternoon, and Diana was strolling through the galleries of the Jeu de Paume, studying the paintings of the French Impressionists and Postimpressionists—Cézanne, Degas, Gauguin, Renoir, Seurat. In their day, most of them had been vilified and ridiculed by the critics and much of polite society. Henri de Toulouse-Lautrec, an outsider by virtue of his physical deformity, had been locked away for a time in an insane asylum. Vincent Van Gogh, living in lonely poverty, had mutilated, then killed himself. No wonder it was so comfortable in these rooms, she thought. Here, surrounded by the output of marginals and misfits, she felt among kindred spirits. Their vision was bright and colorful, ridiculously hopeful, in spite of the daily contempt with which they had lived. In a harsh world that had had no use for them, these artists had created their own beauty. If she could have slept within its walls, Diana would never have left the museum.

She had visited it for the first time two weeks earlier, instead of going to class. She had not returned to the Institut Lautrec since the day Marcus Desloges had passed judgment on her work, spending her time instead at the Jeu de Paume during the hours the Lennoxes thought she was at the school. She hadn't told Mary and Doug about dropping out, for the simple reason that she knew they would feel obliged to give her pep talks. Diana felt no need of cheering. She was perfectly content. She continued touring and exploring the city. She was still taking her notebook with her on her walks, stopping frequently to sketch. She continued to paint in her room at the Rue Clément Maroi. In these respects, nothing had changed.

It was just that she happened to agree with Desloges. She was a mediocre talent, at best, as he had suggested. Why, then, spend her days quaking with shyness and living in fear of criticism for something that was nothing more than a pleasant, private, therapeutic activity?

Mallory would be proud of her, Diana thought. Well, *maybe* she would, if she understood. Because what Diana had done in walking away from the institute and from those who might echo Marcus Desloges's verdict on her work was to practice what Mallory had always preached. She had refused to allow herself to be judged. In doing so, she had also declined to let this wonderful time in Paris be tarnished.

Desloges had done her a favor. It had been a mistake to get tied up with classes two afternoons a week. Now she was free to spend her time sketching boats on the Seine, or people-watching from the safe anonymity of a sidewalk café, or exploring museums and visiting the work of her dead spiritual brothers, Henri and Vincent and the others. Other girls might yearn for exciting careers, or love, or a raft of children, but Diana's expectations of life were low. This year in Paris—the *gift* of this year—was more beautiful than anything she could have hoped for. When it was finished, she would take home to Minnesota an intact, perfect, precious memory of sights and sounds and experiences that would sustain her for the rest of her days. It was enough.

"You missed your caller," the concierge told Diana as she passed through the alley on her way to the inner courtyard at the Rue Clément Maroi apartment.

"Caller? For me? I think you're mistaken, *monsieur.*"

"I am no such thing!" The little man in the beret was clearly offended at the idea that his professionalism might be in question. "The gentleman came an hour ago, stayed for twenty minutes, then left again—*Mademoiselle Caine,*" he added pointedly.

"This gentleman," Diana asked, "who was he?"

"I called upstairs and he was admitted to speak to the bishop and Madame Lennox. I'm sure you'll be more satisfied if *they* give you the details," the concierge sniffed. He turned his back—his pride, it was clear, mortally wounded.

Diana opened her mouth to apologize and explain that it was quite impossible she should have a caller, since she didn't know anyone in the city. Before she could say a word, however, the concierge slipped into the gloom of his own little flat behind the reception, and Diana was left staring at the closed door. She sensed that she had committed a *faux pas* of epic proportions. She would be lucky if he didn't start waylaying her mail from home. She sighed and headed into her own apartment, where she found Mary Lennox bustling about in the little galley kitchen, preparing supper.

"Mmm . . . it smells good in here," Diana said. "Need some help?"

"No, it's under control. Doug just ran down to pick up a baguette, and we'll eat as soon as he gets back. How was your class?"

Diana hesitated. Well, that was one possibility eliminated. Coming in the door, she'd had the unsettling thought that maybe the Institut Lautrec sent out truant officers to haul in absentee students. But Grenier's life painting was a not-for-credit course, and her fees were paid up. Why would they care whether or not she put in an appearance?

"Class was all right. I went for a walk afterward. Sorry I'm late. I'll go wash up."

Mary turned to the stove, but then let out a cry. "Oh! Diana!"

Diana stopped dead in her tracks and spun around. "What happened? Are you all right?"

"Yes. I just forgot. There was a man here to see you. He was sorry to have missed you, but he left his card." Mary came bounding out of the kitchen, her eyes bright with excitement. "He said he's an art dealer." She shuffled over to the hall table, picked up a rectangle of cardboard and peered at it. "Marcus Desloges, that was it. Oh, Diana. How exciting! Did you know about this?"

Diana took the card and stared at it, stunned. "I—what—I mean, no. He came to the institute a few weeks ago. What did he want with *me?*"

"I don't know. He said he had seen your work and he wanted to talk to you. I told him you were brilliant, of course. And I showed him some of your paintings."

"You *what?*"

Mary clamped a hand over her mouth. "Oh, dear! Did I do something wrong? Doug said we really shouldn't without your permission, but Monsieur Desloges seemed so curious, and—oh, Diana. Don't cry."

How could she not cry? Diana thought. It was humiliating. They had shown him her work. The stupid paintings she did in her room. They weren't for anyone to *see.* They were just something for her to *do.* More wasting of time. He must have seen that. She turned away from Mary, feeling nauseated, her comfortable little world suddenly chucked into a cement mixer. Why on earth had Marcus Desloges come *here?* To tell her yet again how hopeless her work was? Hadn't he already made that perfectly clear? Why go to all this trouble to embarrass her?

Because, Diana realized, her blood turning to ice, she had sketched him that day in the *brasserie.* He was offended that she had used him as a subject without his permission. But she never would have had the nerve to *ask* him. She should have, of course. She knew that now. Desloges was respected and famous, at least on the Paris art scene, a colorful local figure, with that shock of white hair and handsome profile. He had been interviewed and written about in the country's major newspapers and journals. Probably, she thought, famous artists had painted him, just as Toulouse-Lautrec had painted Aristide Bruant in his cabaret. What had she been thinking trying to sneak a sketch of him like that? No doubt Desloges wanted the drawing back to tear it up.

"Diana," Mary said, placing a hand on her arm, "I'm sorry. I'm just so proud of you, that's all."

Diana looked up through a shimmer of tears at Mary's blurred, worried face. "It's all right," she whispered. "It doesn't matter." The turning of a key in the front door announced the bishop's return. She couldn't face them both, not now. "I'm tired," she added, pulling away. "I'm going to my room."

"But what about supper?"

"I'm not hungry. Really, Mary, I'm not angry with you. I just want to be alone."

Paris, France
November 2, 1979

The Galerie Desloges was on the Rue Bonaparte, just off the square at St-Germain-des-Prés. Marcus Desloges had arrived unusually early, determined to get a handle on advance preparations for his next major exhibit, works by the young Spanish sculptor, Orlando Yago. There were pieces to be selected from the stack of photos Yago had sent him, pamphlets and posters to be designed and written, mailers to be sent, customs-and-import papers to be filled out.

But as he reached to unlock the gallery door, Desloges found a notice from the electric company, *Electricité de France*, hanging from its heavy brass knob. It announced that EDF would cut off the power unless his bill, three months overdue, was paid within twenty-four hours. He ripped the tag off the door, cursing. I *paid* that bill, he thought, bristling with righteous indignation.

Or had he? He remembered sitting down a couple of weeks back to tackle an untidy stack of paperwork over which he had procrastinated until finally, the pile was sliding off his desk. Wasn't the electric bill in there? He couldn't remember. He *did* remember that he had fortified himself with a bottle of wine to get through the tedious job that evening, and that by the time he got to the end, his signature had acquired some wild flourishes and he was adding vulgar epithets on the corners of the checks—not out of malice, merely to inject a little fun into the drudgery. But for the life of him, he couldn't remember whether he had written a check to EDF.

Desloges entered the gallery and relocked the front door, then took the stairs two at a time to his office. Shrugging out of his leather coat and slinging it over a chair, he pulled his check register out of his briefcase and began flipping through the pages. *Merde!* he thought. No record of paying the thing. He looked at his desk and sighed. The bill must still be in here somewhere, lost among the fliers, posters, letters, books, art magazines, reviews, directories and—he sighed again—more bills. That was the problem with paperwork. Every time you thought you had it licked, it crept back up on you again, like some particularly insidious infestation of weed. Marie-France had always been a better administrative gardener than he.

He should have hired a bookkeeper long before, if for no other reason than to make sure the damn bills were paid on time. But the thought of someone else in the office, at *her* desk, filled Marcus with such nausea that he shoved the idea away every time it occurred. He was coping just *fine,* he told Jean Grenier whenever his old friend commented on his disorderly office. The professor would merely shake his head, muttering, "Marcus, Marcus..."

Two hours later, Desloges had managed to rearrange the material into a few piles, although his headway had been slowed by the distraction of unread articles and lost correspondence, business cards from potential patrons who needed to be culti-vated and a copy of a glowing review from *The Times of London* on one of his recent exhibits—all items that he thought he had misplaced and had given up hope of ever finding again. Unfortunately, he still hadn't found the electric bill.

He had just decided that he had no choice but to drive over and throw himself at the mercy of some billing clerk when, glancing out the window at the street below, he spotted the girl in the cape. She was standing in the doorway of the antique shop across the street, staring at the front of the gallery, chew-ing on her lower lip and looking decidedly undecided. She shifted her gaze along the street, as if scouting out an escape route, then glanced back at the gallery's front door. Her dark eyes sparkled with each movement and her cheeks were flushed, perhaps from the cold. Coming up the river beyond St-Germain-de-Prés, the wind was whipping her cape around her and sending her long, curled tendrils of hair flying.

She reached to brush a strand from her eyes and as she did, the girl happened to look up. Desloges saw her freeze at the re-alization that he was at the window, watching from above.

They stared at each other, motionless, while he struggled against the grin he felt unexpectedly forming in the muscles of his face. She was, he told himself sternly, a distraction he didn't need at the moment. He had work to do. Of course, he *had* left a message the previous day, saying he wanted to speak to her. But he was busy just now, dammit!—though she was a lovely sight all the same. With those dark eyes and that hair, and her long cape and colorful skirt whipping around soft, brown boots, she looked like a figure out of a nineteenth-century novel. A young Emma Bovary, perhaps.

Get a grip, man! Desloges told himself. She's a sheltered American girl, abroad for the first time in her life, and she lives with a clergyman and his wife, for heaven's sake. And *you*, he added, are an old goat with a business that's going to be in darkness tomorrow if you don't get that bill settled today. Still, she was here now, so there was nothing for it, he supposed, but to see her. He crooked his finger to beckon her over, pointing to the door below. She hesitated, then stepped to the curb, checking for oncoming traffic. Desloges hurried downstairs to open the front door.

She squeezed between two parked cars.

"Bienvenue. Entrez," Desloges said from the doorway of the gallery.

"Non, merci," Diana began.

"Come in, please," he repeated in English, smiling this time. "It's cold out there."

She held back, still unsure. Finally, she stepped past him into the gallery. As he locked the door behind her, her gaze traveled across the walls, curious in spite of her nervousness.

"Well, here you are," he said. She spun around at the sound of his voice, right next to her now. "I'm sorry. I didn't mean to startle you."

"No, it's all right. I just . . ." She glanced back at the walls. "I like this work."

"It's part of our permanent collection, on display between special exhibits. Most of these artists are well established in their respective fields. Their sales help pay the bills and finance the new people we like to show."

"Those two over there—they're Hugo Labelles, aren't they?"

"Yes, they are."

"I read about his work in *ArtForum* a few months ago." Diana studied another canvas on an easel. "And Jeanette St-Cyr? One of her recent works?"

"That's right. How did you know?"

"I understand she's only been experimenting with this acrylic resin for the past year or so."

Desloges leaned against an archway and crossed his arms, nodding. "What about that one over there in the corner?" he asked, indicating a large, brightly colored landscape, a riot of blues and yellows that vaguely recalled Van Gogh but depicted quite a different countryside than the French meadows the Dutchman had preferred. "Do you know who the artist is?" Diana turned to examine it, a crease forming between her eyebrows as she struggled to come up with a name. "I'll give you a hint," Desloges added. "He's a countryman of yours."

The crease vanished. "Thelonius Walker. One of the works from the Mississippi Delta series."

"Bravo! You *have* been around."

"Oh, no. I just read a lot." She walked over to study the Walker from a better vantage point. "He still lives in Paris?"

"Yes. A self-imposed exile, like Josephine Baker in her day—an African-American genius who came abroad to find recognition."

"He must be, what, sixty now?"

"Seventy-two."

"And his inspiration, even after all these years, still comes from his roots." She shook her head. "From memory. It's amazing."

"You're right, Diana, he *is* brilliant. You have a good eye."

She felt her face grow warm, and her tongue tie itself in knots. If she'd been next to the door, she might have been tempted to bolt. What had she been thinking of, coming here? "I—I don't want to bother you. I just dropped by to say I'm sorry."

"You're not bothering me in the least. Why are you sorry?"

"For sketching you that day. Invading your privacy."

"I didn't mind."

"Yes, you did. I could tell."

"Well, actually, yes, I *was* a little annoyed, I admit, but only because I'm a miserable old man and I was having a bad day. You mustn't pay any attention to me."

Diana pulled back her cape to get at the canvas bag slung over her right shoulder. Reaching in with her left hand, she withdrew a sheet of paper. When she looked up, she saw that the dealer's eyes were on her right arm, which hung motionless at her side, the hand hooked in the pocket of her skirt. She'd dropped the cape and stepped forward, holding out the paper. "Here," she said. "You can destroy it. Again, I'm sorry."

Desloges took the drawing, and as he examined it, she tried to slip around him to make her flight for freedom. "Wait!" He reached an arm across her front, gripping her opposite shoulder and stopping her gently in her tracks. Their hips brushed and her skirt rustled against his leg, and Diana's body trembled under his outstretched arm and hand. Desloges stepped away, releasing her. "Don't run off. I wanted to talk to you."

"Why?"

"For one thing, to say *I'm* sorry, too."

"What for?"

"For embarrassing you in front of the others that day."

"You're entitled to an opinion. And anyway, you were right. I know my stuff's not very good. I just—"

"That's not what I said."

"You said—"

"I *said* you shouldn't be in that class, and I'm even more convinced of it after seeing your canvases yesterday."

"I don't understand."

"It's very simple. I don't believe in art schools. Oh, for schoolteachers and academics and, heaven forbid, critics, maybe they're all right. But not for *real* artists."

"I'm not an artist, I'm just a hobbyist."

"Oh, no. You shouldn't say that."

She gave him a hard look. "Don't."

"What?"

"Don't do that."

"Do *what*?"

"Patronize me."

"Why would I patronize you?" She turned away, lips pressed together. "Why would I do that?" he repeated.

"Because," she whispered.

"Because why?"

"Because you think you hurt my feelings. Well, you didn't, so you don't have to bother feeling sorry for me."

"But—why would you think I feel sorry for you?" She closed her eyes, pained. "Because of your arm?" Desloges asked. Her eyes snapped open. "Actually, I didn't even notice it that afternoon," he said. "Jean Grenier happened to mention it later, when I told him how curious I found your work. And as a matter of fact, Diana, I don't feel sorry for you at all. I think you're rather lucky."

"Lucky?"

"Well, perhaps *lucky* is not the right word. But you've been forced to develop and use your two hands independently. Form follows function, and because you function in your own way, the form in which your talent manifests itself is unlike anyone else's. You seem to have developed a style for each hand, in a way that's fascinating. I noticed it when I looked at your sketches. They're very precise and controlled. Yet your painting is loose and fluid, like the work of another artist altogether." Desloges shrugged. "Your injury makes you unique as an artist, and uniqueness is nothing to scoff at."

"It makes me a freak, is what you're saying."

"Now who's feeling sorry for herself?"

She gathered her cape tightly around her. "You know, Monsieur Desloges, when I heard you had come to the apartment, I thought you were a nice man with an unnecessarily guilty conscience. Now I'm not so sure. I have to go." She glanced at the sketch he held in his hand. "Tear that thing up and I won't bother you anymore."

"Why are you running away?"

"Because I don't want you to lie to me."

"I'm not lying. I never lie."

"Oh, really? So tell me, if you don't believe in art schools, why do you lecture at the institute?"

"Because Jean Grenier is an old friend."

"You lie to him?"

"No. He knows how I feel. I think art schools stifle creativity and make artists too timid and self-conscious. They provide some education to amateurs and the merely curious, though, and anything that raises the level of consciousness among the public is probably a good thing. For that reason, and out of friendship, I speak to Jean's students."

"They think you come scouting for new talent."

"I know. I try not to raise expectations. Personally, I've never seen any real vision among those students. Until now, perhaps."

"You think *my* work shows vision," she said, her voice dripping with disbelief. Why was he stringing her along like this?

"I think it shows promise. I'm not saying it's fully developed, but I think there's potential there. This *is* how I make my living," he added, eyebrow arched, arm opening to take in the gallery. "I think I have a right to a professional opinion."

Diana stared at him, then away, thoroughly flustered. Stepping backward, she fumbled for the door handle. "Well, thank you. That's nice of you to say. But now, I'd better—"

Desloges glanced again at the drawing in his hand, frowning. "Wait a minute, please! There's something you can do for me—that's why I came to see you yesterday."

"Do? For you?"

"Yes. A commission." He looked up. "I think I'd like to commission some work from you."

"You're not serious."

"But I am."

"What work?"

Desloges hesitated, glancing at the staircase at the back of the gallery. "Look," he said, "I have a problem today that I need to take care of, so this isn't the best time to discuss it, but would you come back tomorrow? And bring your sketching materials?"

"You mean it?" she asked, incredulous.

"Absolutely. Please, won't you come back?"

Diana was flabbergasted. "Well . . . I guess. If you're sure."

"I'm sure."

She opened the door, then turned, disbelief pushing aside hope once more. "You're not just trying to be nice, are you? Because you don't have to—"

"Don't worry, Diana. I'm never nice."

17

At Thanksgiving, when most students and faculty were home with their families, gorging on turkey and pumpkin pie, Mallory was in the college-library stacks, researching a poli-sci paper on the origins of the Vietnam War. Her eyes grew itchy and dry from hours of reading on microfiche old newspapers from the Johnson era full of stories about antiwar protests. But as she read, vaguely remembered TV images started flickering across her mind—waves of marching bodies rolling over wide plazas, fists clenched, voices united. Suddenly, a singsong chant began echoing in her brain. She remembered dancing around the living room, reciting it over and over, as if it were some gay skipping song.

"Hey, hey, LBJ! How many kids did you kill today?"

She stopped in midchant and turned to her mother. *"Mommy? Who's LBJ?"*

"Lyndon Baines Johnson. The president."

"The President kills kids?" Mallory's eyes grew wide.

"Not children, honey, and he doesn't kill anyone with his own hands. But he sends young men to fight in Vietnam, a place we have no need to be. A lot of those boys die."

"He shouldn't do that!"

"No, I don't think he should, either. That's why those people on TV are marching—to say it's wrong. If you think something's wrong, you need to stand up and fight for what you believe."

"We should march."

"We could, but there are other ways to fight."

"Like what?"

"Like with words. Daddy and I have both written letters to the president and to our congressmen, telling them we don't agree with this war. And we fight with our votes, too." Her mother picked Mallory up on her lap and kissed her hair. *"Mr. Johnson won't be president much longer,"* she said, *"and then maybe the boys will come home."*

Mallory snuggled in her mother's arms, breathing in her delicate perfume, slowing down long enough for once to let herself be rocked. She felt warm and safe, protected from a world that was sometimes, it seemed, too sad.

The microfiche screen had gone blurry. Mallory blinked, and tears flowed over her cheeks. She wiped them away hurriedly and glanced around, but the few people in the library, mostly foreign students probably as lonely as she was, appeared to be lost in their own projects. Even the acne-faced boy who'd stared at her when she first came in had given up trying to catch her eye and was hunched over a book, picking at a pimple on his chin as he read.

Mallory turned to the historical yearbook at her elbow, flipping through summaries of events for the sixties, trying to fix the time when she and her mother would have had that conversation. In 1968, she saw, Lyndon Johnson had announced he would not seek a second term in office. She would have been seven. She scanned the chronology of events, trying to bring back the memories, but little of this had made any impact on a second-grader. Right here in Los Angeles, Bobby Kennedy was shot on his way to the Democratic nomination. Richard Nixon went on to win the presidential race. *"Going from the frying pan to the fire,"* her mother had said ruefully. She never did see the boys come home, Mallory thought.

At the movies that year, the yearbook said, *Rosemary's Baby* portrayed devils on the home front, while *2001: A Space Odyssey* predicted an eerie future of death and rebirth. Something called *The Beatles White Album* dominated the music charts, led by a long song with a chanting refrain. Mallory slouched in the hard wooden library chair, closing her eyes as something else stirred in her memory.

A hot day. Bright sunlight and wheeling sea gulls. The smell of seawater and coconut oil. People singing "Hey Jude."

She opened her eyes. Not 1968, she told herself. A few months later. Memorial Day, 1969. She flipped forward in the yearbook to the entries for 1969, trying hard to recapture the time. The Vietnam War ground on. A man walked on the moon, and Ted Kennedy drove off a bridge at Chappaquiddick. In Los Angeles, Charlie Manson turned mansions into slaughterhouses. Half a million kids turned up at Woodstock for three days of sex, drugs and rock and roll. But none of this meant anything to her, then or now, she thought, and there was nothing in this book about a little girl who saw her home and her parents vaporized in front of her eyes. That, apparently, had been a world-shaking event to no one but her.

Mallory closed the yearbook with a sigh and pushed back her chair, its legs scraping noisily along the floor. The dweeb across the room shot her a curious look, then went back to picking his zits. Mallory rose and headed for the reference desk, where a gray-haired librarian was flipping through cards in a long file box. What was it with librarians, she wondered, that they were always so absorbed with card catalogs? After a minute or two of being ignored, she cleared her throat and the woman finally peered up over half glasses. "Can I help you?"

"I'd like to look at the *Los Angeles Chronicle* for 1969, please."

"That would be on microfiche."

"I know. I'm on the machine now."

"I see. The *Chronicle,* you say. Date?"

"I'm not sure."

"You need a date. It's a big newspaper. The 1969 issues will be on more than one film."

"Well, May, I guess. After Memorial Day, whenever it was that year. And then all the issues for the month or two following. To start, at least."

"You don't have a page reference?"

"No, but I'm sure I'll find it."

"What exactly are you looking for?"

Mallory froze. What should she say? That she was looking for her past? For her lost childhood? For the reason she was a screwed-up eighteen-year-old orphan living alone without a friend in the world? "I'm looking for anything that might have been written about..."

The librarian was pulling down a bound *Los Angeles Chronicle* index from a shelf behind her. She stopped and looked back at Mallory, one eyebrow raised. "About...?"

"About a murder."

The woman appeared to be taken aback for a second, then made a quick recovery. It probably wasn't the strangest research request she'd ever received, Mallory thought. "Do you have a name?" the librarian asked.

"Mallory Caine."

"Is that the victim's name or the murderer's?"

"Oh! No, neither. I thought you meant did *I* have..." Mallory flushed. "Look, maybe I could just go through the index and jot down any references I find?"

The librarian sighed and handed over the heavy volume, nodding to a table nearby. "Sit there. Bring back the index and the dates when you find the references, and I'll retrieve the microfiche."

"Thanks." As the librarian returned to her card catalog, Mallory lugged the big book to the table and settled in a chair. Opening it to K, she scanned the lines of fine print until she came to "Knight," her birth name.

Her fingers traced the letters on the page. Ever since arriving in Los Angeles, she'd toyed with the idea of changing her surname back to Knight, losing the name of the adoptive father she despised. More than once, she'd stopped at a phone booth to check the Yellow Pages listings for lawyers, intending to contact one and see what it would take to erase the mark of Harold Caine from her life. But each time she'd reached for the telephone to make an appointment, she'd withdrawn at the last moment. She'd told herself it would complicate her college registration, given that her high school records were all in the name of Mallory Caine. But there was more to it than that, she knew. Underneath the hesitation lay fear and anger. Fear of declaring a heritage that might turn out to be as black as the

Rev had always claimed. Anger at parents who had abandoned their two little girls for reasons Mallory was afraid to explore.

Taking a deep breath, she ran her gaze down the listings for "Knight" in the index. Knights of Columbus, Olivia Knight, Patrick Knight, Philip Knight, Richard Knight, Selena Knight, Knights Templar... She froze, her eye flicking back up the page. Philip. And Selena. Both of her parents were here. She began copying the references to articles about her father, categorized under various headings:

Knight, Philip B. (architect)
—awards received by
—designs of
—murder of
—speeches

Farther down were the entries for articles written about her mother:

Knight, Selena R. (née Cooper) (landscape architect)
—awards received by
—designs of
—murder of

Her mother had received awards, so she must have been good at her job. Why had she forgotten that? Mallory wondered. She *did* remember seeing her mother sitting at her drafting table poring over seed catalogs. She also recalled her working in the little yard at their old house, mixing loam into poor California clays, holding the soil in her cupped hands and breathing in a humusy smell that made Mallory's nose wrinkle. Her mother would often take her and Diana on long walks through parks and public gardens, pointing out sea lavender and rock roses and St. Catherine's lace, although Mallory was always more interested in chasing the fish in the koi ponds. And now, here was Selena Knight in the *Index to the Los Angeles Chronicle*, her brief life cataloged and defined, not as the mother of two little girls in whose hearts and lives she had left a gaping hole, but as someone who had designed beautiful outdoor living spaces, won awards and been murdered.

Mallory finished copying the indexed references to her parents, then retrieved the microfiche records for the dates the articles had appeared. There were, she was astonished to discover, only three articles on the actual explosion—a brief one that appeared the day after it happened; a longer one two days later speculating on the mystery of why a professional couple might have been murdered and containing the first suggestion that it was a question of a drug deal gone bad, and finally, a wrap-up piece:

EXPLOSION IN ESMERELDA CANYON
DRUGS ARE SUSPECTED MURDER MOTIVE

Newport Beach—Newport Beach P.D. and Orange County Sheriff's sources say that the professional couple murdered in last week's spectacular destruction of an Esmerelda Canyon luxury home may have been dealing drugs and run afoul of mob-world suppliers.

Deputy Sheriff Rod Flynn confirmed yesterday that a quantity of both heroin and hashish were found in the trunk of Philip and Selena Knight's car, parked in the driveway of their brand-new house, which was destroyed in a deliberately caused propane explosion. The couple had just returned from the beach and were inside the house at the time of the blast.

"We suspect they had gone to the beach to meet their supplier and hadn't yet unloaded the drugs they purchased," Deputy Flynn said.

The suspects in the murder, who have not been identified, apparently used the couple's absence to rig a line from a swimming-pool propane heater to the house. When the couple returned, police speculate, the propane was ignited by means of a remotely initiated spark, possibly caused by a ringing telephone.

"There was ignition and lift-off," Flynn said. "The entire house went straight up and came back down again in pieces no larger than a baseball."

The couple's two young daughters, Diana, 10, and Mallory, 8, were outside the house at the time of the blast, and both children received serious injuries. The younger child, however, was able to tell police that her parents had gone into the house moments before the explosion. Minute traces of human remains were found in the rubble, and county fire and coroner's officials speculate that the couple was killed instantly.

Philip Knight, a respected architect, received local and national honors for his work on the Westwind Park housing development in south Orange County, a master-planned community by Quad-A Homes. Selena Cooper Knight, a British-born landscape architect, had also received recognition for her work on the Westwind project, which critics said set a new benchmark of design excellence for residential communities. (See separate article)

Associates on the Westwind project told police that the couple had a darker side, however, and had been known for some time to be involved in recreational-drug use. Quad-A officials said the Knights had recently been fired from the project, despite the professional recognition their work had garnered, because of problems related to drug use.

The article went on to speculate that Philip and Selena Knight had turned to drug dealing after they were fired from the housing project as a means to earn money and to meet the costs of completing their new home.

Mallory's fingers traced the pictures on the screen, shadowy microfiche negatives of her parents at an award ceremony, and other photos that she recognized as Diana's and her elementary-school pictures. She pressed her lips together, fighting tears. Since the explosion, she had not seen her parents' faces. There had been nothing to remember them by—no photos, no personal items, no mementos of any sort. Everything the family owned had been utterly destroyed in the blast, except for the boat, the car, some plastic beach toys and the bikinis the two little girls had been wearing that day. Her parents didn't even have a grave, because there'd been nothing left to bury. That ugly pseudo-Tudor monstrosity now standing in Esmerelda Canyon, Mallory thought, was the only memorial to mark their deaths.

She searched the index again to see if she had missed any articles, but after these three, it seemed, the matter was closed. There were no further newspaper references to the murder of Philip and Selena Knight, or any suggestion that their killers were ever identified. Having written off the dead couple as disreputable characters, the media had apparently lost interest in them, their killers and their orphaned children.

When the library closed at 10:00 p.m., Mallory had just finished rereading the articles for the fourth time. She dragged herself back to her tiny apartment, not bothering to turn on the light as she entered, heading straight for the bed. Flopping down fully clothed, she curled into a tight ball, face to the wall, and cried herself to sleep.

18

Diana sat at a drafting table in the upstairs office of the Galerie Desloges, poring over the now-familiar photographs of sculptures by the young Spanish artist Orlando Yago. She had first set eyes on the photos almost three weeks earlier, when she had gone to the gallery for the second time, shaky with anticipation and still in a state of disbelief that Desloges might not only be genuinely interested in her work, but even have a commission for her. In no time at all, however, she had forgotten her fluttery innards and Desloges's daunting presence, as the two of them discussed posters for Yago's upcoming exhibit.

"I don't understand why you want drawings," she'd said that morning. "Why not enlarge one or two of these photographs?"

"I could," Desloges said, "but in my experience, photographs can backfire. People look at the photos and say to themselves, 'So, this is what the artist does.' They may like what they see, but decide that they have no need to visit the exhibit, having seen the photos. Or maybe the particular work in the picture doesn't excite them, so they don't bother to come and view the rest."

"What about text only?"

"That's fine for well-known artists. But for someone new like Yago, I want something more stimulating. A visually arresting graphic that suggests the mood and strength of his work, without being strictly representational."

"Color?"

"I'm not sure. Your sketches, especially some of the pen-and-ink ones in your notebook, struck a chord for me."

Diana's face went hot at the memory of how mortified she'd been that day Desloges stood flipping through her sketchbook while the rest of the class looked on. She turned from him now and forced herself to focus on the photographs.

Orlando Yago worked primarily in bronze and copper. The photos in front of her showed semiabstract representations of human and animal figures, some of them almost mythic in appearance. His pieces, which suggested both mass and movement, ranged in size from a few inches to almost six feet.

"These are wonderful," she said. "You want to reach out and touch them. How did you find him?"

"Marie-France and I saw one of his pieces in Madrid five years ago, in a tiny gallery near the Prado. We liked it so much, we bought it."

Marie-France, Diana registered—his wife and partner. He had mentioned her in his talk at the institute. She glanced around. The office walls were covered with photographs of Desloges and a petite, blond woman, arm in arm more often than not, alongside a number of artists and their works. The pictures had obviously been taken at various exhibit openings over the years, as evidenced by the shift in his hair color from black to pure white, the gradual appearance of lines in his still-handsome face and the changing hair and dress styles of the woman at his side. On Desloges's desk, Diana had noticed, was a silver framed photo of the same attractive woman.

"We tracked Yago down to a little town near Toledo," Desloges was saying. "He was twenty-three at the time. He had very few finished pieces, but I knew right away that I wanted to represent him. We kept in touch, and I steered a couple of private commissions his way. This past summer, I went to look in on him again, and we decided it was time to bring his work to Paris. So," he added, waving his hand over the photos, "here we are. The exhibit opens January eighteenth."

Diana felt her heart sink. For five years, he had waited patiently for the right moment to spring this artist, a protégé really, on the Paris art scene. Now that the moment had arrived, she knew how important it would be to Desloges and Yago that everything be perfect. But he was asking *her,* an inexperienced dabbler, to produce a work for posters and pamphlets to draw people in to Yago's first solo exhibit. "I don't know, Monsieur Desloges—"

"Marcus," he said. "Please, call me Marcus. I like to delude myself that I'm not an old fossil, even though my mirror tells me differently."

"You're no fossil," Diana said. Then her smile faded. "But I don't think I'm the right person for this job."

"I do."

"But—"

"Trust me, Diana. I *know,* even though I don't know exactly what it is I need here. If I did, I suppose, I'd be an artist instead of just a flogger of other people's talent. But over the years, I've learned to trust my instincts, and they tell me that what I need right now is you." As he said this, Desloges's hand went to her arm and their knees brushed under the drafting table. An awkward silence settled over the double entendre he had uttered, and Diana was surprised to see his cheeks become inflamed. It was a revelation that the very urbane Marcus Desloges could embarrass himself. He removed his hand and pushed back his chair. "There's no need to feel pressured," he said. "Just see if it works for you."

"I'm flattered that you think I can do this, but . . ."

"You need to believe in yourself, Diana."

"You sound exactly like my sister."

"Then you have an intelligent sister."

"She is. She got all the self-confidence, too. You'd like her."

"I like *you,* and I like your work. So what do you say? Will you do it?"

"I'd hate to take it on and then disappoint you."

"The only way you could disappoint me would be to say you won't try. Look, we have several weeks before anything has to be sent to the printers. I can always go with photos or plain text if necessary. You don't have to feel that the fate of the universe is riding on your shoulders. All I want you to do is study these photographs, do some sketches and see what comes to mind. Just have fun, all right?"

Diana looked back at the photos, sighed deeply, then nodded. "All right."

As November rolled on toward December, Marcus began to look forward to the mornings when he would arrive at the gallery and see the lights on in the upstairs office, telling him Diana was there. He had given her a key so she could have access to the Yago photos whenever she wanted. Although he knew he could trust her to take them home and not lose them, he told himself and her that it was better to keep the pictures at the gallery for safekeeping, as long as she didn't mind coming in to work on her sketches. She said she didn't, which made Marcus irrationally pleased.

Paperwork suddenly became appealing. Never, since Marie-France had stopped working almost two years earlier, had the bills been paid and gallery correspondence answered so promptly. He and Diana would sit on their respective sides of the room, saying little. But Marcus was acutely conscious of the girl's presence, and watched her surreptitiously from time to time. He was fascinated by the way she became lost in her drawing: right-hand fingers clutching a pencil, flying over the paper, despite the dead weight of the attached arm resting on the drafting table. Her face in profile was a study in concentration as her dark eyes moved back and forth between Yago's photos and her sketchbook. Her left elbow would rest on the table, the fingers of that hand playing distractedly with a small scar on her left cheek, or with a coil of her dark hair. Marcus found himself itching to touch that hair and that scar.

Diana said she was an early riser, and she normally arrived before Marcus, a night owl who'd never seen any good reason to get out of bed before the sun had cleared the city's rooflines. When he came in, she would look up from her art pad and smile. After a couple of days, he would find that she had put fresh coffee on to brew, knowing it was his first ritual of the day. From the start, it felt strangely right to have her here, despite the solitary turn his nature had taken of late.

But finally, inevitably, the day came when he felt intruded upon. He arrived at the gallery later than usual, after spending the morning at the framer's having some canvases mounted.

When he walked in, Diana was dusting the photographs on the office walls. He stopped cold in the doorway. "What are you doing?"

She spun around, startled. "Oh! I was just tidying."

"I didn't ask you to tidy."

"I know. But I was pacing, trying to come up with a solution to a problem, when I noticed that the photos were dusty. So I—"

"Well, don't."

"I'm sorry."

Marcus walked over and straightened the picture she had knocked off kilter when he surprised her. "I have someone who comes in to clean. I didn't hire you to be a charwoman."

"I know that. I—"

"Just leave things alone. I *like* clutter."

"Fine."

"Fine." When Marcus turned around again, she was gathering up her materials. "What are you doing?"

"I think I'll work at home." She looked as if she was struggling between tears and the desire to hit him, although it appeared the latter urge might win out. It was a surprise, coming from this gentle girl. But then, Marie-France had often said that his quick temper was intolerable.

"You don't have to leave," he said.

"I don't have to stay, either, do I? This commission doesn't mean I *have* to work here, does it?"

"No, but don't go. I'm sorry. I overreacted. I just don't like to see you doing a menial job. You're an artist."

"An artist who doesn't like dust. It makes me sneeze."

Marcus smiled. "I'll fire the cleaner and get a new one, I promise."

Diana hesitated, then her features softened. He watched her eyes travel to the framed photo he had straightened. "Marcus?"

"What?"

"Is that Marie-France with you in those pictures?"

"Yes."

"I don't mean to pry but—"

"You're wondering why you haven't met her."

"Yes. Doesn't she come to the gallery anymore?"

Marcus let out a long, slow exhale and settled himself on the edge of the desk. He'd known Diana was curious about the photographs and his references to Marie-France, but she was obviously too polite to pry into his personal life. He wasn't stupid. He knew the girl was inexperienced, lonely and vulnerable, which could lead to her becoming infatuated with him, despite the twenty-five-year age difference. The way she blushed sometimes made him think she might already have done so.

By now, Marcus conceded to himself that he was attracted to *her,* but he found perverse pleasure in playing with that feeling, savoring it, telling himself he could keep the situation under control. It would be folly, of course, to let anything happen between them. His better side accused him of encouraging Diana in more than her art, but even though the nagging voice in his brain told him he was courting danger, he couldn't bring himself to deter her from coming to the gallery.

It wasn't as if he were doing this only for his own benefit, he rationalized. She had talent that deserved to be fostered. He was playing mentor to her protégée, nurturing father to blossoming child. But even as he told himself this, Marcus knew there was only one reason he had kept silent about Marie-France's whereabouts and left Diana wondering—because it was the safest kind of wall between them. Protection from foolish, romantic daydreams, hers and his own. Now, as the Americans would say, the jig was up.

"She passed away thirteen months ago."

"Oh, I'm sorry!"

His fingers traced the curved, beveled edge of his antique rosewood desk. Marie-France's desk, if the truth were known. He had bought it, but she had claimed possession by virtue of the long hours she spent at it. "She...ah..." It wasn't easy to talk about her, even now. "She had lung cancer. She was sick for about ten months, and then she died."

Diana sat down. "You must miss her terribly," she said quietly.

He nodded. "I think I always will. We knew each other all our lives, grew up in the same neighborhood, were partners from the start. Her name was Desloges, too. We had a common great-grandfather. That's why the gallery has only one name on it.''

"But I thought she was your wife.''

"She was, for all intents and purposes. Legally, we were only married two weeks before she died.'' Marcus smiled. "Marie-France was a bit of an anarchist. Didn't believe in pieces of paper. She gave in at the end, mostly, I think, to simplify the legal status of the gallery after she was gone. She knew how much I hated lawyers and paperwork.''

"I think she must have loved you very much.''

"Oh, I know she did.'' In her own way, Marcus added to himself. Never exclusively, though.

Marie-France had been six years older than he. He had been infatuated with her even as a little boy, and she had been kind to him, tolerating his gawky attentions. When he began to dream of a gallery, she was the first to offer encouragement. Marie-France had believed in him enough to pool her inheritance with his after he finished his doctorate in art history, and to leave her job as a bookstore manager when the gallery became successful and he needed her there full-time.

She had also cared for Marcus enough to teach him about love when he was eighteen and she twenty-four, and to remain his lover all their adult lives—although they'd never actually lived together until those last few months, when she was dying and he refused to let her live alone. She'd had other men over the years, too, but none, she said, that she loved more than him. At first, when he found out about someone new, Marcus would rage and storm off, sometimes into the arms of other women. But in the end, he would always go back to Marie-France, and she always came back to him.

Marcus looked at the young woman in front of him now. How to explain such a strange relationship to someone who'd lived the sheltered life Diana had? The answer was, of course, that you didn't even try.

19

Andrew Mulvey Beekman—called "Drew" to distinguish him from his father, Andrew George Beekman, the Orange County real-estate developer—was scheduled to work the Christmas Eve shift at Truffles, the trendy Westwood eatery and watering hole where, at twenty-two, he was a part-time bartender and assistant manager when he wasn't attending senior-year classes at UCLA. Drew called to inform his mother of his shift switch, prompting a burst of bitter complaints.

"You *cannot* be serious!" Asa Beekman cried. "What about the party?" She was referring to her annual Christmas Eve blowout, an intimate affair for fifty-odd of her nearest and dearest friends and relations, featuring both a chamber orchestra and a brass quintet playing seasonal music. The evening's festivities would kick off at 8:00 p.m. with the traditional lighting of the forty-foot Douglas fir, specially trucked down from Colorado each year to grace the massive Beekman living room on Lido Isle in Newport Beach. After music, champagne and hors d'oeuvres would come the main event, a sit-down dinner at midnight. It was the finest re-creation of a nineteenth-century Windsor feast that her husband's money could buy, including roast goose, beef and Yorkshire pudding, minces and plum pudding, and little wrapped gifts of Victoriana antiques at each place setting.

"I'm going to have to miss it, Mother. I'm sorry."

"Why do *you* have to work that night? Let them get some-one else. You must tell them you have have a prior commit-ment, Drew."

"I can't do that. There *is* no one else." He would never ad-mit, of course, that he had volunteered to work the bar on Christmas for the express purpose of avoiding his mother's af-fair.

"Well, then, you'll have to quit the job," Asa said. "Your father would agree, I'm sure."

But the old man wouldn't, Drew knew, and what's more, so did his mother. Andrew Senior had insisted, from the time Drew was old enough to have a paper route, that he earn his own spending money. Asa had coaxed and stormed and pleaded with him, humiliated by the thought of a young Mul-vey-Beekman doing menial work, but on this point her hus-band had stood firm.

"I'll not have a spoiled-rotten ne'er-do-well bearing my name," Beekman Senior had thundered, his Scottish brogue slipping through his deliberately flattened-out speech pat-terns. "He'll learn to stand on his own two feet and make a living. And don't be expecting any fancy, son-of-the-boss po-sitions from me, either, young man," he had added, turning on Drew. "Before I'll hire ye, I'll want evidence of satisfactory work history for other employers, make no mistake about it!"

"Father expects me to put work obligations before plea-sure, Mother," Drew said now. "You know that."

"*I* want you here."

"You'll have to make my apologies. Ariel will be there, won't she?"

Ariel was Drew's twenty-four-year-old sister, a virtual clone of their mother. She had recently become engaged to a young man whose chief occupation seemed to be surfing. Jon Houghton was the bubbleheaded son of one of Asa's wealthy friends who had none of her husband's tiresome obsessions about the work ethic. He would inherit more money than he could spend in three lifetimes, whether or not he ever did a day's work. Asa was thrilled her daughter had landed him.

"People want to see *you*, darling! They ask about you all the time. Goodness knows, you're around little enough these days.

Senator and Mrs. Redman will be here, with their daughter, Courtney."

"Oh, now, *there's* a real magnet," Drew said dryly.

"She's very sweet, Drew. You haven't seen her in years, since she was in braces, but you'd be surprised. She's lost all that baby fat and blossomed into quite an attractive young woman."

"That may be, Mother, but it doesn't change the fact that I can't make it. I'm sorry."

"Couldn't you come after work?"

"I work until 1:00 a.m. By the time I closed up and drove to Newport, your party would be all but over."

"Oh, Drew!" Asa complained. "I *am* going to speak to your father about this."

"Don't. It'll just turn into another row, you know it will. You go ahead and have a terrific party and don't worry about anything else, all right?"

The telephone line echoed the depth of her sigh. "I suppose. But you *are* coming for Christmas Day, aren't you?"

"Sure. I'll be down first thing in the morning." Although, Drew thought, hanging up the phone a moment later, if Truffles had been open on the twenty-fifth, he would have been tempted to volunteer for that shift, too.

And so, he suspected, would Mallory Caine. She always seemed to be available to work when other people wanted time off. When Drew had seen her name on the shift schedule for December twenty-fourth, it had provided all the added incentive he needed to face down his mother's complaints and duck out of her overblown Christmas festivities.

Paris, France
December 17, 1979

After Marcus cleared up the mystery of the absent Marie-France, Diana sensed a subtle shift in their relationship. She found him less intimidating, with feet of very human clay. Despite all his outward success, she realized, he lived with loss and pain and disappointment. Like her, he carried scars, less visible to the eye, perhaps, but no less real than her own. Most people probably had them, she decided.

As Diana became more relaxed in his presence, she felt *him* begin to relax, as well. They'd gone for lunch that day, and Diana had found herself telling him about the murder of her birth parents and her own injuries, about Mallory, about their adoption by the Caines and their life in Minnesota. Not even when she'd told him how her parents' criminal activities had led to their murders did he make Diana feel shamed or pitied, for which she was deeply grateful.

A few days later, Marcus had invited her to accompany him to an opening at another gallery of a new exhibit by a group known as the Alsace school. Not long after that, when Ambassador Pannet had sent invitations to the Lennoxes and Diana to attend an embassy-sponsored Georgia O'Keeffe show, she'd invited Marcus. Before long, whenever he had a few hours free, Marcus and Diana were traipsing around galleries and museums all over the city. He patiently explained artists and schools and techniques she had never encountered before, although whatever his personal tastes might have been, he never made judgments. Instead, he left her to form her own opinions, only nodding when she saw connections and discordances, offering enough alternative points of view to force her to examine closely what she liked and what she didn't, and why.

In between, of course, he had his gallery to run, and she had the Yago project, but they found they could work side by side in comfortable silence. By the time December arrived, Diana's daily treks to St-Germain-des-Prés had become a part of a life that was just about perfect. *Almost* perfect, she thought, except—

Except that she still hadn't come up with a satisfactory design for the Yago posters and brochures. Marcus never pressed, but she knew his printing deadline was rapidly approaching. She'd done dozens of sketches in ink, graphite, conté and watercolor. With his agreement, she had settled on India ink as the medium, and on a loosely massed collage of drawings to represent the movement and power of Orlando Yago's work. But as the deadline drew closer, something was still missing. Marcus was trying hard, she sensed, not to show his disappointment.

"Don't worry about it, Diana. I always told you it was the experimentation that was important. We'll work out something for the posters, but in the meantime, this has been a very interesting exercise, and I have no regrets for having suggested it. I hope you don't," he added, lifting her chin with one finger.

She couldn't bear to look at him. Although many times over the past weeks she had wished for his touch, he had kept a respectable distance. Now that their collaboration was drawing to a close by virtue of the calendar and the demands of a printing schedule, Marcus had finally reached out to her, simply and spontaneously. But all Diana felt was shame and inadequacy. She didn't deserve his kindness. If she couldn't pull off this commission, she knew she would never be able to face him again.

Diana hadn't shown up at the gallery for five days. On the second day that she'd failed to appear, Marcus had telephoned the apartment on Rue Clément Maroi, worried that something might have happened to her. Diana had come to the phone but seemed evasive, saying only that she wasn't feeling well. He'd decided not to press.

As the days passed and he continued to arrive to a darkened gallery, Marcus told himself that it was for the best. Losing her work for the exhibit was a disappointment, but that was nothing compared to the emotional danger he had courted. He had come to depend on her being there, and to look forward to their outings together, but it was stupid to tie his well-being to a situation that was just temporary. Not only that, but if he cared about her, as he now admitted to himself that he did, he had to realize how hurtful it would be for her to get caught up in any foolish fantasy of a long-term future for the two of them.

Diana deserved better than Marcus Desloges. She was young, just starting out in life. She'd had so little joy and affection in the past that he wanted happiness for her now. She deserved some fine, young man who could offer her a lifetime of protection and stability. He himself had lived over half of his life already, and a chaotic, tangled life it had been, too. He was emotionally bruised, set in his ways and opinionated. He had a temper. And, he reminded himself for the ten-thousandth time, he was old enough to be her father. It was best to let this thing—this infatuation, this whatever it was—end here and now.

But by the fifth day of staring at her empty chair, Marcus was ready to put a fist through the office wall. Suddenly, at midafternoon, he grabbed his leather coat, tore down the stairs, flipped the door sign to *Fermé* and locked it. He ordered a glass of wine at the café next door, and then a second. When even that couldn't numb the clawing at his gut, he got into his car and drove to Rue Clément Maroi. The wizened, bad-tempered concierge harrumphed when he recognized Marcus, then called up to the apartment. Marcus was granted entry, but when the door opened, it was Mary Lennox who stood on the other side.

"Mrs. Lennox—how are you?"

"I'm fine, thank you, Monsieur Desloges. Come in, please."

Marcus stepped into the apartment. The first thing he noticed was the overwhelming, coppery odor of acrylic paint hanging in the air. "I don't want to bother you," he said. "I was concerned that Diana might be ill."

Mrs. Lennox hesitated. "No, not ill. She's not here, though."

"Oh. Well, I won't keep you. Just tell her I stopped by to say hello, will you?"

"Stay for a moment, would you, Monsieur Desloges? My husband is out, too, but there's something I think we need to discuss." Her normally smiling face was set in a stern expression. A frisson traveled the length of his spine, as if he were a little boy caught writing obscenities on the bathroom wall.

"Has something happened to Diana?" he asked.

"I'm not sure, but I'd be lying if I told you we weren't worried about her."

"Why?"

Mary sighed. "Come in and sit down, please." She took his coat and hung it in the hall. When they had settled in the front room, she played with the rings on her fingers before looking at him. "Monsieur Desloges, I think you know a little of Diana's history, do you not?"

"About her parents' murders? Yes, she told me."

"My husband knew her parents slightly. After they were killed, he helped arrange the girls' adoption and kept an eye on them as they grew. The adoption, unfortunately, turned out to be less than ideal. Diana's sister reacted by rebelling, but Diana withdrew into herself. She became painfully shy, almost reclusive. These past few months, Doug and I have been amazed and gratified to see how she's begun to open up and blossom. I think the kindness you've shown her has had a lot to do with it. She seemed happy."

"Seemed?"

"Yes. But for the past while, she's been extremely tense. Lately, she's been acting strange."

"How so?"

"She's hardly slept or eaten in almost a week. She stays in her room day and night, painting, but she won't let us look at what she's working on, or talk to us about it." Mrs. Lennox paused, then added, "Mallory, Diana's sister, once told me that Diana takes her emotional pain out on her canvases."

Marcus felt a cold worm of anxiety stir in his gut. "You think she's in pain?"

"She's in some sort of turmoil."

"Why?"

"That's what I was hoping you could tell me. You see, Monsieur Desloges, I suspect Diana has fallen in love with you. I don't know if you've done anything to encourage or discourage her, but I'm terribly afraid she's going to be hurt, and in Diana's case, one can't predict what that might do to her psyche."

It wasn't a worm he felt inside, Marcus thought, it was the snake of his own malfeasance—a cobra—and it was squeezing the air out of his chest.

"Am I wrong?" Mary asked.

Marcus looked up and took her steady gaze head-on. "Nothing has happened. Nothing *will* happen."

"But you *are* aware of the problem?"

He sighed. "I'm aware that there is the *potential* for a problem, if it's allowed to develop. I have no intention of doing so."

"Good. Then perhaps you can help us."

"In what way?"

"My husband and I have been invited, and Diana, as well, to visit the south of France for three weeks and spend the Christmas holidays with friends. She's been hesitating about going, but I believe she can be convinced, as long as there's nothing to hold her here. I think a break would be the best thing for her right now, don't you?"

"It's—a good idea," Marcus said. A *terrible* idea, his mind screamed.

"I'm glad you agree. We plan to leave next week, so perhaps you could get whatever drawings you need from Diana before then and make it clear to her that her work for you is done . . . ?"

Marcus nodded.

"Good," Mary said, sitting back briskly. "Now, can I get you some coffee?"

"No, thank you. I should be off."

"Diana will be back any minute. She said she had an errand to run, but she left over an hour ago."

"Tell her I said hello. Or better yet," Marcus said, rising, "perhaps you shouldn't mention this visit. I'll just call and tell her I'm going ahead with the material I have at the gallery."

"Whatever you think." Mrs. Lennox followed him to the hall, where she handed him his coat. "Please don't misunderstand, Monsieur Desloges. My husband and I think you've done Diana a great deal of good with your encouragement of her art. It's unfortunate, the way things turned out on the emotional level, but we're only human, after all. You mustn't blame yourself."

"Ah, but I *do,* Mrs. Lennox." He shrugged into his coat, but before he could say goodbye, the door opened and Diana walked in.

"Marcus! What are you doing here?"

When he saw her, it was only with great difficulty that Marcus restrained himself from putting his arms around her. If Mary Lennox had not been standing at his elbow, he would have lost the battle. Diana's eyes shone with a fevery brightness and were ringed with dark, sleepless circles. Her skin, except for two crimson spots on her cheekbones, was as pale as

new ivory, and she bristled with a nervous energy as perceptible as the buzz of a telephone wire.

"I was in the neighborhood," Marcus said, "and I dropped
in to see how you were."

"I'm well."

"Good, good. Mrs. Lennox tells me you're off to the south
next week."

"I'm not—"

"I'm glad you'll get a chance to relax in the sunshine. You've
been working much too hard in that dreary old place of mine."

"I like it there."

"I'm taking a break myself."

"You're going away?"

"Yes. I usually head off to Grindelwald with friends for
some Christmas skiing," Marcus said. It was only half-true. He
had gone two years earlier with Marie-France, just before she
got sick. Last year, after her death, he hadn't been able to face
the idea. Jean Grenier had asked him several times about this
year, but Marcus had been stalling on his answer. Why? he
asked himself. What else had he thought was going to happen
if he stayed in Paris for the holidays? With whom had he
planned to spend them?

"I have to be going now," he said. "I'm glad to see you're
feeling better, Diana."

"Wait! Don't you want to ask about the Yago project?"

"What about it?"

"That's what I've been doing," she said. "I'd almost given
up, but then I had an idea. It took me several tries before I had
what I wanted."

"You didn't have to go through so much for this exercise."

"It's not just an exercise. Is it?" she asked, her expression
turning wary. "You meant it, didn't you, about it being a real
commission?"

"Yes, of course, but—"

"Well, then, would you stay and see what I have for you?"

Marcus glanced at Mary, who looked as perplexed as he.
"All right."

Diana slipped out of her cape, which Mary took and hung
up. Diana withdrew a folder from her canvas bag and opened

it to reveal a pile of clear acetate sheets onto which had been transposed the India ink drawings she had done of Orlando Yago's sculptures. "I had these made up at a print shop just now," she said.

"I don't understand. What for?"

"Just wait. I have to get something ready. You can come in a minute."

Diana disappeared down the hall, leaving Marcus and the bishop's wife mystified. A few minutes later, they heard her call, and the older woman led Marcus to Diana's bedroom. There were art materials everywhere and several paintings stacked, face-in, against one wall. Near the window stood an easel with a canvas mounted on it, its back to the doorway. Diana was waiting on the other side, her left arm hugging the right in the self-protective posture Marcus had seen so often before. Her eyes darted nervously from the easel to Marcus and back again.

When he came around to join her, he saw that the canvas was an acrylic wash of color. It started out gleaming yellow-white at the top, then deepened down the canvas, tone-by-tone, as broad, swirling brushstrokes passed through a warmer yolk-yellow to vibrant oranges, bleeding scarlets and crusty reds, ending up at the bottom as a rich burnt sienna. Superimposed on the canvas, she had tacked the clear acetate sheets, creating an India ink parade of Yago's surreal sculptured figures, cavorting and galloping on a background that subtly evoked memories of bullfighting posters—the bloody ring under a hot Spanish sky. It was extraordinary.

"My God," Marcus breathed. "You did it!"

"It's stunning!" Mary exclaimed.

Marcus turned to Diana. His mouth hung stupidly open, he knew, but he couldn't help it. She was brilliant! She was wonderful! She was beautiful!

She was young.

He closed his mouth and turned back to the easel, forcing himself to breathe deeply and get a grip. "How did you know to do this?" he asked.

"It was too flat before. It needed something."

"It needed this. You had the movement and the power in the drawings, but not the raw emotion. Now, it's all there."

"You really like it, Marcus?" Her voice was a nervous whisper.

Marcus swung around to her once more. The hell with it, he thought. He took her curly head in his hands and kissed her right in the middle of the forehead, one firm, enthusiastic, but appropriately chaste, kiss. Surely even the bishop's wife could not object to *that*. Then he stepped back. "I love it! And do you know who else will love it?"

"Who?"

"Orlando Yago. That young man is going to be thrilled at what you've done for him. As a matter of fact," he added, "I think you two young people are going to get along very well indeed." The idea of Diana and Orlando meeting, Marcus suddenly realized, was very unsettling.

20

Los Angeles, California
December 24, 1979

"Truth or dare."

Mallory paused in her table wiping and glanced over to the long wooden bar at the center of the restaurant. "What?"

"Truth or dare," Drew Beekman repeated. "Let's play."

"Now, why would I want to play games with you?"

He shrugged. "Something to do. You don't look like you're in a hurry to get out of here."

It was true, Mallory thought. It might be Christmas Eve, but she had neither warm house nor tree nor loved ones to run home to. At least here in Truffles there were lights and music. She glanced around the empty eatery. It was fifteen minutes to closing, but after an early-evening rush of customers dropping in for drinks and a bite after work or last-minute shopping, the place had been like a morgue all night. By eleven-thirty, Drew, in his capacity as acting manager, had let the rest of the staff go home, leaving just himself and Mallory to hold the fort until one o'clock.

"I'm cashed out and everything's cleaned," she said. "I won't hold you up. You want to close early?"

"No. I haven't got anywhere to go. I want to talk to you."

"What about?"

"I don't know. Anything. You."

"What about me?"

"Where you come from, to start with. You don't sound like a Valley Girl. What do you do when you're not slinging alfalfa sprouts and margaritas in this place?"

"I'm from Minnesota, and I take classes at Westside College and study," she answered. "Happy?"

"Not entirely, but it's a start. How about a Christmas drink, Mallory from Minnesota? On the house."

Careful, Mallory told herself. She'd felt the young barman's eyes on her for weeks, but she'd deliberately avoided making contact or putting herself in situations where he could corner her. Let him chase someone else, she'd thought. Any one of the other girls who worked here—most of them students like her, or aspiring actresses waiting for their big break—would have been happy to go out with him. He was a senior at UCLA, she knew, and his father was some kind of wealthy real-estate developer. That much she'd learned recently from Wendy Ryker, another waitress.

"He likes you, Mallory," Wendy had whispered as they stood near the kitchen hatch, waiting for their orders. "Haven't you seen how he looks at you? And how he always makes up your drink orders first?"

"No," Mallory lied.

"Have you got a boyfriend already?"

"No."

"Well, so?"

"So?"

"Why don't you go for it?"

"It? What *it*?"

"*Him*, girl! Drew Beekman. He's cute and rich. What more do you need?"

Mallory had taken her food orders from the shelf and turned away with a shake of her head. "You can have him."

The last thing she needed, Mallory had decided, was to get involved with some arrogant rich guy. She still hadn't gotten over the sting of Gunnar Anderson. She'd never been much good at these courtship rituals, and whatever cockiness she might once have possessed had been knocked right out of her by the experience with Gunnar.

As if that weren't bad enough, she was floundering like a fish out of water in a place she'd thought would feel like home but never had, not from the first moment she'd arrived in L.A. In Ferry Falls she'd been an outsider, marked by the scandal of her parents' deaths and her own rebellious behavior, destined never to feel a sense of belonging. But neither did she seem to fit in here, among all these tanned, too-beautiful Californians, with their lazy speech and wild, irrational optimism.

She had no reason for optimism or self-confidence, not after looking into her past and finding it as painful and disappointing as Bishop Lennox had feared she might. However warm her memories of a previous life with her natural mother and father, she had learned to distrust them. Memory was a vague, unreliable thing, she'd come to believe, especially a child's memory. How could she have known how weak and irresponsible her parents were, how their actions would cost them their lives and steal forever their children's sense of security? As much as she disliked the Rev and hated carrying his name, Mallory had come to despise Philip and Selena Knight even more.

"What'll it be, Minnesota?" Drew asked. "Wine? Kahlua? Margarita?"

Mallory hesitated, then tossed her table rag onto the bar and pulled up a stool. What the hell, she thought. She hadn't had a drink in months, since the last time she'd seen Wiley Dixon, and she could use a little numbing tonight. "Margarita—although I should warn you, I'm underage."

"How old are you?"

"Eighteen and a half."

Drew glanced at the door, then shrugged. "I don't think anyone's going to arrest us on Christmas Eve for one little celebratory drink." He dropped ice and margarita mix into a blender, then added tequila, put on the lid and flipped the switch. As the mixture blended, he slid two large goblets from an overhead rack, dampened the rims and dipped them in a bowl of salt. "So?" he said, looking up. "Want to play?"

"Truth or dare? Don't you have anything better to do?"

"Nope. And that's the truth. There. I answered your first question. Now it's my turn to ask."

"I didn't say I would play."

"Scared?"

"Not of you."

"Good. First question—why didn't you go home to Minnesota for Christmas?"

Mallory shrugged. "No one to go home to."

She felt a niggle of guilt at the thought of Frances, who had written and asked her please to come. Franny had even offered to send a plane ticket—the Rev *couldn't* have known about that—but Mallory had begged off, claiming too much schoolwork. She missed Franny, and wished they could visit, but the thought of the Rev was enough to hold her back. The only good thing about spending this Christmas alone was that she wouldn't have to sit through multiple church services and the Rev's droning sermons.

Drew snapped off the blender and filled the two glasses, which turned frosty. Hooking a wedge of lime on the edge of each, he slid a drink across the bar to her. "You don't have any family left back there?"

"Not really. And that's two questions."

"Right. Sorry. Your turn. Merry Christmas," he added, lifting his glass to hers.

Mallory returned his toast, and took a sip. Putting down her drink, she passed her tongue over her lips, licking away salt, then trailed her finger around the rim of her glass, watching him watch her.

Drew was nice-enough looking—no Gunnar Anderson, but not hard on the eyes, either, with his shiny, walnut-brown hair cut short, and eyes of an almost identical hue. His features were regular, his skin smooth, his teeth white and even. He wore the same Truffles open-necked navy knit polo shirt that she did, and it hung loose on a lean frame. From the muscle definition on his arms, she guessed that he must spend time on a tennis court.

"Are you a spoiled rich kid?" she asked, surprising herself as well as him with the question.

"Why? What have you heard?"

"Oh, no. That's not how you play. I ask the question, you have to answer."

"All right. I don't think I'm a spoiled rich kid. My parents have money, but I have to work for my own food, clothes, entertainment and transportation. My mother slips me a few bucks, when my father doesn't catch her at it, and she buys me clothes sometimes, which I usually return, because I don't like them. Does that make me a spoiled rich kid?"

"Probably."

"Fair enough. Now my turn."

"No, it's my turn again," Mallory said.

"Why?"

"You asked your question, 'Does that make me a spoiled rich kid?' Now I get to ask."

Drew's eyes narrowed. "You're very sneaky, Minnesota."

"No, I'm just smart. Next question—why aren't you at home with Mummy and Daddy on Christmas Eve instead of slumming around here, playing stupid games?"

"I'd be playing games *there,* too, believe me."

"What games?"

"Dutiful-son games. Stupid social games. And that's two questions, so now I get two."

"Okay, fire away."

"Don't you have any family at all?"

"I have a sister, but she's in Paris right now."

"What about your parents?"

"Pass."

"You don't want to answer that one?"

"Nope."

"The game's called Truth or *Dare.* "

"So what's the dare?"

"I dare you to chug that margarita."

"You think you're going to get me drunk?" Mallory shook her head. "You don't want to make this challenge, rich boy. I can drink you under the table."

He grinned. "You could, hmm? Okay, fair enough. In that case, I dare you to go out with me."

"What? When?"

"Now. Tonight. We're closed," Drew added, checking the wall clock. "Go and lock up the front and flip that door sign, would you?"

Mallory slipped off her bar stool and walked to the door, dodging overhanging asparagus ferns and weaving around backgammon tables. After she had locked it and turned the sign to Closed, she returned to the bar, where Drew was bagging the night's receipts. His preoccupation with the tally gave her time to think as she sipped her drink. He wasn't so bad, really, and considering that this was just about the longest conversation she'd had with anyone in months, it hadn't been terrible.

She thought about her tiny apartment, sparsely furnished and undecorated for the holidays. Why bother with festive decorations? she had thought. It would only remind her that she was alone. The last thing she wanted right now, she had to admit, was to drive home to that empty apartment, past twinkling Christmas lights and houses whose chimneys were smoky from warm fires lit in living room hearths. She had a long, lonesome Christmas Day to look forward to. Hanging out for a few more hours with Drew Beekman might not be a bad idea. Then she could sleep till noon or later, get up and work on school assignments, and before she knew it, the day would be over.

Drew locked the night-deposit bag, then drained his margarita glass. A few grains of salt wedged themselves in the smile lines at one corner of his mouth. Mallory reached over the bar and brushed them away with her fingers. Drew caught her hand before she could retrieve it. A grain of salt was left on one fingertip. He kissed it away, then closed his hand over hers and looked up. "So, do we have a date?"

"It's 1:00 a.m.," Mallory said. "Everything's closed. What did you have in mind?"

"We could go for a drive and look at Christmas lights."

"We could," she agreed.

"We could drive down to the Santa Monica pier and watch the night fishermen."

"We could do that, too."

"If we get hungry, I know a great all-night taco stand."

"That sounds good."

"And if we get cold," Drew said, bringing her hand up to his lips again, "we could always go back to my place and watch *Miracle on 34th Street.*"

His breath on her fingers and his warm gaze on her face set Mallory's insides to dancing. After almost six months of being alone and wanting to keep it that way, the fact that he could set off this reaction was more like a *Miracle on Santa Monica Boulevard*.

She blinked, like someone startled awake after a long, deep sleep. "Maybe we should just start with those Christmas lights."

Drew Beekman's Volkswagen camper had seen better days, he had to admit. Its body was chipped, revealing naked steel underneath, and what rusty-red color remained of the original paint job was only an anemic reminder of its original hue. The van's exhaust was an embarrassment, its engine sounded like a rhino with pneumonia and a kid on a sugar high could easily outrun the thing. His mother had wanted to replace it for his birthday with something more "appropriate," but Drew had bought and paid for this old clunker with his own money, and he had a perverse, almost parental pride in it. He had refused her repeated offers, and on this, as on little else, he and his father had agreed.

After locking the back door of Truffles, Drew opened the rear of the van to load Mallory's Yamaha inside.

"What's this, rich boy?" she asked. "A loaner from the garage while they fix your Jag?"

"This is my pride and joy, I'll have you know."

"Really."

Drew grunted as he slammed the door. "Yup. She may not be fancy, but she's all mine and she gets me where I need to go."

They climbed into the front seats and Drew headed the wheezing thing down the block to the Wells Fargo Bank, where he dropped the canvas bag containing the restaurant's receipts into the night-deposit box. Walking back to the van, he saw Mallory studying him. She was frowning, and he had the uncomfortable feeling that she was finding him wanting. He felt a flash of annoyance. Who did she think she was, this lonely, apparently friendless girl from *Minnesota* of all places? Drew Beekman was not accustomed to being judged harshly, especially by the girls he dated. He had the phone numbers of plenty who would have taken her place in a flash, despite the eccentricity of his mode of transport. Some of those girls were prettier, and all of them were better-dressed and more sophisticated than she was, and they had fathers whose money ensured they wouldn't be caught dead waiting tables.

Right. And he wouldn't have traded a chance to get to know Mallory for any ten of them. There was something about her, he thought, something that went beyond a nice, long-legged body in tight jeans, wild blond hair, or piercing, almost-black eyes. It was the mystery of the contrasts in her—the alternating brashness and caution in her manner, and the flashes of defiance and fear in those eyes. All the other girls he dated were open books by comparison, and not very interesting books at that.

"So, we cruise for Christmas lights?" he asked, climbing into the van.

"Sure, although I've seen a few already. You Californians don't overdo it much, do you?"

Drew headed the van east. "Hey, people grow up under the influence of Disneyland out here. If there's one thing we do well, it's gaudy, overblown display."

He proved it by driving up and down residential streets in the west end and on into the winding lanes of Beverly Hills. Although many of the household lighting displays had been extinguished, there were enough residents apparently unconcerned by whopping electric bills to keep theirs lit all night. Drew showed her front lawns transformed into wonderlands, with artificial snow, gingerbread houses, running miniature trains, tethered hot-air balloons, scores of life-size, animated figures and enough twinkling lights to illuminate Las Vegas.

"Is one of these your family's house?" Mallory asked.

"No, although theirs is almost as tacky. My parents live south of here, in Newport Beach."

Her head spun around. "In Orange County?"

"Yeah. Do you know it?"

She turned away again. "No."

"I don't live with them anymore. I have a place just off campus."

"You don't get along with your parents?"

Drew shrugged. "We get along all right."

"But?"

"I don't know. My mother's got her clubs and charities, and my father's always been tied up with his business. My sister and I were raised by nannies. We don't have what you'd call a real warm, fuzzy family, except when appearances call for it."

"I know what you mean."

"You do?"

She nodded. "My sister and I were adopted and raised by a minister and his wife. The Rev was never very keen on having us, but he used to make us put on the 'one, big, happy family' display for his parishioners."

"Is that why you left home?"

"Pretty much."

Drew nodded. "I've been thinking along the same lines."

"Leaving here?"

"Yes. My father insisted I find my own jobs up to now, but my parents expect me to work for his company after I graduate in the spring."

"You don't want that?"

Drew shook his head vehemently. "Not on a bet! The idea of building suburban tract housing bores me to tears."

"What do *you* want to do?"

"I'm interested in politics and diplomacy. My parents think I'm crazy, but I'd like to work in Washington."

"So? What are you going to do about it?"

"I'm not sure. I applied for a senate internship and I'm waiting to hear. I haven't told my parents, because they'd make sure I didn't get it."

"Can they do that?"

"Sure. They're big political contributors. Greases the wheels of business, you know, to have friends in high places."

"But that could work to your benefit."

"It *could,* if my parents would support me on this. Senator James Redman is a friend of theirs, and he's vice chairman of the Senate Foreign Relations Committee. That's the committee I'd like to work for, but my parents would make sure my internship application was shredded if they found out."

"Bummer. Aren't families great?"

"As opposed to what? Athlete's foot?" Mallory laughed, and Drew smiled to himself. Progress, he thought. "Hey, Minnesota, I'm starving. Have you seen enough lights?"

"For a lifetime."

"Good. I think we're beginning to draw attention, anyway." He glanced in his rearview mirror and noted the private-security patrol car that had been trailing them for the past block and a half. The good citizens of Beverly Hills did not take kindly to riffraff in the neighborhood, and the van looked more like an escapee from Watts than Newport Beach. "Let's hit that taco stand I was telling you about."

Mallory was intrigued, almost in spite of herself. Drew Beekman had grown up with nannies, summers in Europe and millionaires and political leaders sitting across from him at his parents' dinner table. These facts emerged casually, almost disparagingly, from their conversation over tacos and burritos at the grungy little Taco Loco stand just off Wilshire Boulevard. He seemed no more concerned about the contrast between his background and their current dining location than he was of the salsa he was dripping on his obviously expensive suede jacket. His manner of speech reflected the fancy private schools he had attended, and yet when it came time for college, and he could have gone to any Ivy League school he wanted, he had chosen UCLA, a public institution.

Drew Beekman was heir to a fortune, from the sound of things, but what he was most proud of was that he had been made assistant manager of some tacky jungle eatery and bar, and that he owned a stinky, ugly, rusting bucket of German automotive technology. Go figure, she thought. The guy was a mystery.

When they finished eating, they climbed back into the van, cruising westward through the uncharacteristically quiet streets of west L.A. and Santa Monica. It was unusual, Mallory knew, for roads in this sprawling, car-loving city to be deserted, but 2:30 a.m. on Christmas morning was apparently one of those rare occasions.

When they reached the double-decked Santa Monica pier, the arcades, the Ferris wheel and the carousel with its red and gold horses were shut down and dark. Drew's promised night fishermen were there, however—Vietnamese and Mexicans mostly, cutting bait and casting lines into the deep water at the end of the pier, beyond the crashing surf. Mallory and Drew stood at the steel railing below the harbormaster's office, watching them reel in snapper and bonita, tossing the fish into water-filled buckets.

Mallory turned her face to the breeze off the water as the tarred wooden planks under her feet rumbled with the vibration of waves crashing around pilings beneath the pier. The night air was cool but clear, the sky full of stars. Far out over the water, at the extreme southern edge of the horizon, she searched for the dim glow of lights that would announce the tip of Santa Catalina, but she couldn't find them this far north. Suddenly, though, an old, forgotten song came to mind— "Twenty-Six Miles Across the Sea." And then, the memories came rushing in.

She and Diana were playing in the surf when Mallory looked back and saw her daddy reach his hand down to her mom, sitting on the blanket, and pull her to her feet. Next thing Mallory knew, they were dancing.

"You guys!" She laughed, running up to them. "What are you doing? This isn't a ballroom!"

Her parents each grabbed one of her hands and swung her around with them as they danced, singing that song she had heard them sing before about "the island of romance."

"What's romance?" she asked.

"Love, honey," her mom said. "And that's where Daddy and I got married, over there on Santa Catalina." She pointed across the water, and Mallory made out the bumps of the island.

"You did?"

"That's right, my love," her mother sang.

They danced on and on in the warm sand.

Mallory shivered.

"Are you cold?" Drew put an arm around her shoulder.

She shook her head, not trusting her voice. She could feel him watching, so she forced herself to look at him, mustering a smile. He returned it, but a shadow of concern flickered across his forehead. Unzipping his jacket, he opened it wide, then moved behind her and wrapped it and his arms around the big fisherman knit sweater she had pulled over her Truffles shirt and blue jeans when they'd left the bar. Mallory stiffened briefly, then warmed to his touch and settled into it, liking it. Wanting it. Needing something that would push aside memories. Needing to forget.

He leaned against her back, his body warm. Crossing his arms in front of her, Drew held her by the opposite elbows, settling his chin on her shoulder. They looked out over the water, swaying ever so slightly with the rhythm of the surf as the waves rolled under them, one after another. His breath was gentle and reassuring on her neck, and when he began stroking her hair, humming softly, Mallory closed her eyes, lost in the comfort of his touch. His hand moved down to her cheek, cupping her face as his thumb continued to stroke and their bodies continued to sway. Drew pushed her hair away and brought his lips to her ear, and when he began to nuzzle her lobe and her neck, Mallory felt the stirring inside of a familiar ache. She leaned into him, arching her neck as he held her tighter. When he turned her head toward him, she offered her lips willingly.

Their kisses started easy, casual and exploratory, feeling each other out, obviously liking what they found. But as one kiss followed another, the intensity grew. Drew loosened his grip enough for her to pivot her body to face him, and then wrapped her up once more. Under the camouflage of his jacket, with her back to their nighttime companions on the deck below, their hands began to move. Mallory gripped his narrow hips as he pressed against her, backing her into the railing, his hands traveling over the cables of her sweater. He was just slipping them underneath, when they heard a slap on the wooden boards behind them, then an exclamation.

Pulling apart, a little breathless, they looked over to one side of the pier, where a fisherman had just landed a large ray. It flopped and wriggled as the man tried to withdraw the hook from its mouth, prompting laughter and incomprehensible words of advice and encouragement from his fishing companions.

Mallory and Drew watched the antics for a moment, and then turned to each other, smiling. She took a deep breath. "It's awfully late. We should be going."

He nodded, and they headed up the pier, arms entwined. "Do you want to go to my place?" he asked.

She debated with herself. Her body voted yes. Her cautious mind said maybe. Her bruised heart said be careful.

"I think I'd better go home," she said.

It took the longest half hour of Mallory's life to make it back to her tiny place in Westwood. If the bucket seats in Gunnar Anderson's T-bird had been a nuisance, they were nothing compared to the enforced isolation of the widely spaced seats in the cab of the Volkswagen. She and Drew couldn't even hold hands as they traveled.

But the length of the drive, physical separation and the late hour turned out to be better than a cold shower for dampening her ardor. After Drew lifted out her bike from the back of the van and rolled it next to her door, it was obvious that he was ready to pick up where they had left off on the pier. But after a couple of brief kisses, Mallory put her hand on his chest. "We have to stop."

"Why?" He moved his lips to her neck.

"We just do. Please? It's going on four o'clock, and I'm dead tired."

He straightened and sighed. "Okay. But I want to see you again, Minnesota. Is that all right with you?"

She nodded, smiling sleepily. "S'okay by me, rich boy."

"When?"

"Whenever. I have to work again tomorrow."

"I don't. But anyway, it's not at work that I want to see you." His face brightened. "I know! Come with me later today, to my folks' place."

"Your parents'? I don't think so."

"What else are you going to do?"

"Sleep. Work on school assignments."

"You need a holiday. I can't promise brilliant company, but there'll be turkey and all the trimmings."

"No."

"Come on, Mallory, it's Christmas."

"I know that."

"You don't want to be alone today, do you?"

She laid a hand on his shirtfront. "I've had a nice Christmas Eve *and* morning, Drew, but now, I'm beat. I'll probably sleep most of the day."

"I want you to come with me."

"No. Your family doesn't know me from Adam, and they'll want to have you to themselves, especially today."

"I'd like them to meet you."

"Another time."

He frowned, but Mallory could see he was getting the message that she wasn't going to give in. She hardly knew Drew Beekman, however pleasant their groping kisses had been. As for his family, she doubted very much that they would welcome a Christmas guest the likes of Mallory Caine.

"Can I call you later?" Drew asked.

"I don't have a phone."

He growled and took her by the shoulders, shaking gently. "You don't make things easy, do you?"

"I wouldn't want to be easy. Look, I'll see you at work sometime, and then," she said, shrugging, "we'll see. Okay?"

"No, but I guess I don't have much choice, do I?"

"Guess not."

He kissed her once more, then let her go, backing away reluctantly. "Merry Christmas, Minnesota."

"Merry Christmas, rich boy. And thanks for a nice time."

21

Newport Beach, California
December 25, 1979

Andrew Beekman—formerly of a tough, working-class neighborhood of Glasgow, Scotland, now of Newport Beach, California—watched his wife across the breakfast table. Asa Mulvey Beekman was as close as one came to California aristocracy—one of *those* Mulveys, a grand-niece of old Otis, who had almost single-handedly transformed Los Angeles into the state's richest, most powerful city, outstripping San Francisco. The feat was accomplished on an economic tripod of real-estate speculation, oil and massive water-diversion projects, and Otis Mulvey had been at the center of them all.

Asa's branch of the clan, admittedly, was known as "the poor Mulveys." Having grown up in an unheated, cold-water flat in Glasgow, Beekman always found it difficult to reconcile his wife's comfortable Hancock Park upbringing with the concept of poverty. He knew, however, that the astute eyes of Asa's girlhood friends would have noticed the shabby furniture and frayed carpet edges in the house her father had inherited but could never quite manage to keep up in the style it demanded.

Andrew Beekman had arrived in California in 1946. He had emigrated not long after he was demobbed from the Royal Navy, having spent five freezing war years serving on a convoy ship in the North Atlantic. It was that experience that firmly convinced him to shun dismal prospects in Glasgow and move to a place where he would never feel the cold again.

He'd arrived in southern California in the middle of a building boom, when houses couldn't be built fast enough to accommodate the influx of people looking for postwar dream careers in oil, food processing, show business or the new aviation and technology industries that were taking the state by storm. Beekman had gone to work as a carpenter, putting in eighteen-hour days, rising swiftly to site foreman. By 1949, he had started his own small construction company, beginning with five employees, increasing by 1952 to a hundred and twenty, and then to almost three hundred employees in 1955, as he grabbed piece after piece of the endlessly expanding housing-construction pie.

By this time, Andrew Beekman was a millionaire several times over—on paper at least, since most of his profits were plowed back into the Beekman Development Corporation. He'd retrained his tongue not to roll its thick, Scottish R's and had taken golf lessons so he could hobnob with powerful people who were in a position to send more business his way. He'd studied and copied their dress and manners. He'd built himself a house on Lido Island, the richest enclave of rich Newport Beach.

And he *was* invited places by the old-money elites. They invited him to large charity functions, where his contributions were sought—though never to small private dinners. They invited him to the occasional open cocktail party, where he was careful to nurse one drink all night so as not to loosen his tongue and turn back into the working-class, profanity-spouting Scotsman he had once been. They even invited him now and again to have lunch or play golf at some of the best country clubs in the area—but never to join those same clubs. As the tenth anniversary of his arrival in California approached, Andrew Beekman had worried that, well as he'd done, his accomplishments had peaked. He could wear all the fine suits he wanted, but he was still a big, gruff working man who knew everything about the business end of a hammer but nothing about making his way in genteel company.

And then he'd met Asa Mulvey. She was twenty-three, living for the summer in a beach house with one of her rich Mulvey cousins, and working as a receptionist in his lawyer's office.

"Just for fun, so I won't be bored to tears," she told Beekman. Afterward, of course, he came to understand that Asa was working because she needed the money—over and above the small allowance her father could afford to give her—in order to keep herself in the expensive clothes she favored. And she was in Newport in the hopes that a summer spent mostly in a swimsuit might snag her a rich, vacationing bachelor. None of the eligible candidates in Hancock Park, it seemed, had taken Asa's bait.

Andrew Beekman was not exactly what the Mulveys had had in mind for Asa, but as soon as Asa spotted him, she'd decided he was just what *she* had in mind. He was wealthy, reasonably good-looking and desperate enough to put up with Asa's sharp tongue and undisguised greediness, and to let himself be molded into something acceptable. They were married that September. If it was not a union made in heaven—Beekman found her neither particularly attractive nor interesting—it was at least mutually beneficial. He had the money, she had the social cachet of her name, and between them, they had ambition to burn.

Asa stared back at him now. Her mouth was open, but her hand, ferrying an English muffin, had frozen in midair, halfway between the pristine porcelain caps on her teeth and the Christmas-patterned Spode china on the breakfast table. Recovering, she lowered her hand. "Jim Redman told you *what?*"

"That Drew has applied for a senate internship."

"There must be some mistake."

"Apparently not. The application was passed on to Redman because Drew asked to work for the Foreign Relations Committee. Jim wanted to know how we felt about it before he made his decision."

"You told him it was out of the question, I hope."

"No, I didn't."

"Why ever not, Andrew?"

"Because that would be an admission that we didn't have a clue what our son was up to, and I had no intention of admitting such a thing."

"I see your point. But Drew can't go gallivanting off to Washington. He's going to work for you after he graduates in April."

"I know that."

"Well, what are we going to do? Jim Redman *can't* approve his application."

"I asked him to sit on it for a while. I told him Drew's been having second thoughts."

"Oh, good. Tomorrow you can call and say he doesn't want the internship, after all."

"It's not that simple."

"What do you mean?"

"Redman wants Drew to call him. The boy's almost twenty-three years old, Asa. An adult. He has to make his own decision."

"But Andrew!"

"Relax. I just have to decide how to go about ensuring that he makes the right decision. Leave it to me. I'll take care of it. Don't mention it when Drew comes."

"All right, but make sure you *do* take care of it. I want my son here."

"He's not going anywhere, Asa, except into the business."

"I should hope not." Asa drummed her lacquered nails on the table. "DeeDee Cunningham's daughter, Page, is home from Bryn Mawr for the holidays. Perhaps we should have them to dinner. Better still, maybe Drew should take Page to the New Year's Eve party at the club."

"No, Mother, I'm *not* going to take Page Cunningham out for New Year's Eve."

"Why not? She's a lovely girl, Drew. You used to think so, too. You had quite a thing for her, as I recall. Wasn't it Page you were caught kissing behind the cabana at Ariel's birthday party one year?"

"That was in sixth grade. I haven't seen her in years."

"Perhaps it's time to renew old acquaintances."

"Sorry, Mom. Can't be done."

"Don't tell me you're working at that grotty saloon again."

Drew rolled his eyes. "It's not a saloon, Mother. And no, I'm not working, but I *do* have plans."

"Anyone *we* know?" his sister, Ariel, wheedled. She and Jon Houghton were sitting on a deeply upholstered love seat in the living room across from their mother and Drew. Ariel had her arm around her fiancé's shoulders and had been twiddling his sun-bleached hair, which, as a result, now stood straight up on his head. That, plus the dopey, half-drunk grin on his bland face, Drew decided, made him a perfect example of Monty Python's upper-class twit.

"No," Drew told his sister, "no one you know." Thank God, Mallory hadn't come with him. Christmas or not, it had been an awful day. His father had been testy from the moment Drew arrived, while his mother had been alternately fawning and aggrieved with her son for no apparent reason.

Ariel and Jon had finally shown up at two in the afternoon to open presents, after promising to be there by ten. From their glazed expressions and wandering hands, it was obvious to everyone that they had spent the missing hours humping themselves blind at Jon's beach house. But annoyed as she was, Drew's mother had smiled stiffly and not said a word. She would do nothing, it was clear, to rock the boat before Ariel and her young millionaire were safely married in February.

Andrew Senior was in his den, smoking the after-dinner cigar Drew's mother refused to have in her extravagantly decorated living room. Everyone was full of turkey and exhausted after their respective late nights—his included, Drew thought, crossing his legs uneasily at the remembrance of how Mallory had clung to him as he pressed against her on the Santa Monica pier. He glanced at his watch. Seven o'clock. If he left now, he could be with her by eight.

He rose, stepping over the three beribboned Shih Tzus—his mother's beloved walking mops—that had draped themselves around his feet when he sat down. The dogs were both beautiful and mind-numbingly stupid, the perfect companions for this life-style that his parents were determined Drew should embrace. He had other plans.

"Where are you going, dear?" Asa asked.

"I have to be off."

"Tonight? Where?"

"Back to L.A."

"You can't! It's Christmas."

"I have a lot to do, Mother—assignments and papers to be finished, books to read over the break."

Behind him, his sister snorted. Drew turned and saw her dark eyebrows dancing under flowing blond tresses. "Little Drew's got a *gi-irlfriend!*" she chanted.

"Stuff it, Ariel."

"Drew, please!" his mother said. "Stay over tonight, at least. You can drive back in the morning just as easily."

"Sorry, Mother. I really need to go now."

"But your father wants to talk to you."

Drew frowned. "About what?"

"Oh, I don't know. Things. You should have a talk with him, please."

Drew sighed. This didn't sound good at all. "I'll stick my head in his den before I leave. I'm going to ask Consuela to pack me some leftovers. Is that all right?"

"Of course it is, dear. There's so much food here, after the party last night and the big dinner today. I'm going to have to do triple time with Eric to get back in shape after all this." She pinched her bony arm and shook her head sadly. There wasn't an ounce of fat on her, but Drew suspected that this beefy new personal trainer his mother and her friends had found supplied more than advice on diet and exercise. At the very least, he gave these women the undivided male attention that their busy husbands never had time for. "But *you're* too thin, Drew," Asa went on. "I don't think you eat properly. I'll be so glad when your classes are done up there and you come home where you belong."

Drew said nothing, only bent to kiss his mother's powdery cheek, then straightened and gave his sister and the doofus beside her a farewell wave.

In the kitchen at the back of the sprawling house, Consuela, the cook, was putting away the last of the pots and pans she had used to make the Beekman family Christmas dinner. She was a Chilean refugee, Drew had discovered one day sitting in the kitchen talking with her while his parents were off at a charity function. Consuela had lost her husband and three children to the death squads in that country. She was a genius in the kitchen, and Drew had often heard his mother rave to her friends about how utterly devoted the cook was to her. Drew knew that the ridiculously long working hours Consuela put in came more from a desire to keep busy and to forget her tragic past than any affection for Asa Beekman and her clan.

"Hey, Consuela!" he said, walking over and giving her a hug. *"¡Feliz Navidad!"*

She smiled broadly. *"¡Feliz Navidad!* Mr. Drew. How are you?"

"I'm great. And you? You must be tired, especially after the big bash last night."

"Sí, very tired. But I'm almost finished here, and then I go to bed."

"Good idea. I have something for you."

"For me?"

"Yes. A little Christmas present." From behind his back, Drew brought a small, gift-wrapped box. Consuela opened it and withdrew six cassette tapes of Spanish music.

"Mister Drew, thank you! I will listen to them in my room."

"I hope you like these artists. I went to Tower Records in L.A. They have the best selection of imported music, and I asked some people who were shopping in the Latin American section who the best performers were."

"You should not go to such trouble."

"No trouble."

She patted his hand and smiled sadly. As painful as her memories must be, Drew thought, they would be especially acute at Christmas. "You okay today, Consuela?" he asked, looking closely at her weathered face.

"Sí, okay," she said. "You are nice boy, Mr. Drew."

"You, too, *Señora* Consuela, and one heck of a cook. Thanks for that great dinner."

"It's okay. I pack you some food to take home tomorrow, *sí?"*

"Actually, I'm leaving in a little while."

"Tonight? On Christmas? Why?"

Drew glanced around the kitchen, but they were alone. "Because there's somewhere else I'd rather be," he whispered.

Consuela's brown eyes danced mischievously. "With a girl, no?"

"With a girl, yes."

"She a special girl, Mr. Drew?"

"Yeah, I think she is, and she's by herself today."

"No family for Christmas?"

"Nope. Not in California, anyway."

"Oh, *es muy triste.* Very sad. I know."

"You do, don't you?" Drew said, squeezing her hand.

"I tell you what, Mr. Drew. I pack a dinner for your girl, okay?"

"You don't mind? I know you're tired."

"No, I don't mind," Consuela said, beginning to bustle around the kitchen.

"Thanks, Consuela. I have to see my father, but I'll be back in a few minutes."

"*Sí, sí.* Go. I get everything ready."

Outside the door of his father's lair, Drew hesitated, one hand on the knob, listening to the low rumble of Andrew Senior's voice. He seemed to be on the telephone. "I *told* you I wouldn't make it last night or tonight. That's why you got your present early." There was silence, and then his father spoke again. "*My* present? You didn't have to—" Silence again, then the creak of his leather desk chair. "And do you come gift-wrapped, too?" Beekman asked, his tone bemused. "I see. Well, that's a difficult offer to refuse. I'm not sure. I'll try. It might be late, though.... All right, in a while, then."

Drew heard the phone cradled, then the creak of leather again. He raised his hand and rapped his knuckles twice on the carved oak door, turned the handle and walked in. His father's chair spun around, his expression startled, then stern. "Drew! What are you doing?"

"I just stopped in to say goodbye, sir. I'm heading back to L.A."

"Now?"

"Yes. I've got a lot of work to do."

"I see."

"So, anyway—" Drew held out his hand. "Merry Christmas, Father."

"Sit down."

"Sir?"

"Sit down. We need to have a talk."

Drew settled uneasily in a hard, straight-backed chair on the other side of his father's massive desk. "About?"

"About your future. You'll be graduating in April, won't you? No problem with your grades?"

"No problem."

"Well then, I think it's time we started thinking about where you'll be starting out in the company. I *had* planned to put you in a junior sales and marketing position to start with—"

"Father, I—"

"But I've been thinking lately that you could handle something more responsible. Maybe in the planning department. You'd still have to learn the ropes, of course, but I've been pleased by the way you've been working and keeping up your studies at the same time. And, to your credit, you've never come to me for a handout, not once. Most impressive."

"Thank you, but—"

"I don't think that dolt your sister's gotten herself tied up with could have managed as well. Bloody good thing he's got his own money, because I'm damned if I'd have the man working for me."

"Father, there's something I should tell you."

"What's that?"

Drew gripped the arms of the chair, disgusted with himself for feeling so terrified. But he'd never in his life won an argument with the old man, and there was no reason to think he was about to start now, not if his father was set on having him join Beekman Development after graduation. "You know I've always been interested in politics," he ventured.

"Bah! Bunch of bloodsuckers."

"Well, maybe. But I'm interested in foreign affairs, and I'm thinking I'd like to try something in that field."

"Waste of time."

Drew took a deep breath and plunged ahead. "I applied for an internship with the U.S. Senate, Father."

"Yes, I know."

"You do?"

"Jim Redman told me about it last night. How do you think I felt, learning it from him?"

Shit! Drew thought. They say the wheels of bureaucracy in Washington run slowly, but they'd been quick enough in this case. He hadn't realized Senator Redman would know of his application so early, or he might have come last night, after all, to head off just such a revelation. No wonder his parents had been in a strange mood all day. "I'm sorry, Father, but I didn't think you'd approve."

"I don't."

"But it's what I want to do."

"I don't think so."

"You could help me on this."

"I don't think so," his father repeated.

"Father, please! I'm not cut out to be a real-estate developer."

"Nonsense! Of course you are. You're my son. I've spent thirty years building this corporation and you'll inherit it someday. In the meantime, you need to learn the business, and I need a lieutenant I can trust. That's you. Now, I don't want to hear anymore of this drivel about Washington."

"You can't force me to withdraw the application."

"No, but how far do you think it will go if I tell Jim Redman I want you here?"

"Have you already done that?"

"I want you to do it. It's time for you to settle down to serious work, Drew. Find yourself a wife—"

"One of Mother's cronies' daughters, I suppose?"

Andrew Senior shrugged. "The right bride never hurts in business."

Drew glanced at the phone next to his father's elbow. "Especially when you can have your cake and eat it, too, eh, Father?"

"There's work and, if you handle things discreetly, there's play, son. That's the way the world is. Take my advice and get on with your life. You'll be a better man for it."

"I'm getting on just fine with my life now," Drew said, rising. "I have to go."

"Where are you running off to on Christmas Day?"

"Somewhere I'd rather be than here, at the moment."

"A new girlfriend?" Drew said nothing, watching stonily as his father rose and reached into his pocket. Pulling out his billfold, he withdrew what Drew could see were two hundred-dollar bills and held them out. "Here. Take her out. Have a good time. Marry her, if you want. We can see about starting you on a salary before graduation. Just get it into your head, Drew, that it's time to grow up."

"I don't need your money, Father. I can make enough to get by. All I wanted from you was moral support on this senate thing. But I guess that was too extravagant a gift to hope for, wasn't it?"

22

After Drew dropped her off around 4:00 a.m., Mallory had crawled into her narrow bed, exhausted, and slept until almost three in the afternoon. When she finally got up, she opened her Christmas presents. There was a hand-crocheted afghan in orange and lime green from Franny—*and* the Rev, the card said, but Mallory knew better—a navy blue sweater and matching beret from Diana—how French, she thought—and a bottle of Chanel cologne and a book of poems from the bishop and Mrs. Lennox.

She dabbed on the cologne, tried the sweater, and then, after making a cup of coffee, curled up in a corner and wrapped herself in the afghan to read the long letter Diana had enclosed with her gift. It was incredible what was happening to her sister. Here was Diana talking about galleries and commissions and exhibits as if she had been some global jet-setter all her life, instead of the girl who used to be too timid to go to the ShopEasy by herself, for fear someone might talk to her. Who exactly was this Marcus character Diana kept referring to? Mallory wondered, grinning. And what brand of witchcraft were he and the Lennoxes practicing on her sister?

But as she folded the letter after reading it for the third time, Mallory experienced the beginnings of a gnawing fear. She had always worried about abandoning Diana, but what if Diana abandoned *her?* What if her sister never came back from Paris? No, she told herself firmly, that wasn't going to happen. They'd be together again. Seeing how things had worked out so well in Paris, maybe now Diana would have the courage to tackle southern California. For sure, she couldn't want to go back to Ferry Falls. Just the thought of it made Mallory shudder.

Frances had mentioned in her last letter that Gunnar and Janice had had a baby girl in October, and that work had started on a new miniature-golf course next to the Two Loons. It was expected to open in the spring. Good for Gunnar, Mallory thought, not altogether warmly. Wiley hadn't written in weeks. As far as Mallory knew, he was still with Moonbeam on the farm in Massachusetts. How did it happen, she asked herself yet again, that people she loved kept disappearing on her?

She shoved the thought aside and went to work, struggling though James Joyce's *Dubliners* for her English course, and when her brain gave up on that, making notes from *All the President's Men* for an essay on the Watergate scandal. By eight-thirty, Mallory decided it was useless to pretend she was going to get any more work done. She was wondering whether it was too early to go to bed and put the bleak day behind her, when there was a knock on the door. "Who is it?" she called, one hand on the chain bolt.

"Drew."

She opened the door and peered out. "Hi. What are you doing here?"

He nodded toward a huge plastic picnic cooler he held by the handles. "I brought you dinner."

"I already ate," she said, glancing over to her little kitchen counter, relieved to see that she had tossed the empty ravioli can in the trash.

"Well, dessert, then. Can I come in? This thing is heavy."

"I guess." She stepped back reluctantly to let him pass. When she shut the door and turned around, he had pushed aside books and deposited the cooler on the card table that served as her dining area and desk. She saw his eyes glance around the room—a stump-footed L with a tiny kitchen in the short end, and a bed-sitting area along its longer side. A bathroom the size of a closet opened off one wall.

Even if she'd planned to entertain, picking up her clutter wouldn't have done much to improve the place, Mallory thought, embarrassed to have the rich man's kid see where she lived. Her furniture consisted of one twin bed that doubled as a couch, and a card table and two folding chairs. A fifties-vintage veneered step table held her cassette player and tapes.

On the dresser next to the bed, the laminated surface was lifting away in one corner. A goo,enecked floor lamp arched over the bed, and the only other light in the place was a cheap ceiling globe in the kitchen area, whose tiny stove and fridge looked like Salvation Army rejects. Cracked green linoleum covered the floor, although Mallory had splurged at K mart on a large oval rag rug to put next to her bed so she'd have something warm under her feet first thing in the morning.

"Not exactly Newport Beach, is it?" she said.

Drew smiled. "It's got something Newport Beach hasn't got."

"Ants?"

"You."

"Swell." She nodded to the hamper. "What's all this about? *Noblesse oblige?*"

"More like *noblesse* obese. There's enough food in that house to feed an underdeveloped nation."

"So you're playing Sir Bountiful. Aren't you a day early?"

"What do you mean?"

"I thought December twenty-sixth was Boxing Day, when rich lords packed up their castoffs and leftovers for the poor serfs."

He grimaced. "Is it heavy?"

"What?"

"That huge chip you're carrying around on your shoulder."

"About as heavy as your conscience. But don't bother relieving it on my behalf, rich boy. I get along just fine. I don't need your pity."

"Good, because you haven't got it. And would you stop calling me that?"

"What? Rich boy? It's true, isn't it? Get real, Drew. You can drive a clunker and come slumming around here all you want, but it doesn't change the fact that Mummy and Daddy are standing right behind you, ready to pick you up first time you stumble."

"What the hell do you know about it?"

"Nothing, believe me."

"That's right, you don't!"

"No, I don't! So why don't you just take your Goodwill hamper and go find yourself another charity case?"

"Maybe I will. God knows why I thought it would be better here."

"What do you mean, 'better'?"

"I had a lousy day, all right? I couldn't wait to get out of that house, and all I could think of was that I wanted to be with you. Call me stupid, but I thought we felt good together last night."

"What happened at your folks' place?"

"What do *you* care?"

Mallory unclenched fists that she couldn't remember clenching and her shoulders slumped as she exhaled. "I'm a sucker for a hard-luck story. Come on, Drew, what happened?"

"Nothing that hasn't happened a hundred times before. They try to run my life, and I feel like I'm drowning in quicksand every time I go there." He punched his fist into the plastic cooler, then winced. "Dammit!"

"What *is* it?"

He looked at her, his expression miserable. "My father found out about the senate internship thing."

"Uh-oh. What did he say?"

"In a nutshell? NFW—no fucking way."

"Can he stop you from doing it, if they approve your application?"

"I told you last night—one phone call to Senator Redman, and I'm dead in the water. Game over."

Mallory shook her head. "I'm sorry. Maybe life as Richie Rich isn't all it's cracked up to be. I know how much you wanted that internship. And thanks for thinking of me," she added, nodding at the hamper. "I didn't mean to be such a witch, but that's me—Miss Shoot From the Lip and Think Later."

"Aw, you're okay, Minnesota." He reached out and traced her cheek with his finger. "How are you?"

"Well, to be honest, I guess I didn't have such a great day, either."

"I have an idea."

"What's that?"

"Let's declare today officially over and start fresh."

"You're on. Good morning."

"Good morning. Think I could have a kiss to start the day off right?"

Mallory smiled. "I think that could be arranged."

Drew put his hands on her shoulders and they kissed, lightly at first, playfully. Then his arms went around her and he tightened his grip. Mallory felt his neediness becoming intense, but before she could decide how she felt about that, her stomach interrupted any thought of passion with a long, noisy growl. They were laughing even before their lips and bodies separated. "Well," she said, nodding at the cooler, "maybe we *could* explore that Care package of yours just a little."

"I could go for a snack, myself," Drew agreed. He opened the lid and withdrew a bottle that was lying across the top of the well-packed cooler. "I swiped this from my father's wine cellar. Chevalier-Montrachet 1966, one of his favorites. He'll be really ticked off when he notices a bottle missing."

She laughed. "Good move, but expensive wine's wasted on me. I wouldn't know Chevalier-whatever from Thunderbird."

"Well, think of this as your first oenology lesson. Got a corkscrew?"

"There's a Swiss Army Knife here somewhere that has one, I think," Mallory said, rattling through a drawer. She found the tool and handed it to him. "My first oh-who lesson?"

"Enology, the study of wine. My father likes to think of himself as a connoisseur, but only because he figures it hides his working-class roots."

"You a snob about the working class, Beekman?"

"Not me, but my father is." Drew popped the cork on the bottle, and Mallory went in search of glasses.

"So I guess he wouldn't be too impressed by us drinking his Chevalier-whatever out of gas-station giveaways, huh?" she said, returning with two tumblers emblazoned with the Phillips 66 logo.

"Perfect." Drew poured the wine and clinked his glass against Mallory's. "Merry Christmas, Minnesota."

"Happy Boxing Day, Beekman," she corrected.

"Right. I forgot." He smiled over his glass as they drank, then turned to the cooler. "Okay, let's see what we've got here. Turkey, of course. Curried mushroom rolls, wild rice, pâté and crackers, broiled shrimp, rum balls, mince tarts, chocolate meringues, buttered nuts—"

"Get serious! There's enough food here to feed an army."

"Yeah, Consuela really outdid herself."

"Consuela? Wait—don't tell me. The cook, right?"

Drew hefted his shoulders sheepishly. "Sure as heck, my mother could never do this. I don't think she even knows how to boil water."

"Good grief. Okay, forget the turkey and the curried mushrooms. Let's cut to the chase here, boy. Dessert!"

"I'm with you."

Mallory found a plastic tray and they loaded it up with samples of all the sticky goodies Consuela had packed, then took it and their glasses over to the bed. Facing each other cross-legged, the platter between them, they settled in for a sweet feast.

"So what are you going to do?" Mallory asked after a bit, licking chocolate off her fingers.

"About what?"

"The senate internship."

"I don't know. I could call Senator Redman and throw myself on his mercy, I guess."

"Think that'll work?"

"I doubt it. My father gave a bundle to Redman's election campaign last year."

"He owns the man."

"To all intents and purposes."

"Why is your father so dead set against this thing?"

"Because I'm the heir apparent to the Beekman Development Corporation and I'm supposed to get busy learning the business."

"How long is the senate internship?"

"A year."

"Your father couldn't wait one more year for you?"

"Of course, he could, but he's afraid that once I get away from this place, I'll never come back." Drew stuck his finger through the middle of a shortbread, crumbling it. "He's right to think that."

Mallory shook her head in amazement. The Rev had been thrilled to get rid of *her,* but if she'd had Drew's cushy life, she might not have been in such a hurry to take off. "It's hard to imagine someone being so protective that he'd want to build a wall around you."

"Protective of *me?*" Drew snorted. "Hardly. It's his own interests he's worried about. My father's paranoid, doesn't trust any of his company executives. Figures they're all out to steal him blind. He just wants his own personal watchdog inside the organization, another set of eyes to spy for him."

"And that's supposed to be you?"

"That's what he thinks."

"Maybe you'll have to defy him and do what you want."

He shook his head. "You don't know my father. He's got a long arm and a long memory, and he doesn't like to lose. Unless I do what he wants, he'll make sure I'm blocked at every turn. I'd have to move to Borneo to escape his reach." Drew's chin dropped to his chest and he picked at the edge of the plastic platter.

Mallory watched the deep rise and fall of his shoulders, and knew that he was struggling to keep his anger and frustration from erupting in a way that could prove embarrassing. She reached across and brushed his forelock lightly. "It'll work out, Drew. You'll be okay, I know you will."

He looked up at her. His brown eyes seemed weary, but his mouth worked its way to a smile. "I sure like you, Minnesota."

"I like you, too."

He leaned forward and put a hand on her neck, pulling her gently toward him. His mouth was sweet and chocolaty, and as their lips and tongues tasted and explored, Mallory felt herself warming and shimmering inside.

Drew pulled away and put his glass and the tray on the floor beside the bed, then reached for her glass, too, and set that aside. Taking her by the hips, he drew her closer, lifting her legs over his and around himself, and wrapping his own legs behind her so that they were face-to-face, zipper to zipper, up tight one against the other. Mallory's arms went around him and their mouths sought each other out again, lips and tongues hungry, devouring, greedy hands exploring though clothing that soon became a frustrating barrier.

Pulling back once more, breathing hard, they looked at each other, all dusky eyes and bruised lips, and Mallory felt Drew's hands move to the bottom of the navy sweater Diana had sent. She hesitated for only a second, then raised her arms and let him lift it off. He tossed it aside, and as his hands and mouth bent to her breasts, Mallory held his head, arching her back, eyes closed, losing herself in his touch.

When he grew warm from his exertions, Drew lifted his head and pulled his own sweater off, then leaned forward, pushing her gently back on the bed. His legs slipped out from under her and he followed her down, draping himself over her. Mallory hugged him, bare torso to bare torso, and wrapped her blue-jeaned legs around his. She felt the steel of his zipper pressing into her, hard and insistent as they kissed deeper and deeper, rocking together. Then Drew's mouth moved to her neck, her shoulders, her clavicle, her breasts, pausing to suckle and caress.

When his hands traveled to the snap of her jeans, it popped without resistance. The slow slide of her zipper made her ache inside, and when he rose to his knees to tug her jeans off, she gave them up willingly. Mallory sat up, too, and went to work on his belt buckle, lips and tongue tracing a line down from his navel as her fingers worked feverishly, slipping catch from notch, leather from clasp and button from hole on his pants. As she opened them wide and pushed them down over his hips, he pressed himself against her, holding her head in his hands.

"Oh, Mallory. Please, yes," he groaned. And then, "No, wait!"

He bounced backward, whipping off his pants and shorts with one swift movement, then yanked down the bed covers underneath her, and positioned her on the pillow. Her panties were off in a flash, and Drew lay himself on top of her, spreading her legs with his knees as he placed himself to enter. At the moment he did, Mallory stiffened. He opened his eyes and looked down, his expression confused. "Mallory?"

"It's okay," she whispered. "Please, do it."

He pushed himself against her tightness and began to rock. After a while, she felt herself relax and open to him. She held him close as he moved, slowly at first, then faster and faster, his breath hot on her neck. And at the second that he shuddered, it occurred to Mallory that it had taken six months, and another man, to finish what Gunnar Anderson had started that night at the Two Loons Motel.

Drew collapsed against her, spent. She held him close, stroking his hair, kissing him gently when he turned his face to hers. Mallory reached down and pulled a blanket over them, and they lay intertwined, drifting slowly into sleep. They awoke again several times during the night, but if the bed was narrow, they were never far enough apart to be in any danger of falling off. The ever-present ants feasted on the crumbs of the dessert tray left on the floor next to the bed, but neither Mallory nor Drew noticed or cared.

Paris, France
January 15, 1980

There were so many more things he wished he could have shown Diana, Marcus thought. So many things he wished he could say to her. But he'd made up his mind. Once the Orlando Yago exhibit was over, he wouldn't see her again. For now, he would be friendly but businesslike, then bid her farewell and good luck as soon as he could hustle her out of his gallery and out of his life.

In the meantime, however, there was one last thing he wanted to do for her. Of the hundreds of her posters he'd had plastered around the city, he'd made sure that a good number were located in and around the Gare de Lyon, where Diana would be returning by train from her vacation in the south. They would be the first thing she'd see as soon as she arrived.

Orlando Yago flew in from Madrid on January fourteenth, and the two of them were uncrating sculptures the next morning when Diana showed up at the gallery. Marcus had his back to the door when the electronic tone sounded, announcing an entry. He saw the young Spaniard look over his head toward the door and freeze, transfixed. Marcus knew it was her. He'd been steeling himself for this moment, but nothing could have prepared him for the change he saw when he turned around.

It was still Diana, of course, with her flowing hair and cape, and those dark eyes he could have tumbled into. But these cherished features aside, this person at the door was nothing at all like the timid young thing who had cowered under the eaves across the road that first time she had come to the gallery, or the fevered, pale recluse who had left Paris a few weeks earlier. Her skin had taken on a tanned and rosy hue. A new, copper-colored silk scarf around her neck brought out the warmth in her eyes and the auburn highlights in her hair, which shone with good health.

And the way she stood there! Marcus thought—confidently, one hand on the door, meeting his gaze openly and directly, a broad smile on her face. He'd said goodbye to a girl before Christmas and a woman had come back. Diana had had a Riviera romance, he decided. It was the only explanation for such a change.

"Well, look at you," he said, finding his voice at last. "You look magnificent!"

"Thank you," Diana said, closing the door and striding over to him. Before he could react, she stretched up and kissed him, once on each cheek. "So do you. Oh, Marcus! I saw the posters. They're everywhere!"

"We're having trouble keeping them up in some places, and people have been coming in to ask for copies. I'm having extras printed for sale. You'll get a royalty on those, of course." She shook her head, incredulous, and they stood face-to-face, beaming at each other like idiots until Marcus suddenly remembered the young man behind him. He stepped back. "Diana, this is Orlando Yago. Orlando, Diana Caine, the young lady who did the artwork for your exhibit posters."

Orlando came around from behind a crate, a wide smile on his face. When he reached out his hand, Diana took it for her own special, left-handed shake, but Orlando bent and put his lips to her fingers. Marcus watched Diana's color deepen beyond her tan. "I am very happy to meeting you," Orlando said in stilted English. "You are making beautiful picture for me."

Marcus was stunned. The boy was positively articulate in English. His French was actually much worse.

"I'm glad you like it," Diana said. "But it was *your* work that inspired it. Your sculptures are wonderful."

"You like? For real?"

"For real," she assured him.

He was still holding her hand, Marcus noted, annoyed. Not that Diana seemed to mind. She had turned that new, confident smile on the Spaniard and was studying him closely. Well, of course she *would* find him attractive. It hadn't escaped Marcus's notice, ever since he had met Yago at Orly Airport, that every woman in visual range seemed to zero in on him. The fellow was big and broad-shouldered, with obsidian eyes and long, almost feminine lashes that seemed incongruous with his blacksmith's frame. He wore his dark hair cropped short and his sleeves perpetually rolled back to reveal muscular, workingman arms. The large hand that held Diana's was callused and scarred, as befits a man who handles razor-sharp metals and acetylene welding torches every day.

Marcus cleared his throat, and the two young people finally seemed to remember that there was an old goat in the room. They let go of each other, but Orlando's insipid smile lingered. Marcus felt like slapping him. Careful, *mon homme*, he warned himself, there's business to be conducted here. And in any event, if these two youngsters were attracted to each other, so much the better. It would be a painless solution to this problem of how to disengage himself from Diana. Painless for everyone but him, of course.

"What are you guys doing here?" Diana asked. "Can I help?"

"We were just starting to uncrate Orlando's work and reconcile the shipment against the catalog," Marcus said. "If you'd like, you could sit over there with this list and note each piece as it comes out."

Diana nodded and he handed her a clipboard. She settled herself on a chair off to the side while Marcus and Orlando went back to prying open wooden crates with a crowbar and lifting out the heavy pieces, Orlando identifying each one for Diana to check off against the inventory. After forty-five minutes, Marcus was disgusted to note that the burly Spaniard showed not a single glistening of sweat on his forehead, while he himself felt as if he were dying. "Done," he breathed gratefully when the last crate was emptied. "Time for lunch."

While Orlando was off washing his hands, Marcus had another thought. "I really should stay behind, Diana. I have phone calls to make and some papers to go over. Would you mind taking Orlando to lunch?"

"Let me help, so you can come, too."

"No, it's business I have to handle myself. You run along, though. There's nothing more to be done here today. Orlando's never been in Paris before. Perhaps you could show him around, take him to some museums over the next few days. I won't have any time to do it, and frankly, I find that artists get underfoot before an opening."

"But—"

"It would be a big help, and the distraction might keep him from becoming too nervous before Friday's opening. Please? Could I count on you?"

She sighed. "I suppose, if you're sure there's nothing I can do here."

"I'm sure."

When Orlando came back and was told of the plan, he broke into a very wide smile indeed.

Los Angeles, California
January 15, 1980

New Year's had come and gone, with Mallory and Drew wrapped in a haze of physical heat that continued unabated through January. When they weren't attending classes at their separate colleges, they spent their time—especially their night-times—together. Over the snide grumbling of other wait-resses, Drew arranged her shifts at Truffles so that they worked the same hours, and when they got off, they usually retreated to his more comfortable digs in Westwood Village to eat, study and make love. He had the second floor of a small apartment block, and if his furnishings were also on the shabby side, *these* castoffs, like the faded Chinese carpet and the chipped English china, had an obvious pedigree.

By mid-January, when it became clear that they were spending more nights together than apart, Drew began to urge Mallory to move in with him. "You'll live rent-free," he said one day as they lay sprawled across his big double bed. "And it'll mean a lot less running around for both of us."

"My place is closer to work and to my classes," she argued.

"I know, but it's not like you aren't commuting from here most of the time, anyway. I'd move, but your place is too small for two people."

"It's too grungy, you mean."

"That's *not* what I mean."

"Well," she said, rubbing his back, "you *are* a good sport about it when we squeeze into my little bed."

He rolled over and pulled her on top of him, grinning. "I like squeezing in with you. What do you say? Will you give your landlord notice?"

But Mallory resisted, and not just on the question of the apartment. As much comfort as she took from being in Drew's arms—took and *gave*—there were large parts of who she was and what she felt that she held back from him. When he asked about her childhood, she told him about Ferry Falls and being adopted, and about the difficult relationship she'd had with the Rev, but left vague the details of her life before Minnesota and her natural parents' death—the where and the when and the how. She claimed to have little memory of it. She told Drew about her sister and how she missed her, and about Diana's handicap and the growing confidence Mallory sensed in her letters from Paris. But as to the reason for Diana's paralysis, Mallory lied, and said there had been some problem at birth.

When she met Drew's UCLA friends, she made an effort to be friendly and fit in, and not to relive the story of Gunnar and the rat packers. She bought new clothes, imitating the styles she saw around her, and struggled to keep her cynical tongue under control, smiling until her teeth dried out.

But for all that, Mallory felt instinctively that she and Drew would not be together long. They were citizens of different galaxies, and if those two galaxies had temporarily collided by some quirk of fate, they were bound to go their separate ways sooner or later. Probably sooner, if her experience to date was any lesson.

There was the matter of Drew's family, of course, and what they would think of his relationship with this girl without family or connections. The question was postponed, however, because Drew had avoided them since the Christmas blowup with his father over the senate internship. "I'm just going to let it ride," he told Mallory. "If Redman wants to turn me down, he'll have to say so. I'm not going to make it easy for him by withdrawing my application."

"What about your father?"

"I'm not going to make it easy for *him,* either. Let him sweat."

And so, they drifted along.

Paris, France
January 18, 1980

"I think you should put this young Spaniard on the next flight out of town, Marcus," Jean Grenier said, taking a long pull from his glass of white wine. He and Marcus were standing in a corner of the gallery, watching the crowd, dwindling at last, that had packed Orlando Yago's opening.

"Why is that?" Marcus asked.

"Because if you're not careful, he's going to steal the beautiful Diana right out from under your nose."

Marcus turned to the two young people across the room. They were perched side by side on stools, next to a high table. The Spaniard was dressed in a flowing white shirt and tight black pants, like some overendowed matador. Diana was wearing a simple, calf-length dress of burgundy velvet. Orlando beamed as she autographed yet another exhibit poster for an enthusiastic patron, and from the glow on his face, the sculptor seemed as proud of her as of the fact that more than half the sculptures in the exhibit had sold in the last four hours. Given the expressions of interest from other potential buyers, Marcus suspected that few, if any, of Yago's pieces would be returning to Spain with him when the show was over. Grenier could be right, though. In addition to what he would earn from the sales, Orlando might end up taking back the biggest prize of all—Diana.

It was his own doing, of course, Marcus thought. He had pushed them together, and the two had been inseparable for days, popping in and out of the gallery between excursions to the Louvre, Diana's beloved Jeu de Paume, and other museums and sights of Paris. A few hours earlier, just before the opening, Marcus had slipped up to his office to get his tie and had walked in on them, Diana almost invisible inside the big Spaniard's embrace as they kissed. He'd backed out of the room, unnoticed. When the couple had come downstairs a few minutes later, they were flushed and altogether too chatty, as if sexual tension could be camouflaged under a barrage of words.

"They seem to have become close," Marcus said to Grenier, his voice as neutral as he could muster.

"And? What are you going to do about it?"

"Nothing. Why would I? Diana is a twenty-one-year-old woman. She doesn't require a chaperon."

"Yes, she *is* a woman—not at all the timid young girl who came into my class only a few months back. It's quite an astonishing transformation. You are a veritable Pygmalion, Marcus." Grenier turned to his friend, one eyebrow arched. "But now you're letting her slip through your fingers. For a supposedly brilliant art dealer, you really are an idiot in matters of love, you know."

"You have an overactive imagination, old friend. In any event, I happen to know exactly what I'm doing. Are you coming to dinner with us?" Marcus asked, changing the subject.

"You're buying?"

"Yes. I promised them a celebratory meal at La Coupole. The Lennoxes, Diana's friends, are coming, as well."

"Well, I won't pass up a good meal, but are you sure you need one more person there?"

"Actually, I'd be grateful for a familiar face. I'd like to get this night over as quickly as possible and leave the young lovers to their own devices. I need to get things back to normal around here."

Diana leaned her head against the back of the banquette at La Coupole, feeling full after a huge dinner, weary after the long day and a little fluffed after two glasses of wine. But looking around the table at these people—none of whom, even the Lennoxes, she'd known well until recently—she felt happier than she ever had in her life.

Orlando, his big frame wedged into the bench beside her, had a permanent grin fixed to his face. His Paris debut had been a smash, and he was assured of work and sales for a long time. His arm was draped along the back of the seat behind her, and he said little as the conversation swirled around him. His limited French and English appeared to be exhausted, but he seemed content enough, just basking in the glow of success. He had scarcely left Diana's side the entire day, clinging to her arm if she made any move away from him. "Stay, Diana. I am so nervous, I have no words to say to these people."

She knew it was only half the reason he wanted her close by, but she found it odd, all the same, to find herself cast in the role of protector of *anyone*, much less this good-looking, talented man. She kept watching for Marcus, thinking it was really *his* job to steer Orlando through the opening crowds, but Marcus always seemed engaged in some negotiation or another. Once, she'd caught him watching her, but he had just shot her a smile and a nod of encouragement across the room. Well, she'd thought, if translating for Orlando helped Marcus get through the busy opening, she was glad to do it, for both their sakes.

She looked over at him now, sitting on the opposite side of the table between Mary and Doug Lennox. They'd been having an animated discussion about the cathedrals of Paris, but Marcus seemed tired. Even under the soft lights of the restaurant, the lines around his eyes showed deeper than usual, and his smile appeared strained, as it had all day. That wasn't so surprising, she thought guiltily. It had been a stressful period for all of them—Marcus, Orlando and herself.

Marcus's friend, Jean Grenier, had come along for dinner, as well, but his chair had been empty for the past fifteen minutes. He had toddled off to the men's room before coffee was served, and by the weave in his walk, Diana guessed that her old professor had done a little too much celebrating.

Their waiter appeared at the table and returned Marcus's charge card, pausing to whisper in his ear. When the man left, Marcus rose from his seat. "It's been a wonderful day and a wonderful evening," he said, "but apparently, Grenier has fallen asleep in the loo. I'm afraid I'm going to have to take my leave of you all to drive him home. Orlando, my friend, *félici-*

tations once again. I'll talk to you tomorrow. Diana—'' He paused. ''Thank you for a wonderful poster and a wonderful collaboration,'' he said finally, looking more uncomfortable than Diana would have ever guessed he could.

Well, she thought, that certainly sounded like goodbye. Under the circumstances, she wasn't sure what she could do about it, and so she nodded, her gaze dropping uncomfortably to her lap.

''I think we'll be off, too,'' Bishop Lennox said, pushing back his chair. ''This was delightful, but these old bones of mine are done in. Are you about ready to go, Diana?''

She looked up again, and felt Orlando watching her closely. ''Actually, I'm not,'' she said, surprising herself. ''I don't think I want this day to end. You two go on home, though. Don't wait up. I have my key.''

She wasn't the only person she had surprised, Diana noted, watching unanimous raised eyebrows around the table, then a recovering flurry of farewells as everyone bustled to respect the wishes of this new, more forceful young woman in their midst. My gosh, she thought, amused, wouldn't Mallory be proud? Diana really *is* a big girl, after all. She had a chance, she realized, to change her life. Tonight she was determined to do it.

When the others had all gone, Orlando reached over and took her hand. ''I am happy you stayed,'' he said. ''What now, Diana?''

She looked up at his handsome, hopeful face and took a deep breath, for courage. ''I'd like to start with a walk, Orlando.''

24

Marcus stood at a window of his darkened town house, watching a full moon rise above the mansard-roofed buildings across the road. The orb was brilliant against the blue-black sky. But its glow, of course, was only the sun's reflected glory. The lunar landscape, so stunning with its peaks and craters, was actually cold and desolate—as bleak as his own life would be, now that he could no longer bask in Diana's light and warmth.

He looked down the quiet, cobbled roadway. Diana was out there somewhere. With Orlando. In his arms, probably. Marcus leaned against the cool, leaded glass, feeling sick and weary as his mind wandered into places it had no business going, imagining Diana in Yago's hotel room, her body being worked and transformed by his sculptor's hands. This is madness to torture yourself this way, he thought. You let it happen. You *made* it happen. Now, live with it!

He turned away from the window, switching on a lamp, and the room was bathed in its soft yellow glow. His was a crowded, comfortable, overstuffed house, filled with eighteenth- and nineteenth-century antiques that had belonged to generations of Desloges from both his and Marie-France's branches of the family. They had been bankers and shippers and merchants once, wealthy and prominent in their day. But somehow, the clan had winnowed itself down, until only he and his distant cousin remained. Now Marie-France was gone, and Marcus was the last of the line.

The high-ceilinged walls of the town house were double-banked with paintings, many of them old, some of them newer acquisitions. Growing up with his family's collection of nine-teenth-century French oils had sparked Marcus's love of art.

The newer works on his walls, by artists he had supported and developed over his twenty-odd years as a dealer, would be the only Desloges legacy left when he was gone.

His gaze fell to a corner of the room, where a sculpture by Orlando Yago stood on a marble pedestal. It was the first one he had bought, five years earlier in Madrid. Nearby, on a table, was a framed pencil sketch of a white-haired man, seen from behind, leaning wearily on the bar of a *brasserie,* his face reflected in a mirror before him. Marcus stared at the drawing for a moment, then sighed, forcing himself to move.

Picking up his coat from where he had thrown it over a chair, he returned to the front hall to hang it, looking for any activity that would absorb his restless energy. Dreading the long night ahead, his thoughts turned to the alcohol-induced slumber in which he had left Grenier in his own bed, forty minutes earlier. He was just heading to the liquor cabinet, and the very old bottle of cognac that he had been saving for some appropriate celebration or disaster, when the buzzer on the front door sounded. Frowning, he retraced his steps and opened the door. And there she was.

"Diana! What are you doing here?" Marcus peered over her head. "Where is Orlando?"

"Cruising the clubs of the Boul-Mich is my guess. May I come in?"

"Yes, of course." He stepped back to let her pass, checked the street once more, then closed the door. When he turned around, she was standing in her self-protective stance, looking small and nervous. Marcus felt a flash of anger. "What happened? What did he do?"

"Nothing," Diana assured him. "He didn't do anything, Marcus. We went for a walk after the rest of you left, and then I came here."

"Did you quarrel?"

"No, we simply talked. I thought it was only fair. And of course, I needed to give you time to get Jean Grenier home. I've actually been waiting across the street for about ten minutes. I didn't see your car come in, but I just saw your lights go on."

"I was—" Never mind, Marcus thought. How could he explain why he'd been standing in the dark? "Diana, what's go-

ing on? Why did you come here? Do you need a ride home?''
She had never been to his house before, he suddenly realized.
It hadn't even occurred to him that she knew where he lived,
but of course, his home address was on a card he'd once given
her, and the place wasn't hard to find.

"We need to talk, Marcus. Are you going to make me stand
in an entry hall to do it?"

"I'm sorry," he said, flustered. "Come in." He led her into
the sitting room. He should offer to take her cape, but common
sense, he was happy to note, was getting the better of
courtesy or desire. He had no idea what had brought her here,
but she couldn't stay, that much was sure. Not with the state of
mind *he* was in.

She pivoted in the center of the room, turning round and
round, her eyes wide as they took in the work on the walls.
"How wonderful," she said softly. "All these paintings!"

Marcus frowned, and he stepped forward and placed his
hands firmly on her shoulders. "Diana, stop. How much have
you had to drink tonight?"

"Enough for courage. Not so much that I don't know why
I'm here."

"Which is?"

"To tell you I love you."

He dropped his hands and pulled away. "Don't say that."

"Why not?"

"Because. What about Orlando?"

"What about him?"

Marcus exhaled heavily, and ran his hands through his thick,
white thatch. "I walked in on the two of you in my office this
afternoon. I didn't mean to spy. Neither of you noticed—you
were rather preoccupied at the time—and I left right away."

"Oh, I see. He was kissing me, was he?"

"You were kissing *him,* too, as I recall."

"Maybe I was. It's hard to tell, though, don't you think? I
mean, two sets of lips touch, but who knows who's really doing
the kissing?"

"Are you *sure* you're not drunk?"

"I'm sure. Orlando only kissed me once in your office,
though. It took me by surprise. It might have gone on a little

longer than it should. I didn't want to hurt his feelings, you see. And maybe," Diana added sheepishly, "I was curious, too. But then I asked him not to do it again. You walked out too soon, or you would know that."

"What happened after we left you tonight at La Coupole?"

"I told you. We went for a walk on the Boulevard St-Michel, he said some nice things to me, I told him I was flattered, but I was already in love with someone else. Then I left."

"How did he react?"

"He seemed disappointed at first, but then he noticed that he was getting a lot of attention from some girls in a nearby café. That seems to happen a lot with Orlando, have you noticed?"

Marcus smiled, in spite of himself. "I've noticed."

"Well, there you go. Somehow, I can't imagine he was alone for long after I left."

He nodded. "All right. Let me get my coat and I'll drive you home."

"Why?"

"Because it's not a good idea for you to be here."

"Excuse me? Did you not hear what I said a while back— *twice*, if I'm not mistaken? About being in love with you? Doesn't that mean anything?"

"Oh, Diana." He shook his head wearily. "It means a great deal, but it doesn't make any sense. This, what you're thinking—you and me—it can't happen."

"Why not?"

"Because it wouldn't be right. I'm too old for you. My *gallery* is older than you are!"

"I don't see your point."

"I'm not what you need, not what you deserve. You are a beautiful, warm, brilliant young woman, and you deserve some equally wonderful young man to share a long, happy life with. I am not that man."

"You don't feel the same way about me?"

"That's not the issue here."

"Then what is?"

"I'm no good for you. I'm a middle-aged, bad-tempered, jaded, cynical man. I am not what you want."

"Don't!"

"Don't what?"

"Don't do that—telling me what I want, and what I need, and what I should do. Honestly, Marcus! For as long as I can remember, people have been telling me what to do—my parents, my sister, the Lennoxes. And now you. It's so patronizing, and I refuse to put up with it anymore! I *know* what I want. And as for *you,* you are the least jaded, cynical or bad-tempered man I've ever known." She waved her good arm at the paintings around them. "Look at these. Look at your gallery, and all the unknown artists like Orlando and me that you've helped. That's not the work of a cynic. And the patience you showed Orlando, waiting for five years until he was ready to do what he did today. Your patience with me, when I kept trying and failing to come up with an idea for the poster."

"I loved working with you," he said quietly.

She reached out a hand to his cheek. "So did I. Even if I hadn't fallen *in* love with you, I still would have loved it."

"And I'm glad, Diana. But I still think you're confused about what you're feeling for me. You only *think* you're in love, but one day, you'll see—"

Her face shifted from softness to stone in an instant. "How dare you!"

"What?"

"How dare you try to tell me what I'm feeling? Who do you think you are? Who do you think *I* am? Some feebleminded child? I've got news for you, Marcus Desloges—my arm may not work, but my brain works just fine, and I know who I am and what I'm feeling."

"I didn't mean—"

"I love you. If you can't handle that, tough. But you know what? I think you love me, too. Maybe I'm wrong—I don't have much experience in these things, it's true. If I *am* wrong, all you have to do is say so and I won't bother you anymore. But don't bloody tell *me* what *I* feel!"

"Diana—"

"Just say it, Marcus. Say, 'Diana, I don't love you and I want you to leave.' How hard can it be?"

"I—"

"*Say* it." She was pleading now.

A few words. That was all he needed to say. She filled his field of vision, and he was conscious of nothing but her eyes, her mouth and the hopelessly one-sided war going on inside him. "I can't," he whispered.

She was on him in an instant. He wrapped her tightly in his arms and kissed her, over and over, on her lips, her cheeks, her eyes, her forehead, and then her mouth again. When his tongue slipped between her lips and teeth, she gasped, then softened against him as she eagerly joined in.

He loosened his grip so that he could reach inside her woolen cape. He felt her left hand come up between them and release the catch at the throat. As the cape slipped to the floor, he wrapped his hands around her waist, sliding them over the soft velvet of her dress to the small of her back, pulling her in tighter against himself, stroking the nap of the velvet. Her left hand was around his waist, and the fingers of her right hand also reached out for him, grasping the fabric of his trousers and stroking his thigh with tiny flutters that sent a shiver through his body.

Marcus took her head in his hands, burying his fingers in those curls he had wanted to touch for so long. He kissed her once more, then held her tight, lips at her ear. "I do love you, Diana. I have from the very beginning. I don't want you to leave, but I don't want to hurt you, either."

She pulled her head back and looked at him. "You could never hurt me, Marcus. Every minute we're together is a gift. Don't you know that?" She took his hand and placed it on her breast. "You've taught me so much already. Now, teach me one more thing."

"Are you sure?"

"Oh, yes! Absolutely sure. Please."

When Marcus awoke the next morning and went to the window to look out, it occurred to him that he couldn't remember the last time he had seen a sunrise. Not that he could actually see the sun itself, which was hidden behind the buildings to the east. But overhead, the black roof of the sky was retracting, trailing an edge of navy blue that drifted into violet. Here and there, between the buildings, he saw flashes of crimson and orange. This was true light, he thought, not the moon's pale reflection, and he had missed it for far too long.

He heard a soft stirring behind him and turned to the rumpled bed, where a lithe form under a tumble of deep auburn curls rolled over, opening beautiful dark eyes. "Hi," Diana murmured sleepily.

"Hi."

"What are you doing?"

"Watching the sun come up. The sky is beautiful."

"It looks good from here, too." She patted the mattress and smiled. "Come and see."

Marcus slipped in next to her and scooped her into his arms, burying his nose in the dusky softness of her hair as her lips explored the hollow of his throat.

There was a lot to be said for sunrises, he decided.

25

Mallory was in her apartment after class one day, retrieving her mail and a change of clothes, when Drew swung by to drive her to work. Looking up as he walked in, she waved an envelope, still stunned by what she had found in it. "You'll never guess what I got in the mail today, and what I found out."

"What?"

"My sister got married!"

"Hey, that's great. Isn't it?"

"Yeah, I guess. I don't know."

"Who'd she marry?"

"This guy named Marcus she's been writing about. The art dealer. Look, she sent a picture."

Drew came and sat on the bed next to her, peering over her shoulder at the photo. "Older guy. Your sister's really pretty," he added. "She has your eyes."

"That's about the only similarity between us. She's beautiful, and talented, to boot. He looks nice, I guess, but I still can't believe it."

Drew put an arm around her shoulders. "Are you okay about this?"

"I don't know. I'm still in shock. I suppose so, if it makes Diana happy. But it means she's not coming home."

"You could visit."

"It's not the same. As a matter of fact, though, they sent a plane ticket." Mallory showed him an Air France folder.

"They've asked me to go over there during spring break. Diana said she and Marcus were going to wait to get married until I was there, but it got a little awkward for them to be together, seeing as how she's been staying with Bishop Lennox and his wife. They didn't want to make the Lennoxes uncomfortable, so they decided to do it right away. They've postponed the wedding party until I come."

"I wonder what the bishop thought about it all."

"I got a letter from him, too," Mallory said. "He said he and his wife were a little surprised by the way things developed, but they like Marcus, so I guess it's all right. I trust the bishop's judgment and if he says this is good for Diana and *she's* happy, then I guess I'm happy for her, too."

"So how come you look like you're ready to cry?" Drew asked gently.

That was all Mallory needed to push her over the edge. Intense memories came rushing in—images of herself and Diana playing together as children. Diana being shot through the air in a blast of fire and heat, her arm caught by the heavy front door. Mallory gripping hospital-bed rails, screaming as they tried to pull her away. Or standing, fists up, in front of Diana in the Ferry Falls Elementary School yard, daring bullies to open their mouths *just once more* about her sister's arm. "I'm being selfish, that's all," she blubbered. "I wanted her to be with me!"

Drew held her close and they rocked. "I know, I know," he soothed. "It's hard."

"She's the only family I have."

"You've got me, for what it's worth."

"Oh, Drew, I'm glad you're here, but . . ."

"Mallory? Maybe *we* should get married. What do you think? You want to do that?"

She froze, then sat up, wiping her face. "No, Drew," she said when she could find her voice again. "Thanks for asking, but I don't think it's a good idea."

"Why not?"

"Just . . . I don't know. Because."

"Are you sure? We could, you know."

Mallory shook her head and mustered a halfhearted smile. "I'm sure. You're sweet to offer, but I'm happy with the way things are right now." She took a deep breath, then gathered the letters and ticket. "We'd better get going or we'll be late for work. Just give me a minute to change."

Drew stretched out on the bed, watching while she put away the letters and pulled on her Truffles uniform. "Speaking of weddings," he said, "my mother phoned this afternoon."

"What about?"

"My sister's wedding."

Mallory turned her back to him, not wanting her face to give away the discomfort she felt every time this subject arose. She'd already dodged the engagement party, and in the end Drew, too, had begged off because he'd come down with a brief, but welcome, case of flu. The wedding itself was unavoidable, however, not least because Drew was to be one of the ushers.

"I told her I was bringing you."

"Oh, Drew. We talked about this."

"And you said you'd go if I *really* wanted you to. Well, I do."

"I still think you should go without me. You'll be tied up with wedding-party duties. You don't need me there."

"I *do*. I don't want to go without you." He slipped off the bed and fell to his knees on the floor, clasping his hands in front of him. "Plee-eeze, Mallory! Don't throw me to those wolves all alone!"

She groaned, then sighed deeply. "Okay, already. I'll go."

Drew leaped to his feet and picked her up in an exuberant hug. "All right, Minnesota! That's my girl."

Newport Beach, California
February 2, 1980

Andrew George Beekman was Scottish-born, but he never set out to deliberately fulfill a cultural stereotype. He would have been parsimonious whatever his nationality. His deprived youth and long, grueling climb to wealth and position had guaranteed that he'd eschew extravagance and watch the outflow of every nickel for fear that his funds—the source of his status—

might slip away, leaving him destitute and powerless once more. When it came to the wedding of his only daughter, therefore, Beekman was torn between a desire to do the expected thing for someone of his wealth and standing, and a deep-seated distrust of nonproductive uses of that wealth.

Asa Mulvey Beekman operated under no such constraints, however. Her daughter's wedding would be the highlight of the Newport Beach winter calendar. Even the date had been chosen to coincide with a slow period in the social scene, when there would be few other goings-on to compete with the showy spectacle that she set out to stage. The Newport Harbor Yacht Club had been selected as the venue for the Ariel Beekman–Jon Houghton nuptials, to which four hundred of the families' very closest friends were invited.

The night of the event, Beekman stood watching couples move around the dance floor and decided Asa had outdone herself. Despite the huge outlay of capital he had been obliged to make, he was satisfied that no one could find fault with even the smallest detail of the affair—from the catered gourmet menu, elaborate ice sculptures and huge sprays of imported orchids on the tables, to Asa's Halston original and his daughter's silk, seed-pearl-encrusted wedding gown with its twelve-foot train, also by the same designer. And of course, Beekman thought happily, it was the last expense he would entail in regard to his daughter. She was Jon Houghton's responsibility now, and *he* could deal with Ariel's spoiled whims and pained sulks when she thought she was being denied her due.

Beekman caught sight of his son, Drew, and the girl he had brought to the wedding, wrapped in each other's arms, swaying slowly to the music. Not for the first time that evening, he studied them closely. She was new, someone Drew had never brought around before, this girl with tumbled, fair hair and dark, mahogany eyes, dressed in a skimpy, peach-colored dress. "Polyester," Asa had sniffed, standing beside her husband a while earlier and watching Drew introduce the girl to family friends.

"I think she looks fine," Beekman said. "And obviously, so does our son. They seem quite taken with each other."

"Hmmph! Who *is* she? No one knows anything about her. Did you get a chance to ask about her people?"

"No."

"Neither did I. I tried at one point, but then there were well-wishers coming up, and the photographer, and the caterers, and all." Asa waved her diamond-braceleted wrist in frustration. "Really, Andrew, she doesn't seem his type, does she?"

"Stop fussing," Beekman told his wife. "I'm sure she's just a passing fancy. He'll be settling down soon enough."

Asa turned her steel-blue stare on him. "What about this senate business? Is it all taken care of?"

"Actually, it looks like the problem might go away of its own accord."

"How's that?"

"Jim Redman called a couple of days ago and said that the internships have been put on hold. Everyone in Washington is preoccupied with the hostage crisis, which is why he couldn't get out for Ariel's wedding."

Three months earlier, Iranian fundamentalists had seized the American Embassy in Tehran and were holding fifty hostages captive there. What had been expected to be a short crisis had turned into a long, frustrating siege with no end in sight.

"Redman says they may not even get around to organizing the senate-interns program this year," Beekman added.

"Well, that's a relief," Asa said. She waved irritably in the direction of their son. "Now, if we could just lose this—this *person,* we might find as good a match for Drew as we did for Ariel."

Beekman rolled his eyes. "Let's try for someone a little brighter than Jon Houghton, shall we? In the meantime, there's no harm in letting the boy have his fun."

Despite his dismissive words, Andrew Beekman hadn't been able to take his eyes off his son's new girlfriend. There was something about her, something he couldn't quite put his finger on but which stirred a profound sense of unease deep in his gut. He watched the young couple now, moving slowly across the floor. As they passed one of the linen-draped, circular dining tables, Drew stopped, reached over to the centerpiece and withdrew an orchid. He held it out to her and she took it, her dark eyes dropping as she brought the blood red trumpet to her nose and inhaled deeply. Then she looked up again and gave Drew a warm smile.

Beekman's blood turned to ice. That was it! He knew now what it was about her that had been bothering him all night.

He felt his chest tighten, and his breathing became so constricted that he thought he might be having a heart attack. He slumped into a nearby chair and tore his eyes away from the girl, determined to get himself under control before people noticed something was amiss. DeeDee Cunningham, his wife's best friend, was sitting in the next chair, and she turned to him and began chattering. He smiled and nodded, forcing himself to look at her, although what she was blathering on about he couldn't have said.

After several minutes, Beekman withdrew a handkerchief and passed it over his damp forehead. When he was done, he folded it again, square over square, slowly and deliberately. He tucked it back in the inside breast pocket of his tuxedo, patting his chest to be sure that there was no bulge showing. Then, and only then, did he allow himself to look up once more to seek out Drew and the girl. They were nowhere in sight.

Excusing himself from DeeDee Cunningham, Beekman circumnavigated the room, his eyes roaming even as he stopped to shake hands and accept congratulations from various wedding guests. When he reached the entrance to the hall and still hadn't located them, he glanced at his watch, then stepped outside to look for a telephone.

26

Mallory was in her apartment, drying her hair one Saturday morning, two weeks after Ariel Beekman's wedding, when she heard a knock. She dropped her towel on a chair and raked her fingers through the wet strands as she headed for the door, trying to imagine who it could be. Drew had his own key, but he was away for the weekend, skiing in Tahoe with his buddies. No ski bunny, Mallory had passed on the trip. She had a history paper to finish before she left for France the following Friday to visit Diana and Marcus, and she had also promised to fill in at Truffles for another waitress who was off sick.

When she opened the door and saw who was standing on her step, she let out a whoop. "Wiley Dixon!" She threw her arms around him and he lifted her in the air, spinning on the step. When her feet touched ground again, Mallory stepped back to look him over. "My God!" she breathed. "I can't believe you're here. Why didn't you tell me you were coming?"

He grinned his dopey, bucktoothed Wiley grin and shrugged. "I wanted to surprise you."

"Well, you did that, all right. Come on in."

He walked into the little apartment and Mallory followed, closing the door, then pausing to look him over again. He was dressed in denim, the way she always remembered him, dusty Lee jeans and jacket hanging loose on his gangly frame. But he seemed taller now, his shoulders broader. His black hair was longer, too, curling over his ears and collar, and his face had acquired new shadows and lines. The gaunt hollows under his cheeks were darkened by stubble that she never remembered him having before. Black circles ringed his eyes, as if he hadn't slept in days.

"How've you been, Mal?"

"I've been fine. What about you? I thought you were in Massachusetts. When did you get in?"

"This morning. I drove cross-country. The bike's outside."

"Same old Harley?"

"Same one. Takes a lickin', but keeps on tickin'."

"So what happened to the communal farm and Moonbeam?"

He shrugged. "It was time to move on. I've been drifting for a couple of months now, working my way west. Some sunshine you got out here."

"Unreal, isn't it? Are you hungry? Can I get you something to eat?"

"In a while, maybe." Wiley sniffed at himself and wrinkled his beaky nose. "What I *could* use is a shower."

"You can have whatever you want. Oh, Wiley! It's so good to see you." She hugged him again.

"Really?"

"You bet. I've been dying for a familiar face. This place is just too weird sometimes."

"What happened to the girl who couldn't wait to come to California?"

"Oh, she kind of faded away."

"Have you been okay, Mal?"

"Yeah, but I discovered that it's true what they say—you can't go back. You can only go forward. I'm not sure where I'm going, but I'm beginning to get used to the ride, at least."

"A little rough?"

"Yeah. I'll tell you all about it later. First, what are your plans? Are you going to stick around?"

"I'm not sure, but I brought something to show you. I sold my first story."

"No! Where?"

"Aw, just a little science-fiction magazine, but it's a start, I guess."

"Wiley, you're a real writer! I'm so proud of you. Can I see it?"

"I've got a copy in my saddlebags."

"Bring them in. You're going to stay here, aren't you?"

"I don't know."

"Where else would you go?"

"I don't want to impose."

"Wiley, this is me, Mal. How could you impose on *me?* Admittedly," she added, glancing around, "the place is small and kind of a dump, but you're welcome to stay, if you don't mind camping on a bedroll. For that matter, I'm out so much, the place would be mostly yours. And I'm leaving next Friday to visit Diana. A few days later, and you would have missed me altogether."

"You're going to Paris?"

"Just for a week. Guess what? Diana got married."

"You're kidding. Who to?"

"An art dealer. Look, here's a picture." Mallory showed him the photo Diana had sent, which she had framed and set on her dresser. "He's quite a bit older than she is, but he sounds really nice. The Lennoxes wrote and said I shouldn't worry, that Marcus has been good for Diana and is crazy about her."

"So she's not going back to Ferry Falls?"

"No, thank God."

"How did the Rev and Franny take it?"

"The Rev couldn't care less, I suspect, except that he's lost one of his handmaidens. I phoned Franny when I found out and she's pretty devastated. This came right on top of another crisis between the Rev and his parishioners. It looks like he's been retired against his will, so Franny's really feeling stressed."

"I heard about that. Is she going to visit Diana, too?"

"Are you kidding? You think the Rev's going to let her have any fun? Not a chance. Anyway," Mallory said, brightening, "what do you say? Do you want to apartment-sit while I'm away?"

"You sure?"

"Of course. My place is your place. Go get your stuff. I have to go to work in a little while—"

"You still working at that fern bar you wrote me about?" Wiley asked, heading for the door to retrieve his bags.

"Uh-huh, but just till four today. I'll get us some food for supper on the way home. Go now! Bring in your stuff."

While he was outside, Mallory picked up her towel and finished getting ready for work, feeling stunned but elated. Despite one awkward moment on the banks of the Ferry River, Wiley was still the best friend she'd ever had, and it felt awfully good to see him again. A flicker of anxiety crossed her mind as she wondered how Wiley and Drew would react to each other, but she brushed it away. Drew wasn't due back until the next night, and since they both had classes Monday, it was unlikely she would see him before Monday evening, at the earliest. She would cross that bridge when she came to it.

Mallory's arms were full of groceries when she returned to the apartment that evening. She kicked lightly at the door for Wiley to open it.

"Mal—hi," he said, stepping back.

"Hi there! I brought us some grub. Take one of these bags, would you? I'm losing my grip here."

Wiley grabbed a heavy bag and went into the little kitchen area, but as he was lifting it to the table, he tripped, and the bag fell to the floor. "Aw, jeez! Sorry." He dropped to his knees and scrambled after apples that were rolling in every direction.

"It's okay," Mallory said. But as she closed the door, a heavy, sweet odor assaulted her nostrils. "Have you been smoking dope in here?" He looked up at her, his eyes glassy, his pupils huge and staring. She sighed and shook her head. "Oh, Wiley!"

"Sorry, Mal. I was just relaxing while you were out." He gathered the last of the apples and stumbled to his feet, cradling them awkwardly in his arms. "You've got company," he added, glancing nervously toward the bed-sitting area.

"Company?" Mallory turned and then froze. "Oh, my God! Mr. Beekman! What are you doing here?"

Drew's father's expression was stony. "I came to have a chat, Miss Caine. Your friend let me in."

"Oh—well, have a seat. Wait a minute, let me put down these groceries and clear a chair for you."

"No, thank you. I won't be staying long."

"What did you want to see me about?"

"It's a private matter."

Flustered, Mallory looked at the bags in her arms. She deposited them on the table, then brushed her hands, smoothed her sweater and pushed her hair out of her eyes. She glanced at Wiley, who was swaying, his expression disoriented. She took the apples from him and put them in a bowl, then placed a hand on his shoulder. "Wiley, maybe you should get some fresh air. How about if you go and sit on the front step while Mr. Beekman and I talk? Is that okay with you?"

"Sure, Mal. That's okay. Why don't I go sit on the step?"

"Why don't you?" She led him to the door and watched as he staggered out and settled himself on the top step, leaning heavily against the railing. He was as stoned as a body could get and still remain vertical, she realized.

She sighed again and walked back into the apartment, closing the door behind her, struggling to keep her hands from shaking. What on earth was Drew's father, of all people, doing in her apartment? She glanced warily at Andrew Beekman, who seemed offended by the tacky little place, more cluttered than ever now, with Wiley's saddlebags and assorted items of clothing scattered around. "What can I do for you, Mr. Beekman?"

Beekman looked over and frowned at the door behind her. "Does my son know that fellow is living with you?"

"Wiley only arrived this morning. He's an old friend."

"I see." Beekman held up a plastic bag by one corner. It contained what looked to be a couple of joints and several pills and capsules of various hues. "Does Drew know about your drug use?"

Mallory's insides turned to jelly. "That's not mine."

"Really."

"Absolutely not."

"It was on the bed here. If it's not yours, whose is it?"

"It must—" Mallory hesitated, glancing back. "I don't know."

"You don't know," he repeated dryly. He tossed the bag on the bed. "Well, it doesn't really matter. It's in your apartment. I must tell you, I don't appreciate drugs in my building."

"*Your* building?"

"Yes. I own this apartment building."

"Since when?"

"Since five o'clock yesterday."

"You bought it?"

"That's right. Look, Miss Caine, I have other places to be, so let me get to the point. I want you out of my son's life."

Mallory reared her head. "I beg your pardon? What business is it of yours?"

"It is precisely my business. Drew is my son and heir, and he has responsibilities ahead that are incompatible with a relationship with a person such as yourself."

"'A person such as myself'? You don't even *know* me!"

"You're wrong. I know all about you. You see, Miss Caine, I had you investigated. I know who you are. I know about your parents—what they were, and how they died. I won't have that kind of scandal touching my family. Under the circumstances," he added, nodding to the bag, "I suppose it shouldn't surprise me to find drugs in your apartment."

"I told you—"

"I couldn't care less about your excuses. I also know that you yourself were constantly skirting trouble in Minnesota—no arrests, so far, but it's only a matter of time, from the look of things. I won't have you dragging down my son."

"What would you say if I told you Drew had asked me to marry him, Mr. Beekman?"

"I'd say he had been seduced by a young tramp, and that there was no bloody way!"

"You couldn't stop it."

Beekman took a step forward. "Don't you threaten *me!* You don't know to whom you speak. I certainly *do* have the power to stop you."

"Is that so? What makes you think you can control people's lives?"

"Because in the first place, as owner of this building, your lease gives me the right to evict you for cause." He pointed to the plastic bag on the bed. "There's cause. Consider yourself evicted. You have one week to clear out."

"Fine. I'll move in with Drew. I'm there more often than not, anyway."

"No, you won't."

"Why not?"

"Because Drew won't be around much longer. He's going to work in Washington."

"The internship program was cancelled."

"That's true, but I've arranged a job for him, anyway, on Senator Redman's staff."

"Drew said you didn't want him to go to Washington."

"I didn't before. Now, I think a short stint there might be good for him."

"You're *that* desperate to get him away from me?"

"I am that *determined.*"

"What if he wants me to go with him?"

"You won't go. In fact, the moment he gets back from his ski trip, you're going to tell him it's over between the two of you."

"Now, why would I do that?"

"I can think of several reasons. First, my son's job in Washington is conditional on your departure from his life."

"Drew won't agree to that condition."

"He won't know about it."

"He will, if I tell him."

"If you tell him, then his losing the job will be on your head. Because make no mistake about it, Miss Caine—Drew can have you or that job in Washington he's so desperate to have. Not both. It's your decision."

"Why don't you tell *him* that?"

Beekman shrugged. "Because then he would be angry with me. But *I'm* not the problem here, Miss Caine. *You* are."

"You're a real piece of work," she said, shaking her head. "No wonder Drew hates going home."

"Here's another thought to help you make up your mind," Beekman went on. "I'm going to have people watching you. If you don't clear out of my son's life, the police will be on both you *and* your friend out there faster than you can say 'drug bust.'"

"You're full of it," she said, disgusted and fearful at the same time, not for herself so much as for Wiley. Who knew what else her old friend had gotten into since she had seen him last, and whether or not that plastic bag on the bed constituted his entire stash.

"You don't think I'm serious?" Beekman asked. "Watch me. I will not have you linked to my son, not with your history."

"You'd go to all this trouble just because of what my parents did? I was *eight years old* when they died, for crying out loud!"

"It doesn't matter. It's bloodlines we're talking about. And as a matter of fact, you must be a magnet for trouble, Miss Caine, because your adoptive father was no less disreputable than your birth father, from what my investigators have been able to find out."

"What are you talking about?"

"It seems the Reverend Harold Caine has a history of molesting young boys."

"What?"

"Apparently, it's been hushed up, and more than once. Now, I'm told, he's been forced to retire. I imagine it would be quite a public scandal if the boys' families could be convinced to press charges. And even if they didn't, the story could leak to the press, couldn't it?"

Mallory fell back, reeling. At the same time, all the little pieces of the puzzle of Harold Caine suddenly fell into place. His contempt for women. His devotion to his acolytes. His blind fury the time one of those boys and Mallory were caught kissing in the sacristy. The altar boy who had committed suicide with a shotgun blast in his parents' garage and then, years later, the Rev's sudden, forced departure from another parish in central California.

Frances! Mallory thought. Had she known all along? No, not simple, softhearted Franny, who always believed in his fundamental goodness, despite all evidence to the contrary. Did she know *now* why her husband had been forced out? It had been hushed up, Beekman said, but what if there was a scandal? Poor Franny!

"It's a good thing I decided to have you checked out," Beekman continued, "before you got your hooks even tighter into Drew. You're a bad apple, Miss Caine, from a long line of bad apples. I don't want you contaminating the Beekman-family barrel."

Beekman made a move to leave, but his glance fell on the framed photo on Mallory's dresser. His eyes narrowed. He reached over and picked it up, the muscles in his face twitching.

"Put that back!" Mallory ordered.

"This is your sister—Diana, isn't it?"

"Put it down, I said!" Mallory's heart was pounding frantically. He couldn't touch Diana, could he? Surely not. Living in France, married to Marcus Desloges, she, at least, would be safe from Andrew Beekman's long reach. *Wouldn't* she? "Get out of here!" she cried.

He replaced the photo and headed for the door. "I mean what I say, Miss Caine. You'll take your leave of Drew immediately. If you tell him I was here, the *next* conversation you have will be with the LAPD—you and your friend out there, make no mistake about it. You have a week to vacate the premises."

Beekman paused, hand on the knob as he peered around the apartment one last time, pursing his lips. "I think I'll have the place demolished," he said.

When Beekman left, Mallory was shaking so hard her legs were threatening to give out. Her mind felt as if it were shutting down, and an overwhelming, self-protective lassitude was settling in, sapping her strength. All she wanted to do was curl up in a corner, pull a blanket over her head and withdraw from an ugly world.

But when she heard a bump outside the door, she forced herself to move. Wiley was still there, and she had to take care of him. When she went out, she found him almost asleep on the step, and it was all she could do to get him inside. She steered him toward the bed, where he collapsed, mumbling, then passed out cold.

Straightening his tangled limbs, Mallory rummaged underneath his body until she found the plastic bag. She tossed a blanket over her friend, then took the contents of the bag and flushed it down the toilet. Taking a pair of scissors, she shredded the bag and flushed that, as well, then checked the rest of Wiley's things to be sure there wasn't any other incriminating evidence in case they did get busted. There was no knowing whether Beekman might change his mind and send the police right away, just to be certain his point was made.

She had nothing in the apartment that could get her into trouble, that much she knew. If she had smoked an occasional joint with Wiley back in Ferry Falls, she'd had nothing since, except the odd margarita or bottle of wine with Drew. Escaping her problems by getting blotto had lost its appeal. All it accomplished was to give her a hangover or Sahara mouth afterward. The same old problems remained, only she'd feel weaker, less capable of conquering them. There had to be another way, she'd decided.

Once satisfied that Wiley's pockets and bags were safe, Mallory busied herself tidying the apartment and putting away the groceries she had brought. There would be no happy reunion supper for the two of them that evening. The tasks were therapeutic. Just as surely as an icy wind freezes rain, a cold fury moved in on her, pushing back the tears that had been threatening to fall.

It would be difficult to imagine a more naked act of aggressive power than what she'd experienced a short while ago. Beekman had wealth and influence on his side, and her emotional attachment to Wiley and Drew had given him additional weapons to use against her. Although he couldn't have known about Wiley beforehand, Beekman was astute, sensing quickly that she was protective of him, using that to his advantage.

He had also gambled that Mallory would give up Drew silently rather than allow him, for her sake, to sacrifice the career he so desperately wanted. Well, maybe she would and maybe she wouldn't, Mallory thought. If her affection for Drew was a vulnerability, Drew was also Beekman's Achilles' heel. He had made that much clear by his actions tonight. Mallory knew

27

Los Angeles, California
February 17, 1980

Mallory had made a nest for herself on the floor out of sleeping bags and blankets after Beekman left, but she slept very little that night, her mind racing with images of rage and violence, love and aggression, and of the people in her life, few of whom invoked neutral reactions. At some point, her mind turned to the Rev, and to the stunning—but not really so surprising, she realized—revelation of his secret vice. She pictured the scrubbed, angelic faces of the half-dozen or so acolytes that the Rev had always kept around him, toadying to their parents, offering the boys private classes and excursions, showing them a warmth and interest that Mallory herself had never felt from him. If what Beekman said was true, how could it have gone on under everyone's noses all these years with no one being any the wiser?

When Wiley finally awoke the next morning, she recounted everything that had happened. He stumbled his way through profuse apologies for his own lapse, flinching only a little when she told him she had flushed his stash. Then, Wiley stunned her by revealing he had known about the Rev for years.

"I talked to my mom a few weeks ago," he added. "She told me about the Rev being forced out. You remember the Stewarts? Mrs. Stewart is my mom's best friend?" Mallory nodded. "And you remember their youngest kid?"

"Little Garry?"

"Yeah, but he's not so little anymore. He's about seventeen now, and when he got himself a girlfriend, he caught the Rev spying on them."

"Spying?"

"Following them. They'd come out of the Rialto or be hanging out at the Burger Boy, and all of a sudden, Garry would look up and see the Rev sitting across the street in his car, watching them. One night, Garry and his girl are necking down at the Falls when the Rev shows up and goes ballistic."

"What happened?"

"The Rev sent Garry home by himself. Took the girl in his own car, giving her a lecture all the way about being loose and corrupting good boys. Next day, Garry goes down to the church to give the Rev hell and tell him to take his candle snuffer and put it where the sun don't shine. The Rev apparently bursts into tears, falling all over him, telling him he loves him, and he just wants to protect him."

"My God!"

"Yeah, well—Garry lit out, but he broke down and told his parents that night. It turns out the Rev had been going after him from way back."

Mallory frowned, remembering the time not long after she and Diana were adopted, before the Rev had left his old parish in Rosemont, California, and they had moved to Ferry Falls. She recalled people pounding on the rectory's front door one night and shouting at the Rev when they were let in. Frances had sent her and Diana to their rooms, but going upstairs, Mallory had recognized the parents of one of the boys in the church choir. She remembered a hasty visit with church officials, then the scramble to find the Rev a parish in another state. When she told Wiley about all this, he nodded.

"My stepdad apparently ran a police check on the Rev. Found out he'd had a parish in Connecticut about twenty-five years ago and his favorite acolyte there committed suicide— blew his brains out with a twelve-gauge shotgun. Apparently, there were rumors that the kid had something going on that he couldn't handle. The Rev, coincidentally, had a nervous breakdown right afterward. The whole thing was shoved under the rug, though, and he was just quietly moved out.''

"That's where Franny said they met—Enfield, Connecticut." Mallory exhaled deeply, shaking her head. "Poor Franny! All these years."

"You don't think she knew he was a little odd?"

"Wiley, even *I* knew he was odd, but I never guessed there was anything like this. Did you?"

Wiley shrugged. "Sure."

"What?"

"A lot of the guys did."

"How come you never told me?"

"I figured it might mess up our friendship." He shrugged again. "Anyway, guys coming on to guys—it's not something you feel real comfortable talking about or admitting, you know? Especially when you're a kid. You worry that maybe *you're* a little fruity around the edges, too, and these guys sniff it out or something, so you don't ever want to let on when it happens to you."

"Did it? Happen to you?"

"The Rev hated me, especially after I got to be friends with you. Once, though, he grabbed me from behind. It was that time you and I set off the stink bomb in chapel. I was in his office alone with him. He twisted my arm and put his other arm across my throat. It wasn't his belt buckle I felt sticking into me, I can tell you that. It was like he got off on being in complete control. But I shoved him away and ran. He went for easier targets after that."

"And the parents of the other boys? They really didn't know?"

"Who would suspect? The kids were intimidated, and the mothers loved it when the Rev singled out their little darlings for special attention. As for the fathers—well, I bet some of them picked up his vibes, but it's like 'who cut the cheese,' right? You smell it, you did it."

"They thought that if they made an accusation, people would figure *they* were the sickos?"

"That's about it."

"So it just went on, year after year, parish after parish. My God, Wiley! How can people ignore that kind of abuse of power?"

Wiley shrugged. "It happens all the time."

Drew had scarcely finished putting away his skis on Sunday evening, when his father showed up at his apartment. Drew had neither seen nor spoken to him since Ariel's wedding. Even then, with all the people and activity swirling around, they hadn't exchanged more than a dozen words, the pall of their Christmas Day argument still hanging over them. If he was surprised to see him show up now, Drew was no less stunned by his father's subdued demeanor.

"I don't want to disturb you," Beekman said when he came inside. "I know you've had a busy weekend and you have classes tomorrow. Mother says you went to Tahoe. How was the skiing?"

"It was fine. Can I offer you a drink or something?"

"Well, I wouldn't refuse a wee glass of Scotch, if you had such a thing."

"I'm not sure I do, Father, sorry. I usually just keep beer on hand. Or I might have some wine."

"A beer, maybe. I haven't had one in a while. Will you join me?"

"Sure, I guess," Drew said, mystified. "Have a seat while I grab them."

When he came back, his father had settled into an old, over-stuffed armchair. "I remember this chair," Beekman said, patting the dark green leather arms appreciatively. "It used to be in the library at home. I always wondered where it had gotten to."

"I rescued it from one of Mother's redecorating frenzies," Drew said. "She was getting ready to toss it. Glass?"

"No, the bottle's fine. I'm glad you took it. At least *someone* has something decent to sit on. Those decorators of hers seem to go to great lengths to find her the most god-awful, uncomfortable furniture imaginable."

Drew settled into another chair. "It doesn't even have a chance to get broken in before she gets tired of it and starts redoing things all over, does it?"

Beekman shook his head sadly, then lifted his bottle. "Oh, well, it keeps her busy, I suppose. Cheers, son."

"Cheers, Father." Drew took a swig, then lowered his bottle and studied his father surreptitiously. He seemed older and more tired than Drew could ever remember. For the moment, gone was the taciturn, distant authority figure who told rather than asked, the busy father who never seemed to have time whenever his young son wanted to do something together or show off some little achievement. Now, for the first time in Drew's memory, his father seemed in no hurry at all. "What brings you downtown, Father?"

"Oh, I had a property to look at and I wanted to do it today, when there was less traffic. Since I was nearby, I thought I'd drop in and see how you were."

"You're looking in the city? But I thought you liked to keep most of your development work in Orange County."

"I do, but I own other properties, too. You'd know that, if you came to work for me."

Drew slumped in his chair. *This* conversation again! "Father, I—"

"Never mind. I'm not going to harp on it anymore."

"You're not?"

"What's the point? It doesn't seem to get us anywhere, does it?"

"Look, it's not that I don't respect your wishes and appreciate what you're trying to do for me, but there are other things *I'd* like to do. From the day I was born, my future seems to have been predetermined. You can't imagine how frustrating that is."

"Can't I?" Beekman paused, flicking at a bead of condensation running down his bottle. "Actually, when I was a young boy growing up in Glasgow, my future seemed predetermined, too. I decided to change it."

"You did, didn't you?"

"Yes." Beekman looked up at his son. "And I've been thinking maybe I've been wrong."

"Sir?"

"All I've done is oppose you, Drew, when you've tried to choose your path. But you have a mind of your own, that much is clear. You're hardworking and ambitious. I should be proud of that, even if you *are* wrongheaded and stubborn about refusing what I believe is best for you. I suppose you come by it naturally. You're *my* son, after all."

Drew smiled, in spite of himself. "I guess I am."

"It could be worse," Beekman said, rolling his eyes. "I could have spawned a Jon Houghton. Good Christ, he's an ass!"

"How *are* the newlyweds?"

His father made a dismissive wave of his hand. "They got back from Majorca on Friday, and Ariel and your mother have been holed up with decorators ever since, planning their new house. I don't think *he's* left the beach. I swear the boy's brain-dead."

Drew grinned. Finally, he thought—a subject on which he and his father agreed. But then, his expression sobered and he took a deep breath. "I suppose you heard they canceled the senate-internship program for this year."

"Yes. I spoke to Jim Redman. He said he could still find a place for you on his staff."

"He did?" Drew's hopes soared, then plummeted. "You told him not to bother, right?"

"No, I didn't."

"What?"

Beekman fixed his son with a steady gaze. "I want you to come into Beekman Development, Drew, you know that, but you're a grown man now. You have to make your own decisions."

"You mean, I could go to Washington if I chose and work for Senator Redman instead? You wouldn't block me?"

"I wouldn't block you."

Drew shook his head, stunned. "But, that's great! I want to do it, Father. I really want to give it a try."

"Then you should call Jim Redman tomorrow and tell him so."

"You mean it?"

"Yes. I think you're daft, mind you. I hope you come to re-alize it sooner rather than later. But in the meantime, if you must do this, then you'll do it with my blessing, dammit."

Drew felt his throat tighten. "I don't know what to say. This is so unexpected."

"Your mother is not going to be pleased, I can tell you that, but I'll take care of her. Just don't forget that I'll always have a spot open for you."

"I won't forget. Thanks, Dad."

"You're welcome, son."

When Mallory arrived at Drew's apartment late the next af-ternoon, he scooped her up and planted a deep kiss on her lips before she had a chance to say a word. "I'm glad you're here," he said when they finally came up for air. "Have I got news for you!"

"What?"

"I got it! I got the job with the Senate Foreign Relations Committee. I spoke to Senator Redman this morning, and I'm going to work for him as soon as the term is over."

"How did this happen, Drew?" she asked cautiously. Surely he had to see how fishy it was. "I thought it was a nonstarter."

He grinned and rolled his eyes. "My father. That guy! I had him all wrong, Mal. He backed me up. When Redman said he could take me on, my dad told me to go for it. Can you believe it?"

"Yeah, I can believe it."

"He came to see me yesterday."

"Your father? Here?"

"Yes, and we had this long talk. It wasn't like any we'd ever had before, and the upshot was, he said he was wrong to try to force me to do something I didn't want to. My father!" Drew added, incredulous. "Andrew Beekman, admitting he was wrong. Can you believe it?"

"It's very touching, I'm sure."

Drew frowned. "What's the matter? Why are you acting this way?"

"No reason. So what happens now?"

"I finish my term. I'm going to quit Truffles," he added. "I need to focus on my final papers. Maybe I can get out a little early. My dad agreed it would be the best thing to do, so he gave me a check to cover all my expenses."

"How very generous of him."

"Mallory, what is *wrong* with you? This is the best damn news I could have had, and I thought you'd be pleased."

"Oh, come on, Drew! He bought you."

"Who?"

"Your father!"

"What are you talking about? This isn't even what he wanted me to do. He wanted me to work for him."

"So, aren't you wondering why he had a sudden change of heart?"

"Maybe it's because he's a pretty good guy, after all, and I'm his son, and he wants me to be happy."

"Terrific. Be happy, then." She started gathering books and clothes and putting them into her backpack.

"What are you doing?"

"I have to go."

"Where?"

"Home, as soon as I get the rest of my stuff."

"Why are you taking your things? Oh!" he exclaimed, a light apparently turning on somewhere. "Because you think this is the end of us, is that it?"

"Very good. You figured it out."

"It isn't over, Mallory. Just because I won't be at Truffles doesn't mean we can't be together. I told you before, you should move in with me, and now there's more reason than ever. You don't even have to work. I have enough money for both of us."

"You're leaving town, Drew."

"So? You can come to D.C., too."

"No, I can't."

"Sure you can. You can transfer your credits to Georgetown U or somewhere else and we'll carry on like before, except now, you won't have to work. Please, Mal," he said, grabbing her arms. "I want this job so much. You know that!"

GET ALL 3

We'd like to send you three free books to introduce you to "The Best of the Best." Your three books have a combined cover price of $16.50, but they are yours free! We'll even send you a lovely "thank-you" gift—the attractive picture frame shown below. You can't lose!

FREE!

ONLY FOREVER
by Linda Lael Miller
"Sensuality, passion, excitement, and drama ...are Ms. Miller's hallmarks." —*Romantic Times*

FREE!

SWAMP FIRE
by Patricia Potter
"A beguiling love story ..."
—*Romantic Times*

FREE!

DARK STRANGER
by Heather Graham Pozzessere
"An incredible storyteller!"
—*L.A. Daily News*

©1995 HARLEQUIN ENTERPRISES LTD.

BOOKS FREE!

Hurry!
Return this card promptly to **GET 3 FREE BOOKS & A FREE GIFT!**

the Best of the Best

Affix
peel-off
MIRA
sticker here

YES, send me the three free "The Best of the Best" novels, as explained on the back. I understand that I am under no obligation to purchase anything further as explained on the back and on the opposite page. Also send my free picture frame!

183 CIH AZHX (U-BB3-96)

Name: _____

Address: _____

City: _____

State: _____ Zip: _____

Offer limited to one per household and not valid to current subscribers.
All orders subject to approval.

DETACH AND MAIL CARD TODAY!

BUSINESS REPLY MAIL

FIRST-CLASS MAIL   PERMIT NO 717   BUFFALO, NY

POSTAGE WILL BE PAID BY ADDRESSEE

THE BEST OF THE BEST
3010 WALDEN AVE.
P.O. BOX 1867
BUFFALO, NY 14240-9952

NO POSTAGE
NECESSARY
IF MAILED
IN THE
UNITED STATES

Mallory pulled away and went on stuffing her backpack. "Then you should go for it," she said dully.

"Mallory! Look at me! What is the *matter* with you?"

She stopped and turned to him. "You just don't get it, do you? If Daddy says stay, you stay. If he says go, you go. He buys whatever you need, and life's just hunky-dory. Well, good for you, Drew, but there's no place in that life of yours for me!"

An angry expression crossed his face. "I thought you'd finally lost that chip on your shoulder, Minnesota, but I guess not."

"No, I guess not. It's been a fun seven weeks, rich boy, but I've got to go." She went into the bedroom to collect the rest of the toiletries and clothes that had accumulated there.

Drew followed her and watched as she moved around. Then, he sighed. "Come on, Mal, don't leave."

"I have to." She glanced at the window. "Someone's waiting for me."

"Who?" When she didn't answer, Drew went over and looked out. "The guy on the Harley out there? Who is he?"

"An old friend of mine. He got into town on Saturday."

"He's staying with you? At your place?"

"That's right."

"He couldn't go somewhere else?"

"I don't want him anywhere else."

"Oh, great! Why didn't you say so in the first place, and tell the truth about why you're packing up here? It doesn't have anything to do with me going to D.C. Jesus! I go away for two days, and the minute I'm gone, you're screwing someone new."

She refused to rise to his bait. "I told you—Wiley and I go way back."

"I'll bet," Drew snorted. "I guess I shouldn't be surprised. It was pretty obvious you had some history. So, do you love this guy, or what?"

She paused, reflecting. "There's not much I wouldn't do for him."

"Yeah, right," Drew said bitterly. "I'm sure you do a *lot* for him. Does he know you did it for me, too?"

She glared at him. "I'll tell you one thing—I sure as hell wouldn't trade him for anyone named Beekman."

"That seems pretty clear."

She tightened the straps on her backpack and turned to go. "Have a great life, fella. And don't forget to thank Daddy."

"I won't! He's a damn great man, for your information!"

"Sure he is. And you're his son."

Book Four

Ambition and Desire

28

It was his last feature assignment, and damned if Ian Gallagher hadn't been bamboozled. It was the kind of trap a rookie would have fallen into, not a senior investigative reporter with twelve years of hard-knuckle experience and a Pulitzer Prize under his belt. Tapped on the shoulder at the relatively young age of thirty-four to join the editorial board of the second-largest-circulation daily in the country, Gallagher had already moved his gear that morning into the coveted outer office at the *Los Angeles Chronicle.* But he'd delayed taking up his Metro editor functions for one more day in order to cover a conference that might provide an important piece to an investigative puzzle he'd been working on for two months—the complex relationship between a pharmaceutical company and a California research institute, and their link to a controversial heart drug, Ritaxin.

Developed by Schiller Pharmaceuticals, Ritaxin had originally been approved by the FDA for limited use, and only with high-risk patients in whom other antiarrhythmic drugs had failed. That restriction had later been eased on the basis of additional research conducted by Western MediSearch of Los Angeles. As a result, Ritaxin had become one of the most widely prescribed medications for heart-rhythm problems, and Schiller Pharmaceuticals had reaped a financial bonanza. New evidence, however, suggested that Ritaxin might be causing more deaths than it was preventing.

Gallagher's request for an interview with Dr. Norton Cook, president of the testing company, MediSearch, had been denied. Now, speaking before an American Medical Association meeting, Cook had announced the expansion of MediSearch facilities and the creation of a new program of research into human autoimmune diseases, the expansion financed in part by grants from Schiller Pharmaceuticals. A payoff, Gallagher wondered, for a clean bill of health on Ritaxin?

After his announcement, Cook had answered questions but ignored Gallagher's efforts to be recognized from the floor. When the doctor began making moves toward the exit, Gallagher jumped to his feet, but his way was blocked by MediSearch staff members, who had formed a human barricade. Mentally kicking himself for falling into such an old trap, Gallagher was about to corner one of the staff doctors, when he heard a voice call out from behind.

"Dr. Cook! Excuse me, Dr. Cook! Hold up there, would you?"

Gallagher turned to see a young, blond woman in a prim navy suit waving frantically at the departing MediSearch president. Her hair was tied back conservatively and her white blouse, severely buttoned to the throat, was softened only by the small bow that flapped with the energy of her movement. Her dark eyes flitted from left to right as she sought a way to escape the crush of people at either end of her row of folding seats. Finding none, she jumped to the seat of one and stepped forward, her skirt hiking up to reveal long, lean legs as she hurdled over the backs of the chairs that separated her from her quarry.

Dr. Norton Cook was silver-haired, handsome and urbane. He was also close to sixty years old, Gallagher estimated, but clearly not immune to the charms of a pretty girl, especially one as determined to meet him as this young lady seemed to be. Cook and everyone else in the room watched, lips turning up as she gamboled across the chairs. She was carrying a canvas backpack, but Gallagher also caught sight of a tape recorder dangling by a strap from her shoulder. A reporter? Gallagher thought he knew most of the L.A.-based press corps, but he'd never seen her before. And despite her textbook dress-for-success outfit, she looked barely old enough to be out of high school.

Landing in front of the doctor with one final, leggy leap, the girl smiled and spoke, although what she was saying Gallagher couldn't hear. The doctor, however, returned her smile, inclining his head toward her. When she indicated the microphone in her hand, he nodded, then waved away the aides at his side and led her, one hand on her back, to a corner where she could ask her questions unhampered by background noise. How bloody thoughtful of him, Gallagher thought glumly. She had to be doing a slush piece for one of the local glossies.

But as he watched their conversation, Gallagher saw the doctor's indulgent smile begin to waver, then fade altogether. Suddenly, Cook's head snapped up, his expression turned angry and he wheeled away.

"Are you denying it, Doctor?" the girl called after him.

"This is rubbish! I have no comment!"

Well, well, Gallagher thought, how interesting. Cook left the hall, the remaining members of the audience streaming out behind him, including the phalanx that had blocked Gallagher's way. He approached the young woman, who was busy unplugging the mike from her Sony tape recorder, coiling the cord and loading it all into her backpack.

"Hi, there," he said.

She glanced up, then returned to doing what she was doing. "Hi."

Gallagher nodded toward the door. "Looks like you upset the good doctor."

"Looks like."

"What did you say to him?"

"Just asked a couple of questions."

"Mind if I ask *what* questions?" She looked at him again, frowning now. "Ian Gallagher," he added, holding out his hand. *"L.A. Chronicle."*

"Mallory Caine." Her grip was firm when they shook, but she released his hand quickly.

"So what got Norton Cook so hot and bothered, Mallory?"

"I'd just as soon not say, if you don't mind."

"Are you a reporter?"

"A stringer."

"For whom?"

"*Southland Magazine,* at the moment. Maybe."

"Maybe?"

"Yes. I free-lance for them now and again, and a couple of local weekly papers, as well."

"*Southland* assigned you to do a piece on Cook?"

"A profile on Western MediSearch, actually. Part of a bigger feature they're doing on some of the high-tech companies in the region."

"*Southland's* reporting is pretty soft."

"I know. That's why I'm not sure they'll take what I'm planning to give them."

"You dug up some dirt on MediSearch?" She shrugged. "Maybe you and I can do a deal," Gallagher suggested. *That* got her attention.

"You'd buy my piece?"

"I didn't say that."

"But you *could* buy it. You're an editor."

Gallagher was taken aback. The girl was quick—definitely not just another pretty face, as Cook, too, had discovered to his apparent regret. "You certainly read the fine print, don't you? That announcement in the *Chronicle* was only a couple of inches long."

"I know who you are, Ian Gallagher. You won a Pulitzer last year for your series on the Crips and the Bloods. Now they've made you an editor."

"Well, I'm about to become the paper's Metro editor, but at the moment, I'm working on a story of my own on Medi-Search."

"And you want me just to give you what I've got here?" she asked, nodding to her pack with its tape machine inside.

"I don't even *know* what you've got there."

"Stuff you could use."

"So you say."

"That's right. Of course, if you're not interested . . ." She shrugged again and turned away.

"Hold on a minute. Tell you what—I'll buy you coffee and you tell me what you've got. If I can use your information, you've got a deal."

"I get a byline?"

"This is *my* piece!"

"So? You're a big-time editor now. You can afford to be magnanimous."

He grinned and shook his head. "How about 'with contributions from Mallory Caine'? *If,*" he added, "I decide to use your stuff."

"It's a start," she said.

Mallory sat quietly in the passenger seat of Gallagher's BMW, her mind racing as he pulled the car into the parking lot of a Coco's restaurant a couple of miles from the AMA conference. They had decided it would be safer to avoid the hotel coffee shop, since Western MediSearch was obviously onto the fact that the press was looking critically at the company, and Dr. Cook's troops might take undue interest in what she and the journalist from the *Chronicle* had to say to each other.

Waiting for Gallagher to lock the car, she finally allowed herself a close look at this minor hero of hers, whose byline she had been tracking ever since reading his prize-winning series on the Crips and the Bloods, L.A.'s two major street gangs. She'd nearly fainted when Gallagher told her his name, although she'd made a supreme effort to cover her reaction. She still couldn't believe she had met him by chance like this, much less that they were going to discuss business over coffee. Or lunch? she prayed. She'd overslept that morning and had to skip breakfast. Now she was starving. Did *Chronicle* reporters have expense accounts? She hoped so, since she was less than flush in the cash department.

Gallagher was about six feet tall, but he had a large-boned, densely packed frame that made him appear even bigger. He was in his mid-thirties, she guessed by the lines in his forehead and around his eyes, and like most veteran journalists, he looked as if he didn't get enough sleep. With a muddy-brown thatch of hair and wire-rimmed glasses over hazel eyes, he was not the best-looking man she'd ever seen, by a long shot, but he had a nice smile and a solid, thoughtful air about him. He looked like someone people would instinctively listen to and put their trust in. It was probably a useful quality in a reporter or editor.

When they had settled in the restaurant and given their orders—Gallagher *did* amend his offer to lunch, thank goodness—he leaned back in the booth and studied her. "So, how long have you been stringing, Mallory?"

"Almost three years. I was working on the Westside College paper and waiting tables for money, but I started getting squeezed for time and my studies were suffering, so I figured I'd better combine work and pleasure by lining up some freelance gigs."

"Newspaper writing is pleasure?"

"Yeah, I love it. Don't you?"

He nodded. "I guess I do."

"I think I first got the bug when I read Woodward and Bernstein's, *All the President's Men*. All those powerful guys—committing crimes, covering up, abusing their authority in the most blatant ways because they figured they were untouchable. And then somebody brought them down, and made them answer for what they had done. I guess I've always had a problem with authority, so that seemed pretty exciting to me."

"It's heady stuff, all right. How did you get started?"

"I was on campus one day, not long after I read that book, and there was this guy in a wheelchair, stuck in the rain outside the administration building because he couldn't get the front door open. I think it clicked with me because my sister has a disability. Anyway, after I opened the door and helped him in, I walked over to the offices of the college paper and said to the editor, 'This campus is supposed to be handicapped accessible, but it's full of barriers, and what are you going to do about it?'"

"And you found yourself assigned to do a story?"

"Right. I spent one day in a borrowed wheelchair, and then another day with my arms pinned at the elbows, simulating limited strength. A photographer followed me around. We documented all the architectural barriers we could find, and then I took my findings to the administration for their reaction. After the paper ran my articles, the college started cleaning up its act, putting in more ramps and automatic door-openers."

"And you were hooked."

"Yup. I thought, somebody lets you *do* this? Take on the things that frustrate you, and really *do* something about them? Even me, little old Mallory from Minnesota? It was like a light turning on."

Gallagher smiled. "I know what you mean. Maybe we can't change the world, but we can sure embarrass the crooks and the charlatans. You're from Minnesota?"

"More or less. Speaking of crooks..." Mallory said, changing the subject.

"Dr. Norton Cook."

"Right. Do you want me to play the tape?"

Just then, the waiter brought their food. "Maybe not in here," Gallagher said. "Why don't you summarize what you've found out?"

Mallory gave her sandwich a regretful glance, then pushed it aside and leaned forward, elbows on the table. "I suppose you know that Schiller Pharmaceuticals partially financed that new research program Cook announced this morning? And about the work Western MediSearch did on the heart drug, Ritaxin? And how Schiller went on to make a fortune on Ritaxin?"

"I do. You think the new program is a payoff?"

"Of course, don't you?" Mallory asked. Gallagher nodded. "Did you know that after the FDA approved the expanded use of Ritaxin, Dr. Norton Cook was named a member of Schiller Pharmaceutical's board of directors?"

"Yes, but that's not illegal. It could present a conflict of interest if MediSearch does any future FDA work on Schiller drugs. Otherwise, Cook hasn't committed anything more than a possible minor breach of ethics, the kind that goes on all the time in the corporate world."

"What if there's more to it? Ritaxin is coming under fire. It looks like the FDA was right in the first place when they approved it only for limited use, because it has so many side effects. What if MediSearch knew that way back, and falsified the research data? What if Norton Cook himself received a payoff to help Schiller get FDA approval for Ritaxin?"

"A payoff? You mean other than his position on the board of directors?"

"I mean cold, hard cash, Mr. Gallagher."

"My name's Ian. Did he? What did you find out?"

"Have you even seen Dr. Cook's wife?" Gallagher shook his head. "She's a beautiful blonde," Mallory said, "half his age. She used to be his secretary. They have a five-year-old son. This is Cook's second marriage. On a hunch, I went to see the wife he dumped for blondie, and I met their thirty-year-old daughter, Rachel, too. And while at first Mrs. Cook number one was too humiliated to talk, Rachel had plenty to say about her father and the dirty tricks he's pulled."

"What dirty tricks?"

"He'd been having an affair with his secretary and when she got pregnant, Cook decided to dump his wife. Since California has community-property laws, he was going to lose his shirt in the divorce. Now, keep in mind, this was just at the time that Western MediSearch had been contracted to do the additional research on Ritaxin."

Gallagher held up his hands. "Don't tell me. I see where you're headed. Dr. Cook needed money, so Schiller funneled it through the secretary in exchange for a clean bill of health on Ritaxin."

"The secretary who," Mallory added, "may have been beautiful, but who was poor as a church mouse, according to Cook's daughter. Suddenly, she's got a house in Malibu and a Mercedes, and even after the good doctor splits his heretofore modest assets with wife number one, he and the new Mrs. Cookie still end up living a life of luxury."

"And the former wife and daughter have never told anyone else about this?"

"The mother just wanted it all to fade away, but now she's got health and financial problems, and the daughter's mad as hell at her old man."

"You've got this all on tape?"

"Yup."

"We need confirming sources, but we won't find them at MediSearch. I've already tried to get around his office, but Cook's a god to his staffers."

"That may be, but his daughter gave me the names of two former researchers who became disillusioned with the church of Norton Cook. They might be willing to talk."

Gallagher sat back and absentmindedly ran his hands through his already-disheveled hair. "You tipped your hand this morning, you know," he said, frowning.

"I wasn't sure if I'd ever get close to him again, and I wanted to see his reaction."

"Yes, but now he's onto you, and he'll go to ground, trying to cover his tracks. We're going to have to move fast."

"We? Does that mean you're giving me a job?"

He raised his hands, palms out. "Whoa! Hold on, there. I can get you a free-lance fee on this, and depending on what turns up, I might even spring for a shared byline. But there's a hiring freeze on at the *Chronicle*. I'm sorry. This wasn't meant to be a job interview, and I haven't got a position to offer you."

Rats, Mallory thought. She knew it had been too good to be true. "As an editor, though, you can throw more free-lance stuff my way, can't you?" she prodded. Nothing ventured, nothing gained.

He frowned. "I'm not even sure about that."

"Why not?"

"The *Chronicle's* a major national daily, Mallory. Forgive me, but Westside College isn't exactly one of the country's top journalism schools. And even if it were, most of our people start out on small papers and work their way up to us. You should think about a graduate journalism degree. Then, get a little more experience—"

"My senior term wraps up in three weeks. I can't afford grad school, and I need a job. I want to write for the *Chronicle*."

He shook his head, incredulous. "You're not too cocky, are you?"

"I know I can do it."

"What makes you think you're so good?"

"I scooped *you*, didn't I, Mr. Pulitzer Prize?" Internally, Mallory winced. She may have gone overboard in the bravado department—she had a tendency to do that. But Gallagher, she was relieved to see, had the grace to laugh.

"Maybe you did scoop me, at that. But I still can't offer you a job. For that matter," he added, his forehead creasing, "I don't even know if you can write."

Mallory reached into her backpack. "I have my clippings right here."

"You carry your clippings around with you?"

She shrugged. "You never know when you'll meet a big-shot editor."

He shook his head again. "All right, I'll look at them later. But no promises, got it?"

"Got it."

"Good. Eat your sandwich. I want to go somewhere and listen to that tape."

29

The first time Mallory saw the Buck Rogers art deco tower of the *L.A. Chronicle* Building, in the heart of what laughingly passed for a downtown in Los Angeles—a vast city of endless neighborhoods and no real core—she felt instinctively drawn to the place, as if to a spiritual home. But as with most of the happy homes she had seen in her life, she was an outsider there. She felt like some little match girl, nose pressed to the window, gazing longingly at the bustle, excitement and camaraderie inside with no hope of ever being invited in to stay.

Ian Gallagher made good on his word to get her a free-lance fee and a couple of "special to the *L.A. Chronicle*" bylines, and he found Mallory a temporary corner to hammer out her notes when her information on Dr. Norton Cook panned out into revelations of large-scale fraud and malpractice at Western MediSearch. But after a brief flurry of excitement, the assignment ended, and Mallory took her final college exams with no prospect of ever entering the *Chronicle* building again. Despite the nice things Gallagher had said when he handed back her clipping file, she knew no one was going to seek an exception to the venerable paper's hiring freeze for some twenty-two-year-old with academic credentials from a minor school and clippings from a few neighborhood rags.

Lili Dahl, her landlady, was philosophical when Mallory expressed her fears about finding a meaty job in journalism. "You can't get discouraged, Mallory. Why, I attended more cattle calls than you can shake a stick at when I came to Hollywood. Some days, I thought my break would never come, and yet look what happened. I played with the Barrymores and Chaplin! *And* Fairbanks." Lili fluttered her many-ringed fingers, her rheumy, kohl-lined eyes wide with amazement even now, fifty years after her brief fling with movie fame.

Old movie posters and framed black-and-white photos from the prime of Miss Lili Dahl lined the walls of her gingerbread house—south of Wilshire and on the extreme western edge of Beverly Hills, but still technically within its boundaries, she was quick to point out. As a pretty sprite from Ohio who had come to Hollywood in the late twenties, Lili had filled a series of minor roles—the second banana's date in those movie nightclub scenes, or the boss's secretary, or the on-screen confidante to whom Mary Pickford or Clara Bow would confess their secret crushes. In the old posters on her walls, the name Lili Dahl appeared in minuscule type, toward the end of the cast credits. Just the same, Lili was as proud of those posters and photos of herself with the stars as she was of her little house—itself a gift, she told Mallory with a sigh, from Errol Flynn. That sigh covered a multitude of bittersweet secrets, Mallory suspected.

Except for a few character parts when she was older, the bulk of Lili's Hollywood career had spanned a mere ten years. In her late seventies now, Lili, who had never married, had decided to seek a female lodger just at the time Andrew Beekman had evicted Mallory from her grotty little bachelor in Westwood. Responding to a notice in the college housing office, Mallory had been taken aback by the old lady with raccoon eyes, russet tresses and bright red lips, who jangled noisily with every dramatic flourish of her hands. But the room in Lili's house was clean and comfortable, and the rent cheap, given that it was to be paid partly in kind, running errands and hauling out the weekly trash cans that Lili could no longer manage. Mostly, Mallory suspected, the old woman wanted the security of having another person nearby, in this city grown too large and too crazy. With neither the time nor the money to be choosy, Mallory had moved in. Three years later, Lili was still her landlady and probably her closest friend.

Drew Beekman was long gone. After he and Mallory split up, he'd left California to work for James Redman in Washington. Mallory had not seen him in the flesh since, although she'd seen the pictures and social notices a year later, when Drew married Senator Redman's daughter, Courtney. No slouch, that boy, when it came to making the right moves to get what he wanted. More recently, she'd spotted Drew in the background of shots of visiting foreign dignitaries on Capitol Hill, and so she knew that his temporary stint as a senatorial aide had turned into the Washington career he'd dreamed of. As bitter as the memory of her seven weeks with Drew were, given the way they had ended, Mallory took great pleasure from the realization that, in seeking to drive a wedge between Mallory and his son, Andrew Beekman had won the battle but lost the war. Drew had made good his escape from his father's clutches.

Wiley Dixon, remorseful over the problems he had caused her, had disappeared from her life as suddenly as he had reappeared that time. Mallory had tried to reassure him that he was the *least* part of Andrew Beekman's problems with her, but Wiley had been unconvinced.

Or maybe it wasn't just the whole Beekman thing, Mallory thought. Maybe she and Wiley had simply outgrown each other after all those years of banding together for mutual survival in Ferry Falls. She felt like Wendy to his Peter Pan. She had changed since coming to Los Angeles and looking into the black maw of her past and finding nothing there but pain and a sense of powerlessness. In Ferry Falls, she'd been happy to escape with Wiley into their own personal fantasyland. Now, she no longer wanted to escape the real world as much as conquer it. Wiley, however, was still content to retreat into the magical spaces of his imagination, propelled, if necessary, by pharmacological fuels that left Mallory feeling too helpless and out of control.

And so, he'd moved on. Mallory still received cards and letters, but from their postmarks, it seemed Wiley was moving physically away from her as well as psychologically—first to Mazatlán and Guadalajara in Mexico, then by freighter across the Pacific to Fiji, then Thailand, and then Katmandu. But just when Mallory was certain that he was destined to disappear forever into a drugged-out fog in some obscure land, a published story in some magazine or anthology would arrive on her doorstep, the latest mad adventure from the fertile mind of Wiley Dixon, featuring supernatural heroes and villains. And always, there would be a heroine with wild, wheaty hair, a flashing sword and a passion for justice.

Diana, of course, had never returned from Paris. Mallory had been over to visit her twice—the first time after Diana had married Marcus, and the second time fourteen months later, after Diana had surprised everyone, including dubious doctors, by giving birth to a son, named Remy. Whatever misgivings Mallory might have had about abandoning Diana or about her sister getting herself tied up with a much older man had vanished when she met Marcus Desloges and saw how utterly devoted the art dealer was to her sister and, then, to their son. Just thinking about Diana made Mallory feel warm inside, no matter how unresolved her own life felt. She herself was a long way from finding what Bishop Lennox had wished for her—the peace that passes all understanding. But her sister, miraculously, seemed to have found it.

Mallory's only regret was that Frances had not been able to see firsthand how well things had turned out for the injured little girl she had taken in and loved. After the Rev had lost his parish in Ferry Falls, he and his wife had retired to his hometown of Claremont, California.

Mallory had hoped Frances would come to visit, but then, she had been diagnosed with stomach cancer. Mallory began renting a car every Sunday to drive up to see her in hospital. She found the Rev unimproved with time and age. After the first couple of tense meetings, when Mallory had bitten her tongue for Franny's sake rather than confront him about the hushed-up scandal in Minnesota, Caine began staying away from the hospital when he knew she was coming. The nurses told Mallory that even when she wasn't there, his visits were brief and scattered.

Frances, however, seemed unconcerned by her husband's neglect as she lay terminally ill. As a matter of fact, she was the most *cheerful* dying person anyone had ever seen. Maybe it was seeing one of her adopted daughters on a regular basis again. Or maybe it was the attention she received from the hospital staff, all of whom seemed to adore the slightly dotty old woman behind the owlish spectacles. Whatever the case, Franny was in such good spirits that Mallory began to suspect her illness was a long-overdue, if subconscious, act of defiance—daring to precede the Rev to the grave instead of closing her eyes to his rottenness and waiting on him hand and foot to the bitter end.

Frances had had but two moments of victory in her entire marriage, Mallory thought. One was convincing Caine to let her have two little girls to keep her company, the other was her death. And the Rev wasn't fooled. He seemed to take it as a personal affront that his wife had finally walked out on him the only way she knew how.

Frances was a class act, Mallory decided. Once, when they were alone in her hospital room, she had probed gently to try to find out how Franny felt about the Rev's alleged abuse of the young boys in his charge, but she had refused to be drawn in. "I leave judgment to God and others," she said.

"How can you not hate him, Franny?"

"I could never bring myself to hate him. I know what he is, and what they say he did. I know he's not a great man, and that he never loved me, but I'm still grateful for the life I had."

"You don't owe him anything."

"Oh, but I *do* owe him something, dear. I would have been an old spinster rattling around with no one but a cat for company if it weren't for Harold. Instead, I had an active life, and friends, and a certain amount of respect in the community." Frances reached up her shrunken, tube-ridden hand and stroked Mallory's cheek. "And best of all, I had you and Diana. I got to be your mother when your real mother couldn't be there for you anymore. I was a poor alternative, I know, and maybe you would have been better off somewhere else, but you girls were the most wonderful part of my life."

Mallory took up Frances's blue-veined hand and held it between her own. "You're a fine mother, Franny. I should have told you so long ago, and I *do* thank you for everything you did for us. I know how awful I was, but it wasn't your fault. I just felt cheated and angry and pushed around by life—but never by you. You were always on my side, and I love you for it."

"I love you, too, dear." The old lady sighed. "I just wish I could have done more to make your pain go away."

"You did everything you could."

"And I was happy to do it. But," Frances added softly, "I want you to do something for me."

"What's that?"

"Watch over Harold. He has no one else. I know what I'm asking is a lot, but Diana's too far away, and she can't handle him, anyway. You're the strong one, Mallory. Do this for me, please?''

Mallory sighed. ''I don't think the Rev would take kindly to me watching over him, Franny. But I'll do the best I can, I promise.''

When Frances died, a few of the nurses showed up at her funeral, where Mallory and Harold Caine were the only other people in attendance. After it was over, Mallory drove the Rev back to his little retirement-community apartment. There, despite her promise and her best intentions, the two of them had one last battle.

''They say cancer is caused by stress,'' Caine said, shuffling around irritably. ''I'm sure Mother did her best to forgive you, Mallory, but I am struggling to find it in my heart to do the same, after the years of anxiety you caused her.''

''*I* caused her?''

''Oh, please! Don't insult her memory and my intelligence by pretending you weren't a trial and a torment from the first day we took you in. We lifted you out of that mire you were born into. Frances and I sacrificed our lives and our health for you girls, and what thanks did we get? Both of you ran off at the first opportunity. Turned your backs on us. Mother cried for weeks. Diana couldn't even be bothered to come and see her when she was dying.''

Mallory could barely restrain the urge to smack him. ''You awful man! You twist everything. In the first place, Diana couldn't travel because of her pregnancy. You know that, and so did Frances. But she wrote to Frances or telephoned every week—practically every day, near the end. And in the second place, I didn't just 'run out.' You were ready to throw me out long before I left. You counted the days to my eighteenth birthday—*you*, not Franny. I was no angel, but she and I got along just fine when you weren't around.''

Mallory took a deep breath to bring her fury under control. She would *not* give him the satisfaction of seeing her cry, no matter what.

''If you want to talk about stress, how about the stress *you* put her under, with your domineering and your bullying? Treating her like a servant. Not to mention,'' she added, through gritted teeth, "the stress of having the parents of little boys come pounding on the door when you couldn't keep your sick urges under control."

The Rev turned fairly purple and clenched his fists, taking a halting step toward her. Man of the cloth or not, Mallory knew that if he'd had a lethal weapon at hand, he would have used it on her. "You are *still* a dreadful child! You haven't learned a thing!"

"Oh, yes, I have. I've learned to see through you! And you know what else I've learned? I am *not* nothing, no matter what you say!"

Mallory had wheeled around and stormed out. Since that day, she had kept her promise to Franny by watching over him at arm's length, calling the superintendent of his complex every other week to make sure he was physically coping and had what he needed to get by. More than that, neither she nor the Rev could have managed.

30

The Friday planning meeting of the *L.A. Chronicle* editorial board was winding down. Ian Gallagher had been attending the meetings less than a month since taking up his Metro-editor functions, but he never ceased to be amazed at the fact that a newspaper eventually emerged from these tedious, drawn-out gripe sessions.

The *Chronicle* was an old, respectable "gray" paper, with twenty-four Pulitzer Prizes to its name, including his own. Its twenty-three foreign and ten domestic bureaus fed a steady stream of in-depth news and analysis into the paper's wire machines in the big building at Chronicle Plaza, occupying a full square city block in downtown Los Angeles. Founded in 1911, the *Chronicle* had for years been a turgid, WASP-y, family-run paper, toadying to the big-business interests that had created and grown fat on the region's boom. But beginning in the sixties, a new style of critical, investigative journalism had begun creeping into its staid pages, eventually turning the *Chronicle* into a dynamic voice more reflective of the multicultural cosmopolitan city that sleepy Los Angeles had become.

Still, Ian thought, watching the faces around the table, the place had a tendency to smug self-satisfaction. It had some way to go before its editorial board—mostly over fifty-five, exclusively white and male with one exception—could claim to be in tune with the rapidly evolving society around them. New blood would help, but faced with a financial crunch caused by rising newsprint and distribution costs, the publishers had instituted a hiring freeze that was unlikely to be lifted anytime soon.

As the planning meeting droned on, each of the section editors—International, National, Metro, Sports, Business, Lifestyles, Entertainment—was called on in turn by Carson Hoag, the managing editor, to outline stories they had in the pipeline for the next week. The art editor discussed photos and graphics to support various pieces. Grady O'Toole, Op-Ed and Sunday Commentary editor, gave his laconic, sarcastic analysis of what was significant and what was dreck in the breaking news.

"Okay, people, if that's everything for today," Carson Hoag said finally, closing his agenda file, "let's go put out a paper."

"Hold it, Carson! One last item."

All the men in the room looked down the long table to the far end, where Celia Webster sat. She was a thirty-year veteran who had risen from the ranks of secretary to proofreader, reporter and editor in the one part of the paper not dominated by the old-boy network that had held the *Chronicle* in its firm grip from the day the paper had been founded. Her section, now called Lifestyles, had until a few years earlier been the Women's Pages. It was the paper's soft underbelly, containing the comics, Ann and Abby, society notices, recipes and an endless stream of light, puffy stories on fashion, social trends, hobbies, kooks and eccentrics. Anything but hard news. As a result, Celia Webster's section, as well as her job on the editorial board, were avoided like the plague by every ambitious male journalist in town.

"I've got a staffing problem," Webster said now. "Annie Newhouse has been offered a book contract and wants to take a leave of absence to write it. I need a replacement."

Hoag shook his head. "No new hires, Celia, you know that. The publishers are adamant. The paper's just pulling back into the black after three years of deficit operations. They aren't going to agree to any new positions right now."

"I know that, but I'm short-staffed, as it is, and Annie's leaving puts me in a real bind. Her leave would be unpaid, Carson. All I'm asking is to transfer her salary into a short-term contract so I can get someone to fill in while she's gone. Six months, tops."

"No benefits? No health or life or pension?"

"Nothing, just a straight, minimum salary to do some of the gofer assignments—social notices and stuff. I'll move some-one else up to do Annie's features. We'll actually save money," Webster added.

"Hmm," Hoag mused, interested in anything that favored the bottom line. "Got someone in mind?"

"Ian has a name for me," she said.

The men all turned to Gallagher. "Mallory Caine," he said, "the stringer who worked with me on the Western MediSearch story."

Grady O'Toole eyed him with a bemused look. "Ah, yes. Pretty thing. Good legs, nice ass. Maybe I can get her to do some free-lance for me, too, eh, Gallagher? I vote we hire her, Carson."

"Go to hell, Grady," Celia Webster said, before Ian had a chance to make the identical suggestion. She turned back to the managing editor. "What do you say, Carson? Can I offer it to her?"

"All right, go ahead. But make it clear that it's only tem-porary. The freeze remains, and we're making no commit-ments to anyone new."

"Understood," Celia Webster said. She turned to Ian and gave him a big smile and a thumbs-up.

He could have let Celia contact Mallory herself to make the offer of the short-term contract. Instead, Ian dug out Mal-lory's number the minute the editorial meeting wrapped. He hadn't seen her in almost a month, and when he heard her wiseacre voice on the phone, he smiled.

"Hey, Pulitzer! How's the new editor?"

"Swamped, but beginning to find my sea legs. How are you, Mallory?"

"Surviving. I'm back to doing slush pieces for *Southland,* but it beats waiting tables, I guess."

"Well, as a matter of fact, that's why I'm calling."

"You've got work for me?"

"Maybe. Tell you what," he added on an impulse. "Are you free this evening?"

"To work?"

"For dinner."

"Dinner?" Her voice took on a cautious note. Where did *that* come from? Ian wondered.

"If you're free to grab a bite," he said. "I'm a little rushed right now, but I'd like to talk to you about an opportunity that's come up."

"What time?"

"I won't get out of here till late—seven-thirty, eight, maybe. I'll pick you up."

"No, I'll meet you. Just tell me where."

"Let me think ... I know. There's a place in Westwood on Santa Monica Boulevard. Bogart's Café. Do you know it?"

He heard her sigh. "Yes. It was called Truffles until it changed hands a couple of years ago."

"That's the place. But we could go somewhere else if you'd rather."

"No, Bogart's is fine. Eight o'clock?"

"Eight o'clock. I'll see you then." Hanging up the phone, Ian caught himself smiling until he remembered Grady O'Toole's insinuations in the staff meeting. He shook his head. If Grady only knew. The idea of feisty, cautious Mallory as *anyone's* bimbo was laughable. As much as Ian could appreciate a pretty face and great legs—and yes, a terrific little ass, now that he thought about it—Mallory was more than the sum of her physical parts. She had a razor-sharp mind and uncanny radar for bullshit. She worked like a Trojan, her energy never flagging when she was chasing a lead, and she was a decent writer, to boot, especially for someone with so little experience. He'd had no problem recommending her to Celia Webster.

Although accustomed to working alone on his investigative stories, Ian had been busy with his new editorial duties while they were putting together the Western MediSearch story, and he had let Mallory do much of the legwork. Watching her, he'd been amused to see that she had perfected the old newspaperman's trick of never appearing quite as smart as she was. Whether it was because of her midwestern accent, her age or her unsophisticated appearance, people invariably underestimated her in the beginning, thinking she could be bamboozled. She fed that mistaken impression, starting out her interviews on a naive, tentative note, saving her toughest ques-

tions for last. By the time she was done, even the hardest nuts
discovered too late that she had them impaled on their own in-
consistent statements. The girl was *born* to do this work, Ian
decided, however modest her academic credentials.

The two of them had consumed gallons of coffee and lost
several nights' sleep over a two-week period as they pieced together the exposé. In all that time, Mallory had never once
complained about the effort he'd demanded, nor the pittance
she was receiving in payment—her flat-rate free-lance fee
amounting to about fifty cents an hour, after all was said and
done. The money seemed incidental to her, although by the
number of times she wore that same navy suit, he'd guessed she
had little to her name. Up to that morning, however, he'd had
little hope of doing much to help her out. Then, bless her heart,
along had come Celia Webster with her problem in the Lifestyles section. Given the uphill battle that Celia herself had
fought and was still fighting for professional recognition and
respect, she was open to Ian's arguments in favor of Mallory
when no one else on the self-important editorial board would
have been.

The idea that there was anything else involved in his support
for Mallory hadn't even occurred to him before Grady
O'Toole's comments in the board meeting. Ian turned
O'Toole's insinuations over in his mind briefly, examining his
motives, then dismissed the idea with a shudder. Aside from the
fact that she was just a kid, he'd already been burned once,
falling for a firebrand whose searing ambition could immolate
anyone who stood in her path. He wasn't eager to play moth to
anyone else's flame.

But neither, unfortunately, was he attracted to women who
lacked fire and drive. Possessing a formidable intellect and a
photographic memory, Ian Gallagher was driven and ambitious, and he liked his women intelligent and self-directed. Not
for him the clinging, vapid beauties who were as boring as they
were bored. This city, he'd discovered in the six years he had
been living in L.A., seemed to have an inordinate number of
such women, drawn by the false, image-is-all atmosphere of the
place. Since his divorce, he'd dated a few of them and admittedly, they'd provided distraction from the emotional pum-
meling he'd taken when his four-year marriage to Caitlyn Allis

had crashed and burned two years earlier. But so far, he'd met no one likely to take Caitlyn's place—least of all some kid from Minnesota with a yen to be the female version of Woodward and Bernstein.

Ian Gallagher had been a big, quiet fellow growing up in Hastings, Nebraska. He'd excelled in sports and academics, and had worked in his father's hardware store. But it was writing—not power tools—that lit his fires, and after an undergrad journalism program at Hastings College, Ian had left Nebraska for New York City and a graduate degree at Columbia. By the time he'd landed the job of legislative-beat reporter on the *Atlanta Constitution* at the age of twenty-seven, Ian had had a string of positions on three smaller newspapers from Maine to Wyoming, and his reputation as an investigative reporter had grown steadily.

Despite a low-key personal style, Ian Gallagher was neither unresearched nor naive in the area of male-female relations when he set down in Atlanta. But the very first time he laid eyes on Caitlyn Allis, a junior aide to the governor of Georgia, he was bowled over flat by the red-headed beauty with the flirtatious green eyes. It was like getting hit by a Mack truck, slow-drawling Georgia version. Caitlyn was a southern princess, Scarlett goddamn O'Hara all over again, and it soon became apparent that she had set her sights on Ian to play the role of her personal Rhett Butler.

For eight months, they flitted around each other in a tortuous, combative dance of seduction, held at arm's length only because of Ian's instinctive, self-protective caution around any woman who could render stupid as many men as he saw panting after Caitlyn. There was also the small matter of the blatant conflict of interest between his investigative functions and her potential to knock out of his head any thought of criticizing her boss, the governor. In his cooler moments, he always wondered if she wasn't aiming deliberately for that effect with the way she flirted, her languid drawl flowing over him like honey.

Ian squirmed, caught between lust and professional integrity, but before he could compromise himself, the *L.A. Chronicle* came knocking, offering him an investigative beat.

He breathed a sigh of relief at the chance to get out of Atlanta after living in a state of constant, unsatisfied arousal more intense than any he had known since the summer he was fifteen, when the amply endowed Bunny Hooper used to parade in her bikini at the Hastings Community Pool. The night that he received the offer from Los Angeles, he ran into Caitlyn Allis at a gubernatorial reception. After telling her the news, Ian was stunned to see her beautiful face crumple, and he was even more confused when she turned around and ran out into the steamy Georgia night. He caught up with her in the parking lot as she was fumbling to unlock the door of her vintage, cobalt blue Chevy Impala.

"Caitlyn? Wait up! What's wrong?"

"Nothin's wrong. I have to be goin' now, is all."

"Why are you crying?"

"I'm not!" she wailed. The locks clicked open just as two huge tears landed on the Impala's blue paint job.

Ian took her by the shoulders and turned her around, his concern real, his intentions gentle. But at the sight of Caitlyn's shimmering cat's eyes and trembling lower lip, his brain short-circuited and his body kicked into libidinous overdrive. He hesitated barely a second before pulling her against himself, head dropping, mouth seeking hers, kissing her roughly. Her arms flew around his neck, lips and tongue devouring him just as greedily. She pushed herself against him, hips gyrating as he groped and pawed at her like an oversexed fifteen-year-old with Bunny Hooper wet dreams.

"You bad, bad boy," she breathed when they finally came up for air. Ian thought she was referring to his clumsy seduction, but no, apparently not. "How could you think of just goin' off like that? If I hadn'a run into you tonight, would you have left for Los Angeles without sayin' a word?"

"I—I—no," Ian stammered. "But I didn't think you'd be so upset."

"Upset? *Upset?* I could die!"

"You could?"

Her eyes softened, and she took his face in her hands, taking off his glasses and slipping them into his pocket, then pulling his head down close so she could tease his lips with her tongue. "Yes, you big ninny," she said between caresses.

"Don't you *know* how hot I am for you?" At that moment, Ian experienced total meltdown. He became putty, hers to mold to her will, which he prayed would include letting him plaster himself over every inch of her body.

Suddenly, Caitlyn pulled away. He stood, staring, as she reached behind her, pulling open the car door. Flipping the driver's seat forward, she shimmied into the back, her eyes never leaving his as she drew him in behind her. Ian climbed in, pausing only long enough to yank the door shut. By the time he turned around, she was reclined on the seat, her fingers slowly unbuttoning, one by one, the tiny buttons that ran down the front of her dress, playing with herself as she went. He was mesmerized. His fingers reached for his own belt and he undid it, whipping it off so that the buckle wouldn't bruise a millimeter of the perfect white flesh he saw emerging from those parting folds of silk. He sat at her feet, only his hands reaching out to stroke and explore, holding the rest of himself back, relishing the tantalizing ache building inside.

Caitlyn sat up to work on his pants and shirt. Her fingers moved over him with the same slow, deliberate movements that they had over herself, and Ian grit his teeth at the sweet torture. When she had spread his clothing wide, she lay back and raised her arms above her head, a smile playing at her lips as her body arched and writhed, just for him. The gauzy, sheer bra and panties she wore hid nothing. He shifted position, and in the brief moment between the time Ian removed her underthings and lowered himself onto her, it flashed through his mind that she was a natural redhead, in case he had ever doubted it. The inside of the Impala grew as steamy and perfumed as the sultry Georgia summer night outside. Ian knew that any passerby in the parking lot would know by the rocking of the Chevy and its fogged windows exactly what was transpiring inside, but at that particular moment, he couldn't have cared less.

He and Caitlyn eventually moved their passion from the car to her apartment, and by the time the night was over, he had convinced her to go with him to Los Angeles. Much later, Ian realized that she had grown bored after a year in the governor's office, and that even before he'd announced his plans, she'd been looking for an excuse to move on. A low threshold for boredom, in fact, turned out to be Caitlyn Allis's defining character trait. It played against him eventually, as much as it had played *for* him that night.

When Mallory and Ian were seated at their table in Bogart's Café, she spent the first few minutes glancing nervously around the restaurant, on the lookout for faces that might have been there when she and Drew Beekman were working and having their seven-week whatever-it-was. The memory wasn't warm and fuzzy enough for her to be able to think of it as a love affair. Lust affair, maybe.

But along with the name, the staff and the decor had also changed. Gone were the asparagus ferns, the folk music and the backgammon tables where hirsute patrons had wiled away long hours. The laid-back look had been superseded by a hard-edged, black-and-white interior that suggested brisk Yuppie efficiency, and the place hummed to a discreet jazz rhythm.

When their meals arrived, Mallory dug in hungrily while Ian explained why he had called. Suddenly, she looked up from her pasta to his broad smile, her heart jumping a beat. "A contract? To write for the *Chronicle?* Don't joke about this, please, because it means too much to me."

"No joke. It's not a staff position, mind you, just a temporary replacement for someone who's taking a book leave, but you'll get some good experience on your résumé."

"I'll take it! When do I start?"

"You'll have to discuss that with Celia Webster, but I think she'd like you as soon as possible."

"Celia Webster? The Lifestyles editor?"

"That's right. She's the one with the opening."

Mallory slumped in her chair. Damn! There was always a catch.

"What's wrong?"

She looked up at him, grimacing. "Lifestyles, Ian? Yuck! I don't want to write that fluff."

"It's a good place for you."

"Why? Because I'm female?"

Ian frowned behind his wire-rimmed glasses. "No, because you're just starting out and the atmosphere in that section is lower-key and less cutthroat than in some of the others."

"You think I can't compete in hard news, is that it?"

"You know that's not what I think. But the fact is, Mallory, it's a buyers' market in journalism right now. Journalism schools are pumping out hundreds of grads every year. We don't even *look* at them until they've got at least five years' experience on another daily. For that matter, with the hiring freeze, the *Chronicle's* not looking at *anyone* right now. I'll tell you one thing—not many of those J-school grads would turn down the chance you're being offered."

Mallory's stomach contracted. What an idiot she was. Ian was right, of course. He was obviously annoyed, too. Much as she was used to annoying people, keeping Ian Gallagher's respect was important, and not just because he was an *L.A. Chronicle* editor. This was one good guy, she'd long since decided. Although the difference in their ages and positions made them unlikely candidates for friendship, she felt more comfortable with Ian than with anyone since the old days with Wiley Dixon in Ferry Falls. Ian had been helpful and patient, giving praise when it was due and showing her the ropes. As a bonus, he hadn't even tried to hit on her, not once in all their late nights together. It had been a long time since Mallory had felt she could let down her guard where men were concerned— after her disastrous experiences with Gunnar and Drew—but this nice man with the easy style and brilliant mind gave her hope that there might be a few princes out there in the swamp, among all those frogs.

"I'm sorry, Ian. I know what you're saying is true, but there you go," she said, waving a hand. "I'm always in a big hurry to run before I walk." She was relieved to see his face relax into a smile.

"You'll run soon enough. In the meantime, I think you'll like Celia Webster. Can I tell her you'll call?"

"For sure. And I really *am* grateful. I know your recommendation is the only reason she's willing to look at me. I don't know why you're being so nice, but I promise, I won't embarrass you. You'll see. I'm going to write the best fluff this town has ever seen."

He laughed. "I know you will. That's why I recommended you. After all, I wouldn't want the reporter who scooped me getting snapped up by the opposition."

31

Los Angeles, California
September 22, 1983

Mallory stood at the photocopy machine in the *L.A. Chronicle* morgue, copying an entry from *Who's Who*. She'd spent the past four months compiling background material and fact-checking information for society notices, book signings, seniors' events, health lectures, engagements and weddings. Her most substantive assignments had consisted of wire-copy rewrites and filler pieces, none of them longer than a few column inches. Despite the misgivings she'd expressed to Ian about writing for Lifestyles, even a fluff piece would be welcome right about now.

She sighed and held down the thick *Who's Who* volume and pressed the start button, leaving the lid up. The machine clunked to life, its blinding light rolling across her features like some indoor klieg. When the copy dropped into the tray, Mallory leaned over to take a look at it. A corner of the text had been cut off. Releasing another deep sigh, she readjusted the book on the glass and hit the start button once more, setting the machine to humming.

As she stretched to check her second effort, still keeping one hand on the book, Mallory felt a sudden bristle animate her spine, and she turned her head in time to catch a gaze flitting from her backside to her face. It was the senior editor of the paper, Grady O'Toole. In charge of the Op-Ed page and Sunday Commentary section, he was considered the *Chronicle's* resident deep intellectual. She'd seen him around and had been told who he was, but Mallory had never met the man. He was fifty-something, with steel gray hair swept back. His pale green eyes, now fixed on her, were vaguely reptilian. His prominent nose and narrow face seemed elongated, and the deep crevices that ran from either side of his nose to his fleshy lips gave his mouth the appearance of being set in a permanent sneer. He was very tall but round-shouldered, in the manner of one who has spent his life talking down to others.

Mallory straightened and tugged self-consciously at her skirt. "I'm sorry," she said. "Did you need to use the photocopier?"

"No hurry." O'Toole tucked a file folder under his arm. "Please, finish what you were doing."

"I'm done. I just—" She stammered, feeling inexplicably nervous. "I was having a little trouble getting the text aligned."

He approached, leaning past her, his sleeve brushing her blouse front as he lifted the copy from the tray. "Gathering information on Vernon Cunningham, I see. Is Celia Webster planning a major exposé on his bank?"

"No. It's for background on a piece about his wife, Dierdre. She's organizing a charity event on behalf of—" Mallory stopped, realizing that he hadn't been serious and he wasn't interested. A smile played around his lips as he watched her face. "Anyway," she said, retrieving the book from the glass, "I'm all done."

O'Toole nodded, but made no move to give back her copy or step out of the way. Unable to meet his unwavering gaze, her eyes dropped to his pinstriped shirt, suspenders and bow tie. They lent an eastern-establishment air to his persona, the effect carefully cultivated, Mallory decided.

"Vern and DeeDee Cunningham are friends of mine," O'Toole said. "If you need more information, perhaps I could help."

"Thank you, but I'm sure I won't have to bother you."

"No bother—Mallory, isn't it?" He held out his hand. "Grady O'Toole. I'm the senior editor around here."

"Yes, sir, I know who you are." Mallory put her hand in his, and he held on until she was forced to look at his face. Only then did he relax his grip and give back her material.

"I wonder if I could ask you to do something for me, Mallory? I need copies of the three top articles in this file, but I'm expecting a call. Could you make the copies and bring them up?" He handed her the file folder. "You know where my office is? On twenty-seven, next to Carson Hoag's? Good."

He wheeled around and was gone before Mallory had a chance to say a word. She fumed, but went ahead and made the copies. When she arrived at his top-floor office a few minutes later, O'Toole was standing behind his desk, gazing out the window. His view was to the west, and although the ocean could be seen sparkling several miles away, the view was clouded by a thick, brown haze of smog. Mallory hesitated in the doorway, then rapped.

The editor turned and smiled. "Mallory! Come in. Put that over here on the credenza, would you?" The cabinet ran under the window before him. She walked over and dropped the copies. "Look at that," O'Toole said.

"What?"

"Out there. The air quality. It's a disgrace, isn't it?"

She glanced at the sludge spread over the city like a layer of beige whipped cream. "Not too appealing," she agreed.

O'Toole stepped closer and put one hand on her shoulder, the other extending toward the water, as one leg brushed against her hip. His scent, which she had picked up in the photocopy room, was stronger here. The entire office, in fact, exuded an odor reminiscent of Jean Naté, strong and citrusy, with a faint, alcoholic overtone. It was like being cornered by a lemon tree in a singles bar.

"On a clear day, you can see Catalina, but there seem to be fewer and fewer clear days as time goes on." O'Toole turned toward her, his face only inches away. "Are you from Los Angeles, Mallory?"

She hesitated. "I moved here four years ago. From Minnesota."

"I see. Minnesota. That would account for those healthy good looks. On your own?" His hand slid casually from her shoulder to the small of her back.

"Yes." *Get out,* a panicky voice in her head cried.

"That's a big step for a young woman. L.A. can be a tough city. But you look like a girl who can handle herself."

"I'd better get back to work now," Mallory said, slipping away from his touch. She couldn't avoid one last brush as she squeezed around him, especially since he showed no inclination to step aside and make room for her to pass.

"Mallory?" he called as she reached the door. She looked back at the editor. "You come strongly recommended from Ian Gallagher. He says you're very good." O'Toole's gaze followed an unmistakable path from her face to her breasts, and below. He smiled and looked up again, arms opening to take in his surroundings. His was one of only two corner offices among the editorial staff. The other belonged to Carson Hoag, the managing editor. "I have some small influence around here. If there's ever anything *I* can do for you, don't hesitate to come and see me, will you?"

Mallory stared at him, stunned. "I'll be fine, thanks," she finally managed to blurt out. Her face was hot and her heart was beating furiously as she strode quickly across the outer office.

Passing Carson Hoag's door, she almost collided with Celia Webster, who had been in seeing him. "Mallory?" Celia said, puzzled. "I was looking for you a while ago. What are you doing up here?"

Mallory glanced at O'Toole's door, then continued toward the elevator, Celia alongside. "I was making photocopies in the morgue when Mr. O'Toole came in. He asked me to do some for him and bring them up when I was finished."

"It figures," the editor said, frowning. They stood watching the progression of lights over the elevator. "Look," Celia said, her voice low, "I know it's tough when you're dealing with someone senior like Grady O'Toole, but you're not hired to be at his beck and call, and you aren't obliged to make copies for him. That's why he has a secretary."

"I know. He won't catch me twice. I just wasn't quick enough on my feet this time."

The elevator came and they rode down in silence, Mallory fuming as she felt her boss watching out of the corner of her eye. When they got to their floor, Celia asked her to come into her office and close the door. Celia sat down and drummed her fingers on the arm of her chair for a moment, then leaned forward. "Did anything else happen up there?" she asked.

Mallory shook her head disgustedly. "Nothing I couldn't handle." She stared at the wall, a sick feeling in her stomach.

Finally, she took a deep breath and looked at the older woman. "O'Toole implied that I got this job because I was sleeping with Ian Gallagher."

Celia's eyebrows shot up. "*Are* you sleeping with Ian?"

"No, of course not! But O'Toole seems to think so. Where would he get an idea like that?"

"Not from Ian, rest easy."

"Are you sure?"

"Absolutely. I've known Ian Gallagher for six years and he is *not* that kind of man."

"Do other people think that's why I was hired?"

"No, they know me better. I'm not in the habit of hiring anybody's bimbo."

Mallory looked down at her silk blouse and soft flannel skirt, smoothing them. She had spent most of her first two *Chronicle* paychecks on a new wardrobe. She'd tried for a conservative look, but had she chosen badly? Was that why she'd drawn this kind of unwelcome attention?

Celia seemed to read her mind. "It's not you, Mallory," she said. "It's not anything you did, or anything you wore. It's Grady. Look, he may be some hotshot intellectual—although frankly, I've never thought anything he's written was *that* brilliant—but he happens to be a jerk where women are concerned. He's been married three times, and he thinks every female on this paper is his personal plaything. He even came on to me, believe it or not."

"What did you do?"

"I told him to go fuck himself, although I wouldn't recommend that course of action to you. Grady can be vindictive."

"Did he try to get you fired?"

"He didn't have that kind of pull back then and I had my own allies. But he *did* spread the rumor that I was a lesbian. I think he believed it, too. After all, if I wasn't interested in the great Grady O'Toole, I must be, right?" Celia shook her head, grimacing. "The best thing for you to do is avoid him."

"It's not right."

"I know that, but if you go up against him, you won't win."

"But if he's doing this to other women . . ."

"It's an old-boys' club around here, Mallory. You may have noticed that the *Chronicle* has very few female reporters outside of Lifestyles, no female columnists and no one but me on the editorial board. O'Toole wouldn't even get a slap on the wrist. Half the guys around here think horny old Grady's just a hoot. Some of them aren't much better themselves, and they think the *real* problem is women with PMS overreacting to a little harmless flirtation.''

''Is that what Ian Gallagher thinks?''

''No, not Ian, nor the rest of our male colleagues who've evolved beyond the Neanderthal stage. The working environment for women on this paper has actually gotten better in the past few years, believe it or not.''

''Obviously, there's still a long way to go.''

''Obviously. But don't let it get you down, Mallory. We'll get there. You know what they say—women hold up half the sky.''

''Now, if we could only figure out a way to drop it on the Grady O'Tooles of this world!''

Celia laughed, but then her smile faded again. ''One more thing, Mallory.''

''What's that?''

''Don't let Grady affect your relationship with Ian.''

''There *is* no relationship!''

''I know that. What I mean is, don't let that ass put you in the position of second-guessing your every word and action when Ian's around. If you let Grady influence your behavior in any way, then you've given him power over you. You don't want that.''

''You bet I don't. Thanks, Celia.'' Mallory settled back in the chair, feeling a little better. ''You said you were looking for me.''

''That's right, I was. Leona Britten's come down with chicken pox. Can you believe it?'' Britten covered society functions for Life-styles.

Mallory grimaced. ''Yuck. It's supposed to be awful when you get it as an adult.''

''She's sick as a dog, poor thing. She'll be out for a couple of weeks, at least, and I'm going to need you to cover for her, starting tomorrow.''

''What's up?''

"It's that charity reception and fashion show tomorrow in Newport Beach on behalf of the Braemar Children's Home—the one Dierdre Cunningham is organizing?"

"In Orange County? I don't have a car, Celia. I've been thinking about getting one, because my motorcycle's going to die on me one of these days, but at the moment . . ."

"One of our photographers will be going. I'm sure you can get a lift."

Mallory took a deep breath, puffing out her cheeks as she exhaled. Looking up the Cunninghams in *Who's Who,* she'd noticed that Dierdre Cunningham's husband, Vernon, president of the Bank of Newport, was also a director of the Beekman Development Corporation, which meant that Drew's parents, Andrew and Asa Beekman, could well show up at this affair. How could she tell Celia Webster that one of southern California's leading real-estate developers had once threatened to have her arrested?

"I know this is short notice," Celia went on, "but we're under strict instructions from upstairs to increase Orange County coverage throughout the paper. It's the wealthiest, fastest-growing part of the Greater Los Angeles Area, and Orange County advertising revenues have played a big part in pulling this paper back into the black. You have to do this, Mallory. I haven't got anyone else. So get out your fanciest duds and off you go."

"That could be a problem," Mallory said, thinking of the one evening dress she had hanging in her closet at Lili's. It was the peach disco number she bought in Minneapolis for her senior prom with Gunnar Anderson. She had worn it only one other time, to Ariel Beekman's wedding, but it was hopelessly out of style now.

"You don't have a cocktail dress?" Celia asked. Mallory shrugged and shook her head. The editor reached for her Rolodex. "No-o problem. Give me a few minutes to make a call and finish up a couple of little jobs here, and then we're off."

"Off where?"

The gray-haired woman clucked her tongue. "Just leave it to me, Cinderella. You'll see."

* * *

Forty-five minutes later, Mallory and Celia stood on Rodeo Drive in front of the travertine, glass, and bronze facade of an obviously expensive boutique called, simply, Fauve. Mallory had seen it before on her explorations of the city, but she had never been inside. Since the store had no display windows, there was no guessing what it sold. She had decided that it was one of those chichi places that if you had to ask, you were (a) too unhip, and (b) too poor to walk in the door. Funny, she thought, she had never thought of Celia Webster as being either hip or wealthy, but there she was, hand confidently on the door, ready to roll in. Mallory held back.

"Come on," the other woman said. "What's the matter?"

"I can't afford a place like this, Celia."

"Yes, you can."

"No, I can't."

"Look on it as an investment. Come on, trust me," Celia added, grabbing her by the elbow and pulling her in. "You'll be fine."

Stepping inside the doors of Fauve did little to clear up the mystery of what it was all about. Mallory found herself in a sort of lobby, its floors tiled in off-white marble and its walls covered in a textured beige fabric that she guessed was silk. There was a grouping of bleached wooden armchairs off to one side, their plump seats and backs upholstered in ivory damask. On the low marble table in the center of the chairs sat a fantastic dried-floral arrangement in browns and creams and rusts, accented with gilt-sprayed branches. Angled across the other side of the room was an elaborately carved and fluted antique desk in dark, reddish mahogany. Behind the desk, a striking young woman sat smiling at them. Another surreal dried-floral arrangement stood behind her on a marble pedestal, a taller version of the one on the low table.

"Hello, Amy," Celia said to the young woman. "How are you today?"

"I'm fine, Miss Webster. It's good to see you again. Zara's expecting you. I'll let her know you're here."

"Thanks."

The woman disappeared through a side door. Curiosity getting the better of her, Mallory turned to the editor. "Zara?"

"Zara Tate. The designer? This is her store."

"It doesn't look like a store."

"No, that's true. Zara caters to a very exclusive clientele. Her customers don't like to strain themselves flipping through dress racks, so they come here to be outfitted. Zara's more than a designer, in fact, she's a total wardrobe and image consultant. If you'd been reading our fashion columns, you'd know she dresses several Hollywood stars and half the wealthy women west of Texas."

"So what am *I* doing here?"

"Fringe benefit, Mallory. It's a well-established practice that designers give fashion reporters deep discounts on their clothing."

"Is that ethical?"

"There's no direct quid pro quo, if that's what you mean— no promise from the reporters to provide coverage or positive reviews. But it keeps the reporters current on the latest trends, and the designers just write it off as a cost of doing business."

"I'm not a fashion reporter."

"I know, and I told Zara that when I called, but she's an old friend and had no problem with you coming in."

Mallory felt skeptical but before she could say anything more, the door at the back of the room opened and out came a tall, pencil-thin, stunningly beautiful woman. She walked over and hugged Celia, then held out her hand to Mallory. "Hi, there," she said. "You must be Mallory. Zara Tate. Good to meet you."

"Nice to meet you, too."

"Celia tells me you need a dynamite dress in a big hurry."

"I guess so. There's a charity reception in Newport Beach tomorrow that Celia wants me to cover, and they probably won't let me in if I show up in blue jeans."

Zara laughed. "The Braemar Children's Home affair, right? I've got a few pieces in that show and I'll be there, too, as a matter of fact." She stood back and examined Mallory, stroking her chin thoughtfully. "What are you, about a size six?"

"Usually."

"That's what I thought. I have some sample dresses that might do. Most of our clothing is made to order, but we do up samples so clients can see what they're getting. Come on back

and we'll see what we can find. I've got lunch waiting," she
added to Celia, draping an arm around her shoulder.

"Good. I'm starved," the older woman said.

Mallory followed them into a large room behind the reception area. It was furnished with the same quiet elegance as the
front, except that here, instead of marble, the floor was covered in deep, plush, mushroom-colored carpeting. Aside from
the large three-way mirror in one corner and pincushions on a
nearby table, the room looked more like the living room of a
comfortable home than a commercial establishment. There
were several chairs and a sofa grouped in the center, and the low
table between them held a spread of tiny sandwiches, fruit and
pastries. A white-uniformed young man stood by, looking
waiterly.

"Take a seat and help yourselves to a bite while Amy and I
pick out a few things for Mallory to try," Zara said. "Mallory, eat fast, because you're going to have to do all the work
here while Celia and I kick back and gossip."

When Mallory and Celia were settled, the waiter came forward and offered them white wine, but Mallory opted to stick
with soda water. Following Celia's lead, she took a china plate
and a linen napkin, then peered at the tray of sandwiches. She
selected smoked salmon and a bunch of grapes, then settled
back to eat quickly, as ordered.

"So, what's the story here?" she asked between bites. "How
do you know Zara?"

"I met her ten, fifteen years ago in New York when she
staged her first show. I was doing a feature on new American
designers and I thought her stuff was great—elegant, comfortable clothes for real women. Unfortunately, the New York
fashion press didn't agree."

"They trashed her work?"

"Viciously."

"Why?"

Celia popped a whole-egg salad triangle in her mouth and
shrugged. "Any number of reasons," she mumbled. "Most of
those, I suspect, had little to do with the clothes."

"What do you mean?"

"Zara was an odd duck in designing circles. She was mostly
self-taught, with little formal training, never apprenticed in

another house, was female *and* black. To top all that, she was a former model, which meant, by definition, that she had to be an airhead as far as the business was concerned. Then she went ahead and brought out a line of fairly deconstructed, loose-fitting clothes that you could move and breathe in, at a time when prevailing fashion currents were going in the direction of short, tight and fitted. She broke all their rules, and so they made her pay for it with snide reviews.''

''Are you telling Mallory about my auspicious New York debut?''

Mallory was surprised by Zara's voice. She hadn't heard her step in the deep carpet. Celia nodded as the owner took a seat in a chair opposite.

''I was ready to jump off the Brooklyn Bridge,'' Zara said, ''until I saw a copy of Celia's piece in the *Chronicle,* praising my work and lambasting the New York press. I moved out here a month later and I've never looked back. I still don't get much respect from New York, but then, neither does any other California designer.''

''And you're crying all the way to the bank,'' Celia said, smiling.

''Things have gone well,'' Zara agreed. ''Californians are more laid-back and experimental. If I never see Seventh Avenue again, it'll be too soon.''

''Celia says you were a model,'' Mallory said. ''That doesn't surprise me.''

''I worked at it for about eight years. Eileen Ford signed me when I was seventeen, but I did most of my work in Europe. This was over twenty years ago, you see, so there wasn't much call for black models in this country. Things are changing now, but back then, I was considered an 'exotic' in Paris when I was just unemployable here.''

''Over *twenty years ago?* You look like you're only in your twenties now!'' Mallory exclaimed.

Zara laughed. ''I *wish*. On second thought, cancel that. I'd never want to go back to being your age. It's too insecure. I'm having more fun now.'' The waiter appeared at her elbow without asking, handing her spritzer in a wineglass. Zara took a sip, then looked up. ''Well, ready to try on some dresses?

Amy's got some outfits waiting for you in the dressing area through that door.''

Forty minutes later, after trying on half a dozen different dresses, Mallory had settled with difficulty—but with Zara's and Celia's advice—on a versatile black silk number. "Your basic little black dress," Celia said, nodding approvingly.

"Not to be immodest, but I love this dress," Zara said, getting up to adjust it.

Made of a rich, shimmering silk, it had a closely fitted bodice, shirred at the center, and a straight, simple line that fell to the knee. Its spaghetti straps were removable, and there was a matching jacket, as well as a trailing scarf. Mallory watched as Zara looped the scarf through a tiny, concealed tab in the center of the bodice and flipped the ends over her shoulders, letting them drape loosely down her back.

"Okay. You've got this look," the designer said. "Or you can tie the ends behind your neck, and it's a halter dress. Or, hook the ends through the same place the removable spaghetti straps go, straight or crossed, and you've got another dress again. *Or* use the scarf as a shawl, or tie it around your neck, or—well, you get the idea. And then, of course, you've got the jacket, and you can accessorize with jewelry. In short, one outfit, endless looks. No one will ever notice you're wearing the same dress, over and over." Zara stood back, shaking her head in mock amazement. "*Gawd*, but I'm good!"

Mallory stared at herself in the three-way mirror. Gunnar Anderson had thought she was beautiful in that peach polyester thing, she thought. If he could only see her now! She glanced at Celia's beaming reflection in the mirror, then gazed back at herself and sighed. "It's gorgeous," she said to Zara, "but I don't know."

"It was *made* for you, Mallory. And you have to take the shoes, too. They're perfect."

Mallory looked longingly at the black suede Ferragamo pumps that Amy had given her to try with the dress. They were the most comfortable things she'd ever had on her feet that didn't come with laces and rubber soles. She shook her head. "It's all wonderful, Zara, but to be frank, I doubt if I can afford you. What does this dress cost, anyway?"

"It was eighteen hundred dollars when it came out—"

Mallory's head began to buzz.

"But it's from last season's line. So if we discount for that, let's see . . ."

"I don't think—"

"Could you manage two hundred and fifty dollars? You could pay me over time, if you want. I won't charge interest."

"*What?*"

"Too high? Actually, I'm throwing in the shoes, and I'm only charging you for my cost of the fabric, but if that's too much—"

"I'll take it!"

"Good."

"This is so great of you, Zara."

"No problem. People helped me when I was starting out, and now it's my turn. When you're rich and famous, I expect you to do the same."

"In my dreams," Mallory said, rolling her eyes.

"That's right. Don't you *ever* stop dreaming, girl. Just make sure," Zara added sternly, "that when you see yourself in those dreams, you're wearing Zara Tate originals."

Mallory laughed and gave her a hug. "Nothing but."

32

Diana sat on a stool in front of her dressing table, brushing her hair, ears tuned to the conversation across the hall, where three-year-old Remy was engaged in an ongoing commentary on his bedtime story.

"Papa? Those hunters were bad to shoot Babar's mama, weren't they?"

"Papa? Babar's really strong, isn't he?"

"Papa? Do elephants kiss with their noses?"

To each question, Marcus's deep voice responded patiently and the book, as usual, took three times as long as necessary to get through. When their son's light was finally switched off and the door closed, Marcus came into their room, a grin lingering on his lips.

"Maybe you should consider skipping pages," Diana said, smiling.

He shook his head. "I wouldn't dare. He knows every word by heart."

"Not surprising, considering that we've read him the Babar story at least a thousand times. Do you think we'll ever graduate to Astérix?"

Marcus settled behind her on the stool and wrapped her in his arms, resting his chin on her shoulder as he studied her face in the mirror. "I don't care. I'll read Babar to him until my eyes grow too feeble to see the page, if that's what he wants."

Diana leaned into him, safe and warm. A little incredulous, as always. Marcus had given her a life she would never have dared to wish for. When they'd married, she had wanted more than anything to give him back the gift of a life, but the doctors had concluded that her body, internally scarred after the explosion, would never conceive. Marcus had said it didn't matter. When, miraculously, she became pregnant, the doctors said she would never carry the baby to term. Diana had spent nearly six months in bed, desperate to hold on. The baby was born five weeks early, but Remy had proved to be a tiny fighter, imbued with his mother's determination that he survive. Marcus had cried the first time he held his son in his arms.

"Do you ever wonder what might have happened," she asked now, "if I hadn't sketched you in the *brasserie*, that day you came to speak to Jean Grenier's class?"

"I would have ended up right here in this house, a lonely, miserable old man."

"No. You would have met some wonderful woman."

"I *did* meet a wonderful woman." Marcus's hands began massaging her shoulders. "If we hadn't met that day, it would have been another day, and another place. This was meant to be. I know that now."

Diana closed her eyes. "I can't even bear to think about what it was like before."

"Then don't. Just think about me and Remy. We'll always be here for you." He growled and bit her ear lightly. "You're stuck with this old wolf, like it or not."

Diana leaned into him, smiling. "I like it. A lot."

Newport Beach, California
September 23, 1983

Andrew Beekman, sated and limp, lay back on the pillow, hands behind his head, staring at the ceiling. His mistress still straddled him, her body rocking slowly as her mouth and hands traveled across his broad chest, stroking and kissing. Her lips moved to his neck, but when her long, streaky blond hair fell over his nose and mouth, he felt a flash of annoyance. "That's enough, Kira!" he said, shoving her off. "Stop it."

She rolled over and rested on her side, watching him for a moment, then sighed. "You don't have to be such a grouch," she said, lips forming a pout.

Beekman glanced at her, then pulled himself to a sitting position. "I have to go."

"Already? You just got here."

"I have dinner plans."

"I thought we'd have dinner together."

"Can't. I'm meeting my wife and the Cunninghams."

"Goody for you," the girl grumbled.

Beekman took himself off to shower, having no interest in arguing with her. She was twenty-two and beautiful, but he didn't keep her for her brilliant repartee. She had waited on him and Asa at dinner one night at San Domenico. After a quiet chat with the girl while his wife was in the ladies' room, Beekman had dropped back later to pick her up when the restaurant closed.

Kira had been occupying his penthouse condo in Long Beach for almost a year now, the fifth in a line of occupants, each one lasting as long as they could hold Andrew Beekman's interest and endure his cold, controlling nature. She spent her days shopping or sunning or doing whatever she wanted, as long as she was available when he said he was coming. He dropped in several times a week, sometimes staying for the night if Asa was away. Other times, he came at midday or for a few hours in the evening. Often, like tonight, all he wanted from her was a quick release of tension before rushing off to another business or social engagement.

When he returned to the bedroom, she was lying on her stomach, flipping through a magazine. Beekman moved around the room, gathering his things and getting into his suit. "I'll probably see you tomorrow or Sunday," he said as he tightened his tie.

She rolled onto her side, propping her head on her hand. "I'm going to Vegas tomorrow."

"What?"

"Nichols called this afternoon. He said he needs me to go again."

"Nobody told me. This is the third time this month!"

Kira shrugged. "You told me I should do this for him, so I said okay. Anyway," she added, her lower lip drooping again, "it's nice to be taken out someplace for a change."

Beekman's anger erupted without warning. "What's *that* supposed to mean? You're not happy living here?" He strode to the walk-in closet, yanking out clothes and throwing them to the floor. "You're not well taken care of? You think you work too *hard* for all this, do you?"

"No! Don't, Andrew! I'm not complaining. It's just—"

"Just *what?*" he shouted.

"It's just that he's nice to me, and—"

Beekman was on her in a flash. He yanked her to her knees, his face hot as he gripped her roughly by the shoulders. "Is he fucking you, too?"

"You're hurting me!" He threw her back on the bed but continued to loom, fists clenched, breathing fast and heavy. She had her arms wrapped around herself, rubbing her shoulders, and she was crying. "I just go because you *told* me to!"

Beekman studied her, his thoughts swirling. Then he spun around and grabbed his jacket, heading for the living room. "Christ!" he muttered. "I don't have time for this!"

"Andrew, please! Wait!" Kira called as he slammed the front door.

Mallory sat on a chair near the runway at the Braemar Children's Home charity reception and fashion show. In order to read her notebook, she'd propped it on her crossed knees and angled it toward what little light there was in the ballroom, aside from the spots focused on the models. Keeping one eye on the show and on her program, she scribbled in her precariously balanced spiral flip notebook, composing her copy.

She and Bill Preston, the *Chronicle* photographer, were due back downtown by 9:00 p.m. Even if traffic was good and they made it on time, there would be less than an hour to type up her story, have Celia go over it, then get it copyedited and typeset in time for the piece and Preston's photos to make the *Chronicle's* late edition. The two of them had already agreed to make a dash for the door as soon as the houselights went on.

Arriving at the Newport Hyatt forty minutes before the 6:00 p.m. event was to begin, Mallory had walked around, getting her bearings, peeking at the mayhem backstage, and introducing herself to Dierdre Cunningham—who preferred to be called

DeeDee, she told Mallory, peering over Mallory's shoulder to make sure she got the spelling correct.

As they were talking, Mallory wondered nervously if Mrs. Cunningham would remember their meeting at Ariel Beekman's wedding four years earlier, an encounter which Mallory herself had forgotten until she saw the woman face-to-face. It was this woman, she recalled, who'd prattled on about a daughter of hers whom a much younger Drew had once been caught kissing. But, preoccupied and suffering from preevent jitters, Mrs. Cunningham had shown no sign of recognition.

That in itself was not so surprising, Mallory thought, but she was *really* thrown when DeeDee called Asa Beekman over and insisted that Bill Preston take their picture together. Afterward, when DeeDee had run off to talk to the Hyatt manager about some detail or another, Asa had turned and focused her attention on Mallory. "You're from the *Chronicle?* What did you say your name was again?"

"I didn't, but it's Mallory Caine."

"Nice to meet you. My husband is Andrew Beekman. Of Beekman Development Corporation?"

"Yes, I know."

"Of course. You would, wouldn't you? His company is a major advertiser in the *Chronicle*—every weekend, pages and pages of the *Chronicle* devoted to his housing ads. I'm sure it comes to quite a tidy bit of revenue. *My* name, by the way," she added, her smile fixed, "is spelled A-S-A. I *so* dislike it when people add an extra S."

"I'm sure that would be very annoying," Mallory said, making a show of noting it in her book. She was stunned. The woman clearly didn't remember her. So much for her impact on the Beekman clan—Andrew Senior's heavy-handed action notwithstanding.

"That's a marvelous dress, dear. Is it an original?"

"It's a Zara Tate."

"Oh, wonderful! She's here, you know. We're *so* pleased to have her."

"Yes, I was just talking to her backstage. She's a friend," Mallory couldn't resist adding.

"Really? Well, we *must* visit some more, Marjorie." Asa glanced across the room to where Mrs. Cunningham was waving at her. "I see DeeDee needs me right now. She gets *so* flustered!"

"Don't let me keep you, Mrs. Beekman."

"I'll talk to you later, Marjorie."

Mallory nodded. Not if I can help it, she thought. She'd debated mentioning their last encounter, but what was the point? She had no idea what Andrew Beekman might have told his wife about her, but even if he hadn't said a word, Mallory had no desire to be brought up to date on Drew's career, much less his love life. The less she had to do with anyone named Beekman, the better, as far as she was concerned.

Andrew Beekman was sitting with Vern Cunningham in the Hyatt lounge, nursing a drink while they waited for their wives. Suddenly, looking over Cunningham's shoulder, he saw a young, blond woman walk by the door. Her hair was pinned up, and she wore a black dress and jacket with a scarf flipped over her shoulders. He watched her in profile as she paused to speak to a passing bellhop, who pointed through the lobby. The woman nodded and moved on across the plush Oriental carpet, out of sight.

Something ominous arose in Beekman's mind, but the memory hovered in the shadows, just beyond reach. He tried to grasp it, but it remained elusive, a dark image that made him shiver, as if someone had walked over his grave. Beekman took a sip from his Scotch, pondering, then put down his glass and slid back his chair. "Think I'll take a wizz before the wives get here, Vern. Won't be a minute."

In the lobby, Beekman hesitated, glancing around. Going in the direction the woman had taken, he passed an archway and was almost to the elevator bank, when he heard a voice and turned toward an alcove off the lobby. Looking in, he saw that she was on the phone, her back to him. Her hip leaning into the wall, she played with the telephone cord, long wisps of hair caressing her neck as she moved. She seemed completely unselfconscious, oblivious to the effect she created as she stood, storklike, one foot idly stroking the back of the opposite calf. The Ferragamo label, burned into the sole of her shoe, rose and fell with each slow, sensuous movement of her long legs. Beekman watched, fascinated.

"We're all done here, Celia," the young woman was saying. "Barring a major bottleneck on the freeway, I should get back in plenty of time.... The show was okay. I saw Zara. Her stuff was the hit of the night." She laughed softly. "Right, a plug in good conscience.... Okay, see you in a while."

Beekman stepped into the alcove, determined to find a pretext to talk to her. And then what? he asked himself. Asa was going to appear any minute. Get her phone number?

The woman turned around, a smile lingering on her face, but when she spotted him, it vanished. "Mr. Beekman!" she gasped.

It took only a split second of those dark eyes burning into him for Beekman, too, to be shocked into recognition. "You!"

She stumbled back, bumping into the telephone table. One hand went to it to steady herself as she glanced around, searching frantically, it seemed, for help or an escape route. He blocked the only available exit. "Well?" she said, pulling herself upright and crossing her arms. "What are you going to do? Try to have me arrested again?"

"What are you doing here?"

"It's a public place. I have as much right to be here as you."

Beekman watched her show of defiance, feeling both annoyed and amused by the absurdity of it. The snippet! Who the hell did she think she was, speaking to him that way? And yet, her appearance set something stirring within him—a long-buried pain, struggling to free itself from the dark hole to which he had consigned it. He stared, fighting the urge to step forward and touch her.

"Well?" she repeated.

"How are you, Mallory?"

She exhaled a bitter laugh. "What do *you* care? I'm sure you haven't lost any sleep over the past four years, wondering what became of me after you threw me into the street."

"Nor did I need to, it seems, since you've obviously done well for yourself. You've grown quite beautiful, Mallory. You look very elegant this evening."

"And you look like you're surviving just fine, too—more's the pity. So, if that about does it for social pleasantries, would you excuse me? I have to be going." She took a step forward, but he blocked her path.

"Wait! Please, wait," Beekman repeated, his voice softer now. "There's something I want to say to you."

She stopped, but the wary expression never left her face. "I *am* in a hurry."

"This won't take long. I only..." He fumbled, searching for the words. "What happened before, about you and Drew—perhaps I overreacted."

"*Perhaps* you overreacted? I'd say so. It was like going after a fly with a howitzer. It might interest you to know, Mr. Beekman, that I never had any intention of marrying your son. We were fond of each other, but I don't think either of us seriously believed there was a long-term future in our relationship. We would have drifted apart eventually without your interference. As it is," she added, "I can't *tell* you how happy it makes me to think that you, yourself, wrote Drew's ticket out of this place. Out of this life that you'd planned for him, but he never wanted. You won the battle, Mr. Beekman, but you lost the war."

"I know that. I just...I was afraid."

"Well, sure, who wouldn't be? I was the most terrifying eighteen-year-old orphan the world has ever seen. The bad seed. You must have been been petrified!"

The words were brave and sarcastic, but she was trembling, Beekman noticed. Watching her, the old pain clawed at him again. And then, he thought about restitution, a way to make up for what had been wrenched away. To redress the balance, make things right. "You've been hurt," he said gently. "I didn't consider how it was for you. What it must have been like after...after what happened to you as a child." Beekman's voice was scarcely a whisper. "Losing your parents like that, it was a terrible thing."

Mallory could handle his dislike, it seemed, but she was clearly thrown by the idea of his sympathy. Her eyes glistened. "It was awful. I try not to think anymore about my parents, but I always carry inside me what happened to them. I sure as hell didn't need *you* to remind me where I came from."

"I'm sorry."

"It's taken a long time, Mr. Beekman, but I'm finally starting to live my own life, putting those memories behind me."

She held up her hands, palms out. "I just want the past to go away."

"Let me help you."

"Help me? How can *you* help me?"

He thought about the condo. He could have Kira out of it in twenty-four hours. Yes, he thought, that's the solution. It was only right, and there was a perfect symmetry to the idea. "I have a condo in Long Beach. It's yours. I owe you that, at least."

"I have no need for a condo in Long Beach. I live in the city."

"You're married?"

"No, but I work downtown."

"Well, a place in town then. I have buildings in Santa Monica, Westwood—"

"I *have* a place to live. I don't need another one. Why are you doing this?"

"Because it's only right, after what I did to you." Beekman took her hand and held it between his. "Let me take care of you, Mallory, please."

She snatched it back. "I don't need to be taken care of!"

He took her by the shoulders. "Yes, you *do*, and I'm the one to do it. I won't let anything hurt you, ever again."

"Mallory?" At the sound of a voice in the doorway, she shot a glance over his shoulder, her face registering relief.

"I'm coming, Bill!" She pushed past Beekman and headed for the lobby, turning only when she reached a man in a many-pocketed green battle jacket who had come looking for her.

"I don't need anything from you, Mr. Beekman," she said. "I don't want anything of yours. I never did."

33

It was nearly 10:00 p.m. when Ian Gallagher wrapped up the last of his editing tasks for the day and the week. Wearily slinging his sport coat over a shoulder, he switched off his desk lamp and headed for the elevator. When it came, he stepped on and pressed P-1, planning to head for his car and his bed in short order. But as the doors closed and lights overhead began to flash, a sudden impulse seized him, and he hit the button for the *Chronicle* building's fourteenth floor. The doors opened onto Celia Webster's fiefdom. At this hour on a Friday night, it was as deserted as his own section, but he could see by the frizzled, gray head bent over her desk in the glass-walled office that Celia was still at work.

One other person sat at a desk in the middle of the floor, adrift alone in a sea of phones and typewriters and scattered paper. By the location of the desk and the slight resemblance she bore to the stringer he had recommended to Celia, this was Mallory—theoretically. Ian paused, watching, as her fingers flew over her keyboard, a yellow pencil gripped between her teeth, the crease of a frown between her eyebrows. A typical Mallory pose, and additional evidence that the beauty in the black dress—incongruously placed in this Red Cross disaster of an office—was in fact his erstwhile protégée. Whatever happened to the ponytail and the prim blue suit?

When he walked over, she raised her head and pulled the pencil out of her mouth, a broad smile lighting up her face. "Hey, Pulitzer! How's it going?"

"I'm fine, but who are *you?* And what have you done with Mallory Caine?"

She sat back in her rolling chair, all legs and shimmering silk, and gave him a wry look. Then she rose to her feet and turned in a full circle, blond tendrils and the scarf of her dress wafting behind her like kite tails. Facing him again, she struck a hammy pose, one hand on hip, the other stretched out—Marlene Dietrich, Minnesota version. "This is the Lifestyles look. You know, Gallagher, this place is a *lot* spiffier than that Metro section rat hole of yours upstairs. We Lifestyles reporters take our image very seriously."

He laughed. "So, what's with the outfit? A new office dress code?"

"Actually, we're supposed to do a little better than this, but seeing as it's the weekend . . ."

"You're a nut." He cocked his head toward her typewriter. "What are you working on?"

"Want to see?" She ripped the copy out of the roll and handed it to him. Ian sat down on the edge of her desk and began reading:

GULP AND GUZZLE FOR
BRAEMAR CHILDREN'S HOME
NEWPORT LADIES SCHMOOZE

Boob jobs and tummy tucks were much in evidence last night at the annual Newport Beach Daiquiri Dash. The event, held to benefit some grubby little kids nobody really cared about, gave the matrons of this fat-cat coastal community a nice tax write-off for a popular booze-and-bitch affair.

"Abused children?" one guest said, referring to residents of the Braemar Children's Home. "I'll tell you about abuse—my gardener and my cook both quit this week. My mechanic flatly refuses to have the Porsche out of the shop in less than five days and my artificial nails have developed fungus." She sobbed, giving her mascara a dainty dab. "I don't know how I'm going to cope!"

Agreeing that the household-staff problem is a pressing social issue, most guests at the $200-a-head affair were of the view that revised child labor laws were the answer.

"After all," said socialite DeeDee Disdain, "the little beasts need to learn a trade, and we need servants who speak English. It's perfect, don't you think?"

Mrs. Disdain, wife of billionaire waste-disposal mogul Dagwood Disdain, announced that the Braemar Home will henceforth be renamed the Fagan School for Fastidious Filthbusters. The first class of Fagan graduates will be auctioned off at next year's Daiquiri Dash.

"So what do you think?" Mallory asked. "I mean, I know it's not Pulitzer caliber, but..."

Ian rolled up the copy and bopped her on the head with it. "I think you've been inhaling too much correction fluid. What's Celia up to?" he asked, nodding toward the editor's office.

"Blue-penciling my *real* story on the Braemar reception."

"Aha! So *that's* why you're decked out like this year's nominee for best actress."

"Yes. And the award goes to... Mallory Caine! For her stunning performance as a society reporter, in which she manages to avoid foul language, falling flat on her face or gagging over the inane conversation of the Newport society ladies."

"Bravo!"

"Thank you, thank you," she said, taking a bow and settling back in her chair. "What brings you slumming down here?"

"No reason. Thought I'd see who was still hanging around. You guys nearly done for the night?"

Celia emerged from her office. "*All* done," she said, waving Mallory's copy. "This is fine, Mallory. Want to run it down to the copy desk?"

Mallory took the story and looked it over. "Hooray, no blue marks."

"No reason to mess with it. You did a fine job. Now, get it to the boys downstairs, would you? Better take a stick with you," she added, glancing at Mallory's dress. After she left, Celia turned to Ian. "She's a trooper, that one. I've given her every rotten, flunky job in the section, but she never complains or shirks."

"She's paying her dues. We all did."

"I think Mallory's paid more than her share of dues."

"What do you mean?"

Celia shrugged. "I'm not sure. She doesn't say much about her personal life, but you know she's been on her own for a while. She's all spunk and bravado, but I have a feeling this piddling contract is the best thing to happen to Mallory in a long time."

"She's focused, that's for sure."

"It's more than that. You and I have both been ambitious and worked hard at our careers, Ian. But with Mallory, I get the sense that it's not just that she *chooses* to work so hard. This is all she's got in her life."

"She has a sister she's close to, I know that."

"Married and living in Paris. A fat lot of good that does her."

Ian sighed. "And her stint here runs out in two months. Then what?"

Celia glanced at the elevator doors, then back. "Actually, I haven't told her this, but we may get a stay of execution. I had lunch with Annie Newhouse today. Her book's going slower than expected and she might want more leave. She's going to let me know for sure in a couple of weeks."

"You'll extend Mallory's contract?"

"I don't see why not. In fact, I think I'm going to start giving her some meatier assignments. As meaty as we get here in the feel-good section, anyway."

"She'd like that. What about the grunt work?"

"I'll parcel some of it out. It'll keep the rest of these clowns humble."

A ding announced the return of the elevator. The two editors watched as Mallory stepped off. "So what do you think of our girl?" Celia asked. "Quite the fairy princess, isn't she?" Mallory rolled her eyes, suddenly made awkward, Ian noted, by all the attention.

"I don't know," he said. "I think she's more the ponytail type."

"Thanks a lot," Mallory grumbled. "Give a guy a Pulitzer, he thinks he's a fashion critic."

"Can I interest you two in grabbing a bite to eat?" Ian asked.

"I'm starving," Mallory said. "I was too busy writing to eat at that Braemar affair."

"What about you, Celia?"

"Pass, thanks. My feet are killing me and I'm beat. This old girl's for home, as soon as I clean up my desk."

"Okay, then, it's you and me, Mallory."

An odd look flashed across her face, Ian saw, and she glanced at Celia. "Actually," she said, "I need to get out of this dress. Maybe I'd better just pack it in, too."

"Tell me you're not driving your motorcycle in that outfit."

"Hardly. I'll grab a cab."

"I'll give you a lift."

"No, really, it's okay..." *Again,* Ian noticed, Mallory glanced at Celia. What was going on?

"Mallory, are you second-guessing yourself?" the older woman asked cryptically.

Mallory puffed up her cheeks, holding her breath for a second, then let it go with a sharp puff. "Yup, that's what I'm doing, all right."

"I don't suppose anyone wants to tell me what this conversation is about, do they?" Ian asked.

"Nope. But I will take that lift, if the offer's still open."

Ian bowed. "Your carriage awaits, Cinderella."

"In that case, let's go before it turns into a pumpkin."

When they pulled up in front of her house, Mallory was distressed to see her landlady puttering in the flower beds. "Damn." she said. "I keep telling her it's dangerous."

"That's the famous Miss Lili Dahl?" Ian asked. Mallory nodded. "What's she doing?"

"Gardening. She does it at night because she doesn't like the sun on her skin. Seventy-six years old and she worries about wrinkles. It wouldn't be so bad if she'd just do it when I'm home. As it is, I'm afraid she'll fall or get mugged when I'm not here and nobody'll be around to help her. She's so stubborn, though, she never listens." They got out of the car and walked over. "Stick 'em up, Lili."

"Hello! You're back, dear. How was the fashion show?"

"Fine. Why are you out at this hour?"

"The roses needed trimming. They're too leggy."

"It's not safe, doing this at night. What if some thug drove by and decided to rob you?"

The old lady made little thrusting motions with her pruning shears. "I'd poke him where it hurts."

Mallory sighed. "Oh, Lili."

"Who's this handsome man?" she asked, looking up and smoothing her red hair, done up in a Gibson girl coif.

"Ian Gallagher, from the *Chronicle*," Mallory said. "Ian—Lili Dahl."

"Delighted to meet you, Miss Dahl. I've seen some of your movies."

"You have?" she asked, obviously delighted.

"You *have?*" Mallory echoed.

"I think so. I thought you were terrific in *Our Dancing Daughters.*"

"Oh, you saw that! It was one of my favorites, too, even if Joan Crawford *was* absolutely dreadful to work with."

"You worked with her again in *Grand Hotel.*"

"Yes. I was going to turn down the part, but it was a chance to work with the Barrymores."

"John *and* Lionel," Ian said, nodding.

"Yes. They were such dears. A little wild, perhaps, but so very nice to me."

Mallory leaned against the railing of the front steps, arms crossed, shaking her head in amazement as Gallagher charmed her landlady, Lili positively fluttering in response. When Ian glanced over, Mallory raised one eyebrow. He shrugged. "I'm an old movie buff."

"Why are we standing out here in the dark?" Lili said. "Come in. I'll make some tea. Have you eaten?"

"I don't want to put you to any bother," Ian said. "I was just giving Mallory a lift home."

"No bother!" Lili hooked her arm through his. "Come on, Mallory, dear, let me make you both a snack."

The aging starlet leaned heavily on Ian as they went up the steps and into the little bungalow. Inside, Lili walked with him toward the kitchen, the top of her head barely reaching his shoulder. Mallory stopped at the hallway leading to her room. "I'm going to change. I'll be right with you."

Lili turned, smiling. "You go right ahead, dear. I'll take care of Mr. Gallagher until you get back. Doesn't our Mallory look wonderful tonight?" she added to Ian.

He seemed to hesitate, then nodded. ''She's beautiful,'' he said quietly.

Watching his soft hazel eyes behind the wire-rimmed glasses, Mallory experienced a sudden knot in her solar plexus and a distinct sense of déjà vu. It was prom night all over again, with Gunnar and Franny watching her come down the stairs. The knot had less to do with memories of Gunnar, however, than with feelings for Ian, her professional idol who had, miraculously, become a friend and, something she was careful never to let on, a *personal* hero, too. Her eyes fell and she turned away, muttering a thank-you as she beat a hasty retreat to her room.

No! she told herself sternly. Don't even *think* about it. Not with Ian Gallagher.

In the first place, she thought, getting out of the dress and looking for something else to put on, it would never be more than a one-sided attraction. She knew Ian was divorced and unattached, but he dated other women. Mallory had seen him, dressed in a tux and looking terrific, in photos taken at various L.A. social and cultural events, each time with a different but lovely woman on his arm—women older than she and obviously more sophisticated. There was no way a man whose star was rising as fast as Ian Gallagher's would take an interest in some kid from Minnesota with a murky past.

In the second place, there was the matter of people like senior editor Grady O'Toole and his snide insinuations. Building her professional credibility was enough of an uphill battle without risking the suggestion that she hadn't legitimately earned every opportunity she got. Mallory agreed with Celia Webster that a slime-bucket like O'Toole shouldn't be allowed to taint an innocent friendship—and yes, friendship was what she and Ian seemed to have developed, grabbing the occasional quick lunch together, or dropping in to chat now and again. They had an easy rapport, and his respect was important to her. So important that she would never risk muddying the waters by doing anything stupid like coming on to him.

In the four years since the blowup of her seven-week affair with Drew Beekman, Mallory had been on a few dates. A couple of times, in fits of loneliness and physical need, she had let an evening end in bed, but sex had turned out to be the kiss of death for those fragile relationships, bringing neither trust nor intimacy, only hurtful memories. Why would she run the danger of tarnishing her friendship with Ian like that? After twenty-two tumultuous years, Mallory had learned to pigeon-hole everyone: the Very Good (Diana, Wiley, Frances); the Generally Bad (Gunnar, Drew); and the Truly Ugly (the Rev, Andrew Beekman, Grady O'Toole). She protected and cherished her newer relationships with people like Lili and Celia, who also belonged in the first category, as did Ian.

No way, she decided firmly, would she do anything to risk turning this good man into just another bad memory.

Ian sipped a glass of sherry and looked over Miss Lili Dahl's scrapbook—somehow, he could only think of her in those very formal terms. As the old lady bustled around the kitchen, preparing tea and sandwiches, he flipped through the pages of her youth. Old publicity stills showing a pretty young thing with lips like a candy heart, sparkling eyes and brilliant red curls. Shots of her taken on various movie sets, or in Roaring Twenties evening dress next to Pickford and Fairbanks, Lillian Gish, Norma Shearer, Chaplin and the Barrymores. Photos of her with Errol Flynn, one taken on a sailboat, one in a nightclub, one with them lounging on a beach, arms draped around each other. Ian glanced up at the old lady with the kohl-lined eyes and jangling bracelets. My, my, Miss Lili, he thought, smiling to himself. What a life you've led. What stories you could tell.

Out of the corner of his eye he noticed Mallory coming down the hall, and his gaze shifted. Her hair was brushed loose. She had changed into a soft yellow pullover and jeans, and although he usually saw her in office attire, this was a better fit for the Mallory he'd come to know. A little wild, a little wary. Done up in that black dress, she could knock the socks off most men—she'd even thrown *him* for a temporary loop—but it was this look he preferred. Maybe it was their common prairie roots, but every time he saw her in blue jeans, usually when they ran into each other doing weekend overtime, it felt like old-home week.

She blushed and Ian realized he'd been staring. Mallory's gaze dropped to the scrapbook in front of him, and she nodded and smiled, obviously having seen it before. She walked over to the counter and picked up the sherry bottle, poured a glass and took Lili by the elbow, putting the glass in her hand. "Here, I'll finish the sandwiches. Why don't you sit with Ian and tell him who all these people are?"

Lili protested a little, but then settled into a chair next to him, clearly delighted to show off her famous old friends. She brought her russet head low to the photos, and Ian recognized the vanity of an old dear who wasn't about to admit that she needed her spectacles. Gnarled, many-ringed fingers danced over the page as she recounted stories of Hollywood stars and parties gone by, and he asked her questions about the movies she'd worked on.

When her scrapbook reached photos from the thirties, Lili sighed. "The age of the blondes," she said. "Back in the twenties, the most popular actresses were brunettes—Bow, Lillian Gish."

"And one redhead," Ian added.

She beamed. "At least one. But of course, I was never as famous as those others. Then along came Harlow and Mae West, Garbo and Dietrich, and suddenly, all the directors wanted was blondes, blondes, blondes. It hasn't really changed since. I was even asked to dye *my* hair! Can you imagine?"

"But you didn't."

"Absolutely not. I'm a natural redhead and proud of it." Lili brushed her locks indignantly. Somehow, Ian doubted that the color was quite as natural as it used to be. "Don't you think a redhead is more interesting than one more blonde, Mr. Gallagher?" she asked coquettishly.

Ian hesitated, then glanced at fair-headed Mallory. She had stopped what she was doing and was watching him with a bemused look on her face, her expression challenging him to get out of *that* one. He turned back to Miss Lili. "I admire any person with the strength to be herself, no matter what," he said. Looking up once more, he saw Mallory grin and shake her head.

"So do I," Lili said. She drained her glass and leaned back in the chair. As she struggled to rise, Ian stood and helped her to her feet. "If you young people will excuse me, I'm feeling done in. It's my bedtime."

"You won't join us?" Mallory asked.

"Not tonight, dear. But take those in the front room, why don't you? The chairs are much more comfortable in there, and I'm sure you and Mr. Gallagher are worn-out after your busy week. Offer him another sherry, and you have one, too." Mallory nodded, and they said good-night. Lili gave Ian a final, winning smile before toddling off to her room at the back of the house, scrapbook under one arm, her high, wavering voice humming a tune.

When Ian and Mallory moved into the living room, he made a circuit, examining the photos and posters on the walls before settling himself into an overstuffed armchair. "It's like a museum in here. She's a great old girl."

"She's that, all right. But I'm amazed you know so much about her career."

"Film's kind of a hobby for me, especially the old ones."

"All those details—is that the photographic memory kicking in?"

He sighed. "I guess. I've got a head stuffed full of trivia."

"Well, you really made Lili's day. And," Mallory added, grinning, "I was impressed with your diplomatic comeback to her comment about blondes and redheads."

"You don't know *how* diplomatic it was."

"What do you mean?"

"My ex-wife is a redhead. That doesn't make for a great recommendation, believe me."

Mallory was silent as she refilled his sherry glass, then passed him a plate of roast beef sandwiches. "You went through a tough time?" she asked finally.

"It was no picnic. I met Caitlyn in Georgia when I was working for the *Atlanta Constitution*. She was an aide to the governor. I was about to leave to come to work for the *Chronicle* when she and I got involved, and she ended up coming with me. We got married in Las Vegas on the drive out, but the marriage never really took. We stayed together three years, but only because of inertia and the fact that we hardly ever saw each other. Caitlyn was in law school, and I was working long hours."

Ian paused, pretending to focus on eating, remembering when Caitlyn started going off weekends to a cabin at Lake Arrowhead to study, she said, with a female classmate. Ian soon discovered she was playing house with one of her law-school teachers. The professor's wife had come to see him at the paper with photographic proof of the affair, hoping Ian would rein in Caitlyn so that she could save her marriage. The affair died on its own, however, when Caitlyn transferred her sights to other, more personally advantageous quarry.

"When we *did* see each other," he said, "we usually ended up arguing. By the time she finished law school, we were strangers. She moved out the day after she heard she'd passed her bar exams."

"Is she still in L.A.?"

"Yes. She's with a big firm downtown, married to a judge now. Caitlyn always lands on her feet."

"What about you?"

"Me? I'm fine, except for an aversion to redheads. Miss Lili Dahl excepted," he added, smiling.

Ian nodded. They sat quietly for a time, the silence between them comfortable, the diffused amber glow of the lamps bathing them in gentle light. "What's your story, Mallory?"

"What do you mean?"

"I'm curious to know how a prairie girl ended up out here, all alone at the tender age of eighteen? What did *you* walk away from?"

Mallory put down her sandwich and settled back on the couch, crossing her legs and hugging a cushion to her chest. She looked so defensive all of a sudden that Ian almost withdrew the question, but he decided to let it lie. He was curious to know what made her tick. The worst that could happen was that she could tell him to mind his own business.

"I was born here," she said finally.

"In California?"

"Right here in Los Angeles. My parents moved to Orange Country when I was two, and we lived there till I was eight."

"And then they moved to Minnesota?"

"No. They died."

"I'm sorry. What was it? A car accident?"

She hesitated. "Memorial Day, 1969. My sister and I were injured, too. She still has paralysis in one arm as a result."

"Mallory, I'm so sorry. I had no idea."

"There was no other family. My mother was English. Her parents were killed in the London blitz during the war. She was raised by her grandparents, but they were long gone. My dad's parents were gone, too, and he was an only child. With no family left, my sister and I were put up for adoption. A minister and his wife took us, and they were transferred to Minnesota not long after." She waved a hand. "There it is, the story of my life."

"It must have been rough on you," he said, realizing even as he said it that of course it was. It didn't take a genius to figure that out. A few pieces of the Mallory Caine puzzle suddenly fell into place. A few, but not all. "So what brought you back here?"

She shrugged. "I guess adoptions aren't that different from marriages. In this case, I would have to say ours didn't 'take,' either. I barely managed to last through my senior year of high school. As soon as my sister got a chance to go to Paris with old friends and I knew she'd be okay, I left. Maybe it was some kind of homing instinct that brought me here."

She hugged the pillow tighter and looked down, busying herself with finding crumbs on the sofa. Instinctively, Ian knew that there was more to this story, but he wouldn't press. At the moment, Mallory looked as if she needed a hug more than prying questions. But *that,* he decided, would be a mistake, for all kinds of reasons—not least of which was his own ambivalence about the idea of touching her.

"You've done well for yourself," he said. "I admire you for that. And by the way, I should tell you that Celia Webster's really pleased with your work."

Mallory looked up, brightening, and relieved, it seemed, at the change of subject. "That's good to hear. I like working for her."

"Even if it *is* Lifestyles?"

"Even so. I'd rather be doing more writing and fewer Joe jobs, mind you."

"I think she's going to let you run with more substantive pieces."

"I'd love that. I was thinking tonight at that Newport Beach thing that I'd like to do something on the Braemar Home. I was talking to the director, and it sounds like they're doing some important work with children who've suffered abuse.''

"You should suggest it to Celia. Also, on a lighter note, you've got a great subject for a piece right here in Lili Dahl.''

Mallory's face lit up. "Whoa! You're right, I do. She'd make a terrific feature. One of the last surviving witnesses to the golden age of Hollywood.''

"Your only challenge would be winnowing through all her memories and photos to keep the article to a reasonable length.''

"What a great idea." She was all bounce and energy once more, yet Ian sensed he'd only glimpsed the tip of the iceberg. What else are you concealing under that feisty false front, Mallory Caine? he wondered.

The two of them sat in Miss Lili Dahl's memorabilia-crammed living room, talking into the wee hours of the morning, their conversation light, irreverent and impersonal, never straying back into private territory or painful memories. But later, driving home, Ian replayed the evening and his reaction to her, which had somehow undergone a subtle shift.

She was, he reminded himself, just a kid. But despite her mask of carefree irreverence, Mallory was the *oldest* twenty-two-year-old he could imagine, her soul worn and weather-beaten beyond her years. Like Celia Webster, Ian had sensed from the beginning that there were deeper currents running through Mallory Caine than she was willing to let on. She was coming to trust him, however, and he was experienced enough in matters of the heart to know that trust and love were closely intertwined. They were heading into dangerous waters. He had firm rules about not getting involved with colleagues, and Mallory, he sensed, also understood that there were clearly defined limits to their friendship, disregarded only at great risk to one's personal and professional integrity.

He thought about Grady O'Toole, and the women he'd hit on at the paper, and Grady's comments about Mallory that first time her name had come up in an editorial meeting. She'd suffer more than he would, Ian realized, if anything were ever to develop between them. Mallory had the potential to become a solid journalist, but her every accomplishment would be downplayed if she was involved with an editor. No matter how

34

Mallory and her landlady sat at the breakfast table, the morning paper spread open between them, looking at a photo of Mallory's face beaming up at them from the newsprint. She was one of several *Chronicle* employees who had been honored two nights earlier at the California Press Club awards dinner, highlighting the best achievements in print journalism over the past year. Incredibly, although working for nearly two years still under one temporary contract after another, Mallory had won in two categories: a first place in the Feature Series competition, and a second in Humor.

"I'm so proud of you," Lili said, squeezing her arm.

Mallory winced. Lili had a killer grip in those seventy-eight-year-old fingers, and Mallory's left arm, despite having been out of the cast for months now, was still sensitive from the triple fracture it had suffered late last autumn.

The break had happened during a bad landing with a hang glider, and the crash of her first solo flight had put an end to Mallory's brief gliding career. She'd also been forced to sever her attachment to her motorcycle, trading it in for a Ford Escort when she found she couldn't drive the bike with a cast on her arm. But the upside of the accident was the press association prize that she had earned for her hilarious, heart-stopping Lifestyles article, "A Wing and a Prayer."

She hadn't planned to get quite so involved in her work when she'd first suggested the article to Celia Webster. She'd spotted Eagles, a hang gliders' outfitting store, while cruising one

Sunday. After talking to the owners, who had invited her to a competition the next weekend, Mallory had suggested doing a profile on hang gliders. When some of the participants dared her to give it a try, it was the proverbial flag in front of a bull, and the story had turned into a wild, first-person report on the perils of trying to master a lunatic sport.

But as proudly as she bore the war wounds of that effort, Mallory's real sense of accomplishment came from the press association "first" she had earned for her series, "Remembering Danny." She'd first met little Danny Wyman two years earlier, while researching a Lifestyles article on the Braemar Children's Home. Danny had been rescued from a psychotic mother, who, in a fit of rage, had sat him on the burning element of an electric stove when he was eighteen months old. When Mallory met him, he still showed the scars of that attack but after months of care and therapy, he was becoming a normal, happy three-year-old. Her article documented Braemar's success with the little guy, who had gone on to live with a loving foster family.

She had been stunned to learn, therefore, that five-year-old Danny Wyman had died of a cerebral hemorrhage on Christmas Day, and she'd fought for the right to do a follow-up story on him. The story had turned into a series, a boxed feature that appeared on the *Chronicle's* front page over three days. Danny Wyman, she discovered, had slipped through the cracks of the legal and child-welfare systems. Although his foster parents had wanted to adopt him, Danny had been returned to his mother when she was released from psychiatric care, her psychosis allegedly under chemical control. Despite social workers' recommendations that the mother not be given custody, Danny had fallen victim to an overcrowded court docket and a judge who had decided to make a snap decision rather than seek additional studies. Three weeks later, on Christmas Day, Danny's mother had swung him by the ankles and bashed his head against a stucco wall because he was making too much noise with a new toy truck.

Mallory had cried every day that she'd worked on the series, but if neither she nor anyone else had been able to save Danny, she at least had the satisfaction of knowing that, in bringing his case to light, she and the *Chronicle* had sparked a debate that had led to the removal of a cavalier judge and an overhaul of custody-review procedures.

"I'm proud of this work, too," she said now to her land-lady. "And guess what? I had a phone call yesterday from an editor at the *Phoenix Sun* about a job opening there."

"Oh, dear! Phoenix? You're going to Phoenix?" Lili's eyes were bright. "Well, if that's what you think you should do, then of course, it's for the best."

Mallory leaned over and gave her a hug. Despite the old woman's clawlike grip, Lili was growing more frail with every passing year. She still made a pretense of puttering around the house and garden, but most of the daily upkeep fell on Mallory, and on the weekly gardener and house cleaner they had hired. Mallory knew it would be impossible for Lili to live alone in her home if she were to move out, but she had no plans to move on. After five years, she and Lili were practically family. Mallory had even taken her along to Paris for the past two years running, when she went to spend Christmas with Diana, Marcus and Remy, her little monkey of a nephew.

"I'm not moving to Phoenix," she said. "But the offer is great, because it gives me ammunition to use with the *Chronicle*. I told Celia about it, and she said to sit tight. She couldn't promise anything, but the hiring situation on the paper looks like it's loosening up at last. She thinks there's a good chance I could get a staff job now, especially after these awards."

"What about your friend Ian? Couldn't he get you something?"

"Oh, Ian . . ." Mallory hesitated. What to say about Ian?

His Metro section had won four press club awards this year, for investigative pieces on the LAPD and on an influence-peddling scam at L.A. city hall. Mallory had wanted to work for him from the start, but now, she wasn't so sure. It was getting harder to keep her feelings hidden, and she didn't even run into him all that often—sometimes not for weeks on end, if one or both of them was especially busy. How could she manage to work for and be around Ian every day without doing something stupid? What kind of a professional relationship would they have then? No kind at all, she decided.

Nor did Ian seem to have any interest in having her in the Metro section. Once, not long after he had driven her home the night of the Newport reception, she had mentioned it casually, almost jokingly. Ian had frozen, and an awkward silence had ensued. Mallory had never broached the subject again, and despite two Metro staff openings over the past year, Ian had not spoken to her about them. Mallory wasn't dumb, she could read the writing on the wall. Ian was nice to her, he seemed to like her, but he didn't think her work was up to his standards. Fine.

For that matter, she thought, it wasn't even clear anymore that he liked her. They'd had an argument a few months earlier, over her stupid hang-gliding accident, of all things. Ian was in Washington, attending a National Press Club conference when it happened. Mallory was at her desk a couple of days later, typing clumsily with one hand, when she looked up to see him glaring at her.

"Hi, there," she said. "You're back. How was D.C.?"

"Fine." Ian cocked an angry thumb at the cast on her arm. "What the hell were you thinking?"

She examined the plaster, rotating it slowly. "Having something readily available for autographs when I meet celebrities?" she suggested. "Want to sign it?"

"No, I don't want to sign it. Jesus, Mallory! Jumping off cliffs? Isn't that going a little too far for a story?"

She leaned back in her chair, one eyebrow raised. "Excuse me? This from the man who was nearly killed in the crossfire between Crips and Bloods?"

"That was different."

"How?"

"I didn't deliberately put myself in harm's way. You did."

"Oh, right," Mallory snorted. "South Central's a *great* place for a nosy white guy to go strolling on a Saturday night."

"I had a guide and I took precautions. You didn't have to throw yourself off a mountain in order to write about a bunch of idiots with a death wish."

"Look, Ian, I did the story the way *I* wanted to do it. What's your problem?"

He stood back, light from the overhead fluorescent fixtures glinting off his glasses. "Go ahead," he said, "do what you want. You're obviously not going to listen to anyone else, anyway." He'd stormed off without another word.

Although they'd bumped into each other a few times since and exchanged neutral comments, there had been no more impromptu visits or quick lunches for Mallory and Ian.

She'd seen him with his date at the press club awards dinner two nights earlier—Mallory had gone with Celia and some other Lifestyles staffers—but although she'd caught his stony look across the room, Ian hadn't come over to their table to congratulate her. Well, she thought, he wouldn't, would he? Not after she'd been vindicated by winning an award for the very piece he thought was so idiotic. The big, stubborn jerk!

Andrew Beekman flipped irritably through his morning paper. The news was bad, as always. It didn't matter which section he turned to, it was all war, mayhem and chaos, the business pages as bleak as the rest. Interest rates were still too high, the national debt was a scandal and those idiots in Congress had nothing better to do than to try to regulate corporations to death.

He was still making money hand over fist in a southern California housing boom that showed no sign of abating, property values skyrocketing year after year. Buyers kept leaping into the market, despite crushing interest rates, for fear things would only get more expensive if they waited. Beekman was tempted to try to slow down some of his new developments in order to reap maximum profit from the bonanza. After all, space was running low, even in the once wide-open, sunny ranch lands of Orange Country. When the land was finally built out completely, the last two precious acres would be worth more than all the preceding developments combined.

It was a gamble, though. The bloody environmentalists were getting more vocal with every new housing tract that went up, whining over gnatcatchers or scrub thistle or some other damn weed or animal. Acres of prime coastal and inland real estate had already been designated for public access or wildlife preserves. Who knew whether they wouldn't eventually bring progress to a complete, grinding halt?

He tossed aside the business pages and turned to the *Chronicle's* first section, with its international, national and regional news. He was almost through his usual cursory flip when, taking a sip from his coffee cup, he sputtered and choked.

"Andrew? What on *earth* are you doing?"

Beekman looked over the paper at his wife, who was regarding him above silver half-glasses, her expression pinched and distasteful. "Nothing," he muttered. "Coffee went down the wrong way."

Asa shook her head and went back to the Lifestyles pages. "Well, stop making that disgusting noise!"

Beekman's glare was daggers, but she was oblivious. He put down his cup and turned back to the photograph on the page that had caused him to choke in the first place. It was the girl—again! The dark eyes stared at him, huge and haunting, shining with alert intelligence. He had always been vulnerable to those eyes.

The gaze in the photograph was direct, the expression confident and strangely sober, despite her smile. It was the mouth, he realized. The eyes were a trick, a distraction. But he knew that mouth. Knew its stubborn line, and its easy transition from smile to critical sneer. She hid behind those eyes, like a thief behind a curtain, trying to lull and distract, but Beekman knew who she was and what she wanted.

He felt his gut roil. He'd tried to make it up to her, hadn't he, when he'd run into her at the Newport Hyatt? But *no,* she'd been too huffy, standing there all done up like some expensive call girl. Who did she think she was, this strumpet who called herself Mallory Caine?

After seeing her that night, Beekman had had her investigated again, a follow-up after the first time, when he'd done what he had to do to get her claws out of his son. She was writing for the *Chronicle,* it seemed, living with some old whore in Beverly Hills—milking *her,* Beekman thought, the way she'd thought she could milk him by latching on to Drew. After that, Beekman had watched for her byline, and he'd been seeing it more and more lately. Now, it seemed, she'd won some kind of award.

Did she think she was going to become powerful enough to challenge Andrew Beekman? Oh, no, he said silently to the photo on the page, don't think you can take *me* on, young lady! Others have tried, but they lost, and you will, too.

* * *

The editors of the *Los Angeles Chronicle* sat around the long boardroom table, preening, Celia Webster thought, like peacocks. It was their Friday planning meeting, and they were flush with hubris after walking away with seventeen press club awards this year, ten of them first-place wins. Virtually every section had had its moment of glory at the dinner two nights earlier. Only Grady O'Toole's Op-Ed and Commentary pages had come up dry, for the third year running.

Celia glanced at him, sitting in his usual place at the managing editor's right hand, wearing a fixed expression closer to a sneer than a smile, looking ready to spit nails. This is killing him, she thought. It was bad enough that he had been shut out, but with Ian Gallagher's Metro section garnering four awards and Carson Hoag beaming at the young editor with almost paternal pride, every paranoid alarm bell in O'Toole's head had to be going off. It had been evident for some time that he saw Ian as the main threat to his ambition to succeed the managing editor when he retired. The fact that Hoag, who had recommended Gallagher for early promotion to the Metro desk, had seen his faith vindicated so quickly only fed the in-house gossip that Ian Gallagher was the new heir apparent.

"Well, it's a proud week for the *Chronicle*," Hoag said, looking around the table. He paused when he got to Gallagher and gave him a big thumbs-up. "Four wins for Metro. Fine work, Ian!"

"I've got terrific people. They've earned those awards."

"Well, I'll be dropping in to thank each of them personally, but I want you to know that the publishers are very pleased with the way you've turned the section around over the past couple of years."

"Thanks, Carson. I appreciate your support."

Grady O'Toole, Celia noticed, had his eyes fixed on the papers he was impatiently flipping in front of him. She could almost hear his teeth grinding.

Hoag's gaze moved down the table to her. "Celia, good show on those Mallory Caine wins. *Two,* for heaven's sake! You've really brought her along."

"She's a hard worker, Carson. But I have to tell you, we're going to lose her if we don't get her into a permanent slot, pronto."

"We wouldn't want that. Is she making noises about leaving?"

"She's been approached by the *Phoenix Sun.*"

"She has?" It was Ian Gallagher who'd piped up, Celia observed. And, she saw by his sudden glance in Gallagher's direction, Grady O'Toole hadn't missed the fact.

"Yes," she said. "I think she'd rather stay here, but she's not going to put up forever with the insecurity of filling in for people off writing books or on maternity or sick leave."

"Have you got any positions coming open?" Hoag asked.

"Maybe in the summer. Annie Newhouse is negotiating another book deal, and a screen option on her last book. If she gets them, I think she'll resign from the paper."

"I've got an opening," Gallagher said.

Celia spun toward him. "What?"

"Bernie Levitz told me yesterday that he's moving back East."

"Do you want to offer the spot to Mallory Caine?" Hoag said.

Ian nodded slowly. "I could."

"Okay, good. Do it. Now, people, moving on," Hoag began.

"Hold on one minute, Carson," Celia said. "I haven't agreed to this. What do you mean, *you'll* take her, Ian? What am I supposed to do if she jumps ship?"

"You're the one who said we should get Mallory on staff, Celia."

"Yes, but on *my* staff is what I was thinking!"

"My, my!" O'Toole sneered, looking from her to Ian and back. "Are we fighting over the delicious Miss Caine?"

"Screw off, Grady!" Celia snapped.

"Calm down, everybody," Hoag said. "Celia, I think we should at least offer the Metro spot to her, don't you? If she doesn't want it, then we'll try for something in Lifestyles so we don't lose her. But frankly, it might be a good thing if she did go over to Ian's shop. Listen up, people. It's no secret that we've been coming under fire for our hiring policies with regard to women and minorities. Now, *we* know it's nonsense. We hire the best man, regardless—'person,' I should say—but I guess it wouldn't hurt if we could point to a few names in hard news to show that we don't discriminate. Also, Mallory Caine's articles have been generating a lot of response in terms of letters to the editor. Not always positive response, mind you, but at least she gets people worked up, and that's good for readership. So, bottom line, if Ian's got a permanent position for her in Metro and Miss Caine wants it, then that's where I'd like to see her.''

Celia fumed, but the discussion was closed. When the meeting wrapped and the others filed out, she fired a glare at Ian. He held back until everyone was gone, then closed the door and turned to face the music.

"I can't believe you did that to me!" she said angrily. "I never would have expected it, not from *you,* of all people! Grady, maybe, but not you.''

"Celia , I'm sorry. I didn't mean to pull an end run. I hadn't planned this at all, believe me. It happened so fast, I'm still not even sure how I feel about it.''

"*Twice* last year you had openings. She wouldn't admit it, but I know Mallory was hoping you'd offer one to her. You passed her by, while I leaped through hoops to keep renewing her contracts. Now, she gets some recognition, and you come raiding. Dammit, Ian!''

"Nobody wants to see her leave, do they?"

"I could probably have managed something for her now.''

"'Probably' isn't good enough, Celia. Christ! Mallory's been working for next to nothing for two years now. She didn't even have health insurance when you let her go jumping off a goddam cliff last fall!''

Celia opened her mouth for a sharp retort, then shook her head and grinned. "As if I could have stopped her and you know it, too, you big dope.''

"Yeah, I guess.''

"Why don't you just 'fess up, Gallagher?" she said, settling herself on the edge of the long table.

"What do you mean?"

"It scared the hell out of you when she got hurt.''

"Well, yeah, of course. She could have been killed.''

"And?"

"And what?"

"*And* that would have made you very unhappy, because you're crazy about her."

"Get outta here! She and I have hardly spoken in months. And by the way, I'm not sure she'll be interested in any job offer from me. I don't think I'm one of her favorite people these days."

"Well, what do you expect? Even *I've* noticed how crummy you've been to her lately."

"I haven't," he protested.

"This is old Auntie Celia you're talking to, guy. Why don't you come clean?"

Ian hesitated, then slumped in a chair and exhaled deeply. Pulling off his glasses and setting them aside, he rubbed his eyes, then looked up wearily. "I don't know if I can work with her, Celia. That's why I didn't offer her one of those jobs last year. I hadn't planned to do it now, either, but it just slipped out after you mentioned that Phoenix business."

"You've got a problem with her work?"

"You know that's not it."

"Yeah, I do. For what it's worth, I suspect it worries Mallory as much as it does you."

"Has she said anything?"

"Are you kidding? Wild horses wouldn't drag it out of her, but I'm not blind."

"So what do we do?"

"Well, in the first place, as much as it infuriates me to say so, you have to make the offer now that Carson's given the order."

"I really *am* sorry, Celia."

"You should be. But, to be fair, I realize that Lifestyles was never Mallory's first choice, so I guess it's only right."

"And then?"

"And then, you take things one step at a time. She's a pro, Ian. She's not going to do anything to embarrass you or herself. She's already dealt with Grady—"

Ian's head snapped up. "Has O'Toole hit on her?"

"Of course, he has, more than once, I think. But Mallory can handle Grady, and she didn't want you to know about it, so don't let on I mentioned it, all right?"

"That son of a bitch!"

"Forget Grady. He'll hang himself in his own noose one of these days. You just worry about doing your job and let Mallory do hers. And as for the rest," Celia added, rising heavily and heading for the door, "things will take their proper course. Just remember, Ian, that it worked out fine for Ben Bradlee and Sally Quinn at the *Washington Post*."

He looked dubious, but managed a smile. "Thanks, Celia. You're a great sport."

"The hell I am," she said, one hand on the door. "I'm going to go and steal someone from *your* section!"

35

It was almost seven o'clock on a Wednesday evening, and Mallory was sitting in Ian Gallagher's glass-walled office as he read the copy for her latest story. His loafer-clad feet were up on the desk and he was slumped wearily in his chair, head resting on one hand. He looked tired, she thought, his hair mussed and his shirt wrinkled after a long day.

Lately, she'd noticed, the lines around his eyes and mouth seemed deeper, and he was quieter than ever. She put it down to stress and a heavy workload. Part of her was tempted to walk behind him and offer a shoulder massage to relieve the tension she saw reflected in his face, but that would be a violation of the ground rules she had set for herself where Ian was concerned—no more personal revelations, no after-work drinks or one-on-one socializing, and, above all, no physical contact of any kind.

There were times when she wondered whether she had done the right thing in accepting his job offer the previous spring. She'd been stunned when he'd approached her about the opening—her transfer to Metro, Ian said, approved by both Celia Webster and Carson Hoag. Professionally, Mallory knew it was a good move. She had made the most of her stint on Lifestyles, and she'd even come to enjoy the lighter pieces, finding laughter as good an antidote as any to whatever ailed her. Stories like the one on hang gliding had been an adventure, despite her broken arm, and she'd had a ball profiling a string of quirky characters, like the Covina man who built life-size statues of Jesus out of toothpicks, or the guy in the Mojave Desert who painted portraits on toilet seats. He'd gotten his start, Mallory had discovered, during World War II, depicting Hitler for airmen at a nearby base, branching out afterward to portray anyone a customer disliked enough to want to sit on. She had to agree it was cheaper than psychotherapy.

And then there was the feature she'd done on Lili Dahl that had garnered so much response and had led to a flurry of television interviews for her landlady. Mallory had even taken her to a studio in Burbank to be interviewed by Roger Ebert, and Mallory found herself fascinated by the workings of that branch of the media.

She'd done good work in the past two years, and she'd been recognized and rewarded for her efforts. But when the Metro job was offered, Mallory had decided it was time to get down to doing the hard news she'd always wanted a shot at. The fact that the opportunity included working with Ian Gallagher was a mixed blessing. On the one hand, he was the best editor on the paper, and she could only get better at her craft working under his guidance. On the other hand, there was the very real risk of making a fool of herself. In the end, she'd decided that by laying down ground rules for herself and sticking to them, she could manage. So far, the plan was working.

Ian took a deep breath and lowered the text. "All hell is going to break loose when this gets out," he said. "Are you sure about your source?"

Mallory nodded. "He's a former Internal Affairs investigator in the Orange County Sheriff's Department. We can't identify him, Ian, because he's already been subjected to threats and intimidation, and he's worried about his family. But if what he says is true, then there's a thread of corruption in that department that leads straight to the sheriff himself."

"Are you sure this guy's not just looking for an ax to grind, after getting a raw deal himself?"

"Of course, he's got an ax to grind. When he caught a couple of rogue deputies red-handed, stealing evidence in a drug case, he wouldn't settle for seeing just them brought down. He wanted to round up their paymasters, too, but Sheriff Fisher blocked the investigation. When my guy objected, they put him in a dead-end job until he got fed up and quit."

"So it looks like Sheriff Craig Fisher's on the take, too."

"That's right. My source figures he owes it to himself and all the other honest cops in the department not to let him get away with it."

"You checked out his information on Fisher's real-estate holdings?"

"Yup. A Realty contact confirmed that he owns three expensive houses in Orange County, none of which he should be able to afford on his sheriff's salary. He's also got, I discovered, a yacht under his wife's name, berthed in Newport Harbor. If you ask anyone about it, they say it's the wife who comes from a big-bucks family back East, but I checked it out with a few phone calls, and the rumor doesn't hold up. Her father's a retired line repairman in Idaho. She has one brother, and he's a bus driver. So where did all this money come from? My source has photographic proof of Fisher's ties to John Nichols, who's rumored to be the king of the narcotics trade in the Tijuana–L.A. corridor."

Ian nodded. "Okay, it looks like you're on to something, but I want you to do more digging before we run with this. Let's start by looking into Fisher's backers, the main contributors to his election campaigns. If they include Nichols or any of his known associates, then we'll know we're on the money."

"Fisher's been reelected twice to the office, and both times were landslides."

"I know, and he was handpicked by the former sheriff when the old guy retired, which means we could have a line of corruption that goes way back. I remember hearing rumors when I first came out here eight years ago, that every elected official in Orange Country was in the pocket of the real-estate developers. That's nothing new for southern California, but if there's drug money at play, too, it puts a whole new wrinkle on things."

"You think there might be a link between the developers and drug runners?" Mallory asked, little alarm bells beginning to ping in her brain.

"Who knows? I did an investigative series a couple of years ago called 'Who Owns Malibu?' and I came up with some disturbing connections. Maybe it's time to see who owns Orange County."

"So, I should check out people like Andrew Beekman?"

"Maybe. He's certainly one of the biggest developers down there. First, though, I want you to follow through on this Sheriff Fisher business and see where it leads. We'll think about expanding the search later." Ian reached across the desk and handed back her copy. Their hands brushed as Mallory took it from him, and they both pulled away quickly.

"I'll get on it first thing in the morning," she said, rising to leave.

"Mallory?"

"What?"

"It's good work you're doing."

She felt her stomach contract. "Thanks." She stared at the paper in her hand, feeling guilty, knowing she should disqualify herself right now from any investigation potentially involving Andrew Beekman. But how could she explain? "Ian," she began.

"Yes?" When she looked up at him, he had already poised his pencil over another piece of copy on his desk, but his eyes were fixed on her. "What's up?"

She racked her brain for an opening, finding none. It was all in the past, her run-ins with the Beekman men, father and son. Ancient history. What was the point of a big confession now? This idea of looking into Orange County developers might not even pan out. Why anticipate trouble, and in the bargain violate her code of no personal revelations?

"I just wanted to say thanks again for taking me on."

He nodded slowly as Mallory turned and left his office.

Later, waiting for the elevator to head for the garage and home, Mallory considered again the professional ramifications of working on any story involving Andrew Beekman. What if she had to approach him directly for an interview? He'd be hostile, of course. What about her? Could she be an impartial investigator where he was concerned? And what if she uncovered any dirt on him? Could she use it? What about the spillover effect on Drew?

She'd been thinking about Beekman's son a great deal lately, having spotted him several times on television. He was working in Washington for the secretary of state, and one of the *Chronicle's* international affairs reporters had interviewed him for a piece on tensions in Eastern Europe. Drew had also been featured in a recent *Time* magazine article on the next generation of movers and shakers in Washington.

She detested Beekman Senior, but Mallory's feelings about Drew had also hardened around the bitter memory of how he had treated her that last time they'd met, jumping to false conclusions about Wiley, demeaning her. In the final analysis, he'd turned out to be his father's son, after all, she decided.

Searching her purse for her car keys in the underground parking lot, Mallory heard a click and a rustle. She froze, straining her ears. It wasn't the first time she'd sensed that she was being followed. She often had the spine-tingling feeling of being watched, but whenever she spun around to see who was there, she found nothing but shadows and echoes.

At home with Lili Dahl, the phone sometimes rang in the evening, but when Mallory picked it up, there would be only silence on the other end, then, after a moment, a click and the dial tone. Mallory worried that someone might be checking to see if Lili was alone in the house, looking for an opportunity to break in. She'd had the number changed and left unlisted, and for a couple of weeks, the evening calls had stopped. Then, they'd begun again, not frequently enough to justify calling the police or Pacific Bell, but just often enough to be unnerving.

She got mail at the *Chronicle*—sometimes only a few items a week, sometimes a couple of dozen, depending on what stories she'd recently done. Some of the letters were sweet and flattering; some were indignant; many were thoughtful. Every so often, one would arrive from someone who was clearly unbalanced, fixated on her or on some issue she had covered. Occasionally, the tone was vaguely threatening. But the letters were part and parcel of the semipublic persona that came from her name appearing in the paper. Mallory had gotten used to the idea that privacy was, in some respects, inversely proportional to whatever success she was enjoying in her career.

Still, as much as she tried to carry on normally, a strange car in front of her house or following her on the street for too long set off a tremor of paranoia in the subterranean levels of her mind. As did noises in the deserted canyons of the parking garage.

She finally located her keys and was about to unlock the door of her little white Escort, when a figure appeared out of nowhere, making her leap.

"Oh, I'm sorry," Grady O'Toole said blandly. "Did I startle you?"

"Yes! Honestly, Grady, do you *have* to skulk around like that?"

"I didn't mean to. I was just getting in my car over there when I saw you come off the elevator. I thought you would have heard me, but I guess you were lost in thought. Poor Mallory," he said, putting his hands on her shoulders. "You're shaking."

She backed away, shrugging him off. "I'm fine. Excuse me, but I need to get going."

"Why the rush?"

"It's late. I've had a long day."

"Gallagher has you working dreadful hours, doesn't he? Have you even had dinner yet?"

"No, but—"

"Terrible! Well, neither have I, but never mind, we'll take care of that. Let's grab a drink and a bite together, what do you say?"

"Sorry, but no. I still have some background reading to do tonight."

"Oh, come on," O'Toole said, slipping a hand through her arm. "You need to relax. You work too hard."

"I don't—"

"We'll take my car. We can have drinks at my place. It's nearby."

Mallory stood firm. "*No*, Grady."

"Why not?"

"Because I don't care to. Now, if you'll excuse me—"

"I don't understand why you're always so jumpy around me, Mallory." He planted himself squarely in front of her, and his hand reached up, cupping her cheek. "I think you're sweet, you know. Very, very sweet..." O'Toole's head dropped toward her, and she felt his alcohol-tinged breath on her face.

"Grady, don't!" she said, pushing against his chest.

"Come on, Mallory," he coaxed. "Don't be like that."

"She said, back off, O'Toole!"

They both looked up. Ian was approaching down the aisle of parking stalls, his stride rapid, his expression livid. O'Toole stepped away from her, hands raised defensively as the other man pulled up. Ian looked as if he was ready to haul off and belt him. His glance dropped to Mallory. "Are you all right?"

"I'm fine," she snapped.

"Of course she is, Gallagher. No harm done."

"Get out of here, O'Toole! And don't let me see you anywhere near her again!"

"Sorry, old man. Didn't mean to wade in your pool. Just a little misunderstanding. I leave her to you."

He slid past Ian and ambled across the garage in the direction of his reserved parking space. They stood watching as Grady got into his black Jaguar and started the engine. When the car pulled out and headed toward the exit ramp, Ian turned to Mallory. "Are you really okay?"

"Yes. Dammit, Ian! You didn't have to do that."

He looked surprised. "What?"

"Come flying to my rescue, for crying out loud! I could have handled it."

"Oh, right. You *looked* like you were handling it."

"I can take care of myself, Gallagher. I'm not some helpless little thing."

"Oh, well, pardon me!"

"I don't need a bodyguard. It's no big deal."

"Oh, yeah, tough guy? So why do you look like you're ready to burst into tears?"

"I'm *not!* I'm just frustrated—and mad."

"At me?"

"Yes! No," she amended, shaking her head. "At him. And myself, for getting cornered. I hate being pushed around, and I know better than to get caught in a bind like that."

"Don't blame yourself. O'Toole's scum."

"He sure is. Senior editor or not, he doesn't know how close he came to getting a sharp knee in the groin." She wiped her face and leaned back on the car, shaking her head disgustedly.

"Mallory?"

"What?"

"I really am sorry."

"What for?"

"That this happened. I know it's not the first time."

She sighed deeply. "It's not your fault. I'm just embarrassed that you had to bail me out." She looked at him ruefully. "I appreciate it, but you need to stop, you know that?"

"What?"

"Being so good to me."

"Why?"

"Because you've done too much already. You always seem to be popping up, like some guardian angel."

"I haven't given you anything you didn't deserve. And anyway," he added quietly, "I kind of like the idea of being your guardian angel."

She looked at his smiling face, just inches from her own. But as they stared at each other, his smile faded, his expression becoming very serious and very attentive. Slowly, it dawned on her that she was not the only one fighting an internal battle.

"It's so hard, Ian," she whispered.

He nodded. "I know."

They stood face-to-face, saying nothing. He planted his hands on the roof of her car, on either side of her, and he seemed to be breathing deeply. Other than that, neither of them made a move. Mallory watched as his gaze inched down her face, coming to rest on her lips. She found herself watching his mouth, too, her own breath coming in short, rapid takes. They were standing too close. An invisible barrier had been crossed and, like opposite poles of a magnet placed in fatal proximity, there was no resisting the force that drew them together.

The space between them grew narrower and narrower. At the last moment, Mallory's eyes closed, but just as she felt the brushing of his lips against hers, there was a shriek of rubber on concrete. She and Ian leaped apart as O'Toole's black Jag, which had apparently circled and returned, screeched to a stop beside them. The parking-lot lights cast a greenish glow on his reptilian features, pursed now in a smug grin. He nodded, once, as if satisfied to have his suspicions confirmed, then his car shot off in a roar of blue smoke.

Ian's head dropped to his chest. "Shit!" he muttered. He looked at her again. "I'm sorry. You didn't need that to happen."

"Neither of us did. It just feeds Grady's warped mind." She exhaled sharply. "I'd better leave."

"Mallory, maybe we should go somewhere and talk."

"I don't think that's a good idea."

He was ready to argue, she could see, but Mallory pulled back, wrapping her arms protectively around herself. The whole situation was suddenly too frightening. It wasn't O'Toole and his potential for smear and gossip. He would say and believe what he wanted, regardless of what actually happened between her and Ian. What frightened her was the idea of breaking down self-preservational barriers she had worked so hard to build. As difficult as it was to work with Ian every day and hide the way she felt about him, it wasn't half as terrifying as the thought of letting herself believe she could have him, then discovering it wasn't to be. And inevitably, experience told her, that was the way it would turn out. She had survived Gunnar, and she had survived Drew. Ian Gallagher would be another story altogether.

"I can't do this."

"Mallory—"

"No! It would be a mistake. Please, Ian, let me go. I don't want anything to happen that we'd both regret."

He hesitated, then stepped back and opened her car door. When she pulled away and glanced in the rearview mirror, he was still standing there, watching her.

36

As the news ended, Andrew Beekman pressed the remote to snap off the television, then leaned back in the deep leather desk chair in his den, thinking. After weeks of speculation and denial, it had been announced that afternoon that Orange County sheriff Craig Fisher and six deputies had been suspended from active duty pending an investigation into alleged irregularities in the running of the department. In an impromptu press conference in front of his Santa Ana headquarters, Fisher had told reporters that he was the target of a witch-hunt being conducted by the *Los Angeles Chronicle,* and that the allegations against him were without substance.

Beekman had known for months that the paper was conducting an investigation of the county, trying to prove a connection between certain members of the sheriff's department and organized crime. Not content to stop there, however, his contacts said the *Chronicle* was also trying to build a case that the conspiracy ran deeper, involving prominent local business leaders who had made financial contributions to Fisher's election campaigns.

Recently, Beekman himself had been cornered by television reporters after his name appeared on a list of Fisher's backers. He hadn't tried to deny his support for the controversial sheriff.

"I've worked for thirty years," he'd told them, "to build safe, comfortable, family-oriented communities in this county. Part of that effort has to include trying to keep out the gang and graffiti problems that plague neighboring counties. As a strong advocate of antigang measures, Sheriff Fisher has had my support. It's as simple as that, and I make no apologies.''

''What about the allegations that sheriff's deputies, even while they've been coming down hard on small-time hoods, have been turning a blind eye to major drug-running in the Tijuana–L.A. corridor? Operations that run right through and may be headquartered in Orange County?''

''Well, I don't know anything about that.'' Beekman had shrugged. ''But the whole idea seems a little farfetched to me. All I know is that I want to keep our streets clean and safe for our kiddies.''

For now, Beekman knew, the media would be focusing on the investigation into the Sheriff's Department, and that could drag on for months. Although some people he knew were worried about it, he himself had little concern about its ability to damage him or his business interests. Aside from financial contributions to Fisher's election, which he had already explained away, his position was largely unexposed. All he had to do was sit tight and ride this out.

That would be easy enough, he thought, were it not for Mallory Caine's byline on those *Chronicle* stories. In a fit of uncontrolled rage, Sheriff Fisher had already denounced her publicly, but that had only made the pushy young reporter more interesting to her media colleagues. The television-news cameras, Beekman noticed, seemed to zero in on her face during media scrums, and some of the local stations had already used her as a commentator on the crisis in the sheriff's office.

So far, she had never approached Beekman on any Orange County story she had done, which wasn't surprising, given their previous contacts. Beekman felt as if he was waiting for the other shoe to drop, however, now that she had climbed onto this investigative hobby horse. How long would it be before she tried to challenge him? He couldn't help wondering if she had discovered yet the real link between them, a link that far predated their brief, unevenly matched battle over his son.

As difficult as it was to convince himself that a mere girl, even this one, could represent a serious threat to him, the day might come when he would have to neutralize her, once and for all. That being the case, Beekman thought, he should have contingency plans ready.

Los Angeles, California
August 12, 1986

Mallory sat at a restaurant table across from Celia Webster, pushing her lunch around her plate, avoiding her old boss's scrutinizing gaze.

"I never thought I'd see the day when you'd back away from a fight, Mallory, especially when the case is as clear-cut as this one. All you're being asked to do is document the times you've been subjected to Grady O'Toole's sexual harassment."

"Why do you need *my* testimony? You've said yourself that there are at least six other women who are prepared to take a joint complaint to management. What difference does one more make? And what good will it do, anyway? It's not like he hasn't been up to these shenanigans for years, and management's never done anything about it before."

"They might now. The climate's changed. Tolerance for this kind of nonsense is going down, and the last thing management wants is for the paper to be slapped with a class-action lawsuit for not reining in Grady O'Toole. With a united front and testimony from articulate witnesses like yourself, Carson Hoag and the publishers might take punitive action against him."

"Are you going to join in the complaint?"

Celia shrugged. "When these women came to me, I told them that I would confirm that this is a long-standing pattern of behavior with O'Toole, but my complaint against him is a pretty old one, and it won't carry as much weight as yours or some of the others he's hit on more recently."

"Did you tell these women that it had happened to me, too?" Mallory asked.

"No, I said I knew of other cases, but I wanted to approach them myself, first."

"I can't get involved, Celia," she said, shaking her head. "I'm sorry."

The older woman sat back in her chair, her expression annoyed now. "What's the matter, Mallory? Do you think that just because you've had less trouble with Grady lately, you've no responsibility to newer or younger women in a weaker position than you? Exactly the kind who are his favorite target? Are you afraid that rising star of yours might be tarnished if you get involved in a grubby little issue like this? That management might not *like* you anymore?''

"Is that what you think, Celia? Is that the kind of person you think I am?''

"No, dammit. Or at least, I never did before. But why are you so reluctant to do the right thing here? I don't get it.''

Mallory slumped in her chair, staring at the tablecloth. "Because of Ian,'' she said finally.

"What's he got to do with it?''

"You know what Grady's always suspected about Ian and me.''

"Yes. So?''

"Well, a while back, something happened to give him reason to believe he was right all along.'' She told Celia about the incident a few months earlier in the underground parking lot. "It was dumb. It shouldn't have happened, but it did. You once told me that Grady was vindictive. What do you think are the chances he won't try to tar Ian with the same brush if I speak out against him?''

The older woman exhaled heavily. "Zip. You're right. Grady's always felt threatened by Ian, and he'd grab any chance to knock him down a peg in front of management. On the other hand,'' Celia added, "there's a big difference between Grady's predatory activities and a stable relationship between two co-workers. Give yourselves a break, Mallory. Just because a man and a woman have a professional association, it doesn't mean that falling in love is forbidden. If you and Ian are a serious item—''

"We're not, and we aren't going to be.''

"It's none of my business, but mind if I ask why not?''

"Just…because.'' Mallory felt the other woman's laser stare working to sear through every layer of protective camouflage she wore. She sighed. "I'm not good at relationships, Celia. I've been burned before, and I'd rather keep things with Ian the way they are now than run the risk of losing it all.''

"I'm sorry to hear that, because to tell the truth, I've always thought you and Ian were a potentially great team, and not just as journalists. However, under the circumstances, I guess I understand where you're coming from on this Grady business."

"I wish I could help. Grady doesn't scare me anymore, but he was awfully intimidating when I was new and unsure of myself."

"Well, maybe his hunting days are numbered. In the meantime, Mallory, as far as Ian goes, don't think that just because things haven't worked out for you in the past, they couldn't work out now. You might be surprised."

"Somehow, I doubt it."

If dealing in half truths was the same as lying, Mallory thought, then she had, over the years, turned into a liar of epic proportions. At the very least, the kind of personal evasions and omissions of fact that she had gotten into the habit of practicing, even with people she cared about like Celia Webster and Ian Gallagher, amounted to a betrayal of their friendship and trust.

But then again, trust—or rather, her own ingrained inability to trust—was the root of the problem. For years now, she had kept the different parts of her life boxed and separate, revealing little of herself, her feelings, or her background. She was building a professional reputation as a competent investigative journalist with the tenacity of a terrier and, at the same time, a nose for the ludicrous side of the day's news that seemed to feed the public's need for occasional relief from unmitigated gloom. After a couple of recent television appearances and public speeches, she had been approached by an agent, wondering if she was interested in pursuing other career options outside of print media. Mallory had demurred for the time being, but Natasha Keene had given her a business card and asked her to keep it in mind. Incredible as it seemed to Mallory, some people apparently enjoyed listening to her talk about the issues that concerned them, putting her own dry, comic spin on things.

She often thought of her sister, and how Diana's confidence had grown over the years as good things had come her way. In her own case, however, just the opposite was happening. Every word of praise, every award, every positive recognition she received carried with it the fear that some day, someone would expose her as a fraud and a screwup, who'd fooled people into thinking she deserved their admiration and support. If they really knew her, Mallory thought, they'd see her for what she truly was—a messed-up kid with a murky background and a chronic inability to forge a lasting bond with anyone.

Lying awake at night, in those hours just before dawn when anxiety is at its most potent, Mallory's thoughts always turned to Ian and her fear of being diminished in his eyes. Dozens of times after the incident in the parking lot, her resolve had wavered, and she had been tempted to throw caution to the wind and reach out to him. She could feel Ian watching her, waiting for a sign that it was all right to lower the barriers they had both worked so hard to erect. Once or twice, working late, they had stared at each other across the glass walls of his office, but she knew he wouldn't make another move until she did. Not when she had been the one to say no.

Mallory had come close to reversing her decision, and might have, except that recently, she had stumbled across a piece of information about Andrew Beekman that put all other considerations on hold. She couldn't share it with Ian, but knew she had to pursue the matter, even if it meant compromising the *Chronicle's* planned investigation into the developers and others who owned and controlled Orange County. She was in danger of losing it all—her credibility, her career and the one person who had come to mean more to her than all the rest— but she was helpless to do anything about it.

And so, after agonizing for several days, she had telephoned Andrew Beekman and arranged to meet him that Friday. If he was surprised to hear from her, he'd hidden it well.

37

Los Angeles, California
August 15, 1986

Andrew Beekman had suggested they meet in his office or a restaurant, but Mallory wanted to avoid both his turf and closed quarters where their conversation might be overheard. In the end, she had suggested the Santa Monica pier, despite the irony of meeting him at the same place she had gone with Drew that Christmas Eve, nearly seven years earlier. After a moment of hesitation, Beekman had agreed.

The sun was sinking toward the Pacific horizon when she made her way to the end of the pier on Friday evening after work. The usual crowd of fishermen, tourists and lovers were milling along its length, but the pounding surf and steady breeze, Mallory noted, would ensure that anything she and Beekman had to say to each other would remain private.

Arriving a little before their seven-thirty rendezvous, Mallory cast her gaze across the water, her eyes automatically searching the sparkling horizon for the northern tip of Santa Catalina that she knew lay somewhere out there. The words of that song, "Twenty-Six Miles Across the Sea," ran through her mind as her thoughts turned to stories her parents had told about the day in June 1955 when they'd taken a ferry across to the island to be married. It was just a few days after Selena Cooper had arrived from England to wed the ex-airman she had met during his military service at a U.S. Air Force base outside London.

"Your mom was the most beautiful thing I'd ever seen," Mallory remembered her father saying. "I knew the first time

I saw her that I would marry her. It took me a while to convince her to leave England, but the day she finally said yes, your dad was the happiest guy in the world.''

Between what she remembered of her father's stories and what she'd been able to piece together since, Mallory guessed that his young life had been pretty bleak up to then. He had been raised by alcoholic parents, and then by foster families, after his mother and father died in a fire, too passed-out drunk to hear their child's screams. Escaping to military service at eighteen, his life, it seemed, began to turn around the day he met Selena Cooper, orphaned like himself—in her case, in the blast of German bombs over London. It was as if there was a curse on their family, Mallory thought with a shudder, this business of children losing parents, over and over, in smoke and blaze and heat.

After his military service, Philip Knight had returned to the States to attend college, never giving up on his efforts to convince Selena Cooper to follow him back and marry him. Raised by grandparents who were avid gardeners, Selena, when she finally came, fell in love all over, with him and with warm, sunny California and its unique landscape. If Philip Knight wanted to build beautiful houses, Selena wanted to design exciting outdoor living spaces around them. From the minds of these two dreamers had emerged Westwind Park, a residential community with culs-de-sac, open spaces and bicycle paths that was a development standard even now, twenty years after completion.

They'd had everything going for them, Mallory thought. Love and a family, professional success and the respect of their peers in the architectural community. How could it all have gone so wrong? Why would they have needed to turn to a lifestyle that included using and dealing drugs when they had the means to be happy and affluent in their own right? Not for the first time, she racked her brain, trying to understand the mystery behind the horror.

Staring out at the water, lost in thought and memories, she didn't notice Andrew Beekman until he was right beside her. ''Hello, Mallory.''

She spun around. He was dressed in a dark gray business suit, obviously expensive, obviously hand-tailored for his large, barrel-chested frame. He must be in his mid-sixties, she thought, but while his face was more lined than when she'd first met him at Ariel Beekman's wedding and his thin hair was going from gray to white, he still exuded force and power. Instinctively, she took a step back.

"How have you been?" he asked.

Mallory nodded, conscious of his neutral, even faintly curious regard. She had rehearsed over and over what she would say to him—the questions, the demands, the accusations. But now, confronted with this daunting man and his bland expression, she found herself uncharacteristically tongue-tied, not knowing where to begin.

"Why didn't you tell me?" she asked finally.

"Tell you what?"

"That you knew my parents."

He took a deep breath and leaned against the railing of the pier, nodding. "So, you've been looking into my holdings. I was wondering how long it would take you to figure it out."

"Westwind Park was one of your developments."

"That's right."

"When I read the press accounts of my parents' murder, they said Westwind was a project of Quad-A Homes. It was only recently that I discovered that Quad-A was a Beekman Development subsidiary."

"Yes. The company's dismantled now. I never liked the name. It was my wife's idea to use the first letter of all our names—Andrew, Asa, Ariel, and Andrew, Jr. I always thought it was a little too coy."

"Why did you place Westwind under a different corporate entity than the other Beekman projects?"

"It was a marketing decision. Up until then, I had been building lower-cost tract houses. Jane Aznar Brown, who owned the Orange County ranch lands on which Westwind Park was to be built, wanted something different—an upscale model community for the Southland. I had six other Beekman Development projects going at the time, but when she gave me the contract to create Westwind, it was on the condition that I form a whole new design team and corporate identity to market it."

"And it was my parents you hired to head up the design team."

"That's right."

"Why didn't you say so when you came to my apartment that night and told me you'd found out who I was?"

He shrugged. "It didn't seem relevant. At the time, I was more concerned about Drew. All I could think of was that I didn't want him mixed up with Philip Knight's daughter. Everything else was secondary." His expression was stony, and under one eye, a muscle twitched. Andrew Beekman, it was clear, detested even the memory of her dead father. "When Drew brought you to Ariel's wedding," he went on, "I thought there was something familiar about you. Finally, I realized what it was. You look like your father, you see. You have Selena's eyes, but the rest of you—your coloring, your mouth, the way you move—is all Philip."

Mallory shook her head. "I wouldn't know. I can barely remember their faces. As she's grown older, I've realized that my sister must look like our mother, but there was nothing left after the explosion. No pictures, nothing of theirs to hold on to or remember them by."

Beekman stared at her for a moment, then turned away, watching a police helicopter that was hovering over a fishing boat a mile or so out, looking for drug smugglers, perhaps.

"What went wrong?" she asked. "Can you tell me why my parents got mixed up with drugs and dealing?"

"Not your mother."

"What?"

"Not your mother," he repeated. "She was a good woman. The press reports were wrong about her. It was a tragedy that she got caught in the middle."

"What are you saying? That it was all my father's doing?"

"He was not an easy man. A brilliant architect, but so driven to succeed that he had no time or patience for anyone who crossed him. He was high-strung and short-tempered. Your mother tried to help him with his demons, but in the end, she couldn't."

"His demons?"

"Holdovers from a rough childhood, it seems. Alcoholism in the family." Beekman shrugged. "I don't know. Maybe he couldn't help it. Maybe there's a gene that creates a self-destructive, addictive personality.''

"Are you saying he was an addict?"

"Perhaps. He was under a lot of pressure during the Westwind project, and over the six years he worked for me, he seemed to turn to recreational drugs more and more, looking for escape from the tension. I thought at the time it was marijuana, but after they died and the police reported finding heroin, as well…" Beekman shrugged again. "At first, Selena said it was just to help him relax. Later, she became frightened and tried to get him to quit, but he wasn't listening to anyone. His work became completely erratic.''

"Is that when you fired them?"

"Not her. I never fired Selena, only Philip. She quit of her own accord. I wanted her to stay. She was torn, but in the end, she wanted to give him one more chance.''

"Why don't I remember any of this? They never fought, that I can recall. I remember that my father always enjoyed a good party, but I don't remember ever seeing him stoned or drunk or debilitated in any way.''

"He was careful around you children, I think. To give him credit, he was protective of the two of you. And Selena was an excellent mother. She would have left him right away if he'd brought his habits and his uncontrolled behavior home. As it was, it was mainly his work that suffered.''

"The press reported that the police found drugs in the car after the explosion. Maybe he *had* started bringing it home,'' Mallory said.

Beekman nodded. "I told Selena that it was inevitable, especially when he got in so deep with the dealers after he lost his job. If she had left him when I asked her to, she wouldn't have had to die.''

Mallory froze, staring at him. "You tried to get my mother to walk away from him?''

Beekman was silent for a while. "I loved her,'' he said finally, his voice low.

"My mother?"

"More than anything in the world.''

"But—but you had a wife! And children!''

"I know, but I would have given them up for Selena. I would have done anything for her. As Philip's behavior became more unpredictable, I begged her to leave him. She finally agreed, but she didn't get out fast enough."

"That's not possible. She wouldn't have left."

"I told her I would take care of her."

"That may be, but my mother would not have walked out on us. No way."

Beekman turned to face her now. "Selena and I were in love. We wanted to be together. She wanted it as much as I did."

Mallory took a step away from him. "You and my mother— having an *affair*?"

"You make it sound sordid, Mallory, but it wasn't like that. I wanted to be there for her, to make sure nothing ever hurt her again. She'd had a rough time during the war, and then later, resettling in a new country and dealing with a difficult husband. I understood Selena. She and I had many things in common, and when things went bad with your father, she turned to me. I could make her happy and safe when Philip couldn't. She needed that, after everything she had gone through, and I needed her."

"I don't believe you! She didn't love you. She loved my father."

"I know this is not easy for you to hear, but—"

"*No!* Why are you lying?"

"I'm not, Mallory. I was ready to take her in, and you children, too." He stepped closer. "I'd still like to take care of you, for her sake."

"Oh, sure," she said with a bitter laugh. "That's why you evicted me from my apartment and threatened to have me arrested."

"I told you before, I'm sorry. Dreadfully sorry. It was wrong to do that. As a matter of fact, when I went there that night, I didn't know *what* I was going to do. But then I found that fellow in your apartment, and his drugs, and I saw red. It was like the situation with your father all over again. Then you, standing there, so stubborn, looking so much like him. It brought back all those memories. I loved Selena, and Philip Knight destroyed her. I hated him for it. I guess I also hated you that night, because you reminded me of your father, and I was afraid you would hurt my son.''

Mallory shook her head, crying now. ''It's not true. That's not what I remember. My father loved my mother, and she loved him.''

''I know you want to believe that—how much you need to hold on to that belief—but you couldn't have known what was really going on. You were just a little girl, and they tried to keep their problems hidden from you and your sister.'' Beekman took a step closer, his voice growing softer. ''I can guess how terrible it's been for you all these years, Mallory, but it's in the past now. We *both* need to put it behind us. I've carried Selena's memory around with me every day since she died. I couldn't even grieve properly for her, because it was a secret, what we had been to each other. I had to keep it all inside and deal with it alone—the rage and the pain. Guilt, too. I should have watched out for you children, but I was in shock after her murder, and I wasn't thinking straight. I didn't know how I could deal with you or your problems, so I let strangers do it. That wasn't right, I know. But maybe it's not too late.'' Beekman put his hands on her shoulders, drawing her close. ''Maybe we can help each other. Grieve for her together.''

She had stood throughout his entire speech, stunned, but she pulled away sharply now. ''No! You're a lying bastard, Beekman. She *couldn't* have loved you.''

''Your father wasn't the man you think he was, Mallory. Philip Knight was a difficult, arrogant, self-indulgent man, and he ended up destroying his family because of it.''

''I loved him, dammit! I loved them both!''

''Mallory, please . . .''

''No! My father was brilliant, and my mother loved him. I know she did! She would *never* have left him for you.''

''Yes, she would have, if she hadn't died.''

''You're lying. My father may have had his problems, but my mother would never have abandoned him. My memories may be vague and incomplete, but I *do* remember the two of them together. I remember them touching each other, and the way they looked at each other. No one could have come between them, least of all you!''

Beekman pulled back, his face hard now. "Philip Knight was pigheaded and weak, and he wasn't worthy of her. And you *are* his daughter, in more ways than just appearance. You're every bit as stubborn and opinionated and incapable of facing up to reality as he was. If you're not careful, you'll end up just like him."

"You're not the first person to tell me I'm damaged goods," Mallory said bitterly, remembering the Rev and his harangues as he forced her to her knees. "But you're wrong. People like you—you think you can lie and lie, and after a while, people will forget the truth. Well, I won't. There's a lot of the past that I don't understand or remember, but I'm not prepared to accept your version of what happened. Much less that my mother could ever have considered choosing you over my father, whatever his problems."

"You have no idea what you're talking about."

"Really? Well, one thing I *do* know is that you're a nasty piece of work. You're lying about this, and if you could do that, I wonder what other lies you might be hiding behind. Maybe it's time the world saw the *real* Andrew Beekman!"

38

Mallory was sitting at a small conference table in Ian Gallagher's office on a Friday afternoon, going over her latest research notes. She had come in to ask for advice on how to proceed on her latest piece, part of an intermittent series on dubious land-development practices. She and Ian had no sooner sat down than he'd received a call from the managing editor's office, saying Carson Hoag wanted to see him right away.

"Sit tight. This probably won't take long," he said.

She nodded as he rose and headed out of the office, weaving deftly through a maze of people and furniture to the elevators. He still moved like the football player he'd apparently once been, she thought, watching his agile dodging of desks and chairs, and of reporters scrambling to meet deadlines. In his late thirties now, Ian spent too many hours desk-bound to be in top physical condition, but under his big, soft-spoken exterior lay an energy that always seemed to manifest itself just when everyone else's was flagging.

Although he'd been brought onto the *Chronicle's* editorial board at a relatively young age, Ian had earned the confidence of those above *and* below him. Never one to seek control for control's sake, he assigned stories then let his reporters run with their instincts, stepping in to provide ideas and guidance only when it was needed. Despite the demands of running a busy newspaper section and the tension of daily deadlines, he never seemed to lose his temper, prodding and cajoling his staff to produce their best work day after day, saving his wrath for outsiders or management on the rare occasions when someone was foolish enough to try to ride roughshod on one of his people. Metro reporters—even seasoned veterans who might have resented being placed under the authority of a young upstart—had come to recognize Ian's human as well as reportorial skills. Every one of them would have happily walked over hot coals for Ian Gallagher, but no one quicker than Mallory herself.

After a few strained months, their friendship had once again settled into a comfortable place where they could be together and not be burdened by what had almost happened that night in the underground parking lot. It was as if both of them had agreed, without ever discussing it, that if they couldn't be lovers, they had to be friends, and that a relationship limited to the *Chronicle* offices was better than no relationship at all.

Mallory knew that she had been doing her best work since the move to Metro, from breaking the story on the corrupt Orange County sheriff, to coverage of abuse in a nursing home, to investigations into links between prominent developers and local politicians who made zoning decisions that spelled windfall or disaster for those landowners. She was a long way from the gangly young free-lancer who had blustered her way to a *Chronicle* byline on the Western MediSearch story nearly four years earlier. Now, her career was blossoming, and she had the respect and admiration of readers, her peers and—most important—Ian.

Her life was busy, and if it lacked one close loving relationship, she had a group of good friends for the first time ever, most of them *Chronicle* staffers and editors like Ian Gallagher and Celia Webster. Her sister, Diana, whom she visited at least once a year in Paris, was thriving with her little family. Mallory also had the comfort of knowing that her old buddy, Wiley Dixon, who had passed briefly through L.A. once or twice again in the course of his restless treks, had acquired a publisher who thought enough of his fantastic stories to bring them out in book form—even if it meant chasing the author all over the globe and having to piece together pages from his dogeared, overfull notebooks.

She should have been content, Mallory thought, but always, simmering away on her personal back burner, was her desire to understand the mystery of her family's past, a strange and tragic story in which Andrew Beekman—the man, his business and his links to her mother and father—now seemed to have played a prominent part. No matter what article she was working on, she rarely made a trip to the *Chronicle* morgue or the land registry office, or interviewed a law enforcement official or government agent, that she didn't inquire into some aspect of Beekman's holdings or activities. Her file on him, which lay in her bottom drawer along with another containing copies of the old stories on her parents, was growing fat with clippings and notes.

Remembering Beekman's comments about inherited tendencies to self-destructive, addictive behavior, she was beginning to wonder if she was harboring a dangerous obsession. Wasn't furtively hiding a compulsion one of the first signs of addictive behavior? If so, maybe she *was* a candidate for some 12-step program, Mallory thought, because she hadn't told a soul about the truth behind her Beekman fixation, pretending instead it was part of her ongoing research into who owned Orange County and whether shady activities might be as prevalent among landowners there as in other parts of the Southland.

So far, she had uncovered nothing scandalous about him or his company, aside from the usual support of political causes and candidates that benefited his financial interests. Beekman Development was among a number of companies that the *Chronicle* had cited lately in Mallory's articles on questionable, if not illegal, links between business and government in Southland counties. The developers were becoming more and more agitated about the coverage, complaining to the publisher and senior management and threatening to pull advertising.

Although Ian never mentioned it, Celia told Mallory that he had fought several battles at editorial board meetings, where Carson Hoag had asked if it wasn't time to move on to other stories.

Grady O'Toole, Celia said, had jumped on the bandwagon to suggest that Mallory be reined in. Still humiliated from the formal rebuke he had received from Hoag and the publishers over the joint sexual harassment complaint that Personnel had forwarded—a rebuke that had probably killed his chances to succeed Carson Hoag as managing editor—O'Toole seemed to have decided that Mallory and Ian had somehow instigated the problem. He was more obsessed than ever, Celia said, with exposing a chink in Gallagher's shining armor.

Still, Ian had prevailed for the time being, and under his protection, Mallory pressed on with her research, keeping Beekman's feet to the fire, convinced that he hadn't told her the truth about his relationship with her mother. If he had lied about that, she reasoned, what other lies might he be living? And he *had* to have lied, Mallory thought, because memory told her another story altogether.

Sitting in the back seat of the car, riding home from the beach, Mallory leaned over to see what her sister was drawing on her clipboard. She was a little jealous. Her daddy had brought her a clipboard from the office, too, but Mallory got sick if she tried to use it in a moving car. Anyway, she couldn't draw nearly as well as Diana.

At the moment, Diana was working on a picture of the little gray kitten their parents had brought home the day they moved into their new house. The picture was perfect, from the kitten's fluffy body to her blueberry eyes. Diana scribbled a little, and suddenly, the kitten looked as if it had a shadow. Mallory frowned. If she had tried that, it would just look like scribbles, but Diana's pictures always looked like the thing they were supposed to be.

"Ooh!" Mallory cooed. "It's Evinrude!"

Diana looked up. "No, Miss Muffet," she corrected.

Mallory appealed to her mother, sitting in front, her left arm stretched across the back of the seat, massaging her husband's neck. "We're calling her Evinrude, right Mommy? 'Cause, like Daddy said, she sounds like his outboard motor when she purrs?"

Her mother glanced back and gave Diana an apologetic grimace. "I think that battle's lost, honey. The kitten seems to answer to Evinrude already." She turned to Mallory's daddy and gave him a playful punch in the shoulder, smiling. "Do you see what you've done? Now we have a cat named Evinrude."

Mallory bounced forward, hanging over the front seat. "Evinrude! Evinrude!" she sang.

She saw her daddy's eyes smile at her in the rearview mirror, and then she noticed his right hand, stroking her mother's thigh. When her mother saw the path of Mallory's gaze, she put her hand over her husband's and held it still. "Now, stop that," she admonished softly. She was blushing, but there was a smile on her lips.

A few minutes later, they reached their new house. As Mallory unrolled the hose to wash off the sand toys, she watched her mommy and daddy stroll, arm in arm, up the walk to the big oak front door, Diana following behind.

They died with their arms around each other, Mallory thought. The picture she held in her mind was not one of a woman who was getting ready to walk out on her husband.

Mallory's head was bent over her notes when Celia Webster walked into Ian's office. "Hi there!"

"Celia, hi. How are you?"

"I'm fine. Where's Ian?"

"Gone up to Carson Hoag's office."

"Uh-oh. How come?"

Mallory shrugged. "I don't know. Hoag's secretary called a few minutes ago and said he wanted to see Ian right away."

Celia dropped heavily into a chair next to her. "Any idea why?" When Mallory shook her head, Celia frowned. "This doesn't look good."

"What do you mean?"

"I was out for lunch at Di Carlo's and guess who I spotted there with Grady O'Toole?"

"Who?"

"Andrew Beekman."

Mallory felt her blood turn icy.

"Did you know they knew each other?" Celia asked.

"No, but I remember Grady once told me that he was a friend of Vernon and DeeDee Cunningham, who are close friends of the Beekmans, so I guess it's possible they could have been introduced."

"Well, I was just coming to give you and Ian a heads-up," Celia said. "O'Toole and Beekman left the restaurant ahead of me. When I got back from lunch, I needed to see Carson, but I couldn't talk to him because he had those two in his boardroom. They were deep in conversation about something. Ian and I must have just passed in the elevators.''

"Beekman's probably whining about our ongoing critique of developers in Orange County,'' Mallory said, feigning bravado. "He's stomping around, I'm sure, threatening to pull his ads if we don't back off.''

Celia nodded. "I don't like the fact that Grady's involved, though. He wouldn't be slithering in on Beekman's coattails if there weren't something in it for him.''

"You think he's looking for a way to do damage to Ian?'' Mallory asked nervously.

"I think it's a good bet.''

Mallory started to say more, but her eye caught the elevator doors opening and the emergence of a white-faced Ian. As he strode across the floor, one of the Metro staffers approached him, but Mallory saw him brush off the reporter with a curt "not now,'' his lips barely moving. She had never seen him turn anyone away, and she had never seen him looking so angry. When he got to his office and registered the presence of the Lifestyles editor, Ian hesitated at the door. "Celia,'' he said, his voice a cold monotone, "could you excuse us? Mallory and I need to talk.''

"Sure, but is everything all right? I saw Grady and Beekman—''

"Please,'' Ian said, holding one hand on the doorknob. The older woman nodded. When she had gone, he closed the door firmly.

"Ian? What happened up there?'' Mallory asked, her mind reeling with possibilities, none of them remotely palatable.

He turned and faced her, his gaze stony. "We're under new guidelines for stories concerning real estate developers.''

"Guidelines?''

"We'll be having regular 'information sessions' with the community of developers so that they can keep us apprised of their projects and plans. And any information we obtain concerning development issues must be verified with the company involved before anything is published in the *Chronicle*.''

"But that's like fact-checking with the Mafia!" Mallory protested. "They're never going to confirm any negative information we dig up, especially Andrew Beekman. I know he's the one behind this. Celia said she saw him with Grady. They're just trying to tie our hands."

"That's exactly what they've done. But it won't be your problem."

"What do you mean?"

"Effective immediately, you're no longer covering Andrew Beekman, Orange County or any story remotely connected to that area or his business."

"Why not?"

Ian walked over to the desk and withdrew a snapshot from his pocket, laying it down. Mallory looked at it and her heart sank. It was her and Drew Beekman at his sister's wedding. She cringed at the sight of her ridiculously skimpy peach dress, and the way she was leaning into Drew as he gripped her possessively around the shoulders. They looked like two people who couldn't wait to get away, throw off their clothes and jump all over each other—which is about how they were feeling at the moment the photographer had taken this picture, if she remembered correctly.

She took a deep breath and sat back. "Ian, I—"

"Do you have *any* idea how bad this looks?"

"I know how bad it makes *you* look. I'm so sorry. You stood up for me in board meetings, I know, when Carson Hoag wanted to kill the series."

"Yes, I did, because I believed absolutely in your integrity. Grady kept intimating that I was incapable of objective judgment where you were concerned, but I would have backed you against any journalist I know, Mallory. And now, I find out that this has all been a personal vendetta on your part."

"It was bad judgment. I just—"

"It sure as hell was! And thoroughly, utterly unprofessional to have carried on with these investigations when you had such a blatant conflict of interest."

Head buzzing, Mallory rose from her chair and turned to leave.

"Where are you *going*, dammit?" Ian shouted.

She looked at him listlessly. "I presume I'm fired."

"You're bloody close to it! Hoag was apoplectic."

"Well then?"

Ian was breathing heavily, his face shifting between fury and pure, hellish anguish. "I told him that if he fired you summarily like that, before you had a chance to explain yourself, I would quit, too."

"You shouldn't have done that."

"Mallory," he cried. "For God's sake, talk to me! Were you so much in love with this Drew Beekman that you'd risk destroying your career and everything you've worked for, just to get back at his father for breaking you up?"

She frowned. "What exactly did Beekman say about me?"

"That you were involved with his son a few years back, but that he and his wife decided you weren't what they wanted for him. He said he used some pretty heavy-handed tactics to get rid of you, including evicting you from your apartment and threatening you with the police. He seemed embarrassed that he had gone to such extremes, especially since you turned out to be a better person than he'd realized at the time. He said he'd tried more than once to apologize and make amends, but that you were fixated on revenge."

"That's it? That's all he said?"

"What else is there?"

Mallory shook her head, amazed, despite her anger and fear, at Beekman's cleverness. There was just enough truth in his story to be plausible. The fury of a woman scorned and all that. But he hadn't risked calling his own character into question by revealing his alleged connection to her mother. As it was, he came across as an overprotective father. Was Beekman shielding himself, she wondered, or was he reserving ammunition in case there was a second round to this battle?

"Mallory? I'm waiting for some explanation."

She stood rooted to the spot, staring at Ian's troubled face, wishing she could do something—*anything*—to make the past go away. He'd believed in her and stood by her, but she had betrayed him—as always, hurting those who meant the most to her.

"I'll clear out my desk and submit my resignation right away," she said.

"I won't accept it. That's not good enough. I want to know *why* you did this."

"I did it because I'm a screwup, Ian. I always have been."

"That's not true."

"Yes, it is. I'm sorry I hurt you, though. I never wanted to."

He stepped toward her. "I don't care about *that,* Mallory. I care about *you.*"

"Don't. I'm not worth it."

"Mallory, please! Tell me what's going on in your head. How could they mess you up like this? What did they do to hurt you so badly?"

She shook her head, fighting tears. "It doesn't matter. I need to get out of here."

Ian watched her for a moment, then sighed, his frustration evident. "All right, look—take a leave of absence. We'll let this die down, then see how we can salvage things. I'm not giving up on you," he added. She stiffened when he put his hands on her shoulders, so he let them drop.

Mallory turned to the door, pausing before she left. "Somebody once said I was a magnet for trouble, Ian. If you're smart, you'll just let me go, and steer clear of me in future."

39

Mallory cleared out her desk, conscious of a dozen pairs of eyes watching her in a newsroom that had fallen eerily silent. No one, it was certain, had ever heard the kind of shouting that had just gone on behind Ian's closed door, or seen the easygoing editor in such a state of barely contained rage. Mallory knew people were confused and curious, but she had no intention of enlightening them. It was all she could do to hold herself together long enough to get off the Metro floor and down to the underground parking lot.

Throwing her personal files into the trunk of her car, Mallory drove out of the dim lot into bright afternoon sunshine, having no clue where she would go or what she would do, now or in the immediate future. Going home was out of the question. Lili would wonder what she was doing there in the middle of the day. She would cluck and commiserate if Mallory told her what had happened, or chatter on interminably if she didn't. Mallory couldn't face either.

Not knowing what else to do, she headed for the Hollywood Freeway, driving north for miles, through Hollywood and Burbank, North Hollywood and Van Nuys, the road shimmering before her damp eyes as she negotiated the interchange to the Golden State Freeway. One hour drifted into another as she drove on, heedless of her speedometer that edged often past eighty, and of the ticket she would get if the highway patrol pulled her over. At the Simi Valley interchange, she veered right, continuing until she found herself, finally, out of the city on the Foothill Freeway, skirting the Angeles National Forest, both she and L.A.'s brown smog drifting along the lower reaches of the San Gabriel Mountains. She took an off-ramp, chosen at random, and steered the Ford Escort east into the mountains, careening up canyon roads and around hairpin switchbacks, her heart thumping at each steep drop-off that sheared away from the shoulder of the road.

As she climbed higher, a sound arose in the back of her mind, an insistent voice that whispered, *"Go ahead! Sail over the edge and be done with it!"*

Why not? What difference would it make? She had nothing. There was no one whose well-being depended on her. Diana didn't need her. Wiley was doing his thing. The Rev was still alive, but living in a state of senile dementia so advanced that he no longer even recognized her on her infrequent visits, keeping her long-ago promise to Franny. Lili Dahl was the closest thing to family she had nearby, but her elderly friend was becoming more frail all the time. Mallory was home so little that Lili might be better off giving up her house and moving someplace where she could have full-time care and companionship.

Nor did she have a job anymore to fill up the blank spaces in her life. She couldn't go back to the *Chronicle*. No matter that Ian had managed, by the slenderest of threads, to save her job when Carson Hoag had wanted to give her the ax. Her credibility was shot. Ian's trust and respect were gone. It was all part of a lifetime refrain of loss that had grown repetitive and tiresome.

Why not give up this battle she had been fighting since that long-ago Memorial Day, when her inner peace and security had vanished in a blast of noise and heat?

All she had to do, Mallory thought, was release the steering wheel when she came to the next curve. She imagined the scenario. There would be a moment of vertigo as the car flew into space and began its arcing plunge. A rush of wind, then impact. After that, the hurting and the rage would end, once and for all. It was simple, really. Probably painless.

She approached a curve and her foot bore down on the accelerator. Her grip on the wheel loosened as she watched the sky expand up ahead where a yawning chasm loomed. There was a guardrail in front of her, but it would be no match for a ton of steel hurtling at seventy miles an hour. Mallory's hands slid down the sides of the steering wheel until only her fingertips rested on the bottom, guiding the car in a direct path toward the precipice.

But just at the point where she was about to release her hold on the wheel and on life, Ian's face flashed in front of her eyes. What would he think when they found what was left of her at the bottom of a canyon?

She yanked the wheel to the left, negotiating the curve in a squeal of rubber, tires skidding on the loose gravel at the shoulder and sending the car into a fishtail. The Escort careened into the oncoming lane. As Mallory fought to avoid slamming into the wall of rock on the other side, a big rig appeared out of nowhere, traveling straight for her. She struggled to maneuver the car back to its own side of the road. Finally, it responded and the sixteen-wheeler screamed past. The little car lurched in its airstream, then settled into the next straightaway. Shaking uncontrollably, Mallory slowed the car and took a few deep breaths.

When the roaring pulse in her ears died away, her thoughts returned to Ian. Would he feel guilty, as if he were somehow at fault? It was ridiculous, of course. She had brought her downfall on herself. All he had done was believe in her, but Ian's sense of personal responsibility was so well developed that assigning blame to himself was the sort of thing he would do.

Another thought occurred to her. Would he think this had all happened because of her ruptured affair with Drew Beekman? She had cared for Drew, certainly, and she had been bitter when Andrew Beekman went after her so viciously, even threatening Wiley. But the idea that the Beekmans alone could drive her to thoughts of blind vengeance or suicide was a joke.

Still, how would Ian know that? How could he understand the constant, churning rage and anxiety that she lived with? The pain and uncertainty about why Diana's and her childhood had been ripped away. The doubt and self-loathing that came from the critical harangues and corrosive pity she had been bombarded with for so many years. The Beekman men, father and son, were the least part of her personal anguish, but how would Ian know any of that when she had never trusted him enough to share the truth?

Mallory moved her foot from the accelerator to the brake, pulling into a scenic lookout at the side of the road. Shutting off the engine, she stared at the sprawling city laid before her under a blanket of haze. The sun had dropped far below the Pacific horizon when she reached for the ignition key once more.

It was after nine when Ian turned onto his quiet residential street in Pasadena. He had bought his sprawling, ranch-style bungalow several years earlier, not long after his divorce from Caitlyn Allis, looking to get a toehold in the skyrocketing southern California real estate market before prices got even worse. Originally planning to keep it as an investment and rent it out, he'd decided to live in it himself—despite the fact that it was a family home in a family neighborhood and too large for a single person. But in his quieter moments, Ian had a hankering to mount a basketball hoop over the garage and float air mattresses in the backyard pool for the children that his warm Nebraska upbringing had conditioned him to want, if he could just find the right woman. A woman with brains and heart, fire and passion.

After the disaster with Caitlyn, which he had written off as a hormonally induced behavioral aberration, he had met only one woman who fit the bill. But for whatever reason—he guessed he understood now—she was unwilling to let him close, even when he was prepared to throw professional caution to the wind. That young woman, who outshone every other he'd ever met, drove a white Escort, and it was sitting in front of his house.

As Ian got out of his car, Mallory came up the driveway, carrying a file folder under her arm. She was wearing the same clothes she'd had on when she left the *Chronicle,* but she looked rumpled and tired, her face drawn and pale under the streetlights.

"Hi," he said quietly. "I've been worried about you. Are you all right?" She nodded. "Have you been waiting long?"

"An hour or so. I'm sorry to bother you at home but I wanted to do this now, before I lose my nerve. I didn't think it could wait till Monday, and anyway, I won't be going back to the office. I won't take much of your time."

"It's okay. I'm glad you're here. Come in." He unlocked the front door and flipped the light switch, then stepped back to let her pass into the vestibule. When he had closed the door and turned around, she was standing in the hall, her eyes taking in the living room on one side and the dining room on the other. He glanced around, as if seeing it for the first time. She'd been there before, of course, for office parties, but never alone. Did she like it? The house was comfortable and functional, but it seemed to him that it lacked warmth.

"I really don't want to bother you," Mallory said, gaze down now. "I just wanted to show you something, and maybe offer an explanation. I owe you that, at the very least. It's not an excuse, mind you. There *is* no excuse, but—"

"Before you continue, I could use a drink. How about you?"

She hesitated, then nodded. Ian led her into the living room, where a bar stood behind the door of a wall unit. "Red wine okay?"

"Fine."

She dropped the file on the coffee table as she passed it, and his curiosity grew. He opened a bottle of Cabernet Sauvignon, poured her a glass, then filled one for himself. They stood awkwardly for a moment, as if racking their brains to come up with a ritual toast. Somehow, there didn't seem to be much to cheer about. Ian took a long draft of the wine, and she followed suit.

"Why don't we sit?" he said. He led her to the sofa, with its deep cushions and tweedy upholstery. But when Ian went to settle himself beside her, a nervous flutter skittered across her features, so he took a nearby armchair instead and waited for her to begin. She wasn't finding this easy, that much was clear. He offered a delaying tactic, anxious to help her out. "Are you hungry? I could make us something to eat."

Mallory shook her head. "I couldn't eat. You go ahead, though."

"No, I don't think I could handle anything, either."

Mallory stared at her wine for a moment, then sighed and set it down on the heavy glass coffee table. "I wanted to explain about the Beekman thing. It wasn't what you think."

"I don't really know *what* to think. It came as a shock when Carson Hoag handed me that picture of you and the son, and then Beekman said his piece. I gather this all happened before Drew Beekman went to Washington?"

She nodded. "Drew was in his senior year at UCLA and I was a freshman at Westside College. He tended bar in the same restaurant where I was waiting tables. Despite his wealth, Andrew Senior always made Drew work for his spending money. As a matter of fact," Mallory added, "it was the same restaurant where you took me that night you first told me about Celia Webster's contract to work for Lifestyles."

"Bogart's?"

"Yes, but it had a different name and management when Drew and I were there. Anyway, he came along at a rough time for me, being new here and all alone. He was going through his own problems with his father. Misery loves company, I guess, so we hit it off."

"Until the old man found out."

"That's right. Beekman came down like a ton of bricks, just like he said. Instead of arguing with Drew directly and running the risk of alienating him, Beekman went behind his son's back, forcing *me* to break it off by threatening not only myself, but also Drew's career hopes *and* an old friend of mine who happened to be visiting from back home. Unfortunately, my friend had a slight drug habit, and when Beekman found out, he threatened to bring in the police. It was Wiley Dixon. Maybe you've heard of him."

"The fantasy writer?"

"That's him. We grew up together in Minnesota and he was the best friend I'd ever had. I couldn't have survived Ferry Falls without Wiley, so there was no way I would let Beekman bring him down. I did what he wanted and walked away from Drew."

"That must have hurt."

"I was more angry than hurt. I cared for Drew, but I wasn't in love with him."

Ian felt an irrational flood of elation. "You weren't?"

"No. We went out for only seven weeks, and I don't think I ever believed we could have a future together. Once I got over the immediate anger of what his father had done, I put it behind me and got on with living." She paused and took a sip of her wine, then replaced the glass on the table. "The next time I ran into Beekman, I was already working for Lifestyles."

"Is it true he tried to apologize?"

She grimaced. "In a manner of speaking, I guess, but I didn't want anything to do with the creep."

"I can understand that. But you were determined to nail his hide to the wall just the same. I *know* you were, Mallory," Ian added when she began to protest. "There are half a dozen major Orange County developers, but it was apparent to me from the start that you were focusing on Beekman for some reason."

"I was, but not because of Drew or anything Beekman had done recently."

"Then *what?*"

She reached for the file folder she'd brought with her. "Because of this," she said, handing it to him.

Ian put down his wineglass and took the file, settling back in his chair. When he opened it, he found photocopies of old *Chronicle* articles dating from 1969. He skimmed through an extraordinary account of a luxury home in Esmerelda Canyon that had been blown to smithereens in a propane explosion, the owners murdered, their two children critically injured. The couple were the architect and landscaper who had designed Westwind Park for Quad-A Homes. Turning a page, Ian froze at the sight of school photographs the paper had reprinted of the children, Diana, ten, and Mallory, eight—*his* Mallory, he could see by the piercing, dark eyes and wild blonde hair. Only the caption said her name was Mallory Knight, not Mallory Caine.

He looked up, stunned. "You said your parents died in a car accident."

"I didn't, actually. You did, and I let you believe it. I was always made to feel ashamed of them, so I didn't want to tell you the truth."

"Mallory... I don't know what to say. I'm so sorry."

"My parents were employed by Andrew Beekman," she went on. Her eyes were bright, her breathing slow and deliberate, as if she was working hard to maintain composure. "Quad-A Homes and Westwind Park were part of Beekman Development, but I only found that out a few months ago, when I started examining Beekman's holdings and his past activities."

"Do you think he had something to do with their murders?"

"No, I don't see how. The police said they were dealing drugs and that they were killed for stiffing their suppliers. It was supposed to be a spectacular warning to anyone else who might consider trying to do the same."

"Back in 1969, a lot of people were into recreational drug use, marijuana and whatnot."

"The articles say my parents went further, into narcotics. That they were fired when their work began to suffer. But recently, I was told it was only my father who was the problem, not my mother."

"Told by whom?"

"Andrew Beekman. This past summer, I called him and we met. I told him I'd found out about his link to my parents, something he'd conveniently neglected to mention when he was busy kicking me out of his son's life. Beekman said he'd fired my dad, but not my mother. He also said . . ." She foundered, and Ian could see she was in agony.

"What?" he probed gently.

"He said he and my mother were having an affair."

"Oh, God . . ."

"He said she was getting ready to leave my father when they were murdered. But it's not true, Ian. It can't be! I was only eight years old, I know, but I remember how they were together. She could never have left my dad for that awful man." As Ian watched, her tears finally began to fall, that hard-won self-control crumbling at last.

He shifted seats and put his arms around her, stroking her hair softly while she cried. But inside, he was seething, ready to rip someone apart—Beekman, Grady O'Toole, her mother, her father. Not to mention whoever had done such sloppy, superficial police work *and* newspaper reporting that it would be damn near impossible to piece together now, all these years later, what really happened back then. No wonder she'd always seemed so conflicted and wary. And then, as if that weren't enough, he'd guessed from the little she'd said that her adoption had been miserable. Anyone else would have given up long ago, he decided, losing themselves in booze or chemicals.

"It's such a mess," she whispered. "And I had to go and make things worse."

"No. Don't worry about that. It doesn't matter. All that matters is you. I'd give anything if I could make it go away. I'd do anything for you." He rested his lips against the top of her head and sighed. His next words came without thinking. "I love you, Mallory." It was a simple truth, after all, but like so many simple truths, it had somehow gotten buried under stupid fears and pointless conventions. He thought she might run from it even now, but instead, she nodded.

"I love you, too, Ian. I'm so sorry that I didn't trust you. I just hurt you, and I—"

"No, shh," he said, stopping her lips with his own. She resisted for a second, then gave it up, wrapping her arms around his neck.

He yanked off his glasses and set them aside, pulling her close. His hands moved to the soft flesh of her throat, stroking her neck, feeling her body shiver under his touch. Wanting to know everything about her. Slowly, he eased her down on the couch, pushing up her skirt to free her legs and gripping her thigh. Her body arched into his as he kissed her, over and over, tasting damp saltiness from her eyes, her cheeks, her lips. She clung to him like a drowning person. When they paused to catch a breath, he leaned his forehead against hers, agonizing at the brushing of her damp eyelashes against his cheeks. "I'm sorry, Mallory."

"For what?"

"For holding back. For not being there for you."

"You've always been there for me."

"Not the way I should have been. Not the way I wanted to be. It's so stupid. No more, though."

"Ian—"

"Don't shut me out, Mallory. I want things to be different from here on in. And," he added, his voice husky, "I want to make love to you. So much."

She watched his face for a moment, then nodded. "I want that, too. Now. Please, now."

They kissed, hard and long, then Ian lifted his head. "Not here. Come with me."

He rose and led her down the hall, his arm around her shoulders, still half-afraid she would change her mind and bolt. In the bedroom, he backed her against a wall as they undressed each other quickly between kisses. When he stepped away for a second to pull down the bedclothes, he turned to find her still pressed to the wall, watching him with parted lips and eyes that were huge and dark and wet. Her arms hung limp at her sides, but her whole body was trembling. Those long legs that had first caught his eye as she gamboled across rows of folding chairs looked now as if they would crumple at any second.

"Oh, Mallory!" He strode over and scooped her into his arms.

On the bed, she wrapped her legs tightly around his body, taking him in, lips and hands urging him on. But he held himself back while he stroked her, coaxing, wanting her with him all the way. Her breathing came in ragged catches. She moaned, softly at first then more urgently, as if she were caught on a wave rushing headlong out to sea. Her cry, when it came, was in the form of his name. Ian pressed himself into her, riding her arching tremors until they had passed. Then, his hands and lips traveled over her once again. As she drew him deeper, moving with him, he raised his head to watch her face. It was flushed and glimmering, dark eyes locked onto him with a look of need so profound that he wanted to hide her away and never let the world touch her again. Suddenly, without warning, he exploded, and they both cried out—two voices, one aching chord. Then they lay, intertwined and still, floating on the rhythm of a single heartbeat that swept away years of lonely silences.

40

Los Angeles, California
December 4, 1986

It was after midnight, but Lili Dahl couldn't sleep. Insomnia was a common occurrence with old people, she'd heard. It was as if the body and the mind, knowing that time was running out, tried to cram in a little more living, stretching what numbered days remained into long, restless nights.

She was in her side yard, trimming back the bougainvillea. A full moon lit the bloodred, papery flowers that cascaded over the picket fence running the line between her property and her neighbor's. Beautiful as it was, she thought, you had to keep bougainvillea under control or it would take over the whole yard. Mallory had said just yesterday at breakfast that she would get to it this weekend, but Lili hated to see her spend what little free time she had doing yard work, and she didn't trust the gardener not to make a hash of it.

How would she ever manage without Mallory, who did all the shopping and most of the day-to-day chores that the weekly cleaning lady and the gardener didn't handle? She felt terrible accepting rent money, but although she'd told Mallory it wasn't necessary, Lili knew by her bank statements that payments were still deposited on the first of every month. Well, it didn't matter, she thought smugly. She had figured out a way to beat the stubborn girl. Mallory didn't know, but she was going to get it all back when Lili was gone. Not just the rent money, but the house, too, and everything in it.

Why not? Lili had thought the day she'd called her lawyer to change her will. The only relatives she had were a nephew in

Ohio and his four dreadful children. They had visited once, fifteen years earlier, when they'd come out to see Disneyland and used her home as a free hotel, the children nearly destroying it in the process and eating everything in sight. Other than that, Lili only heard from them once a year, at Christmas, when they sent a card with a photo of themselves and their ugly dog. There was never a letter in the card, or even a signature, just a preprinted card with some inane saying like, Happy Ho-Ho-Holidays from the Dahls!

So why not leave it all to Mallory? For the past seven years, she'd been the closest thing to a daughter or granddaughter that Miss Lili Dahl would ever have, even going so far as to take Lili to Paris for the holidays when, otherwise, she would have been alone.

Lili sighed as she stepped back to view her pruning job. It was a terrible thing to outlive everyone you'd once known and loved, she thought. Not for the first time, she wondered what her life would have been, had she accepted any one of the several marriage proposals that had come her way when she was a pretty young thing and men still yearned for her. But she had been swept off her feet by Errol Flynn, and she'd held out the hope every time he came back to her home and her bed that *this* time, he would stay. For six years, they had loved each other passionately, if discreetly, in this little bungalow that he'd bought especially for her. Even after Errol had moved on and then died—Lili's hopes along with him—she had been unable to abandon his memory. Other men had seemed pallid and dull by comparison. If she'd just lowered her standards, Lili thought, she mightn't have ended up alone. But she had no regrets. She'd known great passion once in her life, and maybe once was as much as anyone had a right to ask for.

Lili smiled as she thought of the call that had come a couple of hours earlier from Mallory. By the time Lili had managed to reach the phone, the answering machine was already recording a message, but she'd picked up so that Mallory would know she was fine and not come rushing over in a panic. She was at Ian Gallagher's, she'd said. Lili could hear the blush in her voice when she'd added that she might not make it home that night.

"Well, it's about time! I was beginning to think you'd *never* get together with that wonderful man."

"I beg your pardon?"

"Oh, come now, dear. He adores you. I could see it in his face that time he was here. And you feel the same way about him, don't you?"

There had been no hesitation in Mallory's answer. "Yes, I do."

"Of course, you do. So hold on to him. Love him, and let him love you. It's all that counts for anything, in the end."

"Oh, Lili! You're such a romantic."

"Not at all. I'm a hard-nosed realist. You get that way, by the time you reach my age."

"Well, then, I bow to your wisdom," Mallory said, laughing softly. "Will you be all right?"

"I'll be fine. You just take care of that fine Mr. Gallagher."

"I'll do that. We'll see you tomorrow, okay?"

"Wonderful. Good night, dear."

"'Night, Lili."

Closing her pruning shears now, Lili turned and headed toward the front veranda, feet shuffling in a happy little dance, her high, quavery voice singing a song from her youth: "Don't Sit Under the Apple Tree With Anyone Else But Me." Inside the house, she locked up and turned out the lights, thinking that maybe, finally, she might get to sleep. Even if she didn't, though, she had warm thoughts and memories to keep her company.

She was almost at her bedroom, when she noticed a crack of light coming from under Mallory's closed door. She must have left it on that morning, Lili thought, puzzled. But when she pushed open the door, her heart leaped at the sight of a large man standing there, holding in his hand the framed picture that Mallory kept of Diana. As the man spun around, the picture slipped out of his hand, clattering to the floor.

"What are you doing here?" Lili demanded.

He hesitated. He was an older man, gray-haired and barrel-chested. Well-dressed, but with a hard face, she thought. It shifted into what Lili felt certain was meant to be a reassuring smile. She most definitely did *not* feel reassured.

"I'm a friend of Mallory's," he said, taking a step toward her. "I'm terribly sorry to have startled you." Lili heard the faint burr of a Scottish R. "The front door was standing open, you see. I knocked, but no one answered, and I was worried that she might be injured or some such thing."

"She's not here. But she'll be home soon," Lili added as a cautious afterthought. "I'll tell her you came to call. Whom shall I say...?"

"Perhaps I could wait for her? I'm a very old friend."

"I don't think—" Lili began as she glanced around nervously. Suddenly, she noticed Mallory's desk, its drawers standing half-open, papers hanging out, the top in disarray. A couple of manila files were on the floor, their contents spilled. Mallory hadn't left her room like this. She was always tidy, especially about her desk and the research notes she worked on at home. "You've been going through her things!" Lili said indignantly. "You get out this instant, or I'll call the police!"

"Now just wait."

The man moved toward her, but Lili shuffled back, truly frightened. She turned and tried to run down the hall to the telephone, but he caught her by the arm and spun her around. "Let go!" she cried.

"You don't understand. I'm here to help her! She's going to need me now."

"She doesn't need you!"

"She does! She has to understand that."

"No! You go away! I'm calling the police! *Help!*"

"Shut up, you stupid hag!" The man raised his hand and swung it hard across her jaw.

The last thing Lili felt, going down in a jangle of bracelets and necklaces, was something solid that cracked against the back of her skull. Or was that cracking sound her head? she wondered as the final curtain dropped.

A neighbor who lived across the street from Lili Dahl noticed that her front door was ajar when he went out to pick up his *Chronicle* from the driveway at seven-thirty that Saturday morning. An hour later, he glanced out his front window and saw that the door was still open. When he realized that Mallory's car wasn't in the driveway, he went across to check on the old girl. Finding her lying in her front hall, a pool of dried blood under her head, the neighbor reached for the telephone on the table next to her, then thought better of it and recrossed the street to call 911 from his own phone. He asked for the police and an ambulance, although he knew the paramedics' services wouldn't be required.

Mallory and Ian arose late after a long, loving night and headed together for the shower. They stayed there for a very long time, guilt-free about contributing to the Los Angeles water shortage. Later, in his kitchen, when Mallory suggested she go back by herself to look in on Lili, Ian shook his head. "I'm not letting you out of my sight," he said, smiling as he reached out to her. "We'll go in my car, and then you'll *have* to come back here later."

"You're insatiable." She laughed, even as her own desire flared up once more. It was extraordinary, she thought. Here she was, unemployed, to all intents and purposes, no prospects, no references, not a shred of professional credibility left—and she'd never felt so happy. All the pain, all the rage, all the unsatisfactory relationships and unanswered questions of her life paled in the glow of this incredible thing that was happening between her and Ian. It was a pure, perfect joy— physical, emotional, mental. Her only regret was that they hadn't given in to it long before.

I'll do anything, she bargained with the fates, pay any price. Forget the past, and leave it all behind. Just let this one thing be. Let me have this, and I'll never ask for anything again.

On the drive to Beverly Hills, Ian held on to her hand as if he still couldn't believe that she wasn't going to run away. Or maybe it wasn't that at all, she thought, but just the desire to touch and feel skin on skin, even in a small way, until they could be in each other's arms once more. She glanced at his face as they rounded the corner of Lili's street, drinking him in, but when she saw his forehead crease into a frown, she turned to see what had caused it. Her stomach plunged at the sight of police cars and yellow tape, a crowd and an ambulance, in front of her house.

"Oh, God! Lili!"

Ian pulled up behind a cruiser. Mallory was out of the car, running, before he had turned off the ignition. At the edge of the lawn, a burly LAPD officer stepped in front of her and blocked her advance. "Hold it. You can't go in there."

"I live here!"

"What's your name?"

"Mallory Caine."

"All right, come with me, please, ma'am." He lifted the yellow tape marked "Police Line—Do Not Cross" and led her to the veranda.

"What happened?" Mallory asked.

"It looks like a break-in."

"Where's Lili? Lili Dahl, the owner?" At that moment, the front door opened and a stretcher was wheeled through, carrying a lumpy, black body bag. "Oh, God! No!"

A detective in a suit turned at her voice, and raised his hand for the paramedics to stop the stretcher. "Are you Mallory Caine?" he asked. She nodded, unable to take her eyes off the ugly thing. "I'm sorry, Miss Caine, but it appears Miss Dahl was attacked sometime during the night. I'm afraid she died of her injuries."

"I was just," Mallory said, choking, "I was just talking to her twelve hours ago."

"You were here?"

"No. I phoned a little after ten o'clock to check on her, and tell her I wouldn't be home."

The detective made a notation in a pad. "Ten o'clock last night. And she was all right?"

"She was fine. When did this happen?"

"The coroner's guessing between midnight and 2:00 a.m. Where were you at that time, Miss Caine?"

Mallory turned toward the lawn, where Ian was approaching in the company of another LAPD officer. "With him, at his house in Pasadena. Ian Gallagher."

"He's with the *Chronicle*, too, isn't he?"

"That's right."

The detective nodded. "I met him once, a few years back, when he was out on the streets, reporting."

"How did she die?" Mallory asked, her eyes drawn again to the vinyl bag on the stretcher.

"Looks like she hit her head on a table in the hall."

"She fell?"

"Or was pushed. She has a whopping contusion on her jaw."

Mallory groaned. "So there's no way it was accidental."

"Not likely, given that the house was also trashed."

"It's trashed?"

"Yes. I'd like you to come and take a look, see if anything's missing."

"Just a sec. Can I see her?"

The detective watched her for a moment, then nodded to the paramedics. One of them lowered the zipper on top of the bag. Mallory stepped forward and looked down at poor Miss Lili Dahl, whose flaming red hair was terribly mussed. The kohl around her half-open eyes had run and her lipstick was smeared, probably by the same blow that had swollen and bruised the left side of her jaw. Bereft of her lively energy, she looked very wrinkled and more than a little macabre.

Mallory reached in and gently brushed the hair away from her face, smoothing it and arranging it, then stroked her cold, papery cheek. "Oh, Lili," she whispered. "I'm so sorry I wasn't here." When she stepped back, she felt an arm go around her, and looked into Ian's sober eyes. She leaned into him as they zipped up the bag and took Lili away.

"Detective Williams, isn't it?" Ian asked. The other man nodded, reaching out his hand. "What happened here?"

"Like I just told Miss Caine, it looks to be a break-in. Miss Dahl must have caught the suspect—or suspects—in the act, and she was assaulted, we figure. We'll know more after the autopsy. The house was vandalized. A gang thing, maybe. We're dusting for prints. Miss Caine was with you all night?"

"That's right."

The detective nodded. He turned toward the door, then seemed to have another thought. "Miss Caine, did you know that you were heir to Miss Dahl's estate?"

Mallory's head snapped up. "*What?* No. Who told you that?"

"Her lawyer lives down the street, and he came over when he saw the commotion. He says she changed her will earlier this year, naming you as her sole beneficiary."

"I had no idea. Why would she do that?"

The detective shrugged. "Let's go inside, shall we? Don't touch anything."

They walked through the house, which looked as if it had been turned upside down and righted again. There seemed to be no rhyme nor reason to what had gone on, Mallory thought. Lili owned plenty of old movie memorabilia that would probably be valuable to collectors, but it was largely untouched. Her silver was scattered, but seemed to be all there. She'd had some valuable jewelry, aside from the costume stuff she habitually wore—gifts from admirers, she'd once told Mallory mysteriously—but any of the pieces Mallory had ever seen were still in her room.

Lili's bed had not been slept in. "She was prowling again," Mallory said.

"What?"

"Lili suffered from insomnia. Maybe she was gardening."

"Gardening?" The detective looked at her as if she were insane. "After midnight?"

"That was her favorite time, especially when the moon was full, like last night. I told her not to, but she never listened."

"Did she leave the front door open when she did this?" Williams asked. Mallory nodded. He pursed his lips. "Well, that might explain why there were no signs of forcible entry."

In her own room, Mallory walked around, examining her scattered possessions: books, clothes, files, toiletries.

"Anything missing?"

"Hard to tell, but I don't think so. Wait," she added, glancing at her bureau. "A picture of my sister. It's in a silver frame." She, Williams and Ian looked around for it. Finally, bending down, Mallory spotted it under the bed and reached out. "There it is."

"Don't touch it," the detective said, pulling back her hand. "We'll check it for prints. That's it? Nothing else that you can see?"

She shook her head. "Why would anyone do this to an eighty-year-old woman?"

"Damned if I know," Williams said wearily. "It's these bloody gangs and their sick thrills. Gets worse every year. Recently, they moved into Beverly Hills High. We've had a rash of break-ins and vandalism lately. This time, though, it looks like things went too far."

Later that night, back at Ian's house, stretched out in front of a crackling fire, Mallory lay across his chest and propped her chin on her fist, sighing deeply. Only twenty-four hours into their new relationship, and she had spent both evenings bawling her eyes out. It wasn't an auspicious beginning.

"When Detective Williams mentioned poor Lili's will, do you think he was intimating that I might have had something to do with her death?" she asked.

Ian stroked her back. "I think he had to pose the question, but I doubt you're a suspect. They checked the phone records, and there was a partial message on the machine at Lili's, so they know you called when you said you did. I was talking to Williams, and he said he could see by your reaction to the body that you cared for her. He could also tell you were genuinely surprised about the will. Cops get pretty good at spotting false reactions and Williams is a good cop."

"I still don't know why she changed her will. She has a nephew somewhere. Why would she name *me* as her beneficiary?"

"Probably because, unlike the nephew, you were there for her. And because she loved you. *I* can understand that." He kissed her forehead. "What are you going to do with the house?"

"God, I don't know. I don't want to live in it anymore, not after this."

"Good. I want you to live with me, Mallory. Here, if you want, or we can get another place."

"Oh, Ian, thank you, but that's probably not a good idea."

"Sure it is. Look at the advantages. We can make love morning, noon and night, and if we drive to work together, we can use the freeway car-pool lane."

Mallory returned his smile briefly, then her expression sobered. "I'm not going back to the *Chronicle.*"

"You can go back. You had reasons for doing what you did. Hoag will understand."

"No! You can't tell anyone, Ian."

"But—"

"No. I've seen my parents' names smeared enough. I won't have my mother publicly linked to Andrew Beekman."

He nodded. "All right. But you still don't have to quit the paper. Take some leave if you want. Hoag will calm down and this Beekman business will blow over, you'll see. You'll do other stories—great stories—and in no time at all, the whole affair will be forgotten.''

"I don't know. And anyway, it's not just that."

"Well, what is it then?"

"It's us. How can we work together and be lovers at the same time?"

Ian was silent for a time, watching the fire. "I don't know if we *should* be lovers, Mallory."

She was taken aback, but she sat up, nodding as she tucked her clothes together. "You're right. I don't blame you, Ian. You've worked too hard to get where you are, and—"

He pulled her down again and rolled her onto her back, leaning over, tracing her cheekbone. "That's not what I mean. I want us to be *more* than lovers, Mallory. I want to marry you."

"*What?* After what I did?"

"It's not the end of the world. And I love you. I want to be your husband, and the father of your children, and your companion for life. If you'll let me."

"But—but—"

Ian placed a hand over her mouth. "Just this once, don't argue, please. All you have to do is nod or shake your head."

She lifted his hand aside. "Are you serious. Life? With me?"

"Yup. I want us to grow into doddering senior citizens together. Although, come to think of it," he added ruefully, "I've got a head start on you there. I'll be in a rocking chair, and you'll still be leaping over them."

She grinned. "The only leaping I want to do is into your lap."

"That works for me. So, will you marry me?"

"Yes. In a flash, if you're crazy enough to ask." She pulled his head down and kissed him warmly, then gave him a stern look. "But I still won't go back to the *Chronicle*. I don't want to be a drag on you there, and Grady O'Toole's snide remarks alone would drive me to homicide."

"The hell with Grady! Other married journalists work together. Look at Ben Bradlee and Sally Quinn at the *Washington Post*." But Mallory shook her head. Ian watched her for a moment, then sighed. "You can do anything you want, Mallory. Write for the *Chronicle*, or for another newspaper or magazine. Television, maybe. You could call that agent you told me about. Do a Ph.D. Or,'' he added softly, placing a hand on her stomach, ''we could just get busy making babies. I'd love to have a baby with your eyes.'' He kissed them, one by one. ''Anything. Just say you'll stay with me.''

''Forever,'' she said firmly. ''Loving you is the finest thing I've ever had in my life, Ian. I don't know how on earth this happened, but now that it has, I could never walk away from you again.''

41

Mallory and Ian were married just before Christmas and spent the holidays honeymooning in Cancún. After they returned, she began shopping her résumé around, picking up some free-lance work and re-igniting the interest of the agent who had tried once before to draw her into television.

"The camera loves your face, Mallory," Natasha Keene of PAA, the Performing Arts Agency, said excitedly. "I know I can market you. But your new name..."

"What about it?"

"'Mallory Gallagher' isn't going to cut it, I'm afraid. There's no way to say it without sounding like you've got marbles in your mouth. Could you live with using your maiden name professionally? 'Mallory Caine' has a nice ring to it."

Mallory groaned. "I suppose." Would she *never* be free of the specter of the Rev?

Her new agent sent her to a voice coach to learn to breathe. "So what have I been doing for the last twenty-five years?" Mallory asked dryly.

Celia Webster's friend, Zara Tate, coached her on dress and movement for the cameras. "No checks, stripes or polka dots," Zara warned. "They start vibrating. And no bouclé."

"Really," Mallory said, rolling her eyes. "Can you see me in bouclé? I'd look like a teddy bear, for God's sake."

Zara laughed. "And no white. It shimmers. You're going to need dresses or jackets with lapels for the mike. Outfits that move easily. No wrap skirts that flap open. Oh, and watch out for jewelry that clanks."

"Poor old Lili Dahl couldn't have done this."

"I guess not." Zara paused, her expression sober. "There still hasn't been an arrest in her murder?"

Mallory shook her head. "No. The police think it's part of this wave of vandalism that's erupted at Beverly Hills High, only this time, the prank turned really ugly. They found fingerprints in my bedroom that they figured would trace back to some of the guys known to be involved in gang activities, but no match so far."

"Poor Lili! She sounds like she was a real old dear."

"She was great. I feel so bad. I keep imagining how terrified she must have been that night."

"This has been awful for you, too."

"It has, but Ian's been there all the way." Mallory sighed. "He's such a rock. God, I love him."

Zara smiled. "You deserve a good man. I'm glad you found each other now, when you really needed him. All right," she added briskly, "back to work. When you're on camera, I want you to keep your eyes moving. Makes them look twinkly and alert, interested."

"Check. Shifty eyes."

"Not shifty, Mallory, *twinkly*. Pay attention!"

"Yes, ma'am."

"You want to bridge the distance between you and your audience, so talk to the cameraman as if he were your long-lost brother. Sit tall in your chair, on the edge of it, spine stretched, and keep one but not both elbows on an armrest."

"Good grief! Do I really want to do this, Zara?"

She shrugged. "It's up to you, but I think you're a natural, and you know what Gore Vidal said."

"What?"

"Never turn down an opportunity to have sex or go on TV."

"So long as you twinkle, right?"

As it happened, things progressed surprisingly fast. Natasha Keene found Mallory an opening on a local cable station to do what she called "rip and read," delivering wire copy during brief news breaks every half hour. Within three months, the local NBC affiliate offered Mallory a subhosting spot on a summer-replacement interview show, "Uncommon Passions," featuring personalities from politics and entertainment, as well as items on consumer affairs. The lead interviewer, unfortunately, tended to grab high-profile guests like Jimmy Carter and Neil Diamond, while Mallory had to make the best of scintillating subjects like head lice and the avoidance of IRS tax audits.

"That's okay, Mallory," Natasha reassured her soothingly. "You're taking those lumps of coal and turning them into diamonds. It's all that matters." Mallory suspected at times that her agent's *brain* was a lump of coal.

But when her greedy cohost landed in traction after trying to relive his youth on a surfboard, Mallory suddenly found herself flying solo. "Uncommon Passions," to no one's greater surprise than her own, began climbing in the ratings. It was picked up for syndication that fall by Fleet Productions, and in every market where it appeared, it soon outstripped most of the fifteen or so syndicated daytime talk shows that aired across the country. Fleet offered her a deal in the second season that included renaming the program and giving her a share of the profits, transforming Mallory into a millionaire overnight.

Ian sighed, and went along with her request that they postpone having a baby just a little longer while "The Mallory Caine Show" established itself. "A little longer" turned into several seasons and one Emmy after another. Finally, though, Mallory started to feel secure enough and to have enough control over program production to consider carving out time for motherhood.

Paris, France
November 3, 1990

Diana sat on a bench in the Luxembourg Gardens, watching her son circle a large fountain, his nine-year-old step sure-footed on the bricked edge, his dark eyes flitting back and forth between the remote control in his hand and the miniature sailboat on the water. The toy was a new one his father had brought home a few days earlier, just before leaving on a business trip to Spain to look at Orlando Yago's latest sculptures.

Marcus and Orlando were discussing the timing and content of Yago's third show at the Galerie Desloges. Diana smiled, thinking back to that first exhibit, and how it had launched not only Yago's but also her own career—and her life. She'd had many commissions since—not only posters, but book and magazine illustrations, as well. Orlando, for his part, had enjoyed outstanding success, his work critically acclaimed around the world. The big Spaniard had married a year after Diana and Marcus, and he and his wife and their four children lived well and noisily in a renovated old Moorish fortress near Toulouse. The two families had visited several times, but on this occasion, Remy's schedule had prevented them from accompanying Marcus. Between school, his friends and his beloved soccer team, Remy was the busiest member of the busy Desloges household, she often thought.

She glanced at her watch, then at the dark clouds churning overhead. "Remy! Bring it in now!"

"Aw, Mama! A little longer!"

"No, sweetheart. It's getting cold and it's going to rain. Anyway, Papa will be home soon." Marcus's flight was due in at three, and Jean Grenier had offered to drive to Orly to pick him up. The plane would be on the ground by now. "Come on, my love. If it's a nice day, you can bring Papa tomorrow to see how well you sail your boat."

Remy sighed, but flipped a toggle on the remote that sent the boat gliding toward the edge of the pool. Diana walked over as he lifted it from the water and gave it a shake, all efficiency and cool competence. She reached out and ran her fingers through his tousled dark hair. "When did you get to be such a big fellow?" she asked softly.

Remy glanced around, blushing. When he seemed reassured that none of his buddies were in the park, he snuggled in for a hug. "I just grew, Mama."

They walked home in companionable silence. The wind had picked up, and huge, frigid drops of rain were spattering the sidewalk by the time they reached their door. "This is going to be a storm," Diana said, looking up worriedly. "I hope Papa and Jean get here soon."

But one hour went by, and then another, and still they hadn't arrived. Diana put music on the stereo to drown out the insistent beating of rain against the windows, and she puttered in the kitchen, making dinner for her son, putting a ratatouille in the oven that she and Marcus would share later. "The plane must have been late," she told Remy, trying to keep her anxiety from showing. But when she finally heard the swish of tires on the cobblestones outside and the slamming of a car door, Diana nearly cried out with relief. The buzzer sounded, and she raced to the front hall. Marcus must have left his keys at home. Remy had beaten her to the door, and it stood open, Jean Grenier watching as she skipped down the stairs.

"Finally!" she said, laughing. "I was about to send the Foreign Legion out to find you two." Diana froze at the sight of Grenier's ashen face, her smile falling away as she searched over his head. "Jean? Where's Marcus?"

"Diana...I..."

Her insides turned to ice, and she hardly heard his next words. It didn't matter. She knew what they would be. She reached out for Remy, pulling him close.

"The bulletin came on the radio as I was driving to the airport," Grenier said. "When I got there, they still weren't sure what happened. Bad weather, certainly. Instrument failure, perhaps."

"Where?" she whispered.

"Over the Pyrénées."

"No one...?"

"Search teams are going in, but the wreckage has been spotted from the air. The plane slammed into the side of a mountain. There's not a chance, they said..."

Diana backed against the wall and slid down, collapsing on a step. "Oh, God, no. Please. Marcus..."

Paris, France
November 10, 1990

The memorial service was over. The French minister of culture, the American ambassador and cultural attaché and most of the Paris art community had shown up to pay their respects to Marcus Desloges. Orlando Yago had come up from Toulouse with his wife, the big Spaniard racked with grief and guilt over the loss of his friend and mentor.

Mallory and Ian had stood at Diana's side in the cathedral and at the cemetery while Diana, pale and trembling, went through the motions of accepting condolences. Keeping one arm firmly around her nephew's shoulders, Mallory had kept watch, all her old, protective instincts rushing back. More than once, she had fought down the urge to shove people aside and hustle her sister out of there. But Diana had managed, somehow, to bear up. Only later that night, when they were back at the house and Remy had been tucked into bed, did Diana collapse, crying inconsolably.

The next day, Mallory tried to convince Diana that she and Remy should return to California with her and Ian, even if only for a while. But her sister, much to her surprise, dug in her heels. "No. I'm staying here."

"What will you do?"

"Raise my son and, for now, try to carry on with running Marcus's gallery. He had exhibits lined up for the next eighteen months or so. I want those to go ahead. Jean Grenier has offered to help."

"And after that?"

Diana shrugged. "The Galerie Desloges is Remy's heritage, and this city is his home. I can't uproot him right away."

"But what about *you,* Diana? Is Paris *your* home? Will you stay here forever?"

"I don't know," she said, her voice cracking, her whole body showing the strain. For the first time in years, Mallory glimpsed the old Diana, the frightened girl from the Ferry Falls rectory. "*Marcus* was my home, Mallory. My haven. Now, I'm homeless. But I have our son—his son—to think of. I have to keep going. I don't know how. I just know I have to."

Los Angeles, California
September 18, 1991

If Mallory had to pinpoint the moment when everything she'd worked for in her own life started to fall apart, it would be one day the following autumn, when she was taping a week-long series on the theme "Violence in America" for "The Mallory Caine Show." In the first four programs, Mallory had interviewed sociologists, criminologists, gang members, gun lobbyists and victims of violent crime—all in the interest of stimulating debate on this painful topic. Her guests, the studio audience and the reviewers who covered the series had been variously agitated, outraged and inspired by it. But no one, least of all Mallory herself, was prepared for the reaction that was sparked by the last day's segment on "Children of Violence"—a subject close to her heart, although no one but Ian knew *how* close. The people on the set that day included a nine-year-old boy, paralyzed after a depressed kid came armed to his school, and the boy's mother, both strong advocates of gun control; a researcher on violent content in movies and on TV; and finally, a child psychologist, who specialized in the treatment of children who had witnessed violence in their own lives.

Dr. Harry Zimmer was discussing the symptoms he found in his young patients. "Most children have fears about monsters under the bed," he said, "but for my patients, the monsters are real. Here in Los Angeles, somewhere between ten and twenty percent of all homicides are witnessed by children."

From where she was standing in the audience, microphone in hand, Mallory shook her head. "That's a lot of terrified kids."

"Terrified, yes," Zimmer said, "but it doesn't stop with the shock of the event. Children internalize the experience. It haunts them. The child who sees a stray bullet kill a playmate feels horrible guilt, because he or she is convinced the bullet was meant for them. I had a patient who saw his mother killed, and although he couldn't talk about it, all his drawings showed boys with gaping mouths, screaming silently. Many children develop behavior patterns that can only be attributed to post-traumatic stress disorder, much like returning war veterans."

"What kind of behavior patterns, Dr. Zimmer?" Mallory asked. Solly Yablonski, the floor manager, was signaling her to speak up, she noted out of the corner of her eye, but she was feeling short of breath.

"They may have nightmares and flashbacks. Some withdraw into themselves. Others become pessimistic and highly agitated, engaging in risky, self-destructive behaviors."

"Well, what do you expect?" she snapped.

Zimmer opened his mouth to respond, then hesitated, giving Mallory a curious look. Her face, she saw on the television monitor at the corner of the stage, had gone pale. "It's not surprising," he agreed. "That's why it's so important to get to these children quickly after the trauma."

"Why quickly?"

"Because they need immediate help to deal with the shock before they suffer long-term damage."

There was a silent gap that seemed to stretch into an eternity as everyone waited for Mallory's next question. When she said nothing, shuffles and nervous coughs began to erupt, the anxiety level in the studio mounting perceptibly. The voice of Mallory's executive producer, Shawn McFee, came to her through the receiver in her ear. "Are you okay, Mal? Do you want to cut to commercial?"

She must have shaken her head, because she heard him call on camera three to focus in tight on her. But it was all happening in slow motion, dreamlike and distant. Mallory's ears were ringing as if they'd been assaulted by an explosive blast. In her nose, she was picking up long-forgotten odors—rock dust and hospital disinfectant.

"Nobody did," she whispered at last.

The doctor on the stage studied her, eyes narrowing as he leaned forward in his chair. "Nobody did *what*?"

"Nobody tried to get us professional help, or talk to us about what we were feeling."

"Did something happen to *you*, Mallory?" Zimmer asked gently, the interview tables somehow turned around.

Mallory blinked, then looked up at him. "I saw my mother and father murdered when I was eight years old," she said dully. "And my sister was critically hurt."

She pressed her lips together tightly. The studio audience was hushed, three hundred shocked faces turned in her direction. Her crew, both here on the studio floor and upstairs in the control booth, stood stunned and motionless.

Finally, Mallory wiped her face and looked up, shrugging weakly. "I was the only one in my family left pretty much unscathed. I've never understood why."

Brenda Vasquez had phoned Ian as soon as she realized something strange was happening with Mallory. He raced over to the studios in Burbank, arriving just as the taping was winding up. To the amazement of everyone there, Mallory had managed to pull herself together and finish the show, but for the first time ever, she hadn't waited around to shake hands with the departing audience. They filed quietly out of the studio, looking sober and confused.

Ian returned with Mallory to her office to provide moral support as she and her producers conducted a post mortem, replaying the tape, trying to decide whether or not to air the segment. Mallory's producers, still shaken, deferred to her for the final decision.

"I never meant this to happen," she said, "but maybe it's for the best. It's a miracle that it never came out before, but it would have, sooner or later. I heard just last week that somebody from the *National Enquirer* was digging around in Minnesota, talking to people who knew me back there. They must have been told the rumors about my parents. We'll just beat them to the punch, is all."

"It's going to be a circus for a while, you know," Ian said. "Your whole life, including some bald lies, will be out there for the world to pick apart."

She squeezed his hand. "I know, Ian, and I know this affects you, too, but I don't see how we can avoid it. Not when three hundred people heard what I said in there. And maybe it'll do some good, if it gets people talking about what we're doing to kids by not dealing with the whole issue of violence in this country." She looked around the room at her staff. "That *was* what we set out to do here, wasn't it?"

They all nodded, and she turned to Ian. "I'm sorry," she said quietly. "I thought I would handle it better than I did."

He put a hand to her cheek. "Don't be sorry. We'll ride this out together."

The media, predictably, had a field day. Mallory's face and her tearful admission were replayed and reprinted, over and over. TV, newspaper and tabloid reporters went crazy, digging out adoption records, then tracing the name "Knight" to old accounts of a spectacular crime involving an attractive, professional couple and their two pretty little girls, one of whom had grown up to be a media celebrity. It was front-page news in papers across the country and around the world—only the *L.A. Chronicle's* coverage subdued and buried it on an inside page at Ian's insistence.

Cynics, of course, said it was a ploy to grab ratings, ignoring the fact that "The Mallory Caine Show" was already number one, and so far ahead of the rest of the "nuts and sluts" daytime talk-show pack that it didn't need to resort to gimmicks. Barbara Walters called, asking for an interview to set the record straight, but Mallory figured she'd already done enough blubbering on national television. Considering the veteran interviewer's reputation for wringing tears from solid rock, she decided to give it a miss.

Dr. Harry Zimmer put Mallory in touch with a therapist to help her deal with her emotional scars, warning that it might take time to come to terms with her parents' murders after all these years. Mallory went once, then decided the whole thing was self-indulgent and silly. She had *already* coped, thank you very much. After all, she wasn't living in a refrigerator crate and drinking Thunderbird, was she? What had happened on the set that day was a simple, human reaction to a sad topic, but she had built a good life for herself that included a successful career and a stable relationship. Exactly what problem did she have?

As the days and weeks passed, and as reporters kept digging into her personal life, more and more of it was smeared across the tabloids, and, in most cases, twisted out of all recognition. One day, Gunnar Anderson, his face puffed and his hairline receding, showed up in a newspaper article, quoted as saying that everyone in Ferry Falls always knew Mallory would make something of herself. Yeah, right, she thought. Gunnar was photographed standing in front of the Two Loons nightclub and resort. His dream had come true, Mallory thought, unable to resist a smile, in spite of everything. She'd missed her chance to become an assistant Ferry Falls entertainment mogul.

Another day, someone got wind of her relationship with Drew Beekman. After a brief marriage to Senator James Redman's daughter had ended in divorce, Drew had joined the staff of the secretary of state. He was now a high-profile, peripatetic international negotiator and troubleshooter for the administration. Drew handled the press with his characteristic easy charm, noting that he and Mallory had only dated briefly and hadn't seen each other in years, although he was aware of and admired her work. Drew Beekman—Teflon Man, Mallory thought. Dirt just didn't stick to him. The press, disappointed, moved on.

When the tabloids got to the subject of Lili Dahl and her unsolved murder, Mallory was moved to rage and thoughts of lawsuits, despite Ian's urging that she ignore the outrageous theories they were manufacturing—the worst being that Mallory had had a secret lover among the Beverly Hills High punks suspected of the crime. The lover had become enraged when he lost her to Ian Gallagher, according to this sick speculation, trashing Lili's house when he couldn't find Mallory, the old movie star getting caught in the crossfire of jealous love.

In the end, as Ian had said, they just had to ride out the storm. It took weeks before Mallory's face—at thirty *and* at eight years old—stopped appearing on every single tabloid cover in supermarket checkout lines. Most of her fans stuck loyally by her, sending mountains of mail and faxes, offering prayers and sympathy, urging her to hang in there. Eventually, the story got stale, and other scandals and titillations moved to the media forefront.

She continued with her work, focusing on lighter themes for a while—celebrity interviews, make-overs, silly stunts and practical jokes. Anyone who tuned in to "The Mallory Caine Show" hoping to see the host lose her grip again was going to be sorely disappointed. Everything, Mallory thought, breathing a sigh of relief, was fine once more and showing every sign of getting better.

And then, along had come a fierce one-two punch—a stalker's appearance at her home, and the reintroduction of Caitlyn Allis into Ian's life.

Los Angeles, California
November 28, 1991

Haig Bedrosian had obviously been drinking the night he broke into their Brentwood estate. Ian was working late, and it was almost ten o'clock when Mallory walked in the front door. The house was dark, except for the large entrance hall, with its dramatic, curved staircase, wrought-iron railings and marble floor that gleamed under an overhead chandelier.

One of the last Wallace Neff–designed houses built in Los Angeles, Mallory and Ian's home had the Mediterranean flavor, superior construction and fine detail for which that architect was known. A Realtor had shown it to Mallory not long after her show had gone into syndication, and she had fallen in love with its elegant design and proportions. It had been badly neglected by previous owners, but she must have inherited something of Philip Knight's architectural instincts, because she knew from the moment she set eyes on it that the house was a masterpiece. She had bought it on the spot, and after a year of renovation and redecoration, the Caine-Gallagher residence had been unanimously hailed as a architectural landmark—this, in a city not easily impressed.

Mallory locked the front door behind her and deposited her briefcase on the stairs, heading down the long, tiled hall toward the back of the house, intent on a cold drink. Her housekeeper, Luisa, she knew, would have long since retired to her own apartment above the garage.

At the kitchen, Mallory's hand reached for the light switch, but she hesitated, then froze. There was something off in the air, but the pungent odor she sensed had nothing to do with food gone bad. It was the unmistakable whiff of stale sweat, the petroleum stink of grease and, over that, the piercing, sweetish smell of booze filtered through human pores.

Mallory had always known that there was a defect in her personal response to fear. When adrenaline kicked in, wasn't it supposed to signal "fight or *flight*"? Why was it, then, that her first instinct was always to fight, instead of retreating sensibly until she could figure out the nature of the threat? She wasn't just obstreperous, she'd long since decided. She was downright stupid. This time was no different. "Who's there?" she called out.

She felt a movement of air, and just as her forefinger flipped the light switch, a hand wrapped around her wrist. The overhead lights flashed on, their brilliant glare ricocheting off the room's ivory wood-and-tile walls. The man dropped back a step and shielded his eyes, but his free hand gripped her tighter. Mallory give a sharp yank against his thumb. As it released, she shoved him in the chest and he staggered back against the stainless-steel double doors of the fridge.

"Who are you?" she demanded, her brain still refusing to do the intelligent thing and order her feet to get the hell out. "How did you get in?"

"I won't hurt you," he said, hands half covering squinted eyes.

He could be a soldier from the army of the homeless, Mallory thought. He was taller than she, with a build that might once have been powerful but now looked stooped and malnourished. His tan windbreaker was grease-streaked, its zipper dangling broken and open to reveal a stained denim shirt underneath. He wore olive-green pants, their cuffs frayed over the toes of scuffed work boots. His cheeks and chin were bristled with several days' growth of beard, and sparse, gray hair hung over his ears in greasy stringlets. He could have been fifty, sixty or eighty. It was impossible to tell.

He cowered against the refrigerator, looking, for all the world, like a whipped dog. Mallory unclenched her fists, but kept her elbows bent, hands in front of her, ready to repel any sudden move. When he finally grew used to the light, the man dropped his hands to his sides and looked up. He stared at her with rheumy, bloodshot eyes, slack lips opening and closing over a mouth that was lonesome for some of its teeth. He blinked, and Mallory watched two glistening, wet spheres slither over the hills and valleys of his weathered cheeks, running into deep crevices that ran along either side of his mouth.

"Oh, sweet Jesus!" he said raspily. "Your eyes."

"What about my eyes?"

"They're just like hers."

"Whose?"

"Your mother's."

Mallory stared at this broken-down man, who seemed to have some memory of her mother—or, at least, her mother's eyes. "Who *are* you?"

"You don't remember me, do you? I guess that's not so surprising. You were a little tyke, last time we saw each other."

"Where was that?"

"Esmerelda Canyon."

"At my father's house?"

"That's right. I used to bring you and your sister rock samples—quartz, pyrite, mica. She liked decorating her plasticine sculptures and dollhouses with them, I remember, but you just smashed 'em with a hammer."

Mallory's eyes shifted to a middle distance as she cast her mind back to memories of playing at the house site while her mother worked on the flower beds. Sometimes, she remembered, she would pound glittery rocks into fine powder, reveling in the pure energy of the action, seeing how fine she could grind them down.

"I liked the sparkles," she said. "I used to pretend I was a prospector during the California gold rush." She looked at the man again. "I *do* know you. You were the stonemason my mother hired for the landscaping."

"That's me."

"I'm sorry, I don't recall your name, though."

"Bedrosian. Haig Bedrosian."

"Mr. Bedrosian," Mallory said, nodding slowly, "that's right. I remember now." Racking her brains for something to say, she considered asking how he'd been, but under the circumstances, it seemed a little ridiculous, not least because he looked like hell. "What brought you here tonight? How did you find me?"

"Finding you was easy. I just got one of those maps to the homes of the stars. I decided to come after I saw you on TV a coupla months ago. I don't see much TV, but one day, I was staying in a place, and the box was on. I heard the announcer say something about Selena and Philip Knight. I looked up, and there they were—their pictures, I mean. And then you came on, talking about how they got killed." Bedrosian shook his head. "You shouldn't have done that."

"Done what?"

"Said all those terrible things about them. That was your mom and dad who died. You should've respected their memories."

"I didn't say much of anything. I just said I'd seen them murdered."

"Yeah, but then the news people, they told all that stuff about the drugs, and made out like Phil and Selena were just sleazy characters. You *let* them say it! That was wrong!"

"What do you mean? What was I supposed to say?"

"The truth! Selena Knight was a lady." Bedrosian's eyes misted, but he regarded her fiercely. Mallory was taken aback by his anger. "Your mom was the prettiest, nicest woman I ever knew. How could you let them say that awful stuff about her? Shame on you for doing that!"

"You're saying it was just my dad who was mixed up with the drug business?"

"Your dad . . ." Bedrosian shook his head. "I worked with Phil Knight a lot, not only on his own house. He was one stubborn character. He—"

Just then, the phone rang, and Bedrosian jumped. His feet started shuffling toward the door as it rang a second time. Mallory held up her hand. "I'll let the machine get it. Go on."

Bedrosian hesitated, waiting out the ring. The answering machine was on a desk in the corner of the kitchen. When it beeped, a voice echoed through the stillness. "This is Brentwood Securitech at 10:04 p.m. We're showing an alarm on your household security system. A patrol car has been dispatched."

Bedrosian's eyes went panicky wide. Mallory flew across the room and grabbed the phone. "Hello! I'm here! It's all right!"

"Mrs. Gallagher?"

"Yes."

"What's the code word, ma'am?" the voice asked suspiciously.

Mallory rolled her eyes, exasperated. "Watergate."

"Right," the voice replied, apparently satisfied. "Is there a problem there?"

Mallory glanced at Bedrosian. She didn't know this man from Adam, he'd been drinking and he seemed highly agitated. Still, she thought.... "Everything's fine. There's no need to send anyone."

Bedrosian was backing away, but she waved her hand frantically, pleading with him to wait.

"The car should be there already," the man on the phone said. "It's just as well to have the system checked out right away. There might be a short circuit."

"No! I don't want anyone now."

The front door opened, and Ian's anxious voice echoed down the hall. "Mallory? What's wrong? There's a patrol car out front." His feet pounded up the stairs.

Bedrosian spun around, and yanked open the back door. "Wait!" Mallory cried, dropping the phone. "Don't go!"

"Mallory!" Ian bellowed from above. "Where *are* you?"

"I'm in the kitchen," she called. "I'm okay."

Bedrosian was already outside, heading toward the sprawling back lawn. Mallory flew after him. "Mr. Bedrosian, please! I want to talk to you. You're right about my mother. Andrew Beekman told me the same thing."

Bedrosian stopped dead and spun around, his weathered face full of hate now as he stood, weaving and breathing hard. "Beekman? You'd listen to *Beekman?* He's to fuckin' *blame* for what happened to them! To all of us! He fuckin' destroyed us all!"

A shadow fell across the path of light from the open kitchen door. Mallory glanced back and saw her husband's large frame come barreling through. "It's okay, Ian! I'm all right." By the time she turned around again, Bedrosian was gone.

Ian pulled up alongside her and put out his hand. "What happened here?"

Mallory shrugged him off and started after the older man.

"Mallory! For crying out loud, stop!"

She ignored his protest, her eyes straining to see where Bedrosian could have gotten to. He was an old guy, and maybe half-drunk, to boot. How could he move so damn fast? At the sound of a thud and a loud curse, she veered toward the pool house, a second later tripping in the dark over the same chaise longue that Bedrosian had apparently crashed into and shoved askew. She tumbled onto the deck, skidding painfully on the pebbled concrete surface.

"Shit! Ian! Hit the yard lights!" she yelled, rubbing her leg. Her stockings were shredded, one shin already sticky under her hand.

A few moments later, the grounds were illuminated by dozens of strategically placed pot lights, floods and spots, turning the palm- and eucalyptus-studded landscape into a fairyland. She heard Ian running toward her, but her eyes were searching the bougainvillea bushes along the perimeter wall for some sign of Bedrosian. Hopeless. The man was long gone, obviously by whatever route he had used to get onto the property in the first place—probably over the stone wall, which backed onto a rolling slope. But how the heck did he vault an eight-foot, broken-glass-topped barrier? she wondered.

"What were you *thinking?*" Ian asked angrily, crouching beside her. "Why did you run after him? For chrissake, Mallory! It doesn't *matter* what he took! You could have been killed!"

"He didn't take anything. He wasn't an intruder. I mean, he was, but—"

"Mr. Gallagher?" A nervous young patrol guard from Brentwood Securitech suddenly appeared and hovered over them. "Is he gone?"

"I don't know. We need to check the grounds."

"I called the LAPD. They'll be here any minute. Our contract says I'm supposed to secure the premises, but not pursue an intruder if he's left the house. He might be armed."

Mallory groaned. "He's an old man. He's not armed."

"Are you sure?" Ian asked.

"Yes. At least, I don't think he was. He wasn't a thief, Ian. I knew him."

"You did?"

"From a long time ago." At the roar of sirens coming up the street, she turned to the security guard. "I don't suppose you

43

Later, she sat on the counter in their bathroom upstairs, wincing as Ian picked bits of stone out of her leg. "Are you sure you don't want me to run you down to the hospital to get this looked at?" he asked. "Maybe you should get a tetanus shot."

"It's only a scrape. Let's not give the tabloids any more pictures tonight, shall we? They've already had a field day with the police and security cars. How the heck did the paparazzi get here so fast?"

Ian shrugged. "There are people out there who do nothing but monitor the police bands. They've got a list of addresses to listen for. If they hear a call-out to one of them, they're on the phone in a flash. Makes for a nice little finder's fee."

"Good grief! So what did the police say when they left?" Mallory had been forced to sit in the living room, bleeding leg up, while LAPD officers questioned her and completed their search of the grounds.

"The police figure that, drunk or not, this Bedrosian put some planning into that break he made in the stone wall at the back. He found an isolated spot on the slope where the sage is overgrown and where he could work without being spotted. He didn't leave any tools behind tonight, and they doubt he had time to grab them on the run, especially given the shape he was in. Which means," Ian added soberly, "he's been here more than once. This wasn't some impromptu decision he made, Mallory. He's been stalking you for a while. They think he's probably unstable and dangerous. You're damn lucky you didn't get killed, taking off after him like that."

"I just wanted to hear what he had to say about my parents. *And*," Mallory added, "about Andrew Beekman. You should have seen Bedrosian's face when I mentioned him, Ian. He turned positively ugly.''

Mallory noticed a flicker of something cross Ian's own face at the mention of Beekman, a subject that had been touchy with him since the day Mallory quit the *Chronicle*. She wasn't sure what bothered Ian more—the embarrassing confrontation over the Beekmans that had led to her resignation, or the shadow of Drew in her life. She suspected the latter. Ian Gallagher, she had discovered to her astonishment, was insecure about his ability to hold on to a woman. It was ludicrous, but then, insecurities usually were. In any event, the Beekmans were a subject best avoided, she had long ago learned.

''You said Bedrosian was angry at you, too,'' he said.

''Yes, like he felt he had to defend my mother's honor. If I'm not mistaken, I'd say Haig Bedrosian was carrying a torch for her, big time. I was thinking about it just now, and I seem to remember that he was always running to tote things for her back then—pots and tools and stuff.''

''Be that as it may, Mallory, the guy's dangerous. I'm going to get that wall fixed first thing in the morning, and the vegetation on the slope cut back. And then,'' Ian told her, closing a tube of first-aid cream and wrapping gauze around her leg, ''we're going to get additional motion sensors installed around the grounds, *and* a new security company.''

''How about some Dobermans and pit bulls?''

''It's a thought.''

''I'm kidding! Honestly, Ian. Do you want to live in an armed camp?''

He stopped what he was doing. ''I don't want you to get hurt, dammit.''

Mallory looked at his worried eyes, tired and deeply lined. She passed a hand through his hair, suddenly noticing how much of it had turned gray. She leaned forward and kissed him. ''I know, sweetheart. But I really don't think he meant me any harm.'' She sat back and exhaled sharply, her cheeks puffing up. ''I just wish I could hear his story. You said yourself that the news coverage of my parents' murder was pretty superficial. Nobody even did any follow-up, once they'd written it off as just another drug deal gone bad. But what if there's another take on the whole thing? What if they were victims of character assassination, as well as murder? What if..." She sighed. "I don't know what I'm looking for. But I was always made to feel they were worthless."

"*You're* far from worthless, Mallory. You're talented, smart and beautiful. You've done more in your thirty years than most people could in a lifetime. What your parents did or didn't do is irrelevant to the person you've turned into."

"Thanks, guy. I *do* feel good about life now, and especially about us. But I guess I always wanted to believe that there was something in my heritage worth salvaging. That maybe some mistake was made."

Ian was silent for a moment, biting his lip. "Let's go in the bedroom."

She smiled. "Any reason in particular, as if I didn't know?"

"I can think of a couple. Actually, I want to move to a softer perch. And then, I think it's time I told you about some research I did one day."

"Research?"

"Just after we got married. Come on," he said, picking her up in his arms.

"I can walk."

"I know, but I like carrying you."

Mallory wrapped her arms around his neck and rested her head on his shoulder. "Far be it from me to deny the man I love his every desire."

Ian lay her down on the bed, kicked off his shoes and stretched out beside her. Mallory took a deep breath, his familiar scent calming and comforting.

Their house, and especially this room, had been designed to be a retreat from the pressures and demands of high-profile careers and lives. Her eyes took in the Scalamandré draperies and matching love seat in a rich navy and plum pattern. The Heriz carpet that picked up those colors and swirled them around in an intricate Oriental design. The marble mantel and hearth, which flickered with the reflected light of the log fire they lit most evenings. The massive, canopied bed, in which she and Ian had spent so many close nights and sinfully long Sunday mornings. Their home was only a few miles from that ant-infested bachelor apartment she'd lived in when she first came to L.A., but she'd travelled a long way, just the same, Mallory often thought.

Ian shifted onto his side, head in one hand, the other stroking her arm. "Some time ago, I did some checking with the Newport Beach police."

"About what happened at Esmerelda Canyon?"

"Yes. It drove me crazy that the paper had never done a follow-up story after those three pieces you showed me. Sure as hell, if I'd been editor back then, somebody would have been put on it. But the *Chronicle* was pretty cavalier about the outlying counties in those days, and frankly, the *Orange County Register* wasn't any better. Like you said, once the incident was labeled a drug deal gone bad, the papers lost interest."

"I'm surprised any police official in the county would talk to you, after we brought down Sheriff Fisher and his cronies."

"Some people there are a little gun-shy around reporters, but I've got an old Newport Beach contact, Sergeant John Kelsey, who's a real straight arrow. He thought we did the county a favor, even if it did make for embarrassing publicity. They'd never admit it publicly, but Kelsey and the good cops in the county hated Fisher, and they were glad to be rid of him."

"So what did Kelsey have to say?"

"He dug out the 1969 file on the Esmerelda investigation. Normally, those files aren't available to the press or public, of course, but Kelsey was called away while I was in his office, and he 'accidentally' left the file on his desk."

Mallory rubbed Ian's chest. "You sneaky old bloodhound, you."

"This old dog's got tricks you haven't even *seen* yet," Ian said, smiling.

"So, was there anything in the file that wasn't in the press stories?"

He sobered. "I saw all the pictures, including what the police found when they first arrived. There were shots of you and Diana on the ground taken by the first cops on the scene, and then, the two of you being loaded into an ambulance. My God, Mal . . ." He pulled her tightly against him.

Mallory closed her eyes and took a deep breath.

"And there was the house, of course, or what was left of it. It was incredible. It had gone straight up in the air, then come down on the same spot, only in little pieces. They figured it only took a spark to set it off. The police report said you told them you heard the phone ring just before the blast.'' She nodded. ''That would have been enough,'' Ian said.

''I remember thinking I set it off with the garden hose. I had just squeezed the trigger when everything went up.''

''Someone must have been watching, waiting for the right moment to call.''

Mallory shuddered. ''What else?''

''I saw photos of the shredded hose from the propane tank. The fuel tank was completely empty, so although it was damaged, it survived the blast. And there were shots of the car in the driveway.''

''My dad's boat trailer ended up on the hood of it, I remember.''

''That's right. Another picture was taken later, after they'd opened the trunk and found the drugs. There were two white, kilo-size bags—the heroin, apparently—and another containing what the police report said was hashish.''

''What about the investigation? Officially, the file should still be open, since they never found the killer or killers. There's no statute of limitations on murder.''

''Actually, Mallory, they *did* find the killer. Or at least, they were pretty sure they did.''

''*What?*''

''The guy's name was Denny Sweet. He was a known enforcer for one of the main gangs running drugs at that time in the Tijuana-L.A. corridor. That tended to clinch the motivation theory the cops had been working with—that your father had somehow run afoul of his drug suppliers.''

''How did the police know this Sweet guy—'' Mallory paused, grimacing. ''Jeez, what a name! How did they know he was the bomber?''

''They found the missing coupling from your propane tank in his bedroom. He'd removed it to attach the hose and apparently walked off with it.''

''Accidentally?''

Ian shrugged. ''Or on purpose. Some sickos like to keep souvenirs of their kills. Anyway, his fingerprints matched prints lifted from the tank and from a stolen southern California

Edison truck that had been seen in Esmerelda Canyon the afternoon of the explosion. It was later found abandoned in San Diego. Normally, nobody takes any notice of utility trucks, but a hiker saw it go up the canyon road and remembered afterward, because it was unusual to see one out on Memorial Day."

"So was Denny Sweet charged with the murders?"

"No, that's the thing, he couldn't be. He was killed in a shoot-out with police during a drug bust, six months after your parents died. The evidence was found after he was already dead, *then* he was linked back to the Esmerelda Canyon explosion."

"There was no press announcement of a break in the murder case?"

"Not that I could see by the file. If there were, you'd think somebody would have reported it, but as you know, there's nothing about it in the news indexes. The whole investigation just seems to have fizzled out. That happens fairly often, believe it or not. The police get busy with new crimes, and the old files get relegated to the back of a cabinet."

"They didn't look for accomplices, or whoever hired Sweet?"

"What trails they had all seemed to dead-end. Detective Kelsey wasn't around in '69, but he said what information they had probably got rolled into their ongoing narcotics-network investigations, especially after they fingered the late Mr. Sweet as the triggerman. Case closed, to all intents and purposes."

Mallory lay back, frowning at the canopy. "You know, if it had been Philip Knight, award-winning architect whose killers the police were looking for, the investigation and press coverage would have been more complete. But nobody cared about an unemployed Phil Knight who'd found a new career dealing drugs." She glanced at Ian. "Why didn't you ever tell me you'd looked at the police file?"

"Because it's so damned unsatisfying. You were already hurt and frustrated, and there's no way now, so many years later, to figure out the details of what happened. I thought about it, Mallory, I really did," Ian added, rising over her. "I wondered whether it would help you to know that their killer was probably dead. But there were still so many unanswered questions, and you said you wanted to put it behind you."

"I did, and I do. I really do, Ian."

"But what about this Bedrosian business? Is it going to bring it all back? He's probably just some crazy old alkie who was infatuated with your mother."

"I know that. I just want to find out what he remembers. The police will track him down, I guess, and then we'll see."

"And then . . . ? I don't want him disrupting your entire life, Mallory."

She wrapped her arms around him. She knew what Ian wanted her to say—that it wasn't going to become a preoccupation. One more thing for him to compete with. One more thing to distract her from what he really wanted for the two of them, more than anything else. Soon, she thought. She would be ready for that soon.

"Bedrosian's just another piece in a lifelong puzzle, that's all," she said, shrugging.

Ian frowned, then sighed and reached over to dim the lights.

The LAPD were unable to locate Haig Bedrosian. Three weeks after the break-in, they reported to Mallory and Ian that they had found a cheap hotel where he'd stayed briefly, a flophouse, really. The man himself had vanished. He'd left behind recent news clippings on Mallory and her parents, as well as the map he had mentioned, showing the location of the Caine-Gallagher home. The police had found stone fragments from their perimeter wall in the man's room, pieces that he had probably carried back in his pant cuffs. Even more worrisome, they had found traces in the carpet of salt, sulfuric acid and gasoline, as well as bits of wire—all items used in the manufacture of crude explosives.

Haig Bedrosian, it seemed, had spent his life working as a miner and stonemason, and had also done a stint in the late fifties as an explosives technician with the Army Corps of Engineers. After his army service, he had been a subcontractor for Quad-A Homes, working on the Westwind Park master-planned community, where he had met Philip and Selena Knight.

The LAPD paid a visit to Andrew Beekman, who remembered Bedrosian as having had a drinking problem even back then. The mason might well have been obsessed with Selena

Knight, Beekman said. She had been a beautiful woman. The developer added that he hadn't seen Bedrosian in over two decades. He had disappeared one day and had never shown up for work again. Was that before or after the deaths of Philip and Selena Knight? the LAPD detective asked. Beekman couldn't remember. He seemed shaken to learn about Bedrosian's recent break-in at the estate of Selena's daughter, Mallory Caine.

The syndicate which produced "The Mallory Caine Show" found out that a dangerous man was stalking one of their major investments. Fleet Productions hired and were adamant that Mallory use a bodyguard/driver and an armored limo. When a month went by and Bedrosian still hadn't been located, Mallory had had enough.

"I want to hire a private detective to find him," she told Ian one night.

"Leave it to the police. We've got enough to worry about, without going looking for trouble."

"They're overworked and understaffed, Ian, and they haven't got the resources to devote to this. If Bedrosian's left the area, he could be anywhere. His ex-wife told the cops that before she lost track of him completely twenty years ago, he'd ended up in a Pennsylvania mine. Maybe he's gone there."

"Fine. Let him stay."

"That's not good enough."

"Why not?"

"Because I need to know what he was going to tell me about my parents. It's driving me crazy. And I don't trust Andrew Beekman. He's not telling the whole truth. He's a master at selective disclosure, we already know that. I want to know why Bedrosian hates him so much."

"Mallory, please . . ."

"I'm sorry, Ian. I *have* to do this."

44

Los Angeles, California
June 12, 1992

The night Ian asked her to marry him, Mallory had meant it when she said she could never again walk away from him, and she would have sworn back then that he would never walk away from her, either. But eventually, he did. Right into the arms of his first wife. Did Caitlyn Allis steal him, Mallory wondered, or had she herself driven him away? At what point had he made his decision? Could she have prevented it?

She had always sensed, when Ian spoke of Caitlyn, that there was unfinished business between them. He said that his previous marriage was a mistake he'd long since put behind him. But, Mallory reasoned, this was her sober, insightful Ian talking, not some dumb, superficial jock who bounced from one casual relationship to another. If he'd loved Caitlyn enough to believe at one time that he could make a lifetime commitment to her, could it really have been a mistake? And if it wasn't, could he have resisted the temptation to go back and fix things when it became obvious that Caitlyn wanted to try again? Especially when Mallory had become so preoccupied that she had ignored all the warning signs?

She'd known for some time that Ian was restless, frustrated by the demands on her time that came with her talk-show success. Not that he was just sitting at home, waiting for her. He'd been named managing editor of the *Chronicle* when Carson Hoag had retired, another coup in an already illustrious career, and one that had driven Grady O'Toole into alcoholic early retirement.

Ian had his own ridiculous schedule to maintain after landing the top editorial job, running the daily as well as overseeing a long-delayed technological upgrade to bring the paper into the computer age. Juggling their two calendars and keeping them in relative sync took all the ingenuity both Mallory and Ian *and* their respective secretaries could muster. Even the timing of their midday phone calls to each other was pre-planned. Still, they had managed fairly well, keeping most weekends free to be together and wrenching a few days of vacation here and there so that they could visit his family in Nebraska, or Diana in Paris, or relax in the resorts of Cancún, where they had honeymooned.

But always, hanging over them, there was the question of a family. Whoever thought men didn't have a biological clock, Mallory thought, had never met Ian Gallagher. She had known from the start that he wanted children. "Preferably before I'm too decrepit to play with them," he said, only half-jokingly. She had agreed, in principle, but something always seemed to get in the way, and the timing never seemed right. And then, it was just too late.

Mallory suspected that Ian and Caitlyn Allis may have been back in touch even before they ran into her at a Cedars-Sinai benefit dinner. Ian's former wife was, after all, lead defense counsel on a spectacular murder case involving a mother who had shot the man who had sexually abused and murdered her child. The case was receiving national attention, and Mallory knew the *Chronicle* had an inside source. She hadn't asked who it was because she didn't want to know, and Ian wouldn't have told her, anyway. She'd suspected it might be Caitlyn. Ex-wife or not, Ian would have been crazy not to take advantage of such an edge over the competition in the press coverage of the trial. In his shoes, Mallory would have done the same.

It was only the night of the Cedars-Sinai dinner that she knew for certain that Ian and Caitlyn were on friendly terms again, and that maybe she should be concerned about it. In the first place, when she and Ian had arrived at the Beverly Wilshire Hotel ballroom and checked the seating plan posted near the door, Mallory saw that she and her husband were to be on opposite sides of the room. Mallory *didn't* recall, however, seeing Caitlyn Allis's name next to Ian's on the plan. And yet, after they were seated, the counselor was at his left elbow.

In all these years, Mallory and Caitlyn had managed to avoid meeting each other. Mallory knew her by sight and reputation—a very bright, very beautiful, very ambitious lawyer, whose large, green eyes and warm, southern accent were reputed to reduce judges and juries to mush. Caitlyn Allis was a rising legal star, and Mallory supposed she should be admired for that. But the fact was, she had once taken Ian's heart and stomped on it. For that alone, Mallory couldn't stand the woman.

She'd glanced over at Ian and Caitlyn from time to time during dinner, her unease growing as the night wore on. Caitlyn had Kirk Douglas on her other side, but from Mallory's place across the room, seated between the president of Paramount Studios and the CEO of the Great Western Bank, she noticed that Caitlyn hardly exchanged a word with Douglas. She was a rare bird, Mallory thought, to be so unimpressed with Hollywood royalty that she virtually ignored the still-handsome, silver-haired actor—but by the sparkle in her green eyes, there was no doubt that Caitlyn Allis had cornered the only man in the room she considered a prince.

It was after midnight when Mallory and Ian returned home. Upstairs in their bedroom, Mallory slipped out of her shimmering gold dress and heels, and padded to her walk-in closet to hang the dress on the door. Then, leaning against the frame, she waited for him to catch sight of her in her silk underthings, knowing how much he liked to watch her remove them—or better still, remove them himself. She wanted him to want her, especially tonight. They had been making love less and less frequently of late. In six years of marriage, they had endured pressures that would have strained any relationship to the snapping point, but until the Bedrosian business, their bond had remained rock-solid, cemented by love and a shared vision of what they wanted for the future. Now, the future seemed to have receded, pushed back by restlessness and uncertainty on both their parts. For the first time ever, Mallory was forced to consider that it was possible to lose Ian.

He had been quiet all the way home from the dinner. Thinking about Caitlyn Allis? Mallory willed herself to dismiss the thought. Many women found Ian as attractive as she did, and some made no secret of that attraction. Caitlyn obviously fit in that latter category, despite the fact that she'd had him once and let him get away.

As she watched him in their bedroom, Ian seemed pensive and withdrawn, his attention focused elsewhere. He tugged absentmindedly at a corner of his black tie, unraveling the bow. The silk sang as he whipped it through his shirt collar, draping it over the jacket he had already hung on the back of a chair.

Look at me, Mallory telegraphed. But when Ian settled into a chair and bent to untie his shoes without glancing up, she decided to go for the direct approach. She smiled and leaned back farther into the door. "Are you mooning over another woman tonight, Ian Gallagher?"

Ian's head bobbed, and his eyes went wide at her pose. He flushed. "What do you mean?"

"Caitlyn, of course." Mallory cocked an eyebrow. "Now, tell me, how *exactly* did it happen that she ended up next to you?"

"I have no idea."

"It seems a little coincidental. The way she was hanging off you, I thought she was going to drop from her chair and eat you instead of her dinner."

Another time, Ian might have grinned and pounced on her, growling about the fans who were always sending her flowers and marriage proposals. But this time, a scowl flashed across his face and he turned back to his shoelaces.

Mallory's heart dropped in her rib cage. She reached into the closet and fumbled until she found a robe to slip on over her slinky underthings that might have been old rags, for all he'd noticed.

"That's uncalled for," he said finally. "We were discussing legal precedents."

She was dumbstruck. Instead of laughing over the way Caitlyn had thrown herself at him, Ian was annoyed by the suggestion that their conversation had been anything but purely intellectual. Ian had looked up a couple of times during the course of the evening and caught Mallory's eye, giving her a vague smile across the room, but for the most part, he, too, had seemed lost in their conversation.

"We were discussing the social and legal impact of this murder case," he went on, rising to deposit cuff links and glasses on his bureau. "It's bound to be controversial for years to come, and Caitlyn has a unique perspective, that's all."

Caitlyn has a unique angle on seduction, too, Mallory thought, one that just might work on a man like Ian, who had never been known to be attracted to dumb women.

"It was a fascinating conversation, nothing more," Ian went on.

"So why are you so defensive?"

"I'm not." Ian smashed his fist on the top of the bureau and she jumped. "Jesus, Mallory!"

"What?"

He exhaled sharply. "Nothing."

"No, come on. What brought that on?" He stood there, jaw rigid, lips pressed in a tight line. "What's bugging you, Ian?"

"Bugging *me?*"

"Yes, you."

"Nothing's bugging me! No, wait a minute, let me revise that. What's bugging me is what's bugging you."

"And what's that?"

"Christ! I don't know! Whatever it is that makes you so paranoid. If it's not Caitlyn Allis, it's drunken burglars and—"

The lump appeared in her throat faster than she would have thought possible. "That's not fair. You know what I've gone though since Bedrosian broke into this house."

"Ah, hell, Mal! Of course I know. And I've tried to be patient and understanding and supportive, you know I have. But it's been months, and nothing's happened." He raked a hand through his hair, eyes clouded with frustration. "You've got to forget about it, so we can move on."

"*Forget* it? How can I?" Mallory was angry now, her voice rising. "Nothing's resolved. Nothing! It's not just about me, Ian, it's about them—my mother and father and Diana. Nobody paid, goddammit! Sweet wasn't enough. There were people behind him, and they got away with murder." She sank onto the bed, furious tears coursing down her cheeks, the Tiffany lamp shade next to it dissolving in a swirl of colors.

Ian sighed, and the mattress dipped as he settled beside her and wrapped her in his arms. "I know, Mal, I know. But it's so far in the past. I wish something could be done about it so you could find some peace and we could get on with our lives. We did try, you know. Your PIs have tried. But they couldn't come up with anything because there's nothing left to find anymore."

"We haven't tried hard enough."

"We did what we could. It's time to accept that and move on. Somehow, you've got to put it behind you, Mal, or it's going to destroy us, and you, and everything you've worked to build."

"I can't."

"You have to, even if it means finding someone—a professional—who can help you deal with this anger you've got bottled up inside."

Ian had suggested once or twice recently that she go back to the analyst Dr. Zimmer had recommended, or to another. But it didn't take some Couch Canyon shrink, Mallory thought, to figure out where her problems came from—the rage and pain that had dogged her footsteps and sabotaged everything she'd ever had or done. There had been nothing subtle about the way her demons had announced themselves, bursting in with a flash of light and a deafening roar that turned a little girl's home to rubble and her parents to vapor.

Bedrosian had brought it all back. At the studio, she continued to function, and no one there, except possibly Brenda Vasquez, saw the growing tension and distraction in her. Only with Ian had she ever really opened up, and as a result only Ian suffered the effects of withdrawal and isolation that her newfound fury forced on her.

"Listen to me," Ian said, lifting her chin and wiping her damp cheeks. "This can't go on. You're not happy, and frankly, neither am I. I've tried. I want to help you, but I don't know how."

"But you do, Ian, just by being there."

"I don't think it's enough."

"Not enough. For you, you mean."

"For either of us."

"Don't say that."

"Mallory—"

"Please, Ian, don't! I love you so much." She took one of his hands and slipped it inside her robe, pressing it against her chest, where her heart had taken up a frantic beat.

Ian was still for a moment, watching her face. "I love *you*." It was a plea.

She moved his hand farther down, over one silk-covered breast. Ian's eyes closed and he sighed. Mallory slipped her robe off her shoulders and moved onto his lap, straddling him as he sat on the edge of the bed. She cradled his head against her shoulder, and they swayed together. Then Ian raised his head and studied her for a long while.

They kissed, lightly first, lips just brushing, then deeper, more urgently. She felt him growing hard under her as his hands traveled over her body, exploring it, never seeming to tire of the rediscovery. His mouth moved down to her neck, her shoulders, the hollow of her throat. She leaned back and moaned softly as he kissed the V between her breasts. Releasing the front snap on her bra, he slid his hands under it and around her back, caressing her skin as he tasted her nipples one by one, his tongue flicking and teasing. Suddenly, he took one in his teeth so hard that Mallory gasped. Then it was his tongue again, circling, and she felt herself dissolving in his lap, a hot, slow melt.

She fumbled at the buttons of his shirt, fingers trembling. As he shrugged out of it, Ian flipped her back on the bed, whipping off her underthings and the rest of his own clothes. When he lowered himself onto her, she wrapped her legs and arms around him, burying her face in his shoulder, reveling in the feel of him, big and hard-edged, his chest hair prickly and sensuous, the dusk-and-citrus scent of his flesh all-enveloping.

He slipped inside, moving slowly at first, rocking, filling her. But as her hands cupped his buttocks, pulling him, he grew more urgent, moving faster and faster, until he brought her into a state of frenzy. She arched her back, and Ian rose to his knees, lifting her hips, driving now, the tension in his face suddenly more angry than loving. He pounded into her, harder and harder, as if trying to drive out the demons that had come between them. If Mallory could have given them up to him, she would have, gladly. But after they had cried out and given themselves over to the last violent shudder of pain and ecstasy, all she could do was weep silently, knowing that nothing had changed.

They lay sadly for a time, too exhausted to summon words of love or recrimination. When they slipped under the covers a short time later and turned out the lights, Ian rolled away to the far edge of the bed. Mallory lay on her own side, staring into the dark.

A week later, he moved out.

Book Five

Love and Revenge

45

Mallory's assistant, Brenda Vasquez, was supervising the limo driver as he loaded Mallory's luggage into the trunk. Mallory was giving last-minute instructions to Luisa, her housekeeper. "I've left my sister Diana's address and phone number in Paris on the desk in my office, next to the telephone, so you'll know where to reach me in case of an emergency," she said. "Has the pool company come yet to fix the crack in the Jacuzzi?"

"Not yet."

"Well, they promised to get to it, so call them and make sure they haven't forgotten, would you? Oh! And that blue suit I was just wearing? It's got a stain on the sleeve. We had Bette Midler on the show today, and she got so excited at one point that a cup of coffee went flying. Could you take it to the cleaners and see if they can get it out? I love that suit."

"*Sí, señora.*"

"Other than that, you have Miss Vasquez's number." Brenda walked in the door as her name was mentioned and Mallory nodded in her direction. "Call her if anything else comes up."

"Señor Gallagher will be back before you get home? Or is he meeting you in Paris?"

Mallory froze, and she and Brenda exchanged glances. Ian had moved out ten days earlier, on a Sunday, Luisa's day off, and Mallory hadn't been able to bring herself to tell the housekeeper yet. She still couldn't quite believe he wouldn't just waltz in the front door one night, whistling tunelessly, as if nothing had happened. Instead, she had told Luisa that Ian was out of town on business. Chickenshit, she berated herself. This is what happens when you lie.

Then she went and did it again.

"He'll be back in town, but he's going to stay with friends while I'm gone. He'll probably drop around to pick up some things. You've got his office number in case there's any emergency with the house—if the plumbing springs a leak, or there's an earthquake or something."

Luisa nodded, her wide brown eyes giving no hint as to whether or not she knew Mallory was lying through her teeth. Surely she must have noticed that most of his clothes and toiletries were gone, more than he took when he traveled on business. And even if she hadn't, Ian would probably let the cat out of the bag when he came around to pick up the books and the bike he'd told Brenda he wanted when he phoned the studio that afternoon.

His bike! Mallory thought. Get serious, Gallagher! You're not exactly in shape for the triathlon anymore. Or does Caitlyn Allis like long, leisurely rides along the boardwalk at Mission Beach, like you and I used to take?

She turned to the housekeeper. "That's about it. I'll be back a week from tomorrow. Be sure to keep the front gates closed."

Luisa nodded vigorously. One time, she had accidentally left them open, and Mallory had come home from the studio to find a celebrity-homes tour bus parked at her front door. She was lucky she'd had to cope with nothing worse than autograph hounds—although, Mallory recalled soberly, an electronic gate had been no obstacle to Haig Bedrosian.

"And be sure to keep the alarm set. I've notified the security company that I'll be out of town."

"You have not changed the combination? Señor Gallagher will have it, in case I am not here when he comes?"

"No, I haven't changed it." Although, Mallory thought, maybe I should.

She voiced the thought later to her assistant. "Can you tell me why I'm being so damn *reasonable* with him, Bren?" she asked as the limo headed for the 405 Freeway and Los Angeles International Airport. "He walked out on me, the schmuck!

And then he has the gall to go snuggling up with Caitlyn Allis at Spago, for crying out loud, where the whole bloody world can see them. I should take that bike and throw it off the goddam Malibu cliffs.''

Brenda raised one eyebrow. "You're being reasonable for the same reason you gave Luisa that load of hooey about him being away on business—you want him back. And you know what else, girl?"

"What?"

"That language! Sometimes I find it hard to believe that you were raised by a preacher in Minnesota."

"*Raised* is hardly the word. Even 'tolerated' is stretching it. The Reverend Windbag and I never had what you would call a mutual admiration society."

Brenda giggled. "The Reverend *what?*"

"Windbag. And that was about the nicest thing I ever called him."

"You must have been some kid, Mal," Brenda said, shaking her head and grinning.

"You have no idea."

The telephone bleeped from its place on the center-floor console, and Brenda picked it up. "Hello? Oh, hi, Jenny." Jenny Lewis, one of the secretaries in her office, Mallory registered. "Okay. What time did he call? I'll tell her. Yeah, we're on the way to the airport now. Traffic's kind of heavy. Right, see you later." She hung up and turned in her seat. "You had a call."

"I gathered. Who?" Please, Mallory prayed, let it be Ian.

"Renzo Patrini. He called about thirty minutes ago. You want to call him back?"

"For sure. Hand me the phone, will you?"

As Brenda uncradled the car phone from the console, Mallory shuffled the contents of her wallet, trying to locate the private investigator's business card, wondering why she didn't know Patrini's number by heart. She had always envied Ian's photographic memory, but just the same, she thought, she should have been able to recall *this* number. After all, she had been calling Patrini two or three times a week lately, worried that his search for Haig Bedrosian was going the same place as those of the first two private investigators she had hired—nowhere. They had submitted thousands of dollars' worth of expense claims and come up with zilch. Patrini, reputed to be the best in the business, had been on the hunt for several weeks now. Maybe, finally, Mallory thought, there was news.

She listened to the phone ringing on the other end of the line, and watched graffiti-decorated freeway walls spin past the car window, a kaleidoscope of garish colors. Her mind whirling, Mallory flashed back to the face of Bishop Lennox, and remembered the blessing he had invoked for her all those years ago, sitting on the front step of the rectory—a prayer that she find "the peace that passes all understanding." For a while, she'd thought she had. No more.

On the sixth ring, the phone picked up on the other end. "Patrini Investigations."

"Is he in?"

"No, he doesn't seem to be." The obviously bored woman was making no effort to muffle the rasp of what sounded like an emery board. "Can I take a message?"

Mallory glanced at her watch. Three-ten. "I'm on my way out of the country. My flight leaves at four o'clock. Is he going to be back soon?"

"I couldn't tell you, ma'am. I'm just the answering service."

"Did he leave a number where he could be reached?"

"No, ma'am."

"Doesn't he have a car phone?"

"I couldn't tell you ma'am. I'm just—"

"The answering service. Yes, I think you said that." Mallory gritted her teeth. "Well, could you tell him Mary Carter called, and ask him to call me back as quickly as possible?" She and Patrini had agreed that this was the name she would use when she left messages for him.

"Sure thing." The woman was ready to hang up.

"Hold it!" Mallory called. "Take the number, please."

"Uh-huh."

Mallory gave the number of the limo phone. When she had the woman read it back, she had gotten it wrong, of course, and Mallory was tempted to drop the pretense and use her real name. *That* would wake her up.

Although her celebrity status was firmly entrenched in this city of celebrities, she was still amazed at the power of her name and the service it got her, even in snotty establishments where, a few years earlier, she would have felt like an interloper. Now, they brought her champagne and fussed embarrassingly. Generally, the management wouldn't even let her have the bill, even though she could have bought the restaurant if it caught her fancy. The managers only hoped the columnists would report that Mallory Caine had been there. She always remembered to tip big, regardless. She knew from her own years of waiting tables that restaurant staff had long memories and loved to gossip.

Good service was celebrity's upside, but the downside was the loss of privacy, as her every public word and action, not to mention her marriage, were held up to casual scrutiny. Even banal things like buying underwear or tampons, or using a public rest room turned into embarrassing, crowd-drawing events that she'd long since learned to avoid. "Think about it," she told Brenda one day, when her assistant was going on about the joys of success.

And so, tempted as she was to snap Renzo Patrini's answering service to attention, Mallory stifled the urge, fearful as always that someone would find out that she had engaged a private investigator, and why. Soon enough, in any event, the press and the world would know. But if the story broke too soon, it would ruin her hopes that somehow, after all these years, she could find out who had hired the man who murdered her parents, crippled her sister and ripped apart her world.

"Just tell Mr. Patrini I'm anxious to talk to him."

"I'll leave a message, Mizz Carter."

Mallory hung up the phone and opened the limousine's minifridge. "I need a drink," she groaned. "Look at this traffic, Bren. I'm never going to make that flight and my New York connection for the Concorde."

The limo was drifting toward LAX in a lazy automotive stream. Ahead on the freeway, Mallory made out the spinning red emergency lights that signaled an accident, another tourniquet clamped on the city's arterial flow, bringing movement to a quiet standstill. L.A. drivers, unlike those in most big cities she'd visited, rarely bothered to honk their horns—another feature, she supposed, of the city's laid-back style. The big car inched forward, its air-conditioning system laboring mightily to filter out heat, dust and diesel fumes.

Mallory shuffled things in the fridge, while Brenda peered over the top of her reading glasses. She had pulled out program ideas and guest lineups, trying to get Mallory to focus on them before they reached the airport. Michael Keaton's postponement had put a small dent in the works, but the problem wasn't insurmountable. There were plenty of stars kicking around town, looking to flog their latest projects. "Mallory Caine" ratings guaranteed them a wide audience for their pitches, and her flamboyant style often brought additional news copy, whether or not the interview went well. In the perverse logic of show business, as P. T. Barnum had noted, even bad press was good.

Brenda removed her glasses, deciding, apparently, that they weren't going to get much work done on this particular ride. "Relax," she said. "You'll make your plane. And if not, there's always the direct L.A.-Paris flight at six-thirty. I'll just call Diana and let her know you're getting in later."

"Where's the Bollinger?" Mallory hit the intercom to the front seat. "Hector? Did you restock the Bollinger champagne, like I asked?"

The driver's voice crackled from the front seat. "Yes, ma'am. Bottom left-hand side of the fridge."

"Bottom left, bottom left," Mallory mumbled as she rummaged.

Brenda put aside her clipboard and reached past her. "Your *other* left. Jeez, girl! Good thing you're on vacation. You got to relax, you know?"

Mallory slumped back in the seat, exhaling deeply. Brenda popped the cork on the champagne, then lifted a stem glass out of the rack over the fridge and poured. "Thanks," Mallory said, taking it from her. "Are you going to have some, too?"

"Are you kidding? You bet. You're turning me into a nervous wreck."

Mallory's face finally relaxed into a smile. "Not a chance, Bren. You're the calmest person I've ever met, next to my sister. Where's all that hot Latin blood you're supposed to have?"

"I grew up in a house full of hot-blooded Latins, everybody running around all the time, yelling or crying, hugging or laughing hysterically about something. Gimme a nice, calm, boring Anglo anytime."

"Thanks a bunch."

"Not you, girl. You could use a little more calm."

Mallory clinked her glass against her friend's. "Nah, I don't think so. Gotta keep moving, or the owls get you."

"Owls?"

"Ladder of life? Hunt or be hunted?" Mallory shook her head. "Never mind. It's just something Wiley Dixon said to me once, when we were kids."

"Are you going to see him, too, while you're in Paris?"

"I hope so."

"How's his collaboration going with your sister?"

"Great. Diana says they've been having a ball."

Several months earlier, Wiley had been in L.A. and asked Mallory to dig out the old notebook he had given her years before, containing the Avaron and Sagramor stories he'd written as a teenager. His publisher wanted to issue a series of illustrated novels aimed at the youth fantasy market. When Wiley had said they were looking for an illustrator, Mallory immediately thought of Diana. Wiley, always restless and eager for the next adventure, had jumped on a flight to Paris to put the proposal to her.

"Diana and Wiley didn't know each other that well back in Minnesota," Mallory said to Brenda, "but they seem to have hit it off now. Wiley's completely cleaned up his act. He doesn't do drugs anymore, or even drink."

"Sounds like Diana's been good for him."

"They've been good for each other. I think this project has helped take Diana's mind off memories of Marcus." Mallory smiled. "Diana says Remy adores Wiley. It doesn't surprise me. Wiley's so much fun, he's every eleven-year-old boy's dream big brother."

"He's probably been what your nephew needed, after losing his dad. How's Diana been coping?"

"Better than expected, especially lately. When I call her these days, her voice actually sounds happy. You know, sometimes I hardly recognize my sister, she's changed so much since we were kids in Ferry Falls.''

"That's good, isn't it?"

"I suppose. I just find it hard to remember that I don't need to be her protector anymore."

"It might do you good to lean on *her,* for a while, after everything you've been through lately. Does she know about Ian?"

Mallory shook her head. "I figured I'd tell her when I got there. It's too much to get into over the phone. She knows about what happened with the 'Children of Violence' episode last fall, of course, but I didn't tell her about Bedrosian. She's got enough on her plate. I didn't think she needed to worry about me, too."

"Maybe now she'll consider bringing Remy to California, even if just for a visit."

Mallory shook her head. "I doubt it, Bren. I resigned myself long ago to the fact that Diana was never going to come back here. Her way of coping with what happened to our family was to avoid this place and not think about it anymore. And who knows? Maybe she had the right idea. I tried to face those memories head-on, and look what it got me—more pain and uncertainty, and a busted marriage in the bargain." She sat quietly, sipping her champagne. And then, the corners of her mouth lifted in a smile.

"What?" Brenda asked.

Mallory shook her head. "I'm not sure, but when I called Diana yesterday to confirm my arrival plans, she mentioned that she's got news for me. She wouldn't say any more just then, but she sounded excited and nervous. I've got a sneaking suspicion I know what's going on."

"Don't tell me—she and Wiley have become an item."

"I bet. What else could it be?"

"Why would Diana be nervous? Would you have a problem with that?"

"No way. Wiley's my oldest friend, but we never had that kind of relationship. Actually, the more I think about it, the more the idea of the two of them together appeals to me." Mallory took another sip of champagne, then stared out the window, feeling the alcohol work through her system. "I still think I shouldn't be going," she murmured.

"Because of Ian?"

"Yes. And Patrini."

"Has there been any progress?"

"Last time I spoke to him, he said Bedrosian had vanished, but he had a lead." Actually, "a whiff of a hint of a possible lead" was what the PI had said, obviously not wanting to get Mallory's hopes up after the disappointing experience she'd had with the two investigators who'd preceded him.

"And Bedrosian's claim that Andrew Beekman was involved? Has Patrini found any evidence to support it?"

"Nothing you could take to court, so far. But maybe..." She glanced at Brenda. "I'm hoping that's what he's calling about."

"It's been a long time, but if the proof is out there, Patrini will find it, if he's as good as you say he's supposed to be. Meantime, your taking a break isn't going to change things one way or the other." Brenda hesitated. "Mal?"

"What?"

"Do you think you should give Ian a call before you go?"

"What for? He obviously doesn't want to talk to *me*."

"Well, maybe a little distance is what you both need. Get things back in perspective."

"Yeah. But what if—"

"What?"

"Nothing."

"Come on, what?"

Mallory swiveled to face her friend. "What if I'm getting perspective, and he's just getting laid?" Brenda made an obvious effort not to laugh, but it wasn't altogether successful. "You think I'm joking?"

"I think you're telling yourself horror stories, Mal. You guys are going through a rough patch, but that doesn't mean Ian's looking for someone else."

"You're right, he's not. He's found her."

"Caitlyn Allis? Please! Talk about your cool Anglos. I've seen her interviewed on TV, and that woman's so calculating, I think she's got a Popsicle for a heart. She's not Ian's type."

"She's *every* man's type—beautiful, brilliant, rich and successful."

"So are *you*," Brenda argued. Mallory harrumphed, and her assistant wagged a finger. "Listen, girl, people don't program their VCRs for the Popsicle Queen, but they do for you."

"Yeah, well, I can name one guy who's switching channels." Mallory sighed. "And who can blame him?"

46

Ian sat in his office on the twenty-seventh floor of the *Chronicle* building, staring out his window at the western horizon, watching the tiny T-shapes of aircraft taking off and landing at Los Angeles International Airport. He glanced at his watch, then back at the airport. Mallory was on one of those planes, on her way to visit her sister.

Remembering that morning to call to make sure he'd be able to get into the house while she was gone, he had considered waiting until she was finished videotaping and speaking to her directly. He'd decided to leave a message with Brenda Vasquez instead. He wasn't ready to talk to her yet, and neither did he want to upset her just before she left for Paris. Going away was the best thing she could do right now, for herself and for him. They both needed time.

After moving out of their home in Brentwood ten days earlier, Ian had been house-sitting for one of his press colleagues, an ABC television news correspondent who was also in Paris, covering the latest round of Bosnian peace negotiations. The conference was becoming a long, drawn-out affair, and the reporter wasn't due back anytime soon. Even so, Ian thought, it was time to turn his mind to finding a place of his own.

Up to now, he'd avoided thinking about the future, overwhelmed by the sick feeling he carried around like a heavy stone in his gut. A broken marriage was the same as a death, he'd read somewhere, bringing on identical, intense reactions of grief, anger and denial. Add guilt to that volatile mixture, and you had all the ingredients for a first-class emotional train wreck. The fact that it was his second run around the breakup track didn't make it any easier.

As a matter of fact, Ian thought, this time it was far worse. He and his first wife hadn't been married long when they began drifting apart, and the legal ending to their marriage, when it came, had been anticlimactic. This time, he had lost something more profound, and carried the added burden of being a two-time failure, incapable of sustaining the love of a woman with whom he had thought he could spend the rest of his life. It wasn't Mallory, admittedly, who'd walked away. But he'd lost the battle for her mind and her heart, squeezed out not so much by her career, which was demanding enough, but by a past whose grip on her he couldn't overcome. He *had* tried, but in the end, he'd been forced to admit defeat.

The question was, had he done everything he could? Would he have kept trying if he hadn't encountered Caitlyn again, recently widowed and looking for comfort?

No, he couldn't blame her. He was responsible for his own actions, and anyway, his and Mallory's problems predated Caitlyn's reappearance in his life. He hadn't even spoken to his former wife until a few weeks ago, when she'd called him at the *Chronicle* to comment on a piece the paper had run on the murder case she was defending. When Ian had first found out that Caitlyn Allis was going to be involved, he'd considered calling her to get an inside track on the competition, then rejected the idea. They hadn't seen each other in nearly a decade, and major story or not, he saw no reason to change that.

It was Caitlyn who'd called him, to correct a factual error in a piece the *Chronicle* had run. During that first conversation, they'd never strayed from the case, except for brief "how have you been's?" and Ian's expression of sympathy over her husband's death. It had been so surprisingly relaxed, however, that it had seemed natural for Ian to call her a few days later, when he needed more information. After that, they had spoken almost every other day as the case moved to trial.

Then they'd sat together at the Cedars-Sinai dinner. Was Mallory right that Caitlyn had rearranged her seat to end up at his table? Possibly. Ian wouldn't put it past her to shuffle place cards if she didn't like the original seating plan, but it wasn't significant, he'd told himself at the time. He and Caitlyn had moved past their personal history, to a place where they could simply be friends. Since that night, Ian had been forced to admit that he'd been affected by Caitlyn's physical presence, and by the undivided attention this still-beautiful woman had focused on him.

He hadn't spoken to her again before he moved out of his house, nor in the days that followed. The murder trial had wound up and gone to the jury, and after her client was found guilty, Caitlyn had telephoned, "just to hear a friendly voice." Ian was on his way to a meeting, but she sounded weary and stressed, and he'd regretted having to brush her off. Without really reflecting on the wisdom of the move, he'd suggested they have dinner together. Spago was her choice, not his. The restaurant was too trendy, frequented by too many people with a passion for gossip. He'd said yes, anyway.

After a few glasses of wine, Ian admitted to Caitlyn that he and Mallory had separated.

His former wife was sympathetic. "I'm so sorry, Ian. It must be a terrible time for you. I know from the media how much Mallory's been goin' through this past year. I can only guess at the strain *you've* been under."

"I've wanted to be there for her."

"'Course you have. That's the kind of man you are. You've always been a tower of strength."

He shook his head. "I don't know about that. I wasn't much help to her, and I don't feel too rock-solid myself these days."

Caitlyn placed her hand, warm and soft, over his on the table. "I know what it's like to suffer a loss. You feel like you're dyin' inside, don't you?"

He nodded, soothed by her shimmering empathy. "I never asked how it's been for you, Caitlyn. You've gone through a pretty rough time, yourself. I really meant it when I said I was sorry about your husband."

"I know you did. I'd like to think you've forgiven me for the awful way I treated you when we were married."

"There's nothing to forgive. We both made mistakes."

"No, *you* didn't. It was me. I was young, and too stupid to know what I had, and so I went and carelessly destroyed it. I never said it at the time, but I want you to know, Ian, I *am* sorry."

"So am I, Caitlyn." He squeezed her hand. "I'm sorry for a lot of things."

Suddenly, out of the corner of his eye, Ian noticed a woman watching him. It was Season Garner, a soap actress he had met at Mallory's studio. She waved to him cheerily, and he kicked himself for having agreed to dinner at this particular restaurant.

"Coffee?" Caitlyn asked as the waiter came around to collect their plates.

"Pass. As a matter of fact, Caitlyn, if you don't mind, I'd like to leave."

"What's wrong?"

He hesitated, then sighed. "There's someone here from the television studio where Mallory's show is taped, and the woman's a gossip. I just—"

"I understand. Don't say another word. We'll get out of here right now. We're both tired, and this place is too noisy, anyway."

She really *was* a kinder, gentler Caitlyn, he thought, to be so understanding when he was giving her the bum's rush out of the restaurant. He drove her to her home in Hancock Park, and she invited him in for the coffee they'd not yet had. Ian knew it was a poor idea to accept—they were both under stress and vulnerable—but he had nevertheless. The coffee even got put on to brew, with the best of intentions, but they never got around to drinking it.

When Ian awoke a few hours later and felt a soft body nestled against him, he reached out to hold her close. "Mallory," he murmured. But as she moved, he sensed a cloying floral scent—definitely not Mallory. He opened his eyes to see two emeralds staring at him in the light of a dim lamp. He recoiled, startled.

"It's just me, darlin'."

"Caitlyn! I'm sorry. I . . . I was disoriented."

"It's all right. Old habits die hard, I know." He frowned, but she raised herself over him and kissed him. "Don't worry about it. I'm not offended. I understand what you're goin' through." Her lips moved to his chest, and, to his unease, began working their way down.

He took her head in his hands. "Caitlyn, stop, please."

"Why?"

"I should be going. It's awfully late."

She glanced at the clock radio next to the bed and smiled. "Actually, it's early. The sun will be up in a few hours. Why don't you just stay?"

"It's not a good idea. I've got a long day ahead, and I need some clean clothes and a shave before I go to work."

"Now, Ian," she chided. "What's the advantage of bein' the big boss at the *Chronicle* if you can't come in late once in a while?"

"There's a Friday-morning editorial meeting I chair. I have to be there."

"All right." She sighed as he rolled away and sat on the edge of the bed, pulling on his pants. "I'll forgive you, if you'll let me cook dinner for you. Tonight maybe, or tomorrow?"

He shook his head. "I'm sorry, it's not possible. I'm speaking at a conference in San Francisco tomorrow, and I need to work on my speech tonight. I won't be back till very late tomorrow evening."

"Lunch then, later today?"

He shook his head. "I can't do that, either. I'm supposed to meet a real estate agent, to look at a couple of places." He slipped on his shirt and buttoned it, then stood and tucked himself together, searching the floor for his socks and shoes.

"Ian?" He glanced back at her. She was lying on her side, watching him, the covers pushed to the foot of the bed. "This is a big house, and there's plenty of room. You could move in here, you know."

"That's not a good idea."

She looked away quickly, eyes brimming, lips pressed together as she nodded. Ian sighed and sat back down, covering her and lifting her to a sitting position. She pulled the sheet tight around herself.

"I appreciate the offer," he said, more gently, "but I need to be on my own right now. I have a lot of things to work out, and you don't want to be around me while I'm doing that, believe me."

"Don't be so sure about that."

"Caitlyn—"

She stopped his lips with her hand. "It's all right. I understand. I just—" She shrugged.

"What?"

"I guess I just can't help thinkin' what might have happened if we'd never split up. We'd have had children by now. I'm thirty-eight years old, and I look around at this big ol' empty place, and I ask myself, how could I have been so plum dumb? I know it's probably crazy, but part of me wants to believe that it's not too late to fix things."

Ian watched her, his heart weary and confused. How could it happen that he was hearing *this*, now, from *this* woman? "Caitlyn, I don't know what's going to happen. It's all—"

"Mixed up. I understand." She sighed again and looked up, smiling bravely. "I'm not tryin' to make things hard for you, darlin'. Just do me a favor?"

"What's that?"

"You do what you have to do, but if you need me, don't forget I'm here for you, would you? That's all I ask."

He nodded slowly. "I appreciate that."

Ian turned away from the window and the air traffic, and flipped through his Rolodex, searching for the number of the real estate agent. Despite what he'd told Caitlyn when he'd left her house in the wee hours that morning, he'd been forced to cancel his lunchtime meeting with the agent. His editorial meeting had run longer than expected and he'd been too busy afterward to get away, so he'd rescheduled with the agent for after work. Now, he decided to cancel. He was exhausted after stumbling back to his borrowed house at 3:00 a.m. All he wanted to do was pack up his briefcase, go home and sleep.

He had just found the Realtor's card, when his phone rang. His secretary picked up first, then buzzed him on the intercom. "It's somebody named Patrini, Ian. Do you want to speak to him?"

"Patrini?" Ian frowned at the name, recognizing it. "All right, put him through." The line clicked. "Hello?"

"Mr. Gallagher?"

"Yes."

"This is Renzo Patrini. I'm a private investigator."

"Yes, I know. You're doing some work for my wife."

"That's right. I was trying to reach her, but we've been playing telephone tag. She told my service she was catching a three o'clock flight, so it looks like I missed her."

"She's going to be out of town for the next week."

"Maybe I could talk to you."

"I'm not—"

"I'm just across from your building, at Starbuck's."

Ian looked down to the street and into the coffee shop across the way, where he could just make out the tiny figure of a man standing at a pay phone near the door. "Do you want to come up?" he asked.

"If you don't mind."

"All right. I'll call the reception desk to have them escort you to my office. Come on over."

Ian announced Patrini to the front desk, watching from his window as the toy man hung up the pay phone, walked out of Starbuck's, dodged between parked cars, jaywalked across the busy street, then disappeared into the front door of the *Chronicle* building. A few minutes later, his secretary showed Renzo Patrini into Ian's office and closed the door behind him.

Patrini was short and stocky, with a head of thick, tightly curled black hair over a low, wrinkled forehead, squinted eyes, pug nose and wide mouth. His entire face and body, in fact, looked collapsed, accordion-style, as if the hand of God had reached out and pressed down on him in a moment of pique.

Ian shook the investigator's hand and showed him to a chair. "I think I should tell you right off, Mr. Patrini, it was my wife's decision to hire you to look for Haig Bedrosian. I haven't been involved at all. And as a matter of fact," he added, "she and I have separated."

"I hadn't heard."

"It happened quite recently. We haven't made any announcement about it."

"Are you getting a divorce?"

"I don't know. It's too soon to say. But to be honest, Mallory's preoccupation with Bedrosian and Andrew Beekman, whom I know she also asked you to investigate, has a lot to do with the problems in our marriage. That being the case, you might want to reconsider whether you should be talking to me about whatever it is that you have to report."

Peering at Ian, Patrini pursed his lips, which flattened out like cymbals. He was a noisy breather, Ian noticed, suddenly reminded of a Boston bull terrier he'd once met.

"Do you love your wife, Mr. Gallagher?" the investigator asked.

Ian was taken aback. He moved behind his desk and settled into the big leather chair, leaning back, stalling. Who the hell did this human pancake think he was, asking a question like that? He picked up a pencil and flicked at the eraser, sending little pieces of rubber flying. Then he stopped, tossed the pencil back on the desk and looked at Patrini. "Yes. I do."

"Well, then, I imagine you'd like her to stay alive."

Ian sprang forward in his chair, feet slamming to the floor. "She's in danger?"

"I don't know. Not yet, maybe. Her high profile actually offers some protection, making people think twice before going after her. But if she keeps poking into the corners the way she has, her luck may run out."

"You're being way too cryptic, Patrini. Just what the hell do you mean? Who's going to go after her? Bedrosian?"

"Maybe."

"Have you tracked him down?"

"I wish I had, but he's gone to ground. I'll tell you this, though, he's been collecting materials for explosives, and he's had a real mad on since your wife went public about her parents' murder. Since 1969, the year the murders took place and he hightailed it out of here, Bedrosian's moved all over the country, taking work in mines and stone quarries, never staying in one place for more than eight, ten months. Late last summer, he was in a hospital just outside Little Rock, Arkansas, being treated for cancer. That's where he still was in early September, in a hospital lounge, when he saw your wife on TV. Staff remembered that he got real agitated, although they never knew exactly what set him off. But I found out that it was the day after the "Mallory Caine" episode on kids and violence aired in Little Rock that Bedrosian slipped away from the hospital and started making his way back to California."

"It took him three months to get here?"

"He was not a well man, sixty-four years old, and he'd just had a piece of a lung removed. He hasn't been back for a checkup since, but I talked to his doc, who figured his long-term prognosis wasn't great. Plus, Bedrosian was drinking. I've traced his route through every flophouse and Greyhound bus he saw between here and Little Rock.''

"You think he's dying?"

"That's what the doc figured."

"But if he's that sick, can he really be a major menace?"

"He managed to break into your house once already, didn't he? Plus, the police found ingredients for explosives in his last confirmed location. We know he's an expert, and I've found evidence of further purchases in recent weeks. I've also traced at least three possible sightings of the man, all of them within a fifty-mile radius of your house." Patrini shrugged. "If Bedrosian's dying and looking to settle old scores before he goes, he's got nothing to lose. I don't know about you, Mr. Gallagher, but if the guy were after a woman *I* loved, I wouldn't discount the danger.''

"All right, I agree. But I can't figure out what he *wants* from her."

"Well, she said he was angry at her for bad-mouthing her parents on national television. And what about this," Patrini mused aloud. "Your wife thought Bedrosian was in love with her mother. What if he knows who engineered the explosion in Esmerelda Canyon that killed her parents, and he wants revenge?"

"It's possible, I suppose, although the police believed it was a dead drug enforcer named Denny Sweet who was responsible."

"I know that, but even if it *was* Sweet, he was working for somebody. I think Bedrosian might know who."

"Why do you say that?"

"Because what I was going to tell your wife is that somebody's been trying to buy me off. I got a call yesterday, saying he'd give me double what she's paying if I'd back off the search. When I said no, the guy changed the offer, proposing to pay me to notify *him*, instead of the police or your wife, if I found Haig Bedrosian."

"Who was he?"

Patrini shrugged. "Got me. When I tried to get the guy to meet me to discuss it, he said 'no dice.' Not that I would have agreed, you understand. I don't double-cross my clients. But I wanted to find out who was so interested in keeping Bedrosian under wraps."

"Maybe that's why the first two investigators Mallory hired never found any trace," Ian said.

"Either that, or they just weren't as good as me," Patrini said not too modestly. "On the other hand, I wouldn't put it past some guys to let themselves be bought off."

"If Mallory were here, she'd say your caller was Andrew Beekman. Bedrosian went ballistic when she mentioned his name."

Patrini nodded. "She asked me to see what I could find about Beekman, but I wasn't altogether clear why she was so anxious to pin something on the guy."

"She didn't tell you?"

"She only said that her father and Bedrosian both worked for Beekman, and that Beekman fired her old man. Is there more?"

Ian hesitated, then decided to tell the investigator. Patrini had already proven his loyalty by turning down and reporting the offer to buy off his services. "Beekman told Mallory that he and Selena Knight were lovers. If that's true, he might have wanted Mallory's father out of the picture."

"But something went wrong, and Selena was murdered, too, by accident?"

"Could be. Did you find any dirt on Beekman?"

"Let's say the trail's getting grimier, and now, I may have a real lead. I discovered that he owns a condominium penthouse in Long Beach, registered in the name of A. B. MacGregor."

"MacGregor?"

"His mother's maiden name. But the ownership address on the title deed is the same as the Beekman Development Corporation in Newport Beach."

"What about this condo?"

"It's occupied by a Miss Kira Webber."

"So Beekman's got a mistress," Ian said, shrugging. "What does that prove?"

"Nothing, in and of itself. But Kira Webber's got a major gambling habit, it seems. Loses big every month in Vegas. Hundreds of thousands, I've heard."

Ian frowned. "She sounds like an expensive mistress. Beekman's a wealthy man, but I wouldn't think he's *that* rich—or foolish."

"Precisely," Patrini said, nodding. "Which is why I'm hoping to have a little chat with Kira Webber."

47

‘‘Mama! Wiley's here!’’ Remy Desloges careened past his mother's room on the way to open the front door.

Diana glanced toward the hall just in time to see the blur of her eleven-year-old son whiz by. ‘‘I'll be right there. I'm almost ready,’’ she added, smiling as her voice trailed off. He was long gone and hadn't heard her, anyway.

She returned to her reflection in the mirror, poking at her mass of long, dark curls, smile settling into frown. I should get this all cut off, she thought, not for the first time. So far, she never had. Marcus had always loved her hair—loved to sit behind her on the stool in the evening, after Remy was in bed, brushing it, touching it. Touching *her*. She closed her eyes, remembering the feel of his hands, and where those warm moments would inevitably lead. After he was gone, Diana thought she would die of hunger for his touch. Even now, with the passage of almost two years, her mind turned every day to the memory of him.

Only their son had kept her going through those black weeks and months after the plane crash, when she had struggled to get Remy's life back into its routine as quickly as possible. Forcing herself to keep busy, meeting his needs and the demands of Marcus's gallery, Diana pretended to be strong, not wanting her son to see how afraid she was of being alone. She had dragged herself out of bed every day, when all she really wanted was to scuttle off into a corner and hide. And then, incredibly, after two years of terror that she would stumble and fall from

one moment to the next, she had been offered a safe haven once
more.

Diana opened her eyes again and leaned forward to put on
some lipstick, noticing, as she did, the scar in her cheek and the
tiny lines that were beginning to appear around her eyes and
mouth. This was a face that had lived and showed it, she
thought. Then she paused. She was only three years younger
than her mother had been when she died. Diana examined the
face in the mirror more closely. Even through the haze of old,
half-forgotten memories, she could see the resemblance.

She sat back and slipped *faux* tortoiseshell combs into the
sides of her hair. Rising from the stool, she smoothed down her
flowing skirt, resting her hand briefly on her waist. It was time
to move on. Life moved on, down a twisted path whose turns
and surprises she could never have anticipated—but was
learning to accept. Would Mallory? she asked herself nervously.

Taking a deep breath, Diana headed for the living room,
where Remy and Wiley were engaged in animated conversation. They were sitting around a low table, heads bent over the
pewter Dungeons and Dragons figures that Wiley had brought
from the States, continuing a complicated game of strategy and
imagination that seemed to never end.

Wiley looked up over the boy's head and gave her a smile,
and Diana was struck yet again by how interesting his face had
become as he grew older. It was still long and lean, like his
body, its angles and crevasses made sharper and deeper by the
years he had spent wandering byways and back roads, and by
the substances he'd experimented with along the way before
giving them up altogether. His hair was fully gray. The ravages
wrought by his eccentric life were softened by the bushy mustache he had grown recently, but Wiley appeared to be at least
a decade older than he was. Just the same, this was a face she
would love to portray on canvas, Diana thought, if she could
just find the time and get him to sit still long enough to pose.

Wiley got to his feet and tapped Remy on the shoulder.
"Time to go, buddy. Your aunt Mallory's plane will be land-
ing in an hour, and there's a lot of traffic between here and
Charles de Gaulle."

"Can we play some more when we get back from the airport?"

"Sure." Wiley stepped around the table, leaning down as Diana took his arm and kissed his cheek. When he straightened, he gave her a close look. "You ready?"

She grimaced. "As ready as I'll ever be, I guess."

"Don't worry. She'll be okay about it, you'll see."

"What if she's not? What if she takes it badly?"

"I'll be there with you, and we'll work on her together. She'll come around eventually."

"I'm not so sure about that, Wiley. You know Mallory, when she gets mad about something. She may never forgive me for this."

"Why's Aunt Mallory gonna get mad?" Remy asked, planting himself between the two adults. He looked up at his mother. "Because you're getting married, Mama? Won't she be happy?"

Diana sighed and passed her hand through his curly, dark auburn hair. "I don't know, sweetie. I hope so."

Mallory was flipping through the pages of the *International Herald Tribune* as the pilot announced the Concorde's final approach to Charles de Gaulle Airport. She was about to fold the paper and toss it aside when a photo on the last page caught her eye. She paused to read the article on the current round of negotiations to bring peace to the former Yugoslav republic of Bosnia. A new ambassador-at-large had just been named to head the American delegation to the Paris conference.

Mallory shook her head at the meteoric rise of Drew Beekman, boy wonder, whose photo accompanied the article. He had an uncanny knack for making himself indispensable, taking on the difficult jobs that no one else wanted, earning the gratitude of his political masters. Now, after several months as deputy head of the delegation, slogging through the verbal mine fields of warring Bosnian Serbs, Muslims and Croats, Drew had managed to become one of the youngest ambassadors in the diplomatic corps, and future rewards seemed assured.

Mallory tossed the paper aside, determined, for a few days at least, to avoid all thoughts of slick Drew Beekman and his awful father—wishing, just the same, that she had managed to reach Renzo Patrini before she'd left. She would try again later from Diana's house.

She gathered her things as the wheels of the needle-nosed Concorde touched down on the tarmac and the aircraft began rolling toward the terminal. She was grateful that the supersonic flight was a short one, cutting the usual seven-hour transatlantic flying time in half—even three hours in the narrow, claustrophobic cigar tube seemed too long.

Entering a Paris terminal heavy with the odors of jet fuel and the dark tobacco of *Gauloises* cigarettes, Mallory heard her nephew's voice even before she spotted the two dark heads of Diana and Remy, and Wiley's gray one. "Aunt Mallory! Over here!" They were waiting behind the French customs area. She waved, and as soon as she had cleared customs, Mallory broke into a jog, scooping Remy into a bear hug.

"My favorite nephew!" she cried, as she squeezed him tight and planted a noisy kiss on his cheek that made him blush.

"Oh, Aunt Mal! I'm your *only* nephew!" he said, rubbing his cheek, looking sheepish and pleased at the same time.

Mallory hugged him again, feeling a thrill as always at the sound of his voice, with its barely perceptible French accent. Remy's English was perfect, of course, having been learned at his mother's knee. Until he was six or so, he hadn't even been conscious that he spoke two languages, knowing only that there was one way to speak to his mother and another way for his papa and little friends in the neighborhood. Just the same, there was a lilt there, a roundness to his vowels that always sounded very proper and appealing to her ear.

"Look how you've grown!" she exclaimed. "What a handsome devil you're getting to be." He had Diana's hair and eyes, but there was something about his build, even now, that made Mallory think of his father. He would move with Marcus's easy, aristocratic bearing when he was older, she thought. "I'll bet you're breaking all the girls' hearts at school."

Remy scowled. "Bah! Girls!"

She laughed, and turned to Diana and Wiley, hugging them. "It's great to see you guys. Nice touch," she added, giving Wiley's new mustache a tug. "Makes you look like Sam Elliot."

"Is that good?"

Mallory grinned. "It ain't bad." She studied Diana, whose cheeks were flushed. The two sisters gazed at each other, all their unspoken news waiting for the right, quiet moment when they could be alone. Watching her, Mallory felt a sudden, stabbing ache inside the familiar ache of loss. "Do you know how much you're getting to look like Mom?" she asked quietly.

Diana said nothing, only hugged her again. "Ian couldn't make the trip?" she asked when she pulled away.

Mallory hesitated. "No. Something came up." It was too soon to cast a shadow over their reunion. "I'll tell you about it later. How are the *Avaron and Sagramor* illustrations coming along?"

"Almost done," Diana said, sighing, "but I'm still not altogether happy with them."

"They're terrific," Wiley said, "and the publisher loves them. You're just too critical of your own work." He patted her curly head, and Diana smiled.

They gathered Mallory's luggage and headed for the parking lot. Driving back to the city in Wiley's Porsche—financial success as a best-selling fantasy writer hadn't dimmed his love for fast machines, but it allowed him to play with more expensive ones—the conversation was dominated by Remy's eager chatter, as he brought Mallory up to date on his school, his friends and his and Wiley's Dungeons and Dragons adventures.

Mallory was squashed into the tiny back seat with her nephew, which is where she had insisted she wanted to ride. Now and then, she looked at Wiley and Diana up front, noting his easy smile and Diana's nervous one as they exchanged periodic glances. She reached forward and gave her sister a reassuring squeeze on the shoulder, tempted to tell her not to worry, that she had a pretty good idea what was going on, and she was fine with it. But instead, she decided to let Diana and Wiley break the news in their own good time.

It was Remy, however, who unintentionally let the cat out of the bag when they got back to the house. "Mama says if we go to America after she gets married, maybe I can visit you. I want to swim in your pool."

"Remy!"

Mallory grinned. "That's okay, Di. He can swim in my pool anytime."

"It's not that, it's just that I wanted to tell you—"

"About you and Wiley. Well, sorry, but I kind of guessed already."

Diana bit her lip and glanced at Wiley, who passed a hand through his hair. "Mal," he said, "I think you've got the wrong idea here."

"It's *okay*, you guys. I think it's great, really."

"Mallory, no. You don't understand," Diana said. Just then, the front-door buzzer sounded, and Diana turned to her son. "Remy, get that, please."

Mallory watched him go, then turned again to her sister, puzzled. "He said you're getting married."

"Yes. Oh, Mallory, I *am*, but not to Wiley." She sighed. "I didn't want to break it to you suddenly like this. I *knew* I should have put it in a letter."

"I don't get it, Di. If not Wiley, who are you planning to marry?"

Diana opened her mouth to speak, then her gaze shifted over Mallory's head to the doorway behind her. Mallory turned around to see Remy, with Drew Beekman standing next to him, one hand on her nephew's shoulder.

"Hello, Mallory," he said. "It's been a long time." It was the same old Drew—a few pounds heavier, maybe, and showing strands of gray hair at his temples, but otherwise, with the same smooth, even features and self-confident bearing.

Mallory stood motionless, stunned.

Drew watched her for a moment, before his gaze shifted to Diana, the corners of his lips softening into a smile. "Hi. I got away early. I thought it was only right that I be here when you told her."

Mallory looked around the room from one face to the next. They could have been from another planet, she thought, for all she knew or understood any of them. Diana took a step toward her, but Mallory held up her hand. "No," she said, her voice cold.

Her sister paled, then turned to her son. "Remy, go to your room."

"I didn't do anything!"

"I know. You're not in trouble. Please, just do as I ask. The grown-ups need to talk." He started to object, but seemed to think the better of it and left.

"Mal," Wiley cautioned, "take it easy, okay?"

"Take it *easy?* Are you nuts, Wiley? You knew about the Beekmans! How could you stand by and let one of them get at my sister?"

"Mallory, I love Diana," Drew said.

She spun on him. "You shut up! How dare you?"

"Mallory, no!" Diana said. "Don't speak to him that way, please!"

"He has no right here! I know this guy, Diana. He's no stranger to me, neither Drew nor his family. You don't know about the disaster I went through with these people. You and Marcus were just married when it happened, and I didn't want to rain on your parade. But you *can't* be involved with Drew Beekman!"

"Diana knows about us, Mallory," Drew said. "I told her when we first met that you and I had gone together for a little while."

"You didn't tell her the *half* of it, I'd wager. You didn't tell her how your father came after me, tooth and nail, and threatened to have Wiley arrested in the bargain, too." She turned on her old friend once more. "How could you just stand by while he came sniffing around her, after what Beekman tried to do to us?"

"It's not Wiley's fault," Diana said. "He wasn't here when Drew and I met. It was at an embassy function four months ago, and Wiley was away, traveling in Greece."

"I didn't even *know* that my father had threatened you, Mallory," Drew added. "When Wiley got back to Paris, we realized that we had nearly met once before, that time in L.A., when he brought you around to get your stuff from my place. That was when he told me what my father did." Drew exhaled sharply. "I wish you had said something. I said some terrible things to you that day, but I had no idea what was going on behind my back."

"How *convenient* for you!" Mallory turned to her sister. "Do you know how sick this is, your getting involved with him, of all people?"

"Mallory, I know the two of you had . . . a relationship. But it was so long ago, and you've been happily married to Ian for years, and—"

"That's not the point!"

"Mallory, come on!" Drew said. "It's not as if you ever loved me. You know that, and so do I."

"You weren't in love with me, either. Admit it. You just used me, because you knew it would bug your parents."

"That's not true. I cared about you, I really did. But when I met Diana, I realized that she's the only one I've ever loved, or ever *could* love. I've made mistakes in the past, including a disastrous marriage. I certainly didn't plan to fall in love with your sister, but we *have* fallen in love. I want to spend my life with her, and take care of her—"

"*No!* That's just what your father said!"

"What?"

"Your father! Oh, God! It's disgusting!"

"What are you *talking* about?" Diana cried. She was weeping, and Mallory, too, was fighting tears.

"I've seen Andrew Beekman again since, a couple of times. He came on to me, Diana. Said he wanted to take care of *me*, too. Then he destroyed my career at the *L.A. Chronicle.* And even worse—" Mallory's voice finally cracked, but when Diana tried to touch her, she pushed her away and stood alone in the center of the floor, shoulders heaving, hands clenched at her sides. "Drew's father knew our parents, did you know that? They worked for him, and it was when he fired Dad that they say the drug problems started. And as if that weren't bad enough—"

Mallory paused, rendered physically ill, as always, by Beekman's claim. But Diana needed to understand the kind of people she was dealing with.

"Beekman told me he was having an affair with Mom when she died."

Diana sank into a chair. Drew dropped to her side, putting an arm around her shoulders. He watched her, his eyes full of panic, and then turned to Mallory. "That's not true. It can't be!" Then he hesitated, exhaling sharply. "Oh, shit! Maybe it *can.* My father's always had mistresses, I knew that. It's just one of the things I dislike about him and his whole way of life. But not . . . oh please, not . . ." His voice trailed off.

Mallory addressed herself to Diana. "I don't believe Beekman. I *refuse* to believe Mom had anything to do with that awful man. But don't you see how sick this is? Andrew Beekman is abusive and obsessive, and a liar, to boot, I'm convinced. Lately, I've come to think he might even be worse than that. Maybe he thought he could have Mom if Dad was out of the way. Only something went wrong, and Mom ended up dying, too."

Diana's head shot up. "What are you saying? That Drew's father was responsible for the explosion? Do you have evidence?"

"Not yet, but I've got an investigator working on it. I've spent years trying to figure out this puzzle, Di. I can't buy that it was a drug problem with Dad. It just doesn't fit my memories of him. This is the only theory that makes sense to me, and if it takes the rest of my life and every penny I've got, I'll find out if Andrew Beekman was connected to the explosion that killed them and hurt you ."

"You can't be serious!" Drew exclaimed. "I know my father's a dreadful man in many ways, Mallory, but murder . . . !"

"You *see* now, Diana?" Mallory said, ignoring him. "You see why this is so wrong?"

Diana rocked back and forth in the chair, crying.

Drew turned away from Mallory and held her tightly. "I *love* you, Diana," he pleaded. "Please! No matter what might have happened in the past with our parents, you and I have too much between us—especially now. I don't care if I ever see my father again, but I can't lose you!"

She stopped rocking. She turned and studied him for a long time, then touched her hand to his cheek. "I don't want to lose you, either."

"Diana, no!"

Her sister looked up. "I don't know Andrew Beekman, Mallory, but I *do* know Drew. I know what he is, and how his father tried to manipulate him, too. Drew doesn't deserve any of this. He's a good man."

"Please, Di, you can't—"

"I love him, Mallory! I need him, and so does Remy. And," she added, placing a hand on her stomach, "so does our baby."

48

She had missed the returning Concorde, and the next best connection out of Paris back to New York and Los Angeles wasn't departing until eight that evening. But Mallory decided that spending a Saturday at Charles de Gaulle Airport was preferable to staying at the home of a sister she no longer knew. A sister preparing to marry a man whose name had come to represent all the pain and rage in her life. A sister who was intent on giving birth to yet another Beekman.

Wiley had followed close on Mallory's heels as she stormed out on Diana and Drew. When he couldn't convince her to stay in Paris even for one night to think things over, he had insisted on driving her back to the airport.

"Don't bother!" Mallory snapped. "I'll take a taxi."

Wiley hesitated for only a second, then snatched her purse and threw it in the trunk of his Porsche, slamming the hood before she had time to react.

"Give that back!"

"No! Get in the car. If you're determined to go home, then I'm taking you to the airport."

"Wiley, open the damn trunk."

"Make up your mind, Mal. Either you go with me, or you hitchhike. You won't get far, with no money or credit cards."

She stood on the sidewalk, burning with a white-hot rage, tempted to thrash Wiley for everything he'd done. Not just the purse, but for letting this happen to her sister. Realizing, however, that the only way she was going to get out of here was in his car, she jumped in and slammed the door. Wiley put her other bags in the trunk, and they headed to Roissy-Charles de Gaulle, Mallory in stony silence all the way. When they arrived, she grabbed her purse and bags, and took off toward the terminal at a trot, never looking back. After she had bought her ticket and checked her things, she found Wiley standing behind her. "I'm going to the first-class lounge," she said coldly.

"I'll wait with you."

"It's for passengers only." She strode away, but Wiley followed and grabbed her arm. She shook him off. "I'm warning you, Wiley. If you don't leave me alone, I'll scream for airport security. Unless you want a dozen *gendarmes* to come running, you'll get the hell away from me."

"Mal, come on! This is *me!* I'm on your side. I've *always* been on your side."

"Not anymore. If you were, you wouldn't have let this happen."

"Would you get real? Diana's a grown woman. When I found out about her and Drew, it was all over but the shouting."

Mallory stood, swaying slightly, watching as her old friend's face came into focus at last. "How could she do it?" she breathed.

"You have to be fair, Mal. Diana had no idea what had transpired between you and Andrew Beekman, much less Beekman and your parents."

"She knew Drew and I had had an affair."

"A long time ago, and I think she did hesitate to get involved with Drew when he told her. Give him credit for being honest with her about that. She didn't know the gory details of how his old man broke you up. *Neither* of them did, and by the time I got back from Greece and told them, it was too late. They had already fallen in love."

"If it had been me, and the Beekmans had hurt Diana that way, it wouldn't have mattered if I were in love. I would have sent him packing, anyway."

Wiley sighed. "Diana isn't you, Mal. You know that. That's why you've always tried to shield and protect her."

"That was a mistake, I see now."

"I'm not sure. Your sister's tougher than she used to be. She's changed a lot from that frightened girl who used to hide in the Ferry Falls rectory. Just the same, Mal, she'll never have the strength you do. She's not a person who functions well on her own."

"But a Beekman!"

"I know you hate the old man, but Drew's not his father."

"Baloney. The whole family's rotten," she fumed. "You know the only difference between a dead dog in the middle of the road and a dead Beekman? You'd see skid marks in front of the dog."

Wiley smiled, just a little. "Look, I hate to say this, but I think you're wrong about the son."

"Are you telling me you *like* him?"

Wiley shrugged. "He's kind of straitlaced for me, but he's okay. Drew's a steady, take-charge sort of guy, and even I can see why that would appeal to someone like Diana, who craves stability."

Mallory dropped into a molded plastic chair, and Wiley settled himself into one beside her. "I was praying it was *you* she'd fallen for," she said.

"I'm not Diana's type. And frankly, beautiful as your sister is and much as I like her, she's not mine, either. There's only one of you I could ever go for," he added quietly.

"Oh, Wiley!" she said with a sigh. "I wish I could have been what you wanted me to be."

"Yeah, I know, but what are you gonna do? Life's a bitch. Anyway, you're still my muse."

She looked at him, smiling sadly. "What happens with you, now that the *Avaron and Sagramor* books are finished?"

"I think I'm going to head back to Greece. There's a lady I met there..."

"A lady?" Mallory said, eyebrows shooting up.

Wiley actually blushed. "Yeah. You'd like her, I think. I met her in Crete. She's a teacher, and she's got me interested in Greek myths. There was this daughter of Zeus named Artemis, see? She was a real feisty character, and she had this buddy named Orion, and the two of them had all these adventures. I was thinking of a new series..." Wiley paused. "Does this sound familiar?"

"It sounds great. I can hardly wait to find out how it all ends."

Wiley nodded, and they sat for a while in a silence that was comfortable once again. Almost like the old days in Ferry Falls,

Mallory thought, when the two of them would escape to the Polar Star Café to commiserate.

"Why don't you go back and talk to Diana?" Wiley prodded. "Don't leave things this way between the two of you."

She shook her head. "I can't. Not with what I still have to do. I've lost her. I've lost everything, Wiley." She looked at him wearily. "Ian's left me, too."

"Aw, no, Mal! I'm sorry!"

"It's my fault. After that Bedrosian guy broke into our house and then disappeared again, I became obsessed with finding him. He knows something about what went on between Beekman and my parents, and I can't rest until I find out what."

"Ian couldn't deal with it?"

She shook her head. "It was the last straw. All he ever wanted was a little attention from me, and for us to start a family, but too many things in my life kept crowding him out. He finally gave up and walked away."

"But you're still not going to give up this search, are you?"

"I can't. I've already paid too high a price not to see it through. Every instinct in my body tells me Andrew Beekman had something to do with what happened in Esmerelda Canyon, and I have to prove it."

Wiley nodded slowly. "You could be right about Beekman."

"Why do you say that?"

He let out a long exhale. "As long as you're determined to go down this path, Mal, I might as well tell you that something's always bothered me about what happened that time the old man showed up at your apartment."

"How so?"

"Well, I was stoned out of my gourd that night, there's no doubt about it. I was into quite a few recreational chemicals back then, and so my recollection of exactly what happened is a little vague, you understand."

"But...?"

"But after I left you in L.A., I headed down to Mexico. It seemed the fastest, cheapest way to replace the stash of drugs you flushed after Beekman left. Only, when I went to hide my new supply in the usual place, I discovered that my old stash was still there."

"What?"

"I used to keep my drugs in the gas tank of the Harley, in a watertight container. When I opened it, everything I'd had was still there. Nobody'd found it, after all. I don't know whose stash you flushed down the toilet that night, Mal, but it wasn't mine."

"It wasn't mine, either."

"Could it have been Drew's?"

"He didn't use, and no one else had been in my place," Mallory said, frowning.

"So, if those drugs didn't belong to us, it could only mean—"

"He set me up! Andrew Beekman brought those drugs with him to plant in my apartment and frame me. The son of a bitch!"

She stared at Wiley, blood pounding furiously in her ears. But even as she did, the Charles de Gaulle lounge faded, and Mallory was back in Esmerelda Canyon, one hot Memorial Day afternoon.

"Help me get the beach stuff out of the trunk," her daddy asked.

Mallory and Diana followed him to the back of the car as he opened it and lifted out the beach chairs, blanket and picnic hamper. She stretched to reach pails and shovels, passing them to her sister.

"You girls rinse off the sand toys before you put them away, okay?"

"Aw, Daddy!"

"Come on, now. We don't want to drag all this mess into the house. I think we brought back half of Newport Beach!" Mallory looked at the gritty swirls of sand on the floor of the trunk. "Leave it open," he added, heading toward the house. "I'm going to get the vacuum."

She watched him catch up with her mom on the front walk, the two of them linking arms. Diana followed behind, and a moment later, there was a tremendous BOOM.

Her dad never did come back out of the house. When Mallory opened her eyes again and looked around, his boat trailer was sitting at a cockeyed angle on the hood of the car.

She blinked now and looked at Wiley. "The trunk was open."

"What trunk?"

"The trunk of my parents' car, before the explosion. It just came to me. My dad left the trunk open, because he was going to vacuum out the sand. But Ian saw the police file on the investigation, and he said their pictures showed it closed when they arrived on the scene. It was only later, when they opened it, that they found the drugs my father was supposed to have bought that day at the beach."

"Maybe the force of the explosion slammed it shut?"

"No. When I came to after the blast, I saw that my dad's boat trailer had been thrown onto the hood, but the car was in the same spot, and the trunk was still open. Then I passed out again, and in the pictures taken when the police found me and Diana, Ian said the trunk was closed."

"Somebody came along and closed it?"

"They must have. And not only that."

"What else?"

"I helped my dad empty the trunk just before he went into the house that afternoon. It was *empty*, Wiley! There were no drugs in it!"

"Holy shit! They were planted afterward?"

"That's exactly what must have happened—just like Andrew Beekman planted drugs in my apartment!"

It was almost midnight on Saturday when Ian's flight touched down at Los Angeles from San Francisco, where he had gone to deliver a speech to a conference of the American Investigative Journalism Association. He spotted Caitlyn Allis as soon as he came through the gate into the waiting area. She had obviously been watching for him, because she pushed forward and threw her arms around him, planting a kiss on his lips before he had a chance to react or say a word. Then she gave him a warm smile. "Welcome back, darlin'!"

"What are you doing here, Caitlyn?"

She looped an arm through his. "I was havin' a quiet Sunday, feelin' lonesome, so I thought I'd come and meet your plane."

"How did you know what flight I'd be on?"

Caitlyn started to say something about being as good an investigator as he was, but Ian stopped listening when he caught sight of the burly man who had been serving as Mallory's driver and bodyguard ever since Haig Bedrosian had broken into their house. Her personal assistant, Brenda Vasquez, was standing with him at another of the arrival gates, and next to her, Ian realized, heart sinking, was Mallory—watching Caitlyn hang on his arm.

He extricated himself from his former wife's grip. "Caitlyn, excuse me, please. Mallory's here."

"Oh, *is* she?" Caitlyn said, turning. "Why, so she is."

"I need to talk to her."

Ian started across the floor, but Mallory had spun away and was heading for the exit. "Mallory! Wait!" He picked up his pace, and caught up with her before she had gone far.

Brenda and the bodyguard turned immediately, but Mallory continued for a few more steps before she, too, stopped, shoulders rising and falling in a sigh of resignation. She pivoted toward him. Her eyes were ringed with black circles, and she looked hot and disheveled, as if she'd been traveling for days—which she must have been, he realized, if she'd been to Paris and returned already.

"What are you doing here?" he asked. "I thought you were visiting Diana."

"Change of plans," she said dully. "And you?"

"I had that speech to deliver in San Francisco today."

Mallory nodded. Her gaze shifted to his right, and Ian looked to see Caitlyn standing at his elbow. She smiled up at him, then turned her emerald beams on Mallory. "So *this* is Mallory," she said cheerily, holding out her hand. "We meet at last."

Mallory hesitated, then shook as briefly as was humanly possible. "How do you do? You're Caitlyn, of course. Were you in San Francisco, too?"

"No!" Ian blurted.

"No," Caitlyn confirmed. "I just thought I'd come out and welcome Ian back. Let him know he was missed."

"I see," Mallory said. "Well, if you'll excuse me, I've had a long trip, and I'd like to get home."

"I need to talk to you," Ian said, following as she began to walk away.

"About what?"

Ian glanced around the airport lounge. Eyes were already turned in their direction. "We should discuss it in private."

"I'm dead tired. You've got your welcoming committee to take care of. It'll have to wait."

Ian sighed. "All right. I'll come around tomorrow. Meantime, you should get in touch with Renzo Patrini as soon as possible."

"He's the first person I'd planned to call."

Mallory glanced at Caitlyn once more, nodded curtly, then strode off. Ian watched her go, feeling sick and angry and frustrated. When he felt Caitlyn's arm loop through his again, he extricated himself. "My car's in the parking lot. It's nice of you to come, Caitlyn, but I can make my own way home."

"I figured you would have driven yourself out here," she said, smiling, "so I took a taxi. I know you must be weary, but could I bother you for a ride home? I'll fix you a nice drink, or a bite to eat—"

"I don't think so."

"Come on, darlin'. You're upset right now, but this will all pass. Let me help you get through it. I'm prepared to give you anything your little heart desires, just to make you feel better."

Ian spun around and grabbed her angrily by the shoulders. "You saw her, didn't you?"

"Whatever do you mean?"

"Mallory! That little exhibition when I came though the gate."

"I was pleased to see you."

"You *saw* her, and you knew she'd spotted you, too. Dammit, Caitlyn!"

"Darlin', I do not know *what* you are talkin' about. If I embarrassed you, then I apologize—deeply." Her eyes went moist. "It was a simple, spontaneous display of affection, that's all. Don't be mad at me. I was only tryin' to cheer you up. Let's just get goin', please?"

"No! I'm not driving you home."

"That's not very kind of you, Ian, after I came all the way out here to meet you. Whatever do you expect me to do?"

He reached into his pocket and pulled out his wallet. "I'll pay for your return cab."

''Don't be ridiculous. Put your money away.''

''Let's get one thing straight, Caitlyn. The other night was a mistake. I'm sorry it happened, and I don't blame you, but it isn't going to happen again. You and I have no past worth salvaging, and even less of a future together.''

''Don't say that! We could be good together. I know you, Ian. I know what you want. You want a wife who'll be there for you, and a family. I'm ready now to give you that.''

''There's only one thing I want, Caitlyn, and you can't give it to me.''

She scowled. ''You want *her* back, don't you? You're just not gonna give up hopin' that one day she'll have time for you.''

''No, I'm not giving up, on Mallory, or on our marriage. And if I have to share her with whoever or whatever, then so be it.'' Ian's eyes searched the terminal, but Mallory and her aides were long gone. ''I'm not sure she'll even take me back, at this point,'' he added, turning back, ''but I'm going to keep trying. I should never have left her. I'm sorry, but that's just the way it is.''

The emerald eyes turned hard, and Caitlyn twisted her mouth into a most unattractive sneer. ''You know, darlin', you always were, and still are, the most *tediously* stolid man I have ever met!''

49

After thirty-six hours and two transatlantic flights in as many days, it was no surprise to Mallory that she passed out cold as soon as her head hit the pillow in her Brentwood home. But when her eyes suddenly sprang open at 8:00 a.m. on Sunday morning and she looked around, the bedclothes were in knots. Her demons had followed her even into exhausted sleep, it seemed. She awoke feeling as if she had come out the loser in a long, drawn-out wrestling match.

As the fog in her brain slowly dissipated, she realized that she had been awakened by the ringing phone. Before she could move, the call rolled over to the answering machine, a parallel system to the one in the kitchen. Her heart flipped at the sound of Ian's voice. *"Mallory? Are you there? Pick up if you are, please."*

She lay still, staring at the canopy over the bed, listening to the sigh that slipped across the line before he continued.

"I'm sorry about what happened last night at the airport. We need to talk. I know you're exhausted, so I won't come over to the house until you call and say it's all right. But please, Mallory, do call."

The machine beeped and the line went dead. Mallory glanced at the phone by the bed. Her hand reached out, but she pulled it back. What was the point? Nothing had changed, except for the worse.

She rolled out of bed and stumbled to the shower. Afterward, pulling on shorts and a T-shirt, and feeling revived enough to attempt human speech, she placed a call to Renzo Patrini. Sunday morning or not, the investigator's answering service snapped to attention this time, promising he would call right back. Five minutes later, the phone rang, and Patrini was on the line. "I was hoping you'd call, but I didn't expect you to be back in L.A."

"Long story. Have you got news for me?"

"Yes, ma'am, I do. Can I come over?"

"Please."

Thirty minutes later, Mallory and the flattened-down PI were sitting in her kitchen drinking coffee while he brought her up to date on the same facts about Haig Bedrosian he had relayed to Ian at the *Chronicle* office, plus further information on Andrew Beekman.

Mallory listened carefully. "So, this Kira Webber is Andrew Beekman's mistress," she said, "but she drops big bucks in Las Vegas on a regular basis? This doesn't sound right. Beekman's son once told me that his old man was tight with a dollar. Unless she has another sugar daddy, I don't see where the money's coming from."

"That was my problem," Patrini agreed, "until I realized where the money was going *to.*"

"What do you mean?"

"She gets taken to Vegas once or twice a month by limo, and she always plays in the same two casinos. Both of those casinos, I just found out after peeling back layers of corporate camouflage, trace their ownership back to one John Nichols of Newport Beach."

Mallory's eyes went wide. "Nichols? The gatekeeper on the Tijuana-L.A. drug corridor? Bingo!"

"Yup. The biggest problem these drug guys have is how to recycle the millions of dollars they receive from small-time buyers, most of it in ten- and twenty-dollar denominations."

"And the one place money like that would be inconspicuous is a gambling casino."

"You got it. Kira Webber's probably only one of many players who gets a fee to take Nichols's drug money and lose it in his casinos. The casinos, of course, are legit, so the money is then free and clear for Nichols to use."

"But where does Beekman fit in? Does he know what his mistress is up to?"

"One of my guys tailed Kira to Vegas on Friday, as a matter of fact. He sat next to her at the roulette wheel. They got to talking."

"Please! Don't tell me she confessed to a complete stranger."

"She wouldn't to me, maybe, but you should see this guy I've got working for me. Mel Gibson's twin brother." When Patrini grinned, his face collapsed into layers of folds.

"Still," Mallory said dubiously.

"I'm not saying she just lay down and gave it up to him. But when he got her all warm and interested, she *did* say her boyfriend wouldn't like her messing around. She mentioned that the boyfriend's name was Andrew—"

"Some 'boy'!" Mallory snorted.

"And that although he kept her on a short leash, he *did* know she was in Vegas. In fact, it was because of him that she'd first gotten into the game."

"All right, now we're cooking. So Beekman and Nichols are in cahoots."

"Looks like. On a separate search, I also discovered that Nichols has bought several properties over the years from Beekman Development."

"For cash?"

"No, but at prices well below market value. Then the properties were flipped—resold by Nichols at a substantial profit."

"Which means Beekman may have taken part of the original purchase price under the table, allowing Nichols once again to launder his dirty money."

"That's my guess."

"This is great work, Mr. Patrini. But something still bothers me."

"What's that?"

"Why would Beekman do this? For the past thirty years, southern California developers have practically had a license to print money. Beekman Development made a fortune in the Orange County housing boom. Why does the man need Nichols?"

"Maybe he doesn't, but maybe Nichols needs him."

"I can see why he might. But in order for Beekman to play along, Nichols would have to have his hooks in him."

Patrini nodded. "He owes a debt to Nichols, or Nichols knows something that he's holding over Beekman."

"Blackmail?" Mallory said. Patrini shrugged and started to say something, but she couldn't hear what it was because a racket had suddenly arisen in the backyard. "What the heck...?" She slipped off her stool and went to the door. When she opened it, her ears were assaulted by the ominous *whump-whump-whump* of helicopter blades.

She stepped out onto the patio as the noise level rose, and looked up in time to see a machine drop from the sky and settle on her long, rolling back lawn like some giant dragonfly. On the side, huge stenciled letters identified the aircraft as the KLBC television-news copter. Wind from the props flattened the grass, set palm fronds whipping and ripped papery petals from bougainvillea vines, sending them flying like pink snow-flakes. This had to be a violation of a gazillion city and air-traffic ordinances, Mallory thought.

As she shielded her eyes against the storm, she saw the back door of the helicopter open and Ian step out. He crouched low and scuttled toward the house.

"What are you *doing?*" she cried when he'd reached her side.

"I ran by the office this morning to pick up some work, and all hell was breaking loose. There's a *Chronicle* reporter and a photographer in the helicopter, and we're hitching a ride with the TV newspeople. The station manager owed me a favor."

"Hitching a ride *where?*"

"Newport Beach. It just came over the wire. There's a hostage incident going on at Andrew Beekman's home on Lido Isle."

"*What?*"

"Some guy's threatening to blow the place up."

"Bedrosian!"

"Looks like. Come on!"

Ian grabbed her arm, but Mallory held back. "Why should I go? You think I care if he blows up Andrew Beekman?"

"Beekman's not there, Mallory! The police are trying to find him."

"I know exactly where he is," Renzo Patrini shouted behind Mallory. "I've got him under surveillance. He's at his Long Beach condo with Kira Webber."

"Why don't you call the Newport Beach P.D. and tell them that?" Ian yelled.

Patrini nodded, then pointed to the helicopter. "Is there an extra seat in that thing?"

"Only one, and Mallory's taking it. You'll have to follow by car."

"Why should *I* go?" Mallory repeated.

Ian put a hand on her shoulder. "Because Bedrosian's got Diana, Mallory. And Remy."

She felt the blood drain from her face. "No! How could he?"

"Come on! I'll tell you on the way what I know."

As the helicopter floated noisily over the city, heading for the coast and working its way south toward Newport, Ian gave Mallory the sketchy details that had come over the news wire.

Some time during the night, a man had broken into the Beekman residence on Lido Isle, reportedly armed with a gun and a large supply of explosives. Only the housekeeper was in at the time. Mrs. Beekman was evidently out of the country, at the family's home in Marbella. Andrew Beekman, apparently, had not returned home that night. A little after 8:00 a.m., however, the Beekmans' son, Drew, had arrived unexpectedly, along with his fiancée and her son.

The police had learned this from the housekeeper, who had been given a message to deliver and then released. The message was that the man would blow up the house, killing his three hostages, unless Andrew Beekman turned himself over.

"What are Drew and Diana doing here?" Mallory asked. "I just left them in Paris."

"Is that what happened over there, Mallory?" Ian asked. "You found out that Diana and Drew Beekman had gotten involved?" She nodded. "I didn't realize they even knew each other."

"Nor did I. Not only that, but Diana's pregnant with his child, so you can imagine how well I took it. We had a huge fight. That's why I turned around and came back."

Ian exhaled heavily. "It looks like they followed right behind you. There's a red-eye flight from New York to Orange County Airport that gets in a little after 7:00 a.m. They must have been on that."

"Great," Mallory said grimly. "My sister finally gets it in her head to come home, and this is the welcome she gets."

The helicopter approached Newport Beach and circled high over the triangle of Lido Isle, which floated between the mainland and the crooked finger of the Balboa Peninsula. As the television cameraman took a few shots of the scene below, Mallory made out the flashing lights of dozens of black-and-white police cars. Two cars were stationed across the single bridge to the island, keeping out traffic, while the rest were massed around a large house at the opposite end. It was wedged tightly among other equally expensive properties, whose owners must have thought that the Lido cachet was worth the nuisance of living like sardines, golden cheek by diamond-studded jowl. The Beekman residence fronted on Lower Newport Bay, and several police and Coast Guard boats were massed just off the house's dock.

"How do we get down there?" Mallory asked Ian. "There's nowhere to land on the island."

"The police and air traffic control have given special permission for the pilot to put us down near the Balboa Bay Club across the way. A police boat will take you and me over."

Twenty minutes later, Mallory and Ian stood on a narrow Lido Isle street, watching Newport Beach police S.W.A.T. officers and Orange Country Sheriff's bomb-disposal experts milling around, studying street maps and building plans, relaying messages from the hostage negotiator, who was sitting in a command post set up in a nearby residence and who had already spoken by phone to the man in the house. Ian recognized his NBPD contact, and introduced Mallory to Sergeant John Kelsey.

"Pleased to meet you, Miss Caine," Kelsey said. "Sorry it had to be under these circumstances, though."

"Are you sure it's my sister and nephew he's holding in there, Sergeant?"

"The housekeeper was given the hostages' passports, to prove he had them. Diana Desloges and her son, Remy, right?"

Mallory's shoulders slumped and she nodded. "And Drew Beekman?"

"That's right. The suspect hasn't given us his name, but when Ian here called to let me know you were coming, he said the guy's probably this same Haig Bedrosian who broke into your house last winter. We've checked with the LAPD, and the description the housekeeper gave us seems to fit."

"Has he said what he wants?"

"Apparently, he wants Beekman."

"That's it?"

"Seems to be his only demand."

"So now what happens?" Mallory asked.

"We got a call from a PI, who I gather is working for you, telling us where we could find Andrew Beekman. We've sent someone to pick him up. Meantime, our negotiator is on the phone, trying to get the suspect to give up the little boy as a sign of good faith."

Mallory glanced around the street. All the houses in the vicinity had been evacuated, and from where she stood, she could see at least four S.W.A.T. snipers posed on rooftops around the Beekman house.

"Isn't there anything more you can do?" Ian asked.

"The housekeeper says this guy's rigged explosives all over the house, and he's wearing some kind of vest that's also packed. If we go in before we know exactly what we're dealing with, the whole neighborhood could go up."

"I don't want anybody to move," Mallory said. "I've met this guy, and he's erratic. When he broke into my house, he went from frightened to furious in a heartbeat. I don't want him turning on my sister or nephew."

"We don't want that either, Miss Caine. Why don't you come into the house we're using as a command center and tell us everything you know about this Bedrosian guy, and why he might be so upset with Andrew Beekman. It might help us figure out a way to negotiate a peaceful solution to this."

While Mallory was debriefing the police on what little she knew about Beekman and Bedrosian, Ian stood outside, behind the police line, watching the house, waiting along with the tense S.W.A.T. team for something to happen. When something suddenly did change, there was a flurry of shouts and commands and clicking rifles.

Ian strained to see what all the excitement was about, then made out the small, frightened form of a young boy walking out of the enclosed Beekman courtyard, hands in the air. The moment Remy had cleared the gate, he was snatched up by a masked, flak-jacketed police officer dressed entirely in black, who raced to the back of the police line, the boy half running, half carried along with him.

"Remy!" Ian dashed forward, barging past a couple of patrol officers. They reached out to grab him, but were bowled aside by his momentum.

The boy threw his arms around him. "Uncle Ian!"

"Get him inside!" someone shouted.

"Come with me," Ian said gently, leading him toward the nearby house that served as a command center. "Your aunt Mallory's waiting for you."

"He let me go, Uncle Ian, but Mama's still in there, and Drew!"

"I know. It's going to be okay. We're going get them out, too."

Word had already passed down the line that one of the hostages had been released. Mallory was at the front door when they walked in, and she and Remy threw their arms around each other. "Oh, sweetie!" she cried. "Are you all right?"

"I'm okay. But that man says he won't let Mama go unless Drew's father goes in there. I think he's really mad at Mr. Beekman. Why, Aunt Mal?"

"I'm not sure, Remy. What about your mom? Is she okay?"

Her nephew shook his head. "She's really scared, and she's tired, too. We were up all night on the plane, and I don't think she's feeling very well. She's going to have a baby, Aunt Mal, did you know?"

Mallory nodded, lips pressed together.

"Why did you go away like that?" Remy asked. "You just got to our house, and then you left right away, and you didn't even say goodbye!"

"Oh, honey, I'm sorry! I just . . . it's hard to explain."

"Mama cried and cried after you were gone, and finally, she and Drew decided they should come and talk to you some more. Why are you mad at them, Aunt Mal? Don't you want them to get married?''

Mallory sighed. ''All I ever wanted was for your mom and you to be happy, Remy. Maybe I just didn't understand what you guys needed.''

''Don't you like Drew?''

''I honestly don't know what I think about him. What about you?''

''He's pretty nice. I wish Mama were marrying Wiley, though. I *really* like Wiley.''

''Miss Caine,'' Sergeant Kelsey said, ''we need to talk to your nephew, so he can tell us a little more about what's going on in there.''

She nodded. ''Come and sit down, Remy. Tell the officers everything you saw and heard. It might help them get your mom and Drew out.''

An hour passed, and then another. Young Remy, exhausted after his hostage ordeal and all-night flight from Paris, stretched out on a sofa, his head on Mallory's lap, and fell asleep. When Ian tiptoed in and settled beside her, she looked up at him anxiously. ''Any word?'' she whispered.

He shook his head, keeping his own voice low. ''Not really, except they say Bedrosian's getting agitated. He wants Beekman.''

''Where the hell *is* Beekman?''

''On his way. Sergeant Kelsey says they found him where Patrini said he would be, but they ran into a problem.''

''What problem?''

''They also found Kira Webber, bruised and beaten to within an inch of her life. It seems someone reported to Beekman that she'd been seen talking to a PI in Vegas the other night, and he'd gone ballistic. The police arrived, but the woman clammed up when they tried to question her. They've taken her to the hospital, and they'll probably book her on suspicion of money laundering.''

''And Beekman?''

''Could be in deep trouble now. I imagine she'll talk, eventually, and charges will be laid. He wanted his lawyer and refused to come here, at first.''

"Even though Bedrosian's holding his son?"

Ian nodded. "Swell guy, huh?"

Mallory shook her head, then dropped it wearily against the sofa back. Ian reached over and took her hand, and she was too stressed to remember that they were supposed to be on the outs. "How are you holding up?" he asked.

"I'm all right. I feel guilty, though. They never would have been here if I hadn't thrown such a hissy fit in Paris when I found out about Diana and Drew."

"It's understandable."

She shook her head. "Nothing makes sense to me anymore—if it ever did. I just seem to stumble from one disaster to another."

"Don't be so hard on yourself."

She glanced at him dubiously, but said nothing. They sat in silence for a while, then Ian turned to her. "About last night," he whispered.

"Never mind. I know I haven't been there for you. I don't blame you for looking elsewhere for comfort."

"I'm not looking anywhere. I didn't know Caitlyn would be at the airport, and I sent her home alone after you left. I have no interest in Caitlyn Allis, or in any other woman, except you, Mallory."

Remy stirred, and Mallory stroked his dark curls until his breathing became deep and regular again. Then she sighed. "I feel like I've spent most of my life caught in a labyrinth, Ian. Every time I think I see a way out, I run into another dead end."

"We can find a way out together. I want to be there with you no conditions, no demands."

"You deserve more."

"Don't give up on us. I'm not."

She shook her head. "I don't know if I can go on like this anymore. It's not only us, it's—"

Just then, there was a bustle in the hall, and Mallory glanced up to see Andrew Beekman walk by, accompanied by several police officers. She slid out from under her nephew, propping a pillow beneath his head.

"Mallory, wait!" Ian said.

"Stay with Remy, please?" When Ian began to protest, she touched his shoulder. "I want to hear what Beekman has to say for himself. I'll hang in the background, I promise. Please, Ian, be here for Remy? I don't want him to wake up all alone."

"He's a madman!" Beekman was saying, when Mallory rounded the corner to the kitchen. "How should I know what he wants of me?"

"This Bedrosian seems to believe you were responsible for the downfall of Philip and Selena Knight in 1969, and for some misfortune he suffered himself," Sergeant Kelsey said. "You have no idea what that's all about, Mr. Beekman?"

"Not the slightest. Am I under arrest?"

"Not at the moment, although I understand there may be charges laid out of Long Beach."

"If I'm going to be arrested, I want my lawyer."

Kelsey frowned. "Mr. Beekman, they *did* tell you, didn't they, that your son was being held hostage in your house?"

"Yes, they did. And of course, I'm terribly concerned. Is there any word how he is?"

"Fine, as far as we know. His fiancée's son was released a while ago."

Beekman frowned. "The officers who brought me over said something about a fiancée, but I don't know anything about that. My son and I haven't seen much of each other in recent years. I wanted him to come into business with me, but he chose another career, and—"

"And now, Drew's planning to marry my sister," Mallory said.

Beekman spun around, and his jaw dropped when he saw her. "You! Here?"

"It looks like the chickens have finally come home to roost. We seem to keep running into each other, don't we, Beekman?"

The developer turned to the sergeant. "What is *she* doing here?" he demanded.

"As Miss Caine said, your son's fiancée is her sister. Mrs. Desloges is also being held hostage."

Beekman, for once in his life, was speechless.

"Well?" Mallory said to Kelsey. "Can we get on with it now?"

"Get on with what?"

"The trade."

"Trade?"

"The hostage trade. My sister for Beekman here."

"Miss Caine," Kelsey said, "we're not sending Mr. Beekman in there."

"Why not?"

"Because I refuse to go!" Beekman said indignantly. "I won't be put at the mercy of an insane man!"

"Calm down, Mr. Beekman," Kelsey said. He turned back to Mallory. "No way, Miss Caine, are we giving that guy another life to put in danger."

"But . . . what have we been waiting for, then?"

"We've been negotiating, stalling for time, trying to wear him down, hoping he'll eventually give up peacefully."

"Hoping?"

"Look, Miss Caine, if Bedrosian wants food, or drink, or to talk—fine. But we're not giving him any more hostages, and we're not giving him weapons. Anything but those two things. Now, if you'll excuse us, we'd like to debrief Mr. Beekman, and—"

A sound of splintering glass interrupted Kelsey's words. A police officer came running into the room.

"What happened?" Kelsey said.

"The guy just saw on TV that Mr. Beekman had arrived. He told the negotiator 'no more talking, he wants him now.' Then he threw every phone in the house out the window. We're cut off."

"Shit!" Kelsey cried. "Didn't anybody call the TV cable company to have them disrupt the signal to the house? Well, do it! Now!"

Mallory walked out into the street, where the tension level had risen perceptibly as a result of this latest round of activity from the house at the end of the block. S.W.A.T. team members were crouched and at a ready position all along the fenced perimeter of the Beekman lot. Although the ground floor of the house was hidden by the high wooden fence that surrounded it, the windows of the second floor were clearly visible. Each one, Mallory saw, had a sniper's rifle trained on it from the neighboring rooftops. Their steep angle of fire would make it difficult to hit anything inside, she thought, given the proximity of the houses. On Lido Isle, residents could practically reach out their bathroom windows and shake the hand of the millionaire next door.

The situation was at an impasse, she realized. The police were not going to let anyone else go in, and Bedrosian, once he realized that, was not going to let his hostages out. He was an angry, disturbed man harboring some ancient grudge—a dying man, if Patrini's information on his medical condition was correct, with nothing to lose by going out in an explosive fury.

Behind her, in the house she had just left, was a little boy, victimized by the same deadly curse that seemed to plague generations of her family, who had, one after another, lost parents to early, fiery deaths. Remy had already been struck once, Mallory realized, when his father's plane had gone down in the Pyrénées. No more, she thought grimly. It has to stop.

Her gaze roamed the scene, searching desperately for a solution that had to be here, somewhere. The afternoon sun was hot now, and as she looked up, shading her eyes, a flutter of bright cloth caught her attention. It was an umbrella, she realized, peeking out over what must be a rooftop terrace on the house next door to the Beekmans'. At the edge of the roof, hanging over, a sniper had his rifle trained on the french doors of a second-floor balcony of the Beekman house—the master bedroom, perhaps.

Looking back to the umbrella and the rooftop terrace, she suddenly remembered the cliffs at San Clemente where, years earlier, as a young *Chronicle* reporter, she had watched hang gliders leap off cliffs, slung precariously from their colorful wings. Finally, someone had convinced her to give it a try. Although she had earned a broken arm for her foolhardiness, she would never forget the rush of running into the void, the ground dropping away as she took off.

Mallory crouched and busied herself retying her sneaker laces while her gaze traveled back and forth from the neighbor's rooftop to the Beekman terrace below, calculating the distance. It couldn't be more than eight or ten feet across the gap, with a drop of another eight or so—could it? And if you had a running start?

Her gaze moved down to the front of the neighbor's house. There was one officer stationed there, but he was nowhere near the door, and his attention, in any event, was focused on the Beekman residence. Mallory glanced around, but everyone else was preoccupied, as well. She got to her feet, edging her way up the block.

When Mallory hadn't returned after ten minutes, Ian took a close look at her nephew. Realizing the boy was deep asleep, he rose from the sofa to find out where she was. One of the police officers in the kitchen said he thought she'd stepped outside for a breath of air. Ian searched up and down the block, but she was nowhere in sight.

He was just about to go back into the house, when he heard a shout from up the street. Overhead. He looked up just in time to see Mallory dash past a startled sniper. The officer reached out his arm, too late to prevent her leap from the roof.

"NO-O-O!" Ian roared.

50

The distance between the houses was, Mallory realized too late, somewhat more than the eight feet she'd estimated, but even so, she managed to clear the railing of the balcony on the Beekman place. The momentum of her leap carried her skidding across the tiled floor of the terrace, crashing into the French doors. The locked doors held tight, but a few glass panes shattered. She collapsed in a heap, covering her head to protect herself from flying shards. Once she'd caught her breath and ensured nothing was broken or bleeding, she glanced back at the furious sniper on the rooftop across the way.

"What the *hell* are you doing, lady?"

She ignored him and got to her feet, reaching for the door handle.

"Don't!" he screamed. "It's wired to blow!"

Mallory hesitated, peering through the window. As she did, the soles of her feet registered a nearby vibration, and her eye caught a movement of shadow in the room. Squinting against the reflection of bright sunlight on glass, she suddenly made out Drew Beekman standing in the bedroom, about ten feet from the French doors. Haig Bedrosian was behind him, one hand on his collar, the other holding a gun in his ribs.

"Mallory!" Drew cried. "What are you *doing?*"

"Let me in!"

"He's got the door locked and wired! You can't!"

"I'm stuck out here. There's nowhere else to go!" Mallory looked at the man behind Drew. He looked no less disheveled and stubble-faced than the night she'd found him in her kitchen, but his eyes were more focused now, and angrier. "Please, Mr. Bedrosian, let me come in. You know me. It's

Mallory. I'm not armed, and I came on my own, I swear. I want to talk to you, and see my sister.''

They stood for a nervous few moments, staring at each other through the glass, then Bedrosian spoke to Drew. Drew looked back at him anxiously. "No!"

"Do it!" Bedrosian ordered. "I'll tell you how."

"*You* do it!"

Mallory saw Bedrosian's lips move and heard the low rumble of the two men's argument, but the words were difficult to hear through the glass. She definitely made out the word "sniper," however. Bedrosian was no dummy, and there was no way he was going to get anywhere near a window.

Drew moved to the door. As the other man walked him through the steps of rendering the door safe to open, Drew fidgeted with hardware that Mallory couldn't see. After a few tense moments, he glanced back at Bedrosian, who nodded. Drew opened the door a crack, holding a clip in one hand attached to a coil of wire in the other, lengthening it to make a narrow opening she could squeeze through while he maintained a connection.

Mallory made a move to go inside, but Bedrosian stopped her with a shout. "Hold it! You tell those cops out there that we're gonna rewire this door closed once you get in. Anyone else tries a stunt like that, the place blows, and everyone in it. Understand?"

"Yes, sir." Mallory turned and relayed the message to the sniper on the roof across the way, who in turn passed it on to the command center through the microphone attached to a headset he wore. "Now can I come in?" she asked.

Bedrosian nodded, and Mallory wriggled inside. Once she was in, he instructed Drew on how to reattach and tighten the wires that ran, she could now see, to a plastic-wrapped package packed along the top of the doorframe.

When he was done, Drew turned to Mallory. His forehead was beaded in sweat and his expression was furious. "You are, bar none, the biggest idiot I've ever met!"

"And you want to marry into this family?"

"You could have gotten us all killed!"

"Shut up, you two, and get downstairs," Bedrosian snapped. Drew glared at her once more, then wheeled around and headed out of the room. Mallory followed, Bedrosian hard on her heels.

Downstairs, the curtains were drawn, casting a dark and funerary pall on the living room, despite its lush furnishings. Diana sat huddled in the corner of an overstuffed, brocade-upholstered sofa, her skin a deathly shade of pale. Her dark eyes were ringed and red and swollen, but they went wide when she saw her sister. "Mallory! What are you doing here?"

Mallory walked over and crouched, taking her hand. "I was in the neighborhood and thought I'd drop by. How are you doing?"

"I'm all right. Did you see Remy?"

"Yes, he's fine. He's with Ian."

"Thank God!" Diana slumped deeper into the corner, trembling visibly. Mallory moved next to her on the couch and put an arm around her. Drew settled in a chair on Diana's other side, watching her anxiously.

Bedrosian paced. He was wearing the kind of many-pocketed vest that Mallory had often seen *Chronicle* photographers wear. But Bedrosian's pockets, she saw, were all stuffed with heavy-looking, grease-marked bundles, and there were wires running from pocket to pocket, like some deadly spiderweb. He also had a gun that he kept waving around nervously, but somehow, Mallory felt more intimidated by those oily little bundles.

"Where's Beekman?" he demanded. "Why hasn't he come over? I know he's here." He waved in the direction of a television set in the corner, whose picture was scrambled now.

"Beekman will be along soon," Mallory said, stalling. "The police are questioning him, asking him what he did to make you upset enough to do this."

"I'll *tell* them what he did!"

"You ripped out the phones, Mr. Bedrosian. How are you going to do that?"

He frowned. "It doesn't matter. I just want Beekman."

"Why don't you send out Diana here, and Drew, as a trade?"

"I already sent the boy, and the police didn't keep their end of the deal."

"I came."

"I didn't ask for you!"

"You were mad at me, too, that night you were at my house."

"Sure as hell was. *Am* still. Bad-mouthing your parents like that. Cozying up to Beekman, taking his version of what happened!"

Mallory began to protest, but thought better of it. Safer to let him vent his rage, she decided.

Bedrosian shook a fist at her. "You were always a snippy little thing, not like your sister here. I should've figured you'd be the one to turn on them. But to do it on TV and in the papers like that!"

Mallory took a deep breath. "You're right, Mr. Bedrosian. It's me you should be angry with, and Andrew Beekman. So why don't you let these two go, and deal with us?"

"You think I'm stupid? You think I don't know this is Beekman's son—his only son? Oh, no," Bedrosian said, shaking his head. "We wait. And he'd better come soon, if he wants to see his boy again."

Ian paced back and forth in the hall. "There must be *some* way to break in there and get them out!"

"From what your nephew says, Bedrosian's got explosives salted all over the house, plus whatever he's wearing on his body. We have no idea what kind of detonation device he's using, or whether he's wired any of the hostages. And of course," Sergeant Kelsey added, grimacing, "there's one *more* hostage for us to worry about now, thanks to that stupid stunt your wife pulled. How could you let her do it?"

"Are you out of your mind? Do you think I *knew* she was going to do that? How could your people let her get by them?"

"Our attention was focused elsewhere," Kelsey said dryly. "We don't usually have civilians trying to break *into* hostage situations. Did you know her leap was picked up by a TV camera overhead in a helicopter? It just flashed on a news bulletin. Now the whole country knows Mallory Caine is being held hostage, and we've got a media circus out there to contend with, on top of everything else."

Ian shook his head. "Dammit, Mallory," he muttered.

"Uncle Ian?" The two men were just outside the living room where Remy had been sleeping. He approached them, rubbing his eyes. "What's happening? Where's Aunt Mal?"

Ian hesitated, then sighed. He brushed the boy's hair out of his eyes, then placed an arm around his shoulder. "She had to go somewhere for a little while. You and I are going to wait together, okay?"

He nodded. "Is my mom still in there?"

"Yes, I'm afraid she is."

"I wish that man would let her go."

"Me, too, Remy. I wish he'd let them *all* go."

Another hour ticked by. Every ten minutes or so, the police called on a bullhorn from outside, offering to send in a telephone so that Bedrosian could talk to them, but he repeatedly shouted, "No!"

Mallory and Drew both grew increasingly anxious about Diana. Finally, Drew got out of his chair and approached the pacing older man.

"For God's sake, let Diana go! Can't you see she's exhausted?"

"Sit down!"

"You've got Mallory and me. You don't need her!"

Bedrosian raised the gun in front of the younger man's face. "Sit the hell down! Now!"

"Drew, please!" Diana cried. "Come here." He remained where he was, glaring at the older man. "I'll be all right," she pleaded. "Please, Drew!"

He backed down and returned to his chair, reaching out to feel her forehead. "This is insane," he muttered. "You should be in a hospital. What am I saying? You should be back in Paris, in your own home. We shouldn't even *be* here!"

"No, you shouldn't," Mallory agreed. "Oh, Diana! I'm so sorry. If it hadn't been for me, you *would* be safe at home. You should have stayed there, especially with—" she hesitated, then placed a hand tentatively on her sister's stomach "—with the baby. You had so much trouble carrying Remy to term, why did you take the chance of traveling now?"

Diana covered her sister's hand with her own. "Because you're my sister. I don't want to lose this baby, Mallory, but I *can't* lose you. You and I had no one but each other, for so many years. I couldn't live with myself if I hurt you so badly that we'd never see each other again.''

Mallory sighed and shook her head. ''How could I not see you and Remy? I would have—''

Her sister gasped suddenly, and doubled over. ''Diana!'' Mallory and Drew cried simultaneously.

''I'm having contractions,'' she whispered painfully. ''They've been coming for a couple of hours, but they're getting stronger.''

''No,'' Drew groaned, sinking to his knees beside her.

Mallory leaped to her feet and turned on the old man. ''Dammit, Bedrosian! You have to let her go.''

''Sit down!''

''No! Listen,'' she said, taking a deep breath and forcing herself to speak calmly. ''Look at her, Mr. Bedrosian. You don't want to hurt Diana. You've known her since she was a little girl. You told me you remembered her. How she used to love those sparkly stones you brought for us. How she used to make pretty things with them.''

''She was a nice little girl.''

''Yes, she was, and she's a wonderful woman, too. Just like our mother. Diana's a mother, too, you know. She has that little boy. His daddy died, and he needs her. Please,'' she pleaded. ''Let her go.''

Bedrosian stood staring at Mallory's sister, and something sad flickered through the anger on his face. ''She looks like Selena,'' he said quietly. ''Such a beautiful lady she was.''

''Yes, she was. Diana is Selena's little girl, Mr. Bedrosian. I know you want to do the right thing here.''

His shoulders slumped. ''I just wanted *Beekman,* that's all. Why hasn't he come?''

''We need to find out where he is,'' Mallory agreed. ''Let Drew take Diana out and tell them—''

''No! He stays, and you stay, too.'' He sighed. ''She can go, though. I'll defuse the front door long enough for her to leave.''

Drew helped Diana to her feet, and she leaned heavily on him. ''She can't make it on her own, Bedrosian. Let Mallory take her sister out. I'll stay behind.''

''No! I'm not giving up two. Not until your father comes.''

"Then you need to get back on the phone," Mallory said. "I'll tell you what. Let me take Diana out to the front courtyard and offer to exchange her for a phone, so you can remind the police again what you want. I'll help her go out, and then bring the phone back in. You have my word."

Bedrosian stood, thinking, watching Diana hunched over Drew's arm. Finally, he withdrew to a corner and pulled something that looked like a television remote control out of a pocket. He crooked his finger at Mallory. "Come here."

As she crossed the floor, he pressed a series of buttons on the electronic device, and unsnapped the vest he was wearing, pausing briefly to separate a couple of wired connections. He shrugged out of the vest and held it out to her.

"Put this on," he said, "and don't try anything stupid. If I press a button on this remote, or put a bullet in the vest, it'll set off the explosives in the pockets, which will not only blow out this room, but detonate the rest of the stuff throughout the house."

"I understand," Mallory said. She pulled on the heavy vest, snapping the catches, her nostrils assaulted by the strong, petroleum-like odor of the greasy packets that weighed it down. Bedrosian reached over and reconnected the wires, then pressed the device in his hand a few more times.

"If you try to disconnect the wires or remove the vest now, it'll blow," he warned. "If you try to run, I'll set it off with the remote. Got that?"

"Got it."

"Good. Let's go and I'll deactivate the front door."

Sergeant Kelsey poked his head in the living room door. "Something's happening," he told Ian.

"Wait here, Remy," Ian said. "I'll be right back."

He and the sergeant ran into the street, peering over the heads of the S.W.A.T. line to the courtyard beyond. Ian immediately picked out Mallory's blond head as she stood just inside the gate at the Beekman compound. "Oh, God, no," he groaned.

She was supporting Diana, who appeared to be ill, but what was more troubling was the bulging green vest Mallory had on. It was sprouting wires and looked like the vest Remy had described Bedrosian as wearing. Clearly, he wasn't planning to let her go.

"My sister needs an ambulance!" he heard Mallory call out. "And Mr. Bedrosian wants that phone you offered. You can send one person in with the phone and to help my sister out. But don't make any sudden, heroic moves, please, because this vest I'm wearing is wired and ready to blow, and our friend inside is holding his finger on a remote control."

"Don't worry, Miss Caine!" Ian heard the S.W.A.T. commander shout. "We've got the phone right here, and we're not going to play any games. Tell Mr. Bedrosian we want to talk to him, too, and find a way to solve this peacefully."

"That works for me," Mallory said. "Send in your guy now, but just take it real easy, okay?"

Ian watched as one of the S.W.A.T. officers entered the compound carrying a small metal case that looked like an army field telephone. He laid it at Mallory's feet and offered an arm to Diana. She and Mallory hugged, then she was out. Mallory bent down and picked up the phone. She started to walk away, but paused, looking toward the street. When she made eye contact with Ian, she gave him a sad shrug.

"Oh, Mallory," Ian whispered. She held his gaze for a few seconds longer before turning reluctantly and heading into the house.

Once clear of the compound, the officer with Diana picked her up and carried her at a brisk pace into the command center, where he laid her on the living-room sofa.

"Mama!" Remy cried. "He let you go! Are you all right? Is Aunt Mal okay? I heard she went in there. Didn't he let her go, too?"

"She and Drew are going to come out very soon, I hope. I'm *so* glad to see you again, my love." Diana hugged and kissed him, then looked up. "How are you, Ian?"

"I'm fine. Mallory said you needed an ambulance, Diana. Are you hurt?"

She bit her lip, glancing at Remy's anxious face, then back at Ian. "Not hurt, but I'm expecting."

Ian nodded. "Mallory told me. Are you having problems?"

"I think so."

"Okay. This is Sergeant Kelsey, Diana. Sergeant, can we get that ambulance?"

"It'll be right here. Meantime, Mrs. Desloges, are you up to answering a couple of questions?"

"Anything."

Ian stepped back as the Newport officer debriefed his sister-in-law on what was going on inside the Beekman residence. As he waited, he noticed Andrew Beekman standing off to one side of the room. Until that moment, the older man had been keeping himself separate, waiting in another room of the house. Now, he stood staring at Diana, his expression drawn, his normally fierce eyes sparkling and damp. When the paramedics arrived a few minutes later and wheeled in a stretcher, Beekman edged a little closer, his eyes never leaving the young woman as they lifted and covered her. He watched, fixated, as Diana reached out to her son.

"Sweetheart, will you stay with Uncle Ian a little longer?" she asked.

"Can't I come with you, Mama?"

Ian stepped forward and put a hand on his shoulder. "We'll follow along later, after your mom gets checked by the doctors. What do you say?"

He nodded. "Okay. We'll bring Aunt Mallory and Drew, too, Mama."

"Please," she whispered.

They wheeled her toward the door. Beekman's hand reached out as Diana went by, Ian saw, but she never noticed him in the crowded room. When she was gone, the developer's shoulders slumped.

Haig Bedrosian must have decided that Mallory, for all her faults, made an acceptable spokesperson, because when she got back into the house and opened up the telephone case, he had her put through his latest demand that Andrew Beekman be sent in to face the music. There was no dial on the portable phone, but someone picked up at the other end as soon as Mallory lifted the receiver.

"Who is this?" a female voice asked.

"This is Mallory Caine."

"Mallory, my name is Suzy. Is everyone all right in there?"

"Yes."

"The man who's holding you, his name is Haig Bedrosian?"

"That's right."

"Just tell them to send in bloody Beekman!" Bedrosian shouted.

"He wants Beekman," Mallory relayed.

"We can't send in Mr. Beekman, Mallory. How about some food? Ask him if he'd like some food."

Mallory turned to Bedrosian. "Would you like some food?"

"No! They know what I want!"

"No, Suzy, he doesn't want food. He wants Beekman."

"I'm going to ask you some questions, Mallory," Suzy said, rolling right along, her voice calm. "All you have to answer is yes or no. There's just one other hostage, besides yourself now—Drew Beekman, is that right?"

"Yes."

"Is he wired with explosives, too?"

"No."

"Are you still wearing the vest?"

"Yes."

"Does Bedrosian have a gun?"

"Yes."

"A revolver?"

"No."

"An automatic?"

"Yes."

Suzy went on asking a series of questions, all intended, Mallory realized, to elicit information about the precise nature of Bedrosian's arsenal and to build as complete a picture as possible of what the police would be facing, when and if they decided to storm the place.

After a minute or so of these yes/no responses, however, Bedrosian snatched the phone from Mallory's hand. *"Beekman!"* he shrieked into the receiver. *"Send in goddam Andrew Beekman!"* Then he slammed the receiver into the cradle. Suzy's ears had to be ringing, Mallory figured.

She sat down on a chair, steering clear of a very agitated Haig Bedrosian as he marched up and down the room. Drew, she noted, looked exhausted, but calmer, now that Diana was out of imminent danger.

"I don't have time for this," Bedrosian fumed. "They think I'm playing games here. I'll show them! I'm going to give him back a taste of his own medicine!"

Mallory looked up. "Andrew Beekman, you mean?"

"Of course, Beekman. What do you think this is all about?"

"I don't know, Mr. Bedrosian, but I've been looking for you since you came to my house that night, hoping you would tell me."

Bedrosian stopped pacing and glared at her. "You had people trailing me, trying to stop me."

"No. To *find* you, so you could tell me what happened between Andrew Beekman and my parents. And you—how do you fit in all this?"

"You *know* what happened!"

"No! How would I know, Mr. Bedrosian? I was only eight when my parents were murdered."

"Eight? Is that all you were?"

"Yes."

"I thought you were older."

"Probably because I was such a mouthy kid. But I *was* just eight. And after my mom and dad died, Diana and I were adopted, and we were made to feel ashamed of them. We were told that our parents got involved with drug dealers, and that's why they were killed."

"That's a lie!"

"That's what the papers and the police reports said."

"They were wrong."

"I believe you."

"Then why did you say those things about them?"

"Because at the time, I had no other information, except my own unreliable, childish memories. Andrew Beekman told me, eventually, that my mother was innocent, but he manipulates the truth so much, it's impossible to know what to believe and what not to believe with him. Then," Mallory went on, "just yesterday, I suddenly remembered something I'd forgotten since the day of the explosion. They said my father bought drugs that day, and those drugs were found in the locked trunk of the car after he died. But I *saw* the trunk when we returned from the beach. It was open and it was empty, before and after the blast. I think someone planted those drugs, Mr. Bedrosian, to cover up the real motive for murdering my parents. I'm guessing it was a corrupt cop, on the take from the mob.''

''Of course,'' he said.

'' 'Of course,' '' Mallory repeated, shaking her head ruefully. ''Easy for you to say. It's taken me twenty-three years just to figure out that much, and I still don't know what the motive was. Except that now, I think it's got something to do with Andrew Beekman's involvement with money laundering.''

''Money laundering?'' Drew exclaimed. ''My father? He's a wealthy man in his own right. Don't get me wrong—I can believe a lot of things about him. I know about his lies and his marital infidelities, but money laundering...? It doesn't make sense.''

''It started with Westwind Park,'' Bedrosian said. ''Beekman had half a dozen other housing tracts going up when he landed Westwind, but that contract was a huge feather in his cap. When Jane Aznar Brown announced that she wanted to build a master-planned, upscale community on her land, it became the most prestigious project in southern California. Contract competition was fierce. Beekman was just another also-ran builder up to then, but he craved the respect he would get if he was a partner in Westwind, so he bid low, to make sure he got the contract.''

''Too low?'' Mallory asked.

Bedrosian nodded. ''He got caught in a cash-flow squeeze. Lumber prices shot up, and he started juggling money between his other tracts and Westwind, in violation of every building and banking regulation in the books. Finally, it got so bad, it was go to the mob, or go to bankruptcy court. Beekman couldn't face the humiliation of bankruptcy, so he started taking cash 'investments' from John Nichols and his drug-syndicate partners.''

''How did you and my parents fit in?''

''We were Beekman subcontractors. The problems started when he began making payments to us in cashier's checks instead of company checks, which should have been a red flag, because it meant we were being paid with money that couldn't be traced. That was bad enough, but over time, he got blatant about it, insisting we take payment in cash—small denominations, of course. Some of us did, me included, but not your dad. He refused, and finally quit the Westwind project. He hated Beekman, anyway, by that point.''

"Because Beekman was after my mother?"

"That's right. She had no interest in him, mind you," Bedrosian said. Suddenly, the old man actually smiled. Mallory was astonished. "She was a real lady, Selena was. Everyone thought so. She loved your dad, though, it was pretty obvious."

Mallory exhaled deeply. "I knew it. That was *my* memory, too. And Beekman?"

"He was obsessed with having Selena. He kept after her, until finally, your dad hit the roof and threatened to turn Beekman in to the authorities over financial irregularities."

"And that's when they were murdered?"

Bedrosian nodded. "No way Nichols and his friends were going to see their investments exposed, so they covered Beekman's ass. He's been in their pocket ever since—supporting the political and law enforcement candidates they tell him to, doing little favors here and there."

"But why didn't anyone speak up?"

"Once the lies about drugs started, most people believed it. Only a couple of us who'd worked closely with Phil and Selena knew what really happened, but we were scared. We'd been compromised ourselves and would have lost our businesses—not to mention our lives. That explosion was a pretty spectacular warning."

"My parents were never into drugs, were they?"

Bedrosian shook his head. "I wouldn't swear that Phil never smoked a joint in his life, but who didn't, back then? The rest was just Beekman, spreading lies. He was rich and powerful, so people believed him. But Phil and Selena couldn't have accomplished what they did if they'd been as wasted as Beekman made them out to be. When your parents quit Westwind, they had other irons in the fire, and things were looking bright. I was

51

Bedrosian fell into a long, morose silence.

Drew sat stunned and ashen-faced. Mallory studied him. Suddenly, she felt something click inside, like the dropping tumblers of a lock, releasing the easy affection she'd once felt for this person who had never, after all, intentionally hurt her. She was the one who'd misrepresented why she was breaking off their relationship, letting him jump to the wrong conclusions about Wiley. In the final analysis, Drew's only real crime that day had been wanting, desperately, to believe that his father cared a whit about him and his dreams.

She walked over and sat down, putting a hand on his arm. "Are you okay, Drew?"

"How could I be?"

"It's not—"

"I'll kill him! The son of a bitch! His lies and hypocrisy! I thought I knew what he was, but I never—" He looked up at her, brown eyes brimming. "What he *did* to your parents, Mallory! And to you and Diana. No wonder you hate me."

"I don't hate you, Drew. I never did, not really. My problem is with your father. I've had trouble separating you from him in the past, but no more. God only knows how you managed to turn out as well as you did."

He shook his head. "I'm not so different."

"What do you mean?"

"After you and I broke up, and I went to Washington, I decided I would never come back here and live my father's idea of a life. That's why I married Senator Redman's daughter—to have an ally, because I was afraid of my father. But I never loved Courtney. I used her, and the marriage was empty from the start. I had an affair, and then another. One day, I looked in the mirror and realized I hadn't escaped at all. I had married my mother, and I was turning into my father."

"But you changed your life."

"I threw myself into my career, and *it* became my life—until I met Diana."

"That was a shocker for me, I have to admit. I couldn't imagine how such a thing could happen, unless it was some great conspiracy."

He shrugged. "The American community in Paris isn't that large. She'd been on the embassy circuit ever since the Lennoxes were in Paris. By the time I was posted there, she was well-known in cultural circles, between her own work and Marcus's gallery."

"I guess it was inevitable that you two would meet."

"I realized right off that she was your sister, Mallory, but I didn't court her just to get back at you, I swear."

"I know. Diana is beautiful, like our mother. She was always the nice one with all the talent. It's not surprising you'd fall in love with her."

Drew smiled a little. "That's funny."

"What?"

"She thinks you're the one who got all the charisma in the family."

Mallory gave a wry grimace. "Well, if anyone can give her a straight comparative evaluation, I guess you can."

He shrugged. "It's pretty subjective. I know who Wiley Dixon would vote for. Ian Gallagher, too, I'm sure. It's some kind of weird voodoo that draws people to each other, Mallory. I never regretted the relationship you and I had, except the way it ended. But Diana..."

"She's the love of your life, isn't she?"

"I love her so much, it scares me," Drew said quietly. "But she deserves better than a Beekman."

"She loves you, too, Drew, and maybe there's some kind of justice at work here. If there *is* a great cosmic plan, maybe your role in it is to undo some of the damage your father did." Mallory sat quietly for a moment, then exhaled sharply and hit the arms of her chair. "But that's never going to happen as long as we're stuck in *here*."

She rose and approached the other man. "Mr. Bedrosian," she announced, "I have something to tell you."

He fingered the control device in his hand. "What?"

"Andrew Beekman's not coming to this little party."

"He has no choice!"

"He won't come. Even if he wanted to, the police aren't going to let you have any more hostages. They told me so. That's why I had to bust my way in."

Bedrosian's face hardened. "In that case, his son is dead."

"That would be one way to punish him," Mallory agreed, "but I have a better idea."

Hours after Diana had been taken away in the ambulance, something was still nagging at the back of Ian's mind about Andrew Beekman's reaction to her. There was his former attraction to Selena Knight to explain it, of course, and Diana's resemblance to her dead mother. But another old puzzle kept spinning around in Ian's memory.

He and Beekman had been sitting at opposite ends of the living room since the paramedics' departure. They hadn't exchanged a word—each knowing who the other was, neither having anything civil to say. Remy was dozing again on the couch. When Ian caught the developer staring at the boy, he was tempted to erect a protective barrier in front of his nephew.

Suddenly, however, Ian got up and walked to a wet bar, took down two glasses and wiped them, then rummaged until he found a bottle of Scotch. Pouring some into each glass, he walked over to Beekman.

"Ian Gallagher," he said, introducing himself. "We met once a few years back, at the *Chronicle*." Ian held out one of the glasses. "I decided I needed a drink, and I thought perhaps you could use one, too. I hope the owners of the house don't mind."

Beekman gave him a curious look, then took the glass. "Thank you. That's very kind of you. I'm sure they won't, under the circumstances."

"Here's to a successful resolution," Ian said soberly. He took a drink.

Beekman nodded and followed suit. "I understand your wife went in there voluntarily," he said.

"I'm afraid she did."

"So we're both waiting anxiously on loved ones."

"Yes. Ironic, isn't it? You ended Mallory's newspaper career over her relationship with your son, and now the two of them are in there together, facing God knows what."

"I didn't mean to hurt her, Mr. Gallagher. I hope you believe me when I say that. I felt sorry for her, after what had happened to her family, and I regretted my initial reaction to her when we met. I wanted to make it up to Mallory, but she developed such an obsessive dislike of me that no matter how hard I tried, she wouldn't even have a rational conversation with me."

"She had her reasons. In any event, Beekman, I don't wish any ill on your son, so I hope this resolves itself as quickly and peacefully as possible."

"As do I."

Ian nodded, then turned away and went back to the bar. Sergeant Kelsey had come in and was sitting on a stool, and he shot Ian a curious look. "That was damn sociable of you," Kelsey said quietly.

Ian turned his back to Beekman, leaning on the bar and keeping his voice low. "Do me a favor, would you?"

"What's that?"

"When Beekman finishes with that glass, get your people to lift his prints off it."

"What for?"

"I'd like you to fax them over to the LAPD, Beverly Hills Division. An old lady named Lili Dahl was killed in her house there a few years back, and the police figured it was local gangs. They found some prints but never made a match, and the case is still open."

Kelsey was incredulous. "You think *Beekman* did it?" he whispered. "Get outta here!"

"The prints were found on a picture of Diana Desloges. The place had been wiped clean of any others, but the photo was wedged under a bed and apparently overlooked. You saw Beekman's face when Mallory's sister was brought in?"

"Yeah, but still..."

"We know Beekman's capable of violence, after the way he beat up his mistress in Long Beach. Look," Ian added, "I'm probably wrong. But as long as we're just hanging out here, humor me, okay?''

"You could testify against Beekman and Nichols, Mr. Bedrosian," Mallory argued. "They could still be tried for my parents' murder."

"I've got cancer, Mallory. I'm not gonna live long enough for a case to go to trial. For that matter, if I walk out of this place, the mob will make sure I don't see another day. No," he added, shaking his head, "it has to end here and now."

"So you're going to blow up Beekman's house?" Mallory said, exasperated. "Big deal! As if he can't buy another house."

"He can't buy another son," Bedrosian said ominously, glancing at Drew.

"Well, forgive me, but that's just dumb. Andrew Beekman will go down in history as a successful, upstanding citizen whose son was tragically murdered by a lunatic with a bomb and some vague grudge against a former employer."

"That's not the way it is!"

"Of course not, but that's how it'll be seen. Unless . . ."

"What?"

"Unless we do it my way."

"How so?"

"What does Andrew Beekman really love? His son? His wife? This house? No. What he *really* loves is power—his status as a wealthy, respected community leader. Take that away, and you destroy the man. You tell your story to a wide audience, Mr. Bedrosian, and he loses all credibility. No way the authorities will be able to avoid looking into every aspect of his activities. I can guarantee that the whole country hears what you have to say about Andrew Beekman."

"How?"

"Twenty million people watch my show every day. Those are just the people who like me. There are probably *twice* as many who'd enjoy nothing better than to see me blown away. Talk about ratings! You and I could make one hell of a spectacular finale to "The Mallory Caine Show" if you'd let me interview you on air before you set off your fireworks. It would be the blast heard round the world!"

Bedrosian seemed to turn the idea over in his mind. "I don't want to hurt you," he said finally. "You can go. I'll tell them to let me make a TV statement, like you said. But when I go, I'll take Beekman Junior here. He's an ambassador. That'll be big news."

"Ambassadors!" Mallory said contemptuosly. "They're forever getting shot or blown away. That's not news. Don't be an ass! *I'm* the bigger story."

Bedrosian scowled. "You're not the lady your mother was, you know that?" He waved a hand impatiently. "What the hell! I don't care. You wanna go up with this place, fine. Get on the phone, and tell them to send in a camera so I can say my piece and get it over with."

"Not so fast," Mallory said.

"What now?"

"You have to let him go."

"Mallory, no!" Drew said.

"Shut up, Drew. This is between me and Mr. Bedrosian."

"I am not letting Beekman's son walk. If I can't get at the old man, I'll take his heir."

Mallory dropped into a chair and folded her arms across her chest—a little awkwardly, because of the vest. "Then you'll do it without my help. They'll label you a psycho, and Andrew Beekman will play noble martyr for the rest of his days."

"Why do you care whether any Beekman lives or dies?" Bedrosian shouted.

"Because to me, Drew's not a Beekman. He's a friend, and the father of my sister's unborn child—Selena's grandchild. Diana needs him. For God's sake, Mr. Bedrosian, hasn't she been hurt enough? Do you have to do *this* to her, too?"

Bedrosian swayed slightly, the strain slowly taking its toll.

"Let him go, please?" Mallory pleaded.

"How do I know they'll do what you say—put this on TV?"

"They won't be able to keep it *off,* it'll be such a big story. If we make this tape, it'll be played and replayed, over and over. That's what I want, more than anything! I hate what Andrew Beekman did to my family and to me, and I want people to know what he really is. I'm tired of fighting, Mr. Bedrosian. I need for it to be over, once and for all. And," Mallory added, fighting tears now, "I want the world to know that my parents were good people. That's all I ever wanted."

"That's what I want, too," the old man said quietly.

Mallory wiped her face and took a deep breath. "Okay, then. Let's do it—for Philip and Selena. You owe them that much."

Bedrosian released Drew, but it took a while for the police to find and bring down a television crew from the Lido bridge who would be willing to give up their camera and arrange a remote feed to ensure that Mallory's last interview was captured on tape, safely away from the site of her captor's bombs. All indications were that the KLBC cameraman who donated his equipment would lose it once Bedrosian had finished his story and made his fiery exit, but the story was worth the price of some replaceable machinery.

The video camera was relayed to the front door by a S.W.A.T. team member. Once Bedrosian was satisfied that the courtyard had been cleared, he disarmed the front door long enough to allow Mallory, still clad in her deadly vest, to step out and collect it.

Back inside, she set the camera on a table, checking and re-checking angles and sound until she was sure everything was working. Dusk had fallen, and she had to turn on all the lamps in the place to provide enough light. The picture quality wouldn't be great, she thought, but it would do. This would have to be accomplished in one take only.

Finally, she got on the phone to the command center. "We're set to go and the camera's turned on," she said. "Is the satellite truck picking us up?"

"Hold on," the voice named Suzy said. "I'll check."

Mallory waited, holding the phone and a cordless microphone in one hand while she smoothed Bedrosian's collar with the other. If he was going to be responsible for vindicating her parents, she didn't want him looking like a complete derelict. He was sitting on one of two chairs that she had arranged before the camera, fidgeting as nervously as any of her guests who had never been on television before. Despite her own unusual costume of shorts, T-shirt and bomb-laden flak jacket, Mallory switched into professional mode. With a microphone in her hand and a camera rolling, her main concern, as always, became helping her guest to relax.

"Suzy?" she called again into the receiver. "Are they ready?"

"Hold on. Almost."

"What's the problem?"

For the first time that day, the surefooted woman on the other end of the line stumbled. "I . . . I'm not sure. Technical glitch, of some sort. They say they'll have it straightened out in a minute."

Bedrosian looked at Mallory, his anxiety level rising visibly with every passing second. He was running his fingers up and down the edges of the electronic control, and she was afraid he would jump the gun before he even began his statement.

"It's okay," she told him soothingly. "Happens all the time on my show. Murphy's Law." Come *on*, guys! she telegraphed mentally.

Then Suzy's voice returned. "Mallory? They're all set. The TV crew said you should remind Mr. Bedrosian to look directly into the camera. You start whenever you want."

"Okay. I'm going to hang up the phone now. Nice talking to you, Suzy."

"You, too, Mallory. Good luck."

Mallory hung up the field phone and kicked it out of the way with her foot. Then she moved to the chair beside Bedrosian and gave him a reassuring smile.

"We're ready to roll. I'll do a little monologue, then introduce you. We'll start out real slow and easy. I'll give your name and ask you a bit about yourself, and then we'll move into how you knew my parents. Just relax, and look at me or the camera lens, and tell what happened. If you run into trouble, don't worry. I'll feed you a question if I think you've left anything out."

Bedrosian nodded and swallowed, his Adam's apple bouncing.

Mallory reached over and squeezed his arm. "This is a good thing you're doing, Mr. Bedrosian. The right thing, at last."

He nodded again.

She sat back and turned to the camera, raising the microphone to midchest level. "Here we go, in five . . . four . . ." She marked 'three,' 'two,' and 'one' with her fingers, and then began.

"Good evening! This is a special edition of 'The Mallory Caine Show'—the *final* 'Mallory Caine Show.'

"I'm sitting in the Newport Beach, California, home of builder and developer, Andrew Beekman. My special guest this evening is Mr. Haig Bedrosian.

"Many of you will remember an episode we aired last fall called 'Children of Violence.' On that show, I made an admission that startled many people, including myself. It was something I had never discussed publicly before—the fact that I had witnessed the murder of my mother and father when I was eight years old.

"Since then, thousands of you have called or sent in letters of encouragement and sympathy. You've been terrific, and I want you to know how grateful I am for your support and prayers.

"Among the people who were watching the show that day was Haig Bedrosian. After years of living in fear of reprisal from those who were responsible for my parents' murder, Mr. Bedrosian has come forward to tell us what really happened twenty-three years ago. It's an incredible story of greed, lust and power, and I want you all to hear what he has to say."

Mallory swiveled toward Bedrosian—just in time to see him propelled out of his chair. Afterward, she could never be sure which she'd noticed first. The report of the rifle. Or the blood that spattered across her bare legs.

"Why did you shoot him?" she screamed, leaping to her feet.

The S.W.A.T. sniper rose from his crouch in the doorway, directly behind where Mallory and Bedrosian had been sitting. She suddenly realized why Suzy had been so anxious that the old man keep his eyes on the camera lens.

"He was suicidal, Miss Caine. He was dying, and he had nothing to lose by going out with a bang, taking you with him. This was our best chance, while he was distracted and thinking about what he was going to say. We didn't know how long we would have, once he got started."

"But I wanted his statement recorded!"

The marksman seemed annoyed by her lack of gratitude. After checking to confirm that Bedrosian was indeed dead—as if there could be any doubt, Mallory thought, wincing at the sight of so much blood—the officer backed out the way he had come.

"Just sit tight," he said as he left. "Someone's coming to get that jacket off you. Then we'll get you out before the rest of the explosives in the house are disarmed."

A moment later, another officer wearing a cap saying Orange Country Sheriff—Bomb Disposal Squad came in. The man was short and stocky, and dressed in so much padding that he bore a strong resemblance to the Michelin Man. He grinned, revealing a large gap between his two front teeth.

"Hi, there!" he said cheerily. "Nice vest, but the color's not you at all. What are we trying to say here? Rambo? I don't think so! What do you say we lose this look?"

He walked around her, examining the jacket, rattling on all the while. "What goodies do we have, hmm? Looks like your basic commercial dynamite, blasting gelatin. Ooh! Some kind of gelled flame fuel. Nice. Yucky stuff. Our boy knew what he was doing. Electronic detonators, too." He picked up the remote device that had flown out of Bedrosian's hand, peering closely at it.

"He used that thing to disarm the vest when he took it off himself," Mallory said, trying to be helpful.

The bomb-disposal man nodded. "I bet we could turn on every television set in the neighborhood, brew coffee and speak to NASA with this little rascal, too. The things they sell at Radio Shack these days! We didn't happen to memorize the sequence our friend used to disarm the vest, did we? NASA would be upset if we made a mistake and diverted one of their rockets." He sighed. "No, I thought not. Oh, well! What's life without a challenge?"

He put the remote on a table and returned to examining the explosive-laden vest, walking all around her, bobbing up and down like some fat little bird, probing tentatively at the multi-colored wires. He also whistled between the gap in his teeth, seemingly oblivious to the fact that there was a dead man on the floor and enough home-made explosive packed around the doors and windows of the house to blow them both to Disneyland if he miscalculated and disconnected the wrong wire.

"How did you guys get in here?" Mallory asked, unable to stand his whistling any longer.

He broke into song, which was worse. Then he paused, grinning at her. "Name that tune," he challenged.

Mallory scowled. Was insanity a requirement for this dangerous job? she wondered. Or did doing it *make* you crazy?

On the other hand, maybe he was just trying to distract her. She became aware, suddenly, that her legs felt like jelly and that her whole body was shaking.

"Come on. What tune is it?" he prodded. His singing resumed as he bobbed around her once more, lifting her arms to take a closer look at the complex wiring.

" 'The Wind Beneath My Wings'?" Mallory ventured.

"Bingo! 'Course, I gave you a hint," he added, pumping her elbows.

Mallory snatched them away, but a light went on in her head. "You came across the same way I did, from the roof next door, down to the bedroom balcony."

"Give the lady a cigar. Actually, lacking your gazelle-like grace, we rapeled across on ropes. But you were indeed our inspiration, Miss Caine."

"How did you get through that wired door?"

"You very kindly left some broken panes for me to reach through, and your former incarceree, the young Mr. Beekman, passed on the wisdom of the ages as handed down from our late, messy friend on the floor there. He drew a diagram. The rest, I humbly confess, was awesome manual dexterity on my part." He pursed his lips and frowned. "Hmm . . ."

"What?" Mallory asked nervously.

He spiraled in the air with his fingers. "Pirouette."

"I beg your pardon?"

"Do a pirouette. Good heavens, Miss Caine, no ballet skills?"

"Hardly."

"Well, turn around then, slowly. Lift your arms, please. That's it, keep going."

"I'm getting dizzy."

"Just one second longer. And....stop!" The birdma
reached out his hand slowly. "She loves me. Loves me not."

Suddenly, he yanked out a wire, and it was Memorial Day a
over again. Mallory cringed, waiting for the flash and thur
der.

When nothing happened, the little guy broke into a wid
grin. "She loves me! Unburden yourself, my lady. You'r
free!"

"Good grief! Did you *know* that was the right wire to pu
out?"

"Not precisely," he admitted, "but I had narrowed th
choice to two."

Mallory unbuckled the disarmed vest and shrugged out of i
He laid it aside gingerly, then reached out his heavily padde
elbow. "Your chariot awaits on high, to transport you to yo
rooftop and freedom."

He led her up to the bedroom where she had first come in
Half a dozen officers were waiting outside on the balcony an
the roof opposite to help her make the return trip. They har
nessed her into rapeling gear, then pulled ropes and pulley
taut. Mallory hesitated at the edge before taking off, leanin
back to kiss the little man. "Thank you," she said.

He rubbed his cheek, grinning. "My pleasure. Now, if you'
excuse me, I have *such* a mess to finish cleaning up in there
Houseguests! The junk they leave behind!" He waddled bac
into the house, whistling a gap-toothed tune.

Ian scooped her up the minute she set foot in the street
Mallory held on tight, feeling a warmth and comfort she'
thought was gone forever.

"You're safe," he murmured. "Thank God, you're safe!"

"It's over, Ian. The whole nightmare is over." They rocke
for a moment, and then Mallory looked up at him. "How'
Diana?"

"Fine. They got her contractions stopped, and she's resting
Drew and Remy are inside. They wanted to be sure you were a
right before they headed over to the hospital to see her."

"I'm fine. I'm great. I'm *so* great!"

"I panicked when I heard gunfire."

Mallory nodded soberly. "I wish there had been another way. Wait till you hear what he told us about my parents. I wanted to get it on tape."

"We *have* it on tape," she heard a voice say.

Mallory looked over at Sergeant Kelsey. "You do?"

"Not video, but audio. Everything he said about Beekman and Nichols. We're going to be following up immediately, I can promise you. Us, the Drug Enforcement Agency, the IRS—the whole ball of wax."

"How did you get what he said on tape?"

Kelsey smiled. "The phone."

Mallory's eyes went wide. "There was an open mike on it?"

He nodded. "It was transmitting even when the receiver was on the hook."

She heaved a sigh of relief, then glanced around. "Where's Andrew Beekman now?"

"Taken into custody. He's got a lot of questions to answer—here, in Long Beach *and* in Beverly Hills."

"Beverly Hills?"

"You can ask your husband about that." Kelsey grinned. "Ask him to tell you how he and Andrew Beekman had a drink together this afternoon while you were tied up over at the house."

Mallory peered quizzically at Ian, who only shook his head and smiled. "I'll tell you later. Suffice it to say that Andrew Beekman's in for a change of residence to considerably less opulent surroundings. Meantime," Ian added, "there's a helicopter waiting to take you out of here." He paused, his expression uncertain. "And me, too—if you'll let me come home."

"Please," she said quietly. "Come home, Ian. No more monsters under the bed. Regardless of what happens with Andrew Beekman now, *I* know the truth—and the truth really does set us free."

A few minutes later, Mallory and Ian were floating over the city lights, the *Chronicle* and KLBC reporters with them reveling in their good fortune of getting exclusive access for the duration of the ride. "So, Miss Caine," one of them began when she'd recapped what had happened in the house.

"Knight."

"I beg your pardon?"

"My name is Mallory *Knight*—not Caine." She glanced at Ian, then amended that. "Mallory Knight Gallagher."

The reporters nodded and made a note. "So what are your plans now?"

"I'm supposed to be on vacation. And," she added to the *Chronicle* reporter, "I plan to convince your boss here to take some time off, too. After that, I guess, it's back to the talk-show gig."

"Do you think you might write a book about all this?"

"It's a thought."

"How about a movie?"

"Who knows?"

"There were press reports recently that you were planning your own television production company? Will you go ahead with that?"

Mallory nodded. "Probably. Although," she added, turning to Ian, "I'm more interested in a coproduction or two, right now."

His expression melted, and he pulled her closer. When the two came out of a long kiss, Mallory noticed the reporters exchanging amused looks. "A coproduction?" they asked. "Anything you want to be a little more *specific* about?"

Mallory smiled, eyebrows dancing. "You'll just have to stay tuned!"

Acknowledgments

Fiction writing is a funny business—a solitary act of trying to spin a three-dimensional world out of thin air. When knowledge fails, I, like Blanche Du Bois, have always counted on the kindness of others, and have never been disappointed. I owe a deep debt of gratitude to the Newport Beach and Irvine Police Department SWAT teams, who opened up their training exercises and let me ask endless questions. Sergeant Ken Cowell, Newport Beach SWAT commander, was especially generous with his time. Journalists Robin Abcarian of the *Los Angeles Times* and Tim Appleby of the Toronto *Globe and Mail* inspired me with their love and knowledge of the newspaper business. Fellow writers Jean Femling and Patricia McFall shared rich memories and research on people and places in L.A., while Maralys Willis passed on moving tales of her hang-gliding, daredevil sons. Virginia Landry is my legal counsel with an artist's soul, who always has a devious idea for getting my characters in and out of trouble. Novelists Kathy de Mayo, Linda McFadden and Sally Scalzo served as midwives, helping this story to see the light of day when I was fully prepared to strangle the thing at birth. My agent, Pat Teal, is wise and patient, managing somehow to keep my eyes on the stars and feet on the ground, all at the same time. I feel very lucky to have linked up with the good people at MIRA Books: people like Senior Editor Dianne Moggy, who's a joy to have in my corner, and publicist Stacy Widdrington, who's a trooper and a pleasure to deal with. Editor Amy Moore has been my personal Max Perkins, finding the book amidst the pages, and I'm extremely grateful for her intelligent and sensitive feedback. Finally, family members near and far are a source of unflagging support, and none more than Richard, Anna and Kate, who are the loves of my life.

The dynasty begins.

LINDA HOWARD
The Mackenzies

Now available for the first time, Mackenzie's Mountain and
Mackenzie's Mission, together in one affordable, trade-size
edition. Don't miss out on the two stories that started it all!

Mackenzie's Mountain: Wolf Mackenzie is a loner. All he
cares about is his ranch and his son. Labeled a half-breed
by the townspeople, he chooses to stay up on his
mountain—that is, until the spunky new schoolteacher
decides to pay the Mackenzies a visit. And that's when
all hell breaks loose.

Mackenzie's Misson: Joe "Breed" Mackenzie is a colonel
in the U.S. Air Force. All he cares about is flying. He is
the best of the best and determined never to let down his
country—even for love. But that was before he met a
beautiful civilian engineer, who turns his life upside down.

Available this August, at your favorite retail outlet.

MLHTM

Take 3 of "The Best of the Best™" Novels FREE
Plus get a FREE surprise gift!

Special Limited-time Offer
Mail to The Best of the Best™

**3010 Walden Avenue
P.O. Box 1867
Buffalo, N.Y. 14269-1867**

YES! Please send me 3 free novels and my free surprise gift. Then send me 3 of "The Best of the Best™" novels each month. I'll receive the best books by the world's hottest romance authors. Bill me at the low price of $3.99 each plus 25¢ delivery and applicable sales tax, if any.* That's the complete price and a savings of over 20% off the cover prices—quite a bargain! I understand that accepting the books and gift places me under no obligation ever to buy any books. I can always return a shipment and cancel at any time. Even if I never buy another book from Harlequin, the 3 free books and the surprise gift are mine to keep forever.

183 BPA A2P5

Name	(PLEASE PRINT)
Address	Apt. No.
City	State	Zip

This offer is limited to one order per household and not valid to current subscribers.
*Terms and prices are subject to change without notice. Sales tax applicable in N.Y.
All orders subject to approval.

UBOB-296 ©1990 Harlequin Enterprises Limited

Bestselling author

Sometimes you can go home again.

Widow Lynn Danfort had counted on the support of her husband's best friend to help her raise her two young children. But then he'd left town without warning.

Three years later, Ryder Matthews was back. This time he came courting. But were Ryder's feelings the result of guilt or were they the real thing?

Uncover the truth, this July at your favorite retail outlet.

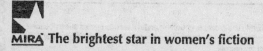

In the blink of an eye, Isabel Gary's life is turned upside down.

Running Away

By *New York Times* bestselling author

Charlotte Vale Allen

When her daughter Denny runs away Isabel's whole world falls apart. Alone, Isabel must deal with the mounting pressures of a competitively cutthroat job, her anxiety over Denny's whereabouts and the mysterious appearance of Brian—who could be her salvation if only she can trust him not to betray her.

Available this July at your favorite retail outlet.

 MIRA The brightest star in women's fiction

Look us up on-line at:http://www.romance.net

If you loved COMMON PASSIONS by

TAYLOR SMITH

Add another one of her passionate stories
to your collection:

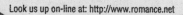